GUILT

a novel

GUILT
Book 1 in the Guilt Series

ISBN-13: 9781973190127

For my dad, Karl Dean Black,
and my sister, Melissa Black Jessop.
As Bea would say, *que en paz descansen.*

One

There's little irony in death.

Angry. Two silhouettes argued away from shore, on a boat—little green, plastic army men, moving and shifting and swinging—and, occasionally, disembodied and disharmonic voices floated over the incessant screams of the waves. One, the figure that faced Jamie, raised an arm in anger or defense, hard to tell, and the second hit the first sharply once on the nose, bitch move, seemed odd given the voices and served only to stun them both. The figures stood calm for a moment, and Jamie almost looked away, got bored.

But then he saw the glint of what looked like a butcher knife, probably wasn't—more likely a fishing knife, given the water, the shore—in the hand of the hooded figure who faced out to sea and for a moment the blade jumped mostly as an extension of the frantic arm, and Jamie imagined terror in the first man's eyes—he couldn't see for sure—and the hand with the weapon rose up and flew down and then suddenly and lightning-like the knife slid into the side of the man's head and dark, gushing blood melted into distended shadows tossed haphazardly from the setting sun. The man crumpled, expressionless and like jelly, almost instantly, which was no surprise, the crumpling, but Jamie let out a shout anyway. And Jamie's friend ran away. Coward. And Jamie saw the hooded figure spin toward shore, eyes wide in the dusk to see the source of the sound, certainly just as shocked to hear that they weren't alone, the killer and the dead man, and for an instant Jamie was exposed until the lamp from the lighthouse panned around again and drenched and blinded the figure, and Jamie dropped to hide in the brush and the bushes and the trees and he yanked at the trousers wrapped jumbled around his ankles, and he didn't bother to sweep the dirt and rocks from his naked butt, just slid his underwear and pants up around his hips. He heard an engine start up and roar, and he crept to his knees to peek through the camouflage and see the boat with the knife and the dead man and the killer head out to sea, to deeper waters, and then the stress and the violence were too much for him and Jamie went to sleep.

Two

Dan's eyes opened. Quick. Sudden. Staring straight ahead and through the ceiling, sweat soaking his sheets. He was lost for a moment, stuck between sleep and awake and not sure which to choose, sentient or knowing. But, before long, the choice was made for him and he remembered clearly and all at once, the dream, then watched helpless as the mist slipped away before speeding back like the bob on some giant pendulum, broken into pieces, undefined and unreachable, then teasingly solid for only a moment before floating gently away again.

There'd been a gong, or a metallic bang like a gong. And then the sound's taunting, unending circling and reverberating until, finally, the ringing fell flat and left nothing but a voided silence. His desk. He remembered his desk. But his computer was gone. The words remained, though; they floated inaccessible in front of him until he heard the clash (that's right, he'd been in his office when it all began). And then he ran. He remembered running, and weighted legs. Or cement. Or the sensation of pushing through still-wet, drying cement until a door. But the block wouldn't open. His hands just palmed the metal of the handle and slid as if the grip was covered in oil or blood. Was it blood? Then all at once he was on the other side. (Had the door finally given way?) The dream dissolved suddenly and too quickly and all he could muster at this point was that he was outside; the rest had melted into nothing more than a feeling of desperation and suffering. But he remembered seeing Ryan and blood and a car, gone, and then the rest of this savage, hiding world evaporated and, for all he struggled to bring the vision back and into focus, there was nothing left.

Dan closed his eyes again, tight, listening to the sound of the light rain on the roof, muffled pings that swaddled him cocoon-like and firm until, finally, he threw back the covers and sat exposed in his bed, pausing only briefly before he pulled his feet loose from the bedding and threw his legs up and over the side where he meant to pin his feet firmly to the ground. But the room kept spinning, apparently unaware he'd stopped moving, and Dan's right foot flew loose, nudging an empty vodka bottle that rolled deliberately across the floor.

He steadied himself with his hands.

"Too slow to break anyway," he heard himself mutter and the comforting rain he'd awakened to became a sudden drum roll on the roof and in his head (still strangely comforting, the cacophony) and he turned to look out the open French doors where dark, weighted clouds now filled the sky and threw oversized drops dancing into the harbor's dirt-blue water. Water. He needed water.

He pushed himself to his feet and crossed to the bathroom, careful of the errant vodka bottle (he'd have to take care of that—later) and opened the cabinet door to pour four or five, six Advil into the palm of his left hand (he didn't count) and into his mouth, downing the pills with a bottle of water that sat open on the sink.

Dan studied himself in the mirror: his cropped hair, his brown eyes. I can do this, he thought.

And with that, he turned and peed. And walked away.

He pulled on a pair of boxers before stepping into the kitchen to guzzle an entire bottle of cold water from the fridge, squeezing his eyes shut as he remembered too late that too much water, especially cold, can be as bad as no water. He grabbed a couple of slices of bread to settle his stomach, and started for the front door, realizing just in time that all he had on were the boxers Susan had given him (Susan, he missed Susan). So he threw on some jeans, a t-shirt and a pair of sandals, and walked out the entrance to unexpectedly clearing skies to head to the coffee house.

He didn't get far.

Dan froze and his heart revved and stopped at once, in an instant. To his left, an older man bent, crouched outside his bedroom, pressed against the window, his hands cupped to shade the sun, surely to see into the darkened room more clearly. Dan opened his mouth to interrupt the prowler, but kept silent when the man straightened himself and moved away and down the road, pausing and standing on tiptoes in what looked like an unsuccessful attempt to reach the bathroom window before he disappeared around the side of Dan's cottage, seemingly unaware he was being watched. Dan started down the road toward the man and peeked around his house's corner, along the side of the building.

Another window opened into the bathroom, the shower more specifically, and the man stood on a crate to get a better view. He crawled off the box and turned, evidently having seen enough, and started back to the road. The man stopped when he saw Dan.

"Can I help you?"

"Nah...eh..."

And with that, the prowler continued calmly to the street and strolled left down the road away from Dan and Dan's house.

"Sir?" Dan called out, stunned, hesitating only a moment before he followed the man. "Sir?"

The stranger didn't stop, just kept walking, not rushing, until he turned left off the street and into the breadfruit trees. Dan jogged the short distance, but as he reached him, the man was already coolly getting into a small motor boat and situating himself.

"Hey, Sir?" Dan shouted, his voice rising an octave in frustration, then he watched as the prowler started the engine and pulled away and into the harbor.

Dan rushed to the edge of the water, again belting out, "Sir!" only to stand and stare as the old man escaped and headed out to sea.

What the? Dan said exhaling, almost silent. But all he could do was return to the road, unclear about what had just happened and more than a little creeped out by their non-altercation. He headed back to his house (coffee could wait) and made sure that all the doors and windows were locked (they weren't) before retracing his and the old man's steps to verify that the predator was, in fact, gone.

He was.

So on with his morning. True to its name, the Water's Edge Coffee House was located in an old house (as were many of the establishments throughout the town) no more than a short walk up Front Street. Really short. Thirty seconds short. Since arriving in the Bahamas almost a week ago, Dan had watched Hope Town's population dwindle, then plummet, coinciding with an increase in clouds and rain, until he rarely saw anyone in the streets. Amazing what nothing more than the potential of a hurricane could do. The coffee house, though, stayed busy, relatively; this was still Hope Town after all. People needed their coffee. Or addicts, some might say…well, their need was a little more desperate.

Dan liked to think his was a controlled desperation.

Inside, a few couples sat at tables situated around the small cafe and glanced at Dan, smiling, as he walked in. He said hello, feeling a bit like Norm on *Cheers, sans* the everyone knowing his name, and crossed directly to the counter where Jamie, the barista, was already ringing him up. The young man, who Dan guessed was about 24 or 25 and who looked just like he'd been plucked out of a Midwestern, conservative college promotional video, had been manning the shop every morning since Dan had arrived. Further enforcing the stereotype, he wore a Notre Dame t-shirt and had short, sandy-blond hair. He smiled and greeted Dan.

"Youse here late," he said, imitating the typical Bahamian lingo.

A visitor could easily forget he was in the Bahamas in Hope Town. The original settlement had been founded in 1785 by British loyalists fleeing what would become the United States after the red coats' loss in the Revolutionary War. Most of the locals, like Jamie, looked British, but sounded more like Americans, with just a pinch of an oh-so-subtle British-Bahamian accent as a reminder.

"Yeah. I want to head over to the library, doesn't open until 11, though," Dan said.

"Figured there was no rush," he added, not mentioning the role an empty vodka bottle may or may not have played in his tardiness. "I want to see if I can find anything about life here in the 19th century."

"Good luck with that," Jamie said, smirking a little, certainly sincere but sounding (and looking) a bit sardonic.

Dan squinted back at Jamie as he pulled money out of his wallet. "Yeah, thanks."

"How's the book?"

"Great," he lied.

Jamie took Dan's American dollars and returned his change in an indiscriminate mix of Bahamian and U.S. coins, then paused immobile, smiling at Dan.

"French press," Dan coaxed. "I don't have a lot of time today." Another lie. Mostly. Dan was eager to get started, though. He'd hardly written more than a few words since he'd arrived.

"Yeah, it's brewing. I saw you coming and got it started."

"Thanks."

"I reckoned that if you didn't want it, I'd just dump it and make something else." Jamie leaned forward toward Dan as if he had a secret. "I'm kinda in charge here."

He shifted back. "Go sit down. I'll bring it out to you. Deck's probably still wet from the rain last night, but it's stopped. I can wipe down a place for you if you'd like."

"Over here's fine." Dan motioned to a table not far from the counter and sat down.

He got out his notebook and stared off across the shop. Dan noticed a woman sitting across the room from him, watching. He smiled at her, and she looked quickly away, shyly, but Dan could see the corners of her mouth fighting a losing battle with a grin. Jamie brought him his coffee and set the mug down with a napkin.

"Thanks." Dan glanced up quickly to acknowledge the boy and then studied the words '*hope*' and '*cholera*' in his notebook. The barista stayed at the side of the table,

12

perhaps trying to think of something else to say, then abruptly turned and walked away to stand instead behind the counter. Dan stopped writing. He put the pad away and tilted the cup quickly into his mouth, but he immediately jerked the coffee away when the almost-boiling liquid washed over his lips.

"*Mmmmm*," he let out and peered, somewhat accusingly, at Jamie. He considered waiting while the drink cooled, but decided against the delay, feeling restless, and started out the front door of the coffee house with a no-eye-contact, "Thanks, Jamie. I'll see you later."

The cholera cemetery wasn't on the way, exactly. It wasn't out of the way, either. Nothing was—just a different way of going. But Dan had made a point of visiting the memorial each day no matter how briefly, and this day was no different. He headed up Lover's Lane, to the east side of the island, then right on Queen's Highway (an exaggeration if there ever was one) toward the town center. The cemetery wasn't much, almost nothing actually. There were no headstones to mark individual graves, just a grassy hill that dropped precipitously down to a thin beach. You'd have no idea what the fenced-in area was except for an old, wooden sign that read:

Cholera
Cemetery
1850's

During a
Cholera
epidemic,
about 100
residents
were buried
here.

Quite picturesque, really, like everything else in the Bahamas. In fact, it was hard to believe there were *about 100* bodies buried there, likely lumped into one large grave. Dan figured the residents had probably started with individual plots, families fighting for the rights of their own lost mothers and fathers. Children. But, given the harshness of life in the 19th century and the lack of understanding surrounding the plague that had afflicted their settlement, the townspeople had probably opted for a mass grave as they'd watched those around them fall one by one to become part of a disease's history, heaped together as a group as ceremoniously as the survivors could muster. Then, with time, forgotten as individuals.

One popular theory of the era was that God was inflicting the disease to dispatch His own Holy vengeance. Of course, that belief injected its own contradictions into the lives of the survivors. On the one hand, they must have felt a terrible loss as they watched their loved ones suffer and, ultimately, die. At the same time, though, they'd surely felt a persistent and inevitable hubris that came with the conviction that they'd been spared God's wrath, almost certainly because of their own moral superiority. Watching the misery and devastation, the lucky ones probably couldn't help but wonder what those suffering had done to deserve such an ignominious end.

Of course, the culprit was God, or the weather. Or bad smells. In short, no one knew. But, Dan thought, understanding why you're afraid is never as important as escaping whatever beast is about to attack, lurking unseen in the husband or wife sleeping peacefully at your side, in the child you cradle in your arms. No clarification could secret away the haunting realization that you could be next. You would never know until the knowing came too late.

And nowhere was safe. Not even your own body.

Dan shivered and moved closer to the white picket fence surrounding the cemetery. This plot and all the contradictions buried there had never left him. He'd been here with Susan less than a year ago when he'd first experienced the suffering. Now he was back, alone, to put those feelings into words. But first, he needed to see if he could find a diary or journal of someone who may have lived, or died, during the outbreak. And that was where the library came in.

A small, converted house held the town's history and a tiny collection of mostly donated books. Inside, a woman in her 30s, almost certainly the librarian, spoke with a shorter, gray-haired woman, dressed in black.

"No, Bea, we still don't have 'The Loves of Anna.' Probably never will."

A thick, withered book rested on a mostly empty bureau next to Dan and he waited more or less patiently, wishing he'd had the forethought to stick it out until his coffee had cooled. He pulled back the tome's front cover and flipped absentmindedly through the pages. Old black-and-white drawings showed Hope Town in the settlement's heyday—hard to imagine the village had ever had a heyday, he thought.

"Sir, I'll be right with you."

Dan dropped the pages closed and looked at the woman standing behind what passed as a counter. "Thanks."

He returned to the book and pulled back the cover again, trying to find his place and glancing between page turns at the two women. The younger one had straight, shoulder-length, reddish-brown hair. She was attractive, but in a tomboyish, *I could beat you at basketball* sort of way. Dan caught himself at once missing Susan and considering the real-life implications of the famous Ross and Rachel break.

"Yes. Well, you're welcome to keep checking, Bea. But I'm telling you, you're wasting your time."

The gray-haired woman turned gruffly from their conversation, and Dan rushed to the entryway to open the door for her. She paused before she got too far and pivoted back to the desk as if to say something more, but instead only shook her head and started again to the entrance. Dan waited there, holding the door open.

As she approached him, the woman glared, perusing him up and down, and spit out, "I suppose you think you're being gracious, but you're really just being condescending," before stomping though the opening.

Dan stood transfixed, his mouth trying, but failing, to form words. He held the open door long enough to watch the elderly woman walk away and climb into the lone golf cart parked out front. Then he closed the entry harder than he'd intended and turned to head back to the counter. The woman in charge behind the barrier stood shaking her head and grinned at him as he walked toward her.

"You haven't been here long, have you?"

"No, I..."

"You'll learn," she interrupted. "That's Mrs. Galson. She's a bit bristly."

"Yes, I..."

"Let's just leave it at that."

"Okay, I was going to say that I think I just figured..."

"You know, she's not even supposed to drive that golf cart into town. She got some neighbor boy to smash down a special path for her around the barriers. Oh that woman! Sometimes I really just want to..." The librarian stopped and studied Dan. "Sorry. That's not what you came here for. How can I help you?"

Dan smiled and, when the woman behind the counter didn't smile back, he continued. "Uh, I'm a writer."

"Good for you."

He stopped. Dan peeked behind him at the door, nostalgic for the amicability of Mrs. Galson, then pressed on. "Well, I'm here to work on a book about the...a historical novel set around the events of the cholera epidemic in the 19th century."

"Oh, well, that sounds interesting." Finally a smile, even if it was more of a smirk.

"Yes, well." He forced a grin. "The thing is, I'm having some trouble finding a lot of information about that time in particular. I thought it might help to find some books or journals written by locals at the time of the outbreak, that could tell a more personal version of what happened. I was—"

"And you thought you might find something here."

Dan glanced around the room they were in and spoke slowly, confused, "Yes, I..."

"Something written by a local at the time of the outbreak. Some kind of memoir to make it all more personal," the librarian said as if she had come up with that brilliant insight on her own and hadn't just rephrased what Dan had said. "And you?" She flipped her head toward him. "What's your name? Would I know your work from anywhere?"

"Dan. Daniel Harris. And maybe, I guess."

"Maybe?" She drove right over his answer; clearly she didn't care. "I'm Cat," she continued, extending her hand as demurely as Dan guessed she could muster.

He reached across the counter. "You're American?"

17

"You can tell?"

"Good guess." Dan smiled.

"Well, yes, I am," she said, whipping the air with her fingers, "but I've been here so long I forget."

"Me too."

"Been here so long or you forget?"

Dan shifted. "No, I..."

She laughed, "I know." Cat leaned into him, smiling seductively and pushing her breasts up into the opening of her collared shirt with her arms. "Listen, Dan. You're not going to get any help from anyone in this town. But I can help you out."

Dan hesitated, thrown by her sudden change in demeanor. He willed his eyes to stay up and forward. Was she flirting with him?

"Okay," he muttered, cautiously. "How?"

"Well, no one here's going to talk to you. About anything. But...if I'm there..." She straightened, seemingly under the impression that her unfinished statement cleared everything up.

The two stood silently for a moment, neither speaking, until Dan finally said, "Now, about that book."

Three

So Ed Wilson was dead.

He'd seen the knife, but never thought the blade would plunge so angrily into his skull. It had. Sudden. Frenetic. He'd processed every moment. Amazing how time was relative and moved snail-like and thick like molasses when death finally came, when all a person could do was observe.

The arm that had held the knife had raised, then lowered, then raised again, at first just an extension of the yelling. Then the hand and the blade had rushed toward him and he'd thought to move, tried. He might have, probably even started. Maybe the slice had been intended for somewhere else. But in the end, Ed had probably helped his killer while trying to evade his own death. He'd felt the initial prick as the cold sharp of the metal pressed against his skull and melted into him until his legs folded and disappeared and he sunk and the emptiness of his life morphed into blood that gushed unstopping from the wound. And he thought he heard a scream or a yell just before life vanished and turned to black.

The killer had fought to wrest the knife out that night, spinning first, drenched in light, then bending and pushing a shoe onto his cheek for leverage, tearing his flesh and leaving a larger, mostly unmistakable oblong hole where the blade had been. Ed hadn't seen the pools of thick red his death had left spreading, or felt the rushed jostling as the boat sped to less visible and deeper waters, or tasted the salty brine as his body was ultimately and too easily tossed over the side of the motorboat. He'd not been there to witness the single tear that had fallen or to watch the desperate mopping of his life and the inevitable erasing of the only reminder of his having been there.

Instead he'd sunk. Ed was thin but muscular in life, and his body had dropped quickly and disappeared into the ocean's depths. The water's currents had washed away what blood remained around his wound, leaving only a discoloration burned in the skin surrounding it, a rust color instead of the slightly blue-white color he was becoming. He'd bided his time obediently for days, fingers and toes and ears gnawed and nipped, but kept safe by the weight of hundreds of tons of water, until the inevitable bloating had settled in and had brought him too quickly to the water's surface where he floated gently, deceptively animated by the rhythms of the ocean.

The night he surfaced had become stormy, and the predictably rough waters had jostled his swollen body. Each wave edged him toward and away from the shore and the harbor—closer with each flow, farther with each ebb.

Closer...farther. Closer...farther.

In time, the sun pushed its way into the sky, and although the hour was still too early for much human activity, seagulls circled and cawed overhead and disturbed the unexpected peace he'd found after his violent end. Dark clouds lurked in much of the sky and gray and ominous shadows slid across Ed's face. The initial chaos of the storm had subsided, but still occasional gusts nudged him in the direction of the shore, moving the ocean and his body along and to land. As Ed crept toward the island and into the harbor, shallow water created even stronger waves, and these pushed his body more quickly.

Closer, closer...farther. Closer, closer...farther.

His progress was slow, but ultimately Ed reached the water's edge and his not-so-final resting place. At first his body jumped violently, excitedly, as water fought land for dominance. But, in the end, brush along a lonely stretch of shoreline snagged Ed's clothes and held him prisoner, even as the oily water wrestled to take him back.

The ocean's rise and fall continued to give life to Ed Wilson, but there was no pretending.

He was dead.

Four

Two things stood out about meeting Cat. One, according to her, she was the only one in Hope Town Dan could count on, a hyperbolic claim in even the most dire of circumstances, better suited for a political rally than a first meeting—as if she were running for mayor of the library and his was the all-important swing vote. And two, she had breasts.

Disregarding item two, her being his only savior felt a bit over the top. With the exception of Mrs. Galson (who, to be fair, had just been told she might never know if Ana would ever love again), Hope Town residents had been almost cultishly welcoming. Cat, though, had turned out to be a bit of a mixed bag.

They'd searched through all the books in the library and were just rounding the final barely stocked shelf (of only four) when Cat tripped over a collection of three volumes, wrapped in a rubber band and marked as the journals of Edward Hawkins, 1849 - 1851. Prone-to-damage documents were apparently stored on the floor. After the standard, *Are you okay?* and *Yes, I just...where did those come from?* (and after she lingered for what seemed to Dan an excessively long recovery against his chest) Cat pushed herself back and motioned to the loosened stack with a nod, "Well, go ahead. Let's see what they are."

Dan glanced at her, not sure why she, as town librarian, seemed to have had no idea about the set. She waited several seconds then, visibly bored, suggested that he stop his reading right then and there and just take the leather-bound books home, reinforcing his suspicion that she was a librarian in name only—her recommendation was certainly contrary to any policy the library might have had.

The two had laughed (a lot) and their joking, coupled with his being a man, had evidently led Cat to assume they were hitting it off romantically. She'd invited him to her house for lunch, which he'd declined, citing a very defensible need to get back to his writing and to review his new, potentially contraband, research material. But when Cat had offered to escort (her word) him to the island's Elbow Reef Lighthouse, Dan had quickly accepted. He and Susan had put a visit off too long before, preferring the romance of the hotel room and only venturing out for occasional and much-needed sustenance. He'd always regretted not having made time to explore the icon.

The lighthouse attracted tourists from all over the world set (at least in Dan's romanticized imagining) on scaling the old building's staircase and visiting the structure's antique lantern room, ultimately to step out onto the lonely circular walkway and recreate (without the requisite emotion, of course) the desperation of all the women who'd come before and their too-often unfulfilled aching for nothing more than to see a husband return from likely death. They'd agreed to meet early the next afternoon at her place and go from there. She'd explained where she lived and they'd separated.

When he arrived the next day, he saw that her house, much like his, was situated somewhat precariously on the water. Although, given that they were on an island (and a thin one at that) her home's location wasn't especially surprising. A short dirt path ran along the side of her house to steps that led to a deck and the building's entrance that faced the harbor. When Dan arrived, the front door was cracked open.

"Cat?"

"Come on in. Just putting some things together for us to take. Water. Snacks. Do you like bananas?"

"Yeah. Sure."

He glanced around the inside of her house. If Dan didn't know better, he'd think he was in a studio apartment in New York City. Cat had great taste, but obviously no maid. The bed was unmade, and clothes were strewn around the room. Used dishes littered the counters and more dirty clothes (did she have any clean ones?) covered a computer and desk not far from the bed. A baseball cap hung from one of the rungs on the desk's chair.

She pranced out of the kitchen and wrapped her arm in his. "Ready?"

"You like the Cards?"

"What?"

Dan pointed at the hat.

"Oh, that. No, not really. You want it? An old boyfriend gave it to me. I never wear it."

"Uh..."

"Here. It will keep that beautiful scalp of yours from getting burned." Cat threw the hat on Dan's head, and he immediately yanked the sports cap off.

"Thanks. I think I'll wash it first," he said, scanning the room. "No offense. Just looks worn and I have a thing about..." There was no way to say this without offending Cat, despite his clichéd *no offense* pre-defense. He pushed the cap back on his head, swallowing a grimace, and forced a smile. "Thanks."

They stepped out the front door onto her deck and Cat, pulling Dan, headed to Queen's Highway.

"Is that your boat?" Dan motioned to the dock extending from her house.

"Oh, yeah. It's mine...we can take it, if you want. But I thought we'd walk. It's such a nice day and the motor's so loud. There's a new path through the trees we can take. It's not far. No more than an hour if we're slow.

"Which I'm not," Cat added, smirking.

Dan shrug-nodded, ignoring her less-than-subtle flirting, and the two continued right down Queen's Highway until they reached a path, also on the right, and headed off through the trees, nothing more than pointing serving as their communication. Apparently, the easy conversation of the library had been a fluke. Finally, Dan spoke up.

"So, you're American." he reminded her, his voice resounding loudly around the silence of the path.

Then more softly, almost a whisper, "...you're not from Hope?"

Cat didn't look at him. "Town."

"What?"

"Town. Hope *Town*. Nobody says Hope, that just sounds stupid. You're already an outsider, silly. Don't draw even more attention to yourself," Cat talked as if they were in the Ozark's and the *Deliverance* banjo boy was close by, keeping a disturbing eye. She grinned at him and leaned her body into his, pushing him playfully.

"Got it." Dan smiled back, ignoring her bluntness and letting her frisky nudge push him farther away. He clarified, "So, you're not from Hope TOWN?"

"No, not really. Although, after a while, you become one of the natives." Now they were in 19th-century Polynesia. "I feel like I've always lived here. I love it. People weren't always so reluctant to welcome outsiders to the island."

Dan nodded.

"How long have you been here?"

"About ten years," Cat mumbled, then scanned ahead as if she were judging the remaining distance to the lighthouse. "We're almost there...race?"

She didn't wait for an answer but instead immediately sprinted down the road. Dan was quick; he'd played football and been a track star in high school, but that was a long time and not enough cardio ago. That and his recent overindulging with the vodka meant she easily left him behind on the dirt path.

Cat turned and jogged backwards. "Come on, Dan. Don't be such a baby."

Dan shook his head, forcing a laugh, but stopped running, ignoring her goading. "No, no," he said, already out of breath, "I'm good."

She stopped and waited while he caught up to her. The path wound a bit, and Dan could see the point of the lighthouse as the weathervane popped into view over the trees.

"See? It's right there." Cat pointed, not sounding winded in the least.

"Yeah, yeah." Dan, of course, sounded like he'd just run a marathon. No drinking later.

Right there turned out to be another 20 minutes, but finally the red- and white-striped, circular column came into more complete view. A white lantern room and outdoor walkway perched atop a pillar surrounded by trees and bushes and other vegetation. Steps at the base climbed to the entrance that faced the harbor and, across the water, Dan's cottage.

"Race you to the top?" Cat crouched as if she were ready to sprint again. "There's a great view of the entire island from up there. You can see everything."

Dan glanced up.

"How about we hold off on that for a minute?"

"Okay," Cat said and feigned a bored child.

"Is there actually still a lighthouse keeper?" Dan motioned to a pair of houses on the hill, just below the building.

"Yes. It's still a working lighthouse. One of the only functioning lighthouses of its kind in the world. It's kerosene."

"Hmmm." Dan said, wondering why the type of fuel mattered. He strolled down the hill toward the water and left the wood walkway to explore closer to the shoreline. Birds circled and squawked overhead. Cat didn't follow.

Dan shouted, "You can probably see my house from where you are. It's white, with a deck. Bluish shutters." When he heard nothing in return, he pivoted to look for her on the hill he'd just come down, yelling again, "Hey, Cat."

She was still at the top, near the lighthouse, dancing to nothing. Dan chuckled and shook his head, continuing on toward the surprisingly rough waves of the harbor. He looked out across the water and saw that the ferry, mostly empty, had just jetted by.

Dan returned to the growth in front of him but stopped, immediately...in the brush...something. The passing ferry had forced pulses of violent waves crashing into shore, jumping and splashing, and a thatch of blue flashed into and out of Dan's line of sight. In one of the water's upswings, Dan caught two empty eyes staring back at him.

He froze.

He darted his eyes around the rocking water, searching the empty waves, confused and wondering if he'd really glimpsed what he thought he'd seen. At first, there was nothing, only pause. Then an arm, a torso, a face, an arm again, a torso bobbed into view. As the rocking softened, Dan shifted forward, cautious. He caught his breath. A body floated trapped in the brush along the water's edge. Waving. Falling.

Dan swayed, feeling suddenly light headed. He panned around the harbor, disbelieving that he'd seen what he knew he'd seen and desperate for confirmation from someone or something else.

And then panic rushed over him. He gasped, frantically realizing that he'd stopped breathing. A sudden rot rushed into his lungs, cutting into his senses and in an instant he felt a persistent isolation and the harbor...the land...the trees...everything collapsed in and around him as an immense void overtook him, stifling, and threatened to suffocate him. The only life he heard was the faint chugging of the disappearing ferry's engine and the aberrant screams from the flock of ever-present birds that circled overhead, taunting and harassing him, their screams stretching into long caaaaaaws that sounded inexplicably as if the creatures were pleading for Carl.

He spun, searching for Cat, calling her name once, "Cat," then again, "Cat," and once more pleading, "Cat!" He rushed to the path he'd just come down, stumbling and catching himself, not falling. He bolted up the hill to the lighthouse, imploring with each step, "Cat!" as he ran, and when he reached the lighthouse, the stairs, he raised his head and shouted once more before he peeked into the building and again shouted her name.

And then he paused. And listened. He gulped fresh air and every other sound pushing around him quickly became nothing more than a soft din behind the chorus of his breathing. He stood and watched the clouds float by.

But nothing.

So he circled back, sprinting to the water, down the wooden walkway, nearly tripping again and almost flying into the dirt and rocks and growth as he jumped from the planks to the muddy shore.

Dan exhaled and held his breath. He squeezed his eyes closed and opened them, blinking to refocus the lingering blur. The body, the man, was stuck forever in a time when age didn't matter—he wasn't old or young, just alive (or in this case, not). He wore jeans (the blue) but his chest was bare, except for a smattering of tattoos splashed across his exposed skin: an eagle holding a large snake in its beak (the serpent wrapped up but stopped just short of his neckline), a sobbing heart torn in two, a blob of, well, a blob. Divots and nibbles infested the man's blue and white, almost luminescent, face and one of his cheeks, the left, hung limply to reveal his skull underneath. Flies danced frenetically around the rotting flesh.

He rested on the man's eyes. They were open and empty, any expression having been drained with his life. Dan's initial conclusion was a relatively calm one; the man was likely the victim of a drowning, probably nothing more than a tourist caught in an undertow. But then he saw something on the left side of the man's head. A softness? He peered closer. Stained, dibble skin surrounded some kind of…opening…where the flesh bubbled out. Easy to miss until you saw it, then un-unseeable.

This man had been murdered.

The air around Dan turned immediately stale.

He stared immobile, feeling instantly nauseated. He scanned the area, desperate and illogical, for a murderer lurking nearby, careful not to move too abruptly and give away his anxiety. Steps sounded behind him and two arms wrapped around Dan's chest and squeezed.

"What are you doing?" Cat laughed.

He jumped and froze at once, then threw out his arms and twirled frantically to prevent Cat from seeing the scene he'd been so intent on protecting her from.

But he was too late.

She stood paralyzed and silent for what seemed like several seconds. Then suddenly and without warning, Cat vomited violently at Dan's feet and, still hunched and bent, let loose a whimper that sounded like sobbing but quickly morphed into louder, pained wails until she drowned out the birds with her own screams.

Five

"Just sit over here. I'll clean up." Dan wrapped his arm around Cat's shoulders to comfort her as he led her up a small incline to a grove of Bahamian pine trees about 20 feet from the water's edge.

"No. Leave it." Cat stopped walking and tucked her head into Dan's shoulder, which hovered just below her eyes. "Birds will get it."

"Exactly. Birds will get it. That's gross." Dan smiled, even chuckled, holding Cat for what he deemed sufficient comforting, then gently pushing her off himself and moving her to sit on a fallen tree.

"I'll be right back," he assured her as he stepped away and back toward the corpse and the remains of her body's reaction to seeing the dead man. Dan studied the vomit that looked like some kind of foamy jello and realized he had no way to clean up something so viscous. He considered simply covering the slime with dirt, but he immediately rejected the strategy when the likely possibility dawned on him that someone's foot, including his own, might squish into the mess. Better just to leave it.

He turned and started up the hill toward Cat. "Any idea who that is? Have you ever seen him before?"

"What?" She raised her head.

"No. I haven't. Probably a tourist." Cat leaned back and almost toppled over, before seeming to realize there was no support to stop her and grasping at the fallen tree trunk acting as her seat. Her legs flashed up and quickly down as she corrected herself, and her startled reaction turned to laughter. She brushed her hair, now in her face, off her forehead with both hands and tucked the errant strands behind her ears. Dan stifled a laugh, finding her uncoordinated fumbling strangely and irresistibly alluring. He opened his mouth to ask if she was okay.

"He wasn't from here," Cat called out. "Anyways, I don't think so. We may not know every...er, be friends with everyone on the cay, but we pretty much *know* everyone."

"Sounds a bit *Village of the Damned*, don't you think?" Dan smiled, but again, nothing from Cat. "Well, we should call someone. Are there police on the island?"

"Yes. Just how backward do you think we are?"

Dan began to answer, but Cat kept talking. "Okay, you're right. We kind of are," she said, grinning and patting her pockets. "A, singular, policeman. We have a constable, Ronnie, uh, Constable Anderson. We should call him. Can I use your phone? I guess I don't have mine down here."

"Sorry, don't have mine, either. Left it at home."

Cat threw Dan a disapproving look. Clearly, she was part of the camp that thought being without your phone was tantamount to a slow and painful death. "My bag, with the water and bananas, it's up by the lighthouse. And chips. My phone's in there."

Dan jogged, then walked, up the hill, grabbed Cat's phone and one of the bottles of water so she could rinse out her mouth, and brought the supplies back, handing the water to her first, which Cat set to the side before grabbing the cell and dialing.

"Getting my exercise today." Dan grinned.

32

No response from her, but he was getting used to that. She held the phone to her ear, and waited a few seconds before saying, "Hi, Ronnie?

"It's Cat.

"Yes, I...

"Oh, really? I'm glad. I...

"Really? Well, isn't that nice.

"Ronnie, stop talking."

Dan chuckled and shook his head, then left her to talk to Ronnie and fill him in about the body they'd discovered. He walked over to the dead man to get a closer look, pulling up his own shirt to cover his mouth as he got closer.

The stink wasn't as overwhelming as he'd imagined or seen in police dramas, probably because of the water, but Dan was still glad he'd skipped breakfast that morning. The stench was, without a doubt, pungent and pervasive, and Dan wondered how the decaying odor hadn't been immediately noticeable when they'd first arrived. He crouched next to the water, holding himself steady with his right palm pressed against the ground, and looked over the body, careful to make sure he didn't fall forward onto the bloated corpse.

The man's face and torso were swollen and his skin was blueish and veined. From this close, Dan could tell that the laceration he'd noticed before appeared likely to be, just as he'd thought, the result of a stabbing. The blade had entered on the side of the man's head near his ear. Odd, he thought, not an easy place to impale someone. If you were going for the head, wouldn't the man's face itself have been easier and more natural? A jab forward? Plus, you'd have the extra benefit of rendering the dead man unrecognizable, or at least less recognizable. Of course, the killer could have been behind the man. Or to the side? Then it might make sense. Or...

Dan stopped. Was he really thinking of pointers to give a murderer?

He whipped his head and scanned the body. Swelling and discoloration had bled into the corpse but, even with the bloating, Dan could tell that the man had put in his time at the gym, hard work that in the end had proved pointless—a blade's a blade, in shape or not. Gases had expanded the corpse's gut and the dead man's stomach pressed swollen against his belt and looked about to burst at any moment. Dan's hand moved reflexively to shield his eyes and he lost his balance. He teetered on the balls and toes of his feet and slammed his fist into the dirt in front of him, saving himself from plunging into the harbor and body, but propelling himself back and almost smashing into Cat's breakfast.

Dan jumped up and moved forward and to the right, darting his eyes over his shoulder at the vomit. He started to gag. Dan shifted again and leaned forward, cautious, this time placing his left hand palm-down on the dirt near the water. He studied the dead man's pockets. In the left, the outline of a small, flat, rectangular object pressed against his jeans' stretched fabric.

With his right hand, Dan stretched to push into the pocket. The stench from the body was thick and overwhelming this close and he felt the rumblings of a gag. When his hand touched the pants and he felt the squishy flesh underneath, Dan's gut tightened and he just had time to whip his head to the left and retch into the ocean, his empty stomach's acid suspended on the surface and sticking to the knee and upper leg of the body. The hat Cat had given to him fell off his head and into the floating refuse and Dan mumbled, disgusted. He paused, then gritted his teeth and rescued the hat, tossing it to the side. He hadn't even wanted the thing.

Pausing to take a breath, which he immediately regretted as the stink forced another wave of nausea through him, Dan steeled himself, and shoved his hand into the man's pocket, pulling out what he saw was a small plastic bag with white powder. He tossed the baggy into the hat he'd just recovered.

He eyed the other pocket. Something bigger, also rectangular, pushed tight against the cloth covering the leg. "Probably his wallet," Dan muttered. "Of course it would be over there."

He repositioned himself on the other side of the body, leaned forward, and braced himself. He held his breath, squinted his eyes and plunged his hand into the folds and pulled back. Dan lunged forward. He was stuck. With his fingers wrapped around whatever he was holding, his fist was too big to get past the opening. He struggled and wrenched his wrist from side to side, determined not to lose his grip on the slimy surface he clung to, but as his fingers slipped he panicked and jerked his arm back, tumbling onto his left side, this time landing squarely in Cat's vomit. He immediately flew to his feet, convulsing his entire body as he did (in a vain attempt to rid himself of the disgust) before jogging away from the scene. He lifted his hand and glanced quickly at the black, leather wallet gripped in his fingers, prying apart the folds and peeking inside. Empty. He grabbed his new cap as he heard Cat calling to him.

"Dan."

Cat had stood from her tree. "Dan, I've been calling out to you. Didn't you hear me?"

35

"No, I—"

"Ronnie will be here any minute. He wasn't busy when I called. He's heading right over."

"Look wh—"

"What's all over you? That's disgusting."

Cat shifted her eyes to Dan's left. He heard the motor of a boat coming closer and glanced over his shoulder to see a heavy-set man with gray-blond hair riding up to the shore where they (including the dead man) waited.

"Oh there he is. Hey there, Ronnie," Cat said and waved. Dan rushed to the unopened bottle of water, twisted off the cap and took a swig, swishing the liquid around in his mouth, then spitting into the bushes before splashing his side in a mostly successful effort to rinse his pant leg clean. He poured what was left over the wallet and hat. The baggy of what was certainly cocaine fell to the ground, and Dan snatched the bag and shoved the drugs into his own pocket. He shook off the leather billfold and pushed the wallet into his other pocket, replacing the empty water bottle against a rock and throwing the baseball cap against the container.

Back at the shore, Ronnie got out of his boat, unsteady, and secured a line around a large rock. He trudged up the hill a short distance, then seemed to decide his trek had been exhausting enough and called out hello to Cat, extending his arms. She crossed to him and gave him a hug.

"Ronnie."

"Cat, so sorry you had to go through this. Must've been awful."

He pressed his lips to her forehead and caressed her hair, holding her tight in his arms, squeezing her into his rather large stomach. Ronnie glanced up, acting as if he'd just realized they weren't alone.

"So, who's this?" Ronnie scrutinized Dan.

Cat started to answer, but this time Dan interrupted her. "Dan Harris." He held out his hand but let the friendly gesture fall when Ronnie didn't reciprocate. He rubbed his palms on the sides of his legs, "We were—"

"No need, Mr. Harris," Ronnie said, sternly, eyeing Dan's side. "Cat can tell me about it all." Cat pulled away from the large man and filled him in about their excursion to see the lighthouse, her beating Dan in a race and, finally, to Dan's finding the body and her throwing up.

"Oh, Cat, so sorry you had to go through this." Ronnie said, his lack of extensive vocabulary or sentiment becoming evident. Dan watched as Cat took Ronnie's outstretched hand and felt an unexpected, but undeniable, rush of jealousy in his own gut.

"Well," Ronnie said and cinched up his pants and brushed his stringy hair to the left, likely doing his best to look official and impress Cat. "I'll just go take a look. Wait for me here."

When Ronnie was several feet away, Dan hurried over to Cat, fanning his shirt as he walked. He began to whisper, "I went thr—"

"Hold on," Cat said and followed Ronnie toward the body, but the policeman turned quickly and stopped her. "Cat, I don't want you to have to see this any more than y'already have." He reached his arm around her and led her the short distance back to Dan.

Ronnie pulled at his pants again and pointed with his lips. "So, that just how you found him? You didn't move the body at all?" Apparently, Ronnie had seen all he needed to see, which couldn't have been much since he'd

37

never even reached the body, only surveyed the scene from a safe and non-exerting distance.

"No, we didn't touch it." Cat spoke up.

"Well, yes," Dan interjected. "I did."

"You moved the body?" Ronnie shifted closer to Dan.

"No, not moved it. But, I touched it…"

"That what happened to you there?" Constable Anderson motioned with his lips to Dan's side.

Dan glanced down. "No…uh that…the vomit. I slipped," he pronounced vaguely. "Anyway, I wanted to see if I could find any identification so I checked his pockets. I found this." Dan pulled the baggy out of his left pocket and started to reach for the wallet.

"You touched the body? What?" Constable Anderson glanced at Cat and smirked. "Why?"

Dan handed the drugs to Ronnie as the situation sunk in. Searching the dead man hadn't been the smartest move, despite his good intentions, and although Ronnie's reaction shouldn't have surprised him, the man's response snapped Dan into the reality of the situation. He suddenly felt more than a little bit threatened and decided that telling Ronnie about the wallet could wait. "I just wanted to know who he was. Cat didn't recognize him."

"No, I don't…Ronnie, I don't think he's from here."

Ronnie held the bag up in front of his face and shook the powder.

"I think it's cocaine," Dan offered.

"Mmmm." Ronnie shook his head, glowering at Dan. "Heroin. Pretty sure it's heroin."

"Well…"

"And you're saying this ain't yours?"

"No, of course not," Dan said, bemused. "Why would I show it to you if it were mine?"

"Mmmm. Dunno. I'm not a criminal." Ronnie studied Dan suspiciously and dropped the drugs, recently declared to be heroin, into his shirt pocket.

"So…did you find anything else?" he continued.

Dan caught himself briefly and then lied. "No."

Ronnie raised his hand to the top of his head and started to move his hair over.

"Ronnie," Dan started.

The policeman froze. He glared at Dan and enunciated, "Constable Anderson."

"Constable Anderson," Dan repeated, precisely. "I just wanted to see who he was. I thought it might help."

"So, Mr. Harris." Constable Anderson lifted his hand to his hair again, but stopped when his cell rang. He pulled the phone out of a holder on his waist and, with the same hand, held up his index finger, turning to look across the harbor. "Hell-o…Yeah, the lighthouse, just south. You'll see us along the water."

The constable snapped the cell shut, pushed his side gut out of the way and fastened the phone to his belt. He glanced at Dan. "Now, why're you here?" Constable Anderson's attention span seemed as lacking as his vocabulary.

"Like Cat said, we decided—"

"No, not *here*," Constable Anderson said, looking annoyed and pointing vigorously to the ground. "And not you two. Yourself, Mr. Harris." He circled broadly with both hands, palms down. "Hope Town. Why're you here in Hope Town."

"Ahh." Dan nodded. "I'm here writing a book. I'm a writer."

"Published?"

"Yes."

"Yes? Well..." Constable Anderson stopped talking. He seemed to be trying to think of something witty as a comeback, a struggle he was apparently losing.

Dan waited patiently (respectfully, he thought), giving the policeman a chance to continue. Then he fought unsuccessfully to bury a smile and said, "Anyway...My wife and I..."

"You're married?" Constable Anderson pulled out a notepad and wrote something down. Cat glanced at Dan.

"Yes. I..."

Constable Anderson looked at Cat.

"Did you know this?"

"No, but..."

"What're you doing here with Cat, Mr. Harris?" He walked closer to the woman and snaked his arm around her, protectively. "You often cheat on your wife?"

"What? No! What? I'm not...We were just..." Dan felt a rush of irritation. "What does this have to do with murder?"

"So, now you're saying it's murder? Why do you say that, Mr. Harris?" Constable Anderson wrote something else down, likely *adultery* since so far only Dan's relationship status had elicited any real response.

"Well, I'm not sure if you got close enough to the body, but..."

"You criticizing my investigation?"

"What investigation?" Dan couldn't suppress the exasperation in his voice. "So far, the only things you've cared about are if Cat is okay and whether or not I'm married. You didn't even walk all the way to the water so you could see the body. If you had, you'd have seen the stab wound on the side of the man's head. Unless the guy fell sideways onto a knife, an upright knife at that, somebody killed him."

Constable Anderson seemed taken aback by Dan's bluntness. "I see. Do *you* own a knife, Mr. Harris?"

Dan shouted a frustrated, "Ahhh!" into the air and started pacing in oblong circles. He stopped and looked to Cat, pleading.

"The man has a...what looks like a *pretty fatal* stab wound on the side of his head, where, I'd like to point out, the vast majority of stabbings turn out to be fatal. I—"

"You don't know that."

"What?" Dan squinted at Constable Anderson, who regarded him straight faced. Dan shook his head and continued.

"Anyway, I was with Cat. We found the man together. Obviously, this all happened before today and I've only been here for...not even a week. It probably happened before I even got here. Most likely, the body just recently washed up on shore and we happen to be the ones to find it."

"So, you got here a week ago?"

Finally Constable Anderson seemed to be listening to Dan. "Yes. Almost. Five or six days ago."

"Which is it, Boss?"

"Six. Five?" Dan struggled to remember which day he'd actually arrived.

"Uh-huh." Constable Anderson paused, then continued. "Well, we'll have to confirm that. But glad to see you're finally cooperating."

Dan lowered his head and chuckled, wondering what he'd been doing up to this point.

"Something funny, Chief?"

"No, I...Listen, all I know for sure is that we found a dead man and he has some kind of a wound...from a knife, looks like...on the side of his head."

"Right. And you know this because you thought putting your hands *and* your DNA all over the body was smart."

"No!"

"No? You changing your story now? You didn't touch the body?"

Dan held his ground silently and glared at Constable Anderson. What he said clearly didn't matter. Maybe this outsider thing Cat had alluded to was actually real.

"So, back to this wife of yours? Why isn't she with you?"

"Seriously?" Dan yelled, exasperated. "We're separated. But, honestly, my marriage doesn't have...*anything*," he mimicked Anderson's earlier palms-down hand circles, "to do with what's happening here. Nothing. Period."

"Someone's got to watch out for Cat. Attractive, single woman. Bald, suspicious, obviously dishonest foreigner pretending to be single. So," he said, not giving Dan a chance to respond, "you contaminated the body. Was Cat with you at the time?"

Dan glanced at Cat, "I'm not bald...not all the way."

He continued, "And no. She wasn't. Not—"

"Not close." Cat chimed in. "But I was close enough to see what he was doing. The smell is so strong. Well, you can smell it, Ronnie. It's awful." Cat walked over to Ronnie and hugged him into submission, a bit of a whine in her voice. "It's just awful."

"Yes...well," Constable Anderson's face turned red and flush. "So your wife."

This was all too surreal. At least Cat was there to flirt Ronnie into distraction, which, thankfully, didn't take much. This comic-book police...guy...seemed more interested in Cat and the fact that Dan was married and, allegedly, cheating on his wife than that a dead stranger had washed up on the otherwise serene shores of Hope Town.

"Susan," Dan said, softly.

"Susan?" Cat cut in. "That's a nice name. You hadn't told me her name yet." Dan glanced at Cat. I haven't told you anything yet, he thought.

"So you're cheating on your wife"

"I am not cheating on my wife!" Dan erupted.

"Boss, calm down. Just trying to get to the bottom of all this."

"Seriously? Get to the bottom of what? Even if I were having an affair, which I'm not, what would my marriage have to do with the decomposing man over there? This is a joke!"

Constable Anderson looked condescendingly at Dan and ignored what he seemed to consider nothing more than a childish tantrum. Anderson pulled at his pants, which hadn't moved, and looked at Cat. "You have anything to add to this, Cat? This man deceive you?"

"No, Ronnie, they're separated. She...let's just say she isn't good for him."

"No, let's not," Dan cut in, wondering how Cat was suddenly privy to anything having to do with Susan.

"So," Constable Anderson looked at his notepad, which probably only had the word *liar* added to the *adultery* from before. He continued, "Let's review. You get to the cay, writing a book, you claim you're separated," the constable rolled his eyes when he said this, "but still, you're on a date with Cat."

Dan opened his mouth to protest, then gave up.

Anderson eyed Dan, but pressed on, "So, you're married, but spending time with Cat, when you find a body, notice a stab wound in the man's head, and decide it's murder. You touch and contaminate the body, making sure your DNA—"

"I wasn't making sure of anything. Just trying to see who he was," Dan said quietly.

Anderson repeated, "Making sure, you now claim without meaning to, though we all know that's just what a killer hisself would say." He studied Dan, then continued, "...making sure that your DNA ends up all over the body. Were you looking for something? Maybe you wanted to throw it to the side? Into the ocean? Make sure we, ourselves, wouldn't find it. That why you're wet?"

Dan fingered the wallet in his pocket but didn't answer, just stared out into the harbor and slowly shook his head.

"Cat calls me, as any concerned citizen would do. Thank you, Cat." He turned, nodding at Cat, and smiled at her. "And I myself come here to inspect the situation. That 'bout right?"

"Yes, that's perfect. Thanks, Ronnie," Cat answered. But Dan couldn't see how that was perfect or that the policeman had actually inspected anything, at least not anything dead.

Constable Anderson shoved his notebook back in his back pants' pocket just as another, larger boat floated toward them, and the driver secured the vessel close to the body. Ronnie stepped about a foot and called out, "Vern, let's get some photos and then take the body over to Marsh

Harbour straight away." Although Dan guessed that by *let's*, Anderson meant Vern.

He turned and spoke to Cat. "Can I take you back across the harbor? I reckon you had a hard day."

"No, thanks, Ronnie. I'm fine. Besides, I came with Dan."

"He can walk. Can't you, Dan?" The policeman leered at Dan.

"No, really. I'm fine," Cat said.

"Sure? No trouble."

"We'll be okay. Thank you." Cat reassured Ronnie, sliding closer to hug him.

Constable Anderson stared sharply and for what felt like several minutes at Dan. "Okay," Anderson said, not letting go of Cat. "But, be careful. I'll contact you both later should I have questions." He looked sternly at Dan. "Which I will. And Mr. Harris, best you just stay on the cay. Don't you try goin' nowhere." Constable Anderson leaned over, hugged Cat one last time and glared at Dan without saying a word before he turned and walked toward the body, presumably to do his part and point aggressively.

"I'm okay, too," Dan shouted, and Cat smiled and giggled softly, crossing to loop her arm into Dan's and start up the hill toward the lighthouse.

"Now, how about we see that view I was telling you about?"

* * * *

"What was that about?" Dan asked as he and Cat climbed the small incline that led to the lighthouse's entrance. Dark clouds, both literal and figurative, had been gathering around the group while Constable Anderson simultaneously caressed Cat and accosted Dan. As the two

45

walked, a gentle rain that belied the ominous sky around them started to fall. Cat purred and pushed her face into the falling water.

"Oooh. I love the rain." She bolted forward and spun in front of Dan, stretching out her arms to take his hands. "Come on. This is so beautiful."

"Cat, what was that about with Constable Anderson?"

She stopped. "Who? Ronnie? Oh, don't worry about him. He's harmless."

"Maybe to you."

Cat started whirling again. Dan shifted back, annoyed.

"Regardless. Cat...Cat!" Dan shouted. Cat froze with her hands in the air. "We just found a murdered man. Don't you feel, I don't know, affected?"

"Affected? Yes, yes. Very affected." She dropped her head and stared at the ground for a few seconds, then looked back up at Dan. "How's that?"

Her mouth curved and she grabbed his hands again. "I'm sure it will hit me hard later. It's just how I deal with things. But, anyways, we shouldn't let it ruin our afternoon. It's over. Done with. We didn't know the guy and there's nothing we can do now anyways."

Dan stared at her. He bobbed his head, glancing at his feet. There was a certain cerebral logic in what she was saying. And maybe he was being a bit of a buzzkill. But still, a man had been murdered, know him or not. Whenever the stranger had been killed, he was, in fact, dead. And now he was alone and pale-blue and swollen and...

"Come on." Cat reached out and pulled at Dan's fingers. The rain had started falling faster and, dragged by Cat, the two ran the short distance to the top of the hill and ducked into the lighthouse. The building was narrow and cylindrical and, as he looked up, Dan felt a bit of a sense of vertigo, almost reaching to Cat for support. Almost.

Dan studied the small room. A metal spiral staircase, broken up by small platforms, wound around the brick interior and ultimately reached (he assumed) the lantern room and the building's *raison d'être*. Dan wasn't claustrophobic—not really—but he couldn't help feeling more than a little nervous about climbing the visibly old and rickety steps. He eyed Cat, who seemed to read his mind.

"Oh, don't worry, my big teddy bear," she said in a voice as if she were talking to a baby. "It will be all right. I'll hold on to you."

"That's what I'm afraid of."

"Oh." Cat acted infatuated relief and raised her clasped hands to her chest. "Finally. You're back."

Suddenly, she darted up the stairs and had nearly finished ascending the first rotation before Dan cautiously started climbing, moving a little more slowly and holding on to the railing. Realizing he was falling behind, he jogged to catch up with Cat, who was already across the first level before the stairs started up again.

Despite his best efforts, by the time he reached the top, Cat had already crawled through a small opening in the round lantern room and stood outside. Dan's height made it awkward to get through the exit but he did, with difficulty, and paused to absorb the 360-degree views. Light rain, really nothing more than a mist at this point, moistened his face.

"Wow!" Dan took in the harbor and the town, careful to stay somewhat close to the security of the building while still clutching the outer railing around the walkway; claustrophobia may not be a problem, but

47

acrophobia...well, who was really thrilled about heights, anyway?

"It's really beautiful," he continued. "You can see everything."

"I told you." Cat leaned against his shoulder. "You know the town didn't want the lighthouse at first."

"Really?" Dan said, stepping away.

"No, they didn't. It cut down on shipwrecks."

Dan turned and looked at Cat, careful not to let go of the metal handrail. "Isn't that a good thing?"

"Not if your main source of income is salvaging those wrecks. Hope Town had more people until the lighthouse was built. I think 1850. 1850...something."

"1864," Dan said.

Cat looked surprised, and he added, "I've done my research."

"Well, I'm impressed." She started around the platform that circled the lantern room. "Did your research tell you what this is called, silly?" Cat jumped and Dan flinched and tightened his grip on the railing. "What we're standing on?"

"No, what?"

"A widow's walk." Cat pivoted to face Dan, looking pleased with herself.

"You know, you shouldn't antagonize him," she continued.

"Who?"

"Ronnie. Constable Anderson. And you shouldn't have touched the body. I don't know what you were thinking. He's not the smartest guy, but he *can* make your life difficult."

"I thought you said he was harmless."

Cat shrugged.

48

"Well he seems to like you. A lot." Dan raised his eyebrows and angled his head to the side.

"Yeah, He does. He has a little crush on me. But, that can help us."

"Us?"

"Well yeah. Us." Cat moved closer to Dan, and dropped her hand on his arm. "I'm on your side, silly. You had to notice how suspicious he was of you."

"Yeah, what was all that?"

"Probably mostly about me. He's jealous." Cat moved away and leaned against the barrier, studying the harbor. "But too, you're just getting here when most tourists are leaving. No one wants to be here if there's a hurricane. We don't really have the services. Plus, developers want to put in a big resort here. People have mixed feelings about that." She spun around, squinting, and crept toward him. "You could be one of them disguised as a writer."

With no warning, the misty rain burst into a downpour and Cat and Dan hurried to the lantern room's small opening. He waited while she ducked and crawled inside, then started in himself. The entrance was flush with the floor of the widow's walk and Dan struggled more squirming in than he had climbing out. Between Cat taking her sweet time and his own wrestling with what amounted to little more than a square hole, by the time he finally reached cover, he was soaked. His shirt hugged tight to his chest.

"Ooh. I like." Cat reached out and ran her hand over Dan's muscles. He pushed her arm away abruptly, tired of her constant advances and suddenly feeling irritated and done with the day.

"Well, what do we do now?" he said.

"We wait," she said, looking serious. "It should stop before too long. We can start down if you want."

Dan motioned for Cat to go first, then followed, stepping carefully. The two waited for the rain to stop, hearing thunder in the distance, the 'before too long' growing into more like half an hour. Then Cat grabbed her bag and they started the hike home, discussing only small, insignificant topics and how they better hurry to get back before the rain started up again, how they were lucky they left when they did.

When the two arrived at Cat's place, she leaned in, standing on her tip-toes, and gave Dan a kiss on the cheek. "Thank you, sir, for a memorable and eventful day."

"You're welcome," Dan said, forcing a smile as he turned away from Cat toward the town center and his house on the other side.

"Dan," she called out to him.

He stopped and pivoted to face her.

"I'm sorry if I overstepped," Cat said, looking downtrodden, but downtrodden mixed with a dash of petulance. "I...

"I just wish you weren't married."

"That's okay. Sometimes I wish I weren't, too."

Cat's face lit up at his words and Dan immediately regretted having said them, wondering where the sentiment had come from.

"Good night, Cat."

"Good night, Dan. And thanks, again." She turned and walked, bouncing, toward her house. "Oh, wait, I almost forgot." She reached into her bag and pulled out Dan's new hat, still a bit wet, rushing back to Dan, who wondered when she'd managed to grab the cap.

"Thanks. Almost forgot it," he said, feeling more sarcastic than he hoped he sounded.

"Well, have a good night, Dan. Talk to you tomorrow?"

"Sure. Have a good night."

Dan shoved the hat in his back pocket and started the short trek home.

Six

The walk back to his house didn't take long, but by the time Dan opened his door and stepped into the living room, the sun was tucking itself in for the night and all he saw across the harbor was the last of the brilliant orange glow silhouetting the lighthouse, the structure's just-then-visible beam circling and casting its warming glow onto the water.

Dan pulled the hat Cat had given him out of his back pocket, the wallet from his front, and crossed to toss them both onto the bed. He paused to take in his home. Cat was right; the day had been memorable and eventful. But beyond that, finding a murdered man had left Dan feeling a kind of blankness, an empty blending of pity and relief like when waiting for a funeral procession of only two cars. And Ronnie's—Constable Anderson's—immediate suspicion of Dan had left him feeling particularly alone and isolated, despite Cat's best, if sometimes annoying, attempts to entice him otherwise.

Maybe a little wine would help.

This had to be a light night, though. Time for Dan to get his life in order and write his book. "And get off this island before I get arrested for a murder I didn't commit," Dan muttered as he opened a bottle of cabernet sauvignon, which the label described as inky—perfect for a writer, even if this writer had no idea what those words meant or how a wine being inky was a good thing.

"*Couldn't* commit," he corrected himself loudly.

Dan poured himself a generous glass, then glanced around the room (to make sure no one was looking) and tipped the bottle into his mouth to take a long gulp, or two—this had been one of those days. Satisfied for the moment, he pushed the cork back into place and crossed to his desk, aka, the kitchen table. He set the goblet down and reached to pull a pen and notepad out of a bag that leaned inconspicuously against the back of the living room couch.

Sitting at his makeshift writing station, he stared at the blank paper. And stared. Staring. Stare-eth. What's a synonym for stare? he thought. Gaze? Gape? Ogle? Lots of Gs. Peer? Kind of, he guessed. But, none of those words truly communicated the sense of vacant seeing he was looking for. Stare it was. Dan started to make note of the word, then wondered why, paused, and instead scribbled '*dead body*', staring (that word again) at the script before jotting down, '*thinks it's me—why*', then *gazing* out across his house's deck to the dark sky and the beam that floated effortlessly across the harbor.

The lighthouse looked so isolated from this vantage point.

Dan returned to his paper and added a '*?*' after the '*why*'. Then, under the original words, '*does he really?*', wondering with his lips as he wrote.

He wasn't sure he should even care, apart from the perhaps too real threat of false arrest. Dan wasn't from the island (didn't even live here, really) and, for all he knew, the dead man wasn't actually killed on Elbow Cay, just carried by the tides from who knows where and, finally, washed ashore in Hope Town Harbour. Dan lifted and tilted his wine glass, but tasted only a hint of *inky* red on the rim of the glass. Empty. How...?

"Oh well," he muttered and crossed to the counter to refill his glass, this time returning with the bottle. He set the wine on the table but before he could sit, his phone rang.

Dan froze, listening. He strained to locate the sound, oddly frantic, even rushing into the bathroom and glancing around the toilet before returning to the bedroom and shaking the linens on the bed. The movement jostled his new hat enough to reveal his phone underneath the bill, and he answered quickly, expecting to hear dead air.

"Hello?" Dan said as he hurried back to the living area and his wine.

"Dan? Is that you?...You sound stressed."

Dan collapsed into one of the table's chairs, feeling better just hearing his wife's voice and grateful she knew him so well that one word could be as revealing as a long conversation. "Susan. It's so good...

"I miss you so much, Susan. It's..."

"Is everything okay?" She sounded worried. Worried was good.

"Yes," Dan let his head fall, "I just—"

"Okay. Then." He heard Susan exhale. "Listen. I only called to let you know that your agent is trying to get a hold of you. He says he really needs to talk to you. He wouldn't tell me why." She sounded sharp. "I've been calling all day. I wish you'd just give this number out. Really. I don't have time to field your calls."

Dan felt like he'd been rescued, only to be hit over the head with a club and thrown back to the proverbial wolves. The day had been overwhelming. But then, to hear Susan talk so abruptly...It was all too much. He took a deep breath and waited. And then answered.

"No. I want to focus. I'm here to work on my book." Dan hesitated. "And us. I miss us. I miss you."

"Yes, I know," she spit out, simply. "You said that."

Dan gazed out the French doors and across the deck that wrapped around the front of his home over the water. Susan was so far away and her response made her seem even farther. All around him, the emptiness of the night crushed against the walls and ceiling of the house. Even the stars felt muted and struggling to be noticed. Dan dropped his hand away from his ear, knocking the phone on the table, and stared straight ahead, seeing nothing.

Finally, he heard a disembodied voice calling out to him. "Dan, are you there?

"...Dan?"

He pressed the phone slowly to his ear again. "I'm here."

"Listen," Susan said. "I just called to tell you to call your agent."

"Okay, but I..." Dan scanned the empty room. "I just really miss you. And Ryan." He paused, a catch in his throat. "I love you."

"Are you drinking?"

"What?"

"Are you drinking?" she repeated, louder. Stern.

Dan opened his mouth, but didn't answer. At first he heard nothing, just an empty silence that couldn't even be bothered to be angry. Then, a quick, emotionless, "Me, too," a click, and Susan was gone.

Dan held the phone to his ear a bit longer, willing Susan back, even this new cold and condescending Susan. He downed his newly poured wine in one long gulp and threw his phone viciously across the room, hitting the device against the wall with a painful thud before he stomped back into the kitchen, to the fridge, where he flipped open the freezer, got out the vodka and filled a large tumbler. Dan downed a large gulp and replaced the cup's missing liquid before returning the bottle to the freezer and slamming the door.

Inhaling deeply through his nose, Dan leaned back on the kitchen counter, then crossed to rest against the open doorway leading to the deck, his insides pounding to reach outside. All he could see was the inky (finally the word made sense to him) night sky. Even the glow that should have emanated from the lighthouse was gone. He paced back into the kitchen, set down his cup and slammed his palms onto the counter, then stomped again toward the doors and the deck. The lighthouse's beam swung around once more and, at last, he could see the light clearly before it disappeared again and reappeared, finally unmissable, like earlier at the water, like the blood, or lack of blood, oozing, not oozing, from the dead man's lifeless head.

Dan shuddered. He hurried back to the table to jot down a quick note about the lighthouse not having been built at the time of the cholera outbreak, which he'd known, but hadn't really realized, returning to the kitchen counter to retrieve his drink, then spinning to pad back across the room and plop down on the couch, tossing his pen behind him toward the table and chairs. The ballpoint landed on the notepad and rolled to a stop just before reaching the edge of the flat surface. Dan held up his fists, lightly shaking them, making a shushing noise to imitate a crowd cheering and spilling his drink in the process.

He licked his wrist and forearm where the liquid had splashed out.

Dan glanced up toward the ceiling. Blank.

Then he shifted forward and relaxed into the cushions, alone, drinking his vodka and staring at the dripping night sky, while light from the island's all-seeing guardian spun into and out of existence until, finally sufficiently sedated, Dan passed out and sunk into sleep, his limp hand opening to release the mostly empty cup that fell lost between the large, soft folds of the sofa.

* * * *

Dan drifted. Deep. Painless. Voided. Rain had fallen throughout almost the entire night and the water's soft staccato had played lightly, rhythmically, occasionally thunderously above Dan's head.

He dreamt of the harbor, of the lighthouse, of the hill that fell down and away from the buildings at the top. He slept with the body, the strangely peaceful and pulsing-with-stolen-life body. Dan fell to his knees, caressing the close-to-bursting forehead of the corpse and wondering what had brought this man here, to this island, ultimately lifeless and gnawed and discovered. Dan felt a rushing, overwhelming compassion for the stranger and the drops falling on the roof were a downpour in his mind, wetting the man's features and melting his individuality into nothing more than a mannequin's smooth skull. Dan tried to protect the man, desperate and leaning forward to shelter the corpse with his own body, but his hand grabbed at nothing and he tipped into the harbor, falling forward and pushing the man deeper and into nothingness, sinking with the stranger, but gently, in slow motion, the air and the water one and like anger. Still, Dan drifted and dropped steadily, all the while fighting to keep his own head above water, again water, and away from his vomit that appeared from nowhere and, at one point, Dan felt his hand wrap around something and he thought it must be the man's arm or leg or any part of him. But when he pulled up and sat back, his fingers were empty and swollen, contaminated, and he stopped and opened his eyes as if nothing had happened, remembering only water. And peace. Then ache.

Seven

Dan felt water. He shifted and glanced down. His cup had tilted and the contents, not water, had puddled at his side, moistening the cushion and pushing the smell of vodka into the air around him and (he pulled the cloth of his shirt up and sniffed) into his clothes from yesterday that he still wore. He squinted and blinked and gazed out the French doors to find that the sun had already risen behind him, tossing well-intended rays bouncing across the glistening harbor. A new day was beginning, like it or not, and life and, perhaps more significantly, death continued unstoppable.

Unexpectedly, Dan woke full of energy and determination. He couldn't help but notice his broken and unusable cell phone when he stood and turned and for a moment he wondered what had happened, until the previous night's call crashed over him and threatened to pull him under. But instead he kept on, repeating his Bahamian morning ritual of water, Advil, and more water, adding a cold shower this time, before heading out of the house with a lingering look to the left to make sure he was alone. He skipped his morning coffee (which he desperately wanted) and instead continued down Front Street to the post office dock.

Back to the lighthouse. Why? Dan wasn't really sure. But he wanted clarity of some kind, and returning to the scene of the crime seemed the most logical place to start.

59

True, the area wasn't really the scene of the crime—more like the scene of the *discovery* of the crime—but the location would have to do.

The post office dock was the busiest of the four or five piers sprinkled around the harbor, all mostly serving as ferry stops. Dan didn't want to take one of the scheduled trips to Marsh Harbour. In fact, he'd been warned against leaving the island, not that Constable Anderson would ever know. But he only wanted to go across the small waterway to the wrap-around edge of the island; he just needed transportation. Luckily, one of the harbor's boaters was always willing to ferry a passenger (for a couple of dollars in thanks) and before long Dan was on his way.

As the two men bounced across the water, his chauffeur leaned back and yelled, "You hear 'bout the body they found over here?"

"Yes." Dan glanced at the boat's driver, surprised he already knew (only a night had passed). "Actually, I found it. Well, we. I was with Cat, the librarian. Do you know her?"

"Ahhh," was all the man said as they sped across the water and Dan noted that the boater shifted slightly away from him, even ducking to fit more completely under the small shelter at the front of the vessel. Dan twisted and watched the shallow wake the boat left behind.

Before long, the two arrived at the other side of the harbor, floating up to the appropriately named lighthouse dock, really just a shed and a short platform. Dan paid the man, who wasted no time in leaving and didn't give him a chance to say he'd need a ride back later or even inquire about the possibility of a return trip. Oh well, he thought, perhaps more exercise wasn't such a bad thing. Dan watched the man speed away and started up the wooden path leading to the lighthouse and the two detached homes that sat at the building's base.

On the trip over, Dan had decided the most logical approach was to skip the shore and, instead, approach the lighthouse keeper directly to ask him—or her, Dan had corrected himself—if he (or she) had seen or heard anything that stood out in the last few days. He walked up to the door of one of the houses and held up his fist, about to knock, when he noticed an older gentleman, dressed in khakis and a button up on the other side of the homes and lighthouse, filling a bucket with water from a hose and eyeing him.

"Something you need?"

Dan stepped off the home's wraparound porch.

"Good morning, Sir. You in charge here?"

"Sure. Something you need?" the old man said.

"My name's Daniel Harris. Dan. I'm staying across the harbor. Just got here this week."

"Mmmm." The lighthouse keeper, Dan assumed, leaned over and picked up his bucket by the handle. "Strange time of year to come. Most people leavin' 'bout now."

"Yes." Dan smiled. "That's what I hear."

The old man started forward. "Mmmm?"

Dan followed, jogging to the man's side and reaching toward the bucket. He repeated, loudly, "I said, that's what I hear."

"Mmmm."

To Dan's surprise, the man stopped walking and handed Dan the pail, apparently happy to be offered the help. "You here 'bout that resort? Already told you people, don't really care much 'bout that. Help save the lighthouse, alls I care 'bout."

"Oh, yeah? No, not here about the resort. I'm just visiting."

"Mmmm. Well," he said, staring straight ahead and wiping his hands on his pants. "I'm Thomas."

"Nice to meet you, Thomas." Dan held out his free hand but Thomas simply motioned to the right. "Right over there."

Dan carried the water *right over there* and set down the bucket. "Are you the lighthouse keeper here?"

"Yep, that's me. Me and my son." He scrutinized Dan. "So...what d'you want?"

Dan stopped, taken aback by the old man's sudden assertiveness. Then he said, "Did you know that a body was found down by the water, down there? Over that way." He leaned and pointed to the spot he and Cat had found the body the previous day.

Thomas crossed to pick up a large boulder and Dan couldn't help wondering if the old guy was just keeping busy. "Yeah, so?"

"You saw the body?"

"Heard a scream. Saw things. People. You." Thomas set down the boulder and pointed at Dan. "A pretty girl. Then Ronnie come over." He brushed a fly away from his face. "Someone drown?"

"You don't know?" Dan studied Thomas's face.

"Don' know what? Eyes not what they was. Just saw something happening, that's all. Didn't really care. Not gonna walk down there for nothin'."

"But—"

"Kinda strange. You're there. Now you're here." Thomas stopped and squinted at Dan.

"I'm just trying to figure out what happened. The man was murdered."

Thomas backed up a few steps and lifted his shirt, fumbling at his side, and darting glances down as he did. "What's goin' on? You think I did it?"

He seemed to finally find what he'd been searching for and pushed out a knife, waving the blade chaotically in front of himself. Dan stumbled back and pressed his palms in the air. "Whoa!"

Thomas continued, "Why would you think I did it? Daniel!" He peeked at the closest house.

"No…I just…"

"Daniel!" the old man shouted again.

"Yes. Sir. I'm right here," Dan answered, confused.

"Nah, not you. The other keeper. He's named Daniel, too."

"Your son?"

"How'd you know that? You spyin' on us?" Thomas said and shifted forward, waving the knife as he did.

"You just told me," Dan rushed out. "Listen, I—"

"He's 'round here somewhere. Don't you try nothin'…Daniel!…Daniel!"

The old man held his eyes on Dan between quick scans around the property.

"It's okay. I'm going. I just…"

"Daniel!"

"Fine. I'm going."

Dan spun and hurried down the same wood pathway he'd used to get up to the buildings. When he reached the trail through the trees, he turned and looked back to see Thomas had already returned to what Dan had figured could only be busy work. He considered going farther down to the dock to wait for a passing boat. But that seemed unlikely, so he started off through the growth, instead. He could always see if Cat was home and fill her in.

"What is with these people?" Dan mumbled, then chuckled, as he stepped off the planks and glanced one last time toward Thomas and his bucket and his weapon. He continued along the dirt path, through the forest of sea grape and mangrove trees, assessing his morning and realizing his investigations at the lighthouse had only left him more confused. Thomas was either a dangerous killer or (more likely) nothing more than an old man freaked out by a foreigner showing up to accuse him of a murder he'd not even known about. Although, Dan had to admit, beginning any process with nothing more than a commitment to gender equality certainly wasn't likely to produce many results.

Dan reviewed what he knew so far. Not much of anything, really. All Dan knew for sure was that a man had been killed, probably somewhere in the Bahamas, and likely in the Abaco Islands. But, he couldn't even be sure about that fact. Could currents carry a body all the way from the states? Or from farther? Maybe? Though certainly not in such relatively good condition.

Dan sat on a rock in the trees along the walkway. He pulled out his notepad and, at the top of a new page, wrote *lighthouse keeper: Thomas, son: Daniel*. He considered his next words, leaning against a tree trunk and closing his eyes.

* * * *

"Ahem."

Dan jerked. He winced.

He'd fallen asleep and his neck pressed awkwardly into the base of a branch. He squinted open his eyes and twisted. Ahead of him, a man he'd never seen before smirked down at him. The creep, Dan had to assume, had been watching him while he slept, and he felt more than a little, well, creepy. He scurried to his feet, his notepad falling to the ground. The man quickly bent to scoop up the papers and read Dan's notes aloud as he did.

"Lighthouse keeper: Thomas. Son..." the stranger said in a British accent.

Dan snatched the pad from the man's hand, shocked at his audacity and still not feeling entirely present, just awake. "Thanks, I'll take that," he said as he studied the hiker, who wore blue shorts and a red jacket, despite the day's heat. Brits, he thought.

"Resting? I do hope I've not disturbed your sleep," the man whispered, or at least pretended to. Although, there's something about an English accent. The man sounded both kind and condescending at the same time.

"No. Just...uh...I was just making some notes."

"Yes. Thomas, apparently a lighthouse keeper, and his son, D..."

"Just some notes."

"Thomas or Daniel?" the Brit continued, this time more clearly taunting Dan. "Are you a lighthouse keeper or his son?

"Or, are you someone else entirely?"

"No, it's just..." Dan stopped, realizing he didn't owe this man any kind of explanation.

After a moment, the Englishman said, "Yes. Well. I'm Victor. Victor Bennett. Perhaps you've heard of me."

The man's name sounded familiar, but although Dan quickly searched his brain for a reason, he couldn't place why. "No," he shook his head and felt a more-than-slight sense of satisfaction.

"Really?" Victor said, clearly incredulous and glancing away dismissively. "I reckon you don't read, then."

Instantly, the name registered and Dan remembered how he knew the man. Victor Bennet, he thought with a slur.

Victor Bennett had been a one-time literary star, a bit of a one-hit wonder as far as authors were concerned. His book, *Time for Breathing* had been lauded as "art of staggering depth and layered intelligence, " and the work had rocketed to the top of every best-seller list (at least every list that mattered), occupying that coveted top spot on most for more than five unheard of years. There was even talk of a film, though the production had never materialized.

Unfortunately for Victor, his 15 minutes plus had run out almost 20 years ago and he'd not produced a thing since, at least not anything publishable. Although, Dan had heard that he'd been actively trying, and failing, to reproduce his celebrity. Even more, there were whispers that he'd actually stolen the original manuscript that had resulted in *Time for Breathing*.

Victor tapped his right foot. "And you are?"

"I'm Dan."

"And you say you're not the son of a lighthouse keeper." Victor smirked and glanced to the side.

"No, I'm not."

"And would you have a surname, Dan?"

"Harris. Daniel Harris."

"The writer?"

Dan nodded.

"Oh." Victor paused. "And you don't know who I am? I'm surprised. I know who you are." He looked away. "Trust me, it doesn't last."

"I..." Dan stopped.

"Do you live here on the island?" he continued, suddenly remembering that he'd heard that Victor Bennett had moved to the Bahamas several years ago.

"Yes, I do. But, shhhh," Victor leaned forward and pressed a finger to his lips. "The press still hound me. I don't like to flaunt who I am."

Clearly, thought Dan. But, although he questioned the existence of any overly ambitious paparazzi pestering the man, he certainly didn't doubt that Victor desperately missed the attention. The Brit had, at one time, been the consistent center of rumors and Dan had often wondered what was real and what was self-generated as part of Victor's vain attempt to remain in the celebrity spotlight. He decided he didn't have the time or the interest in getting to know the man.

"Well...it was nice to meet you," Dan said, extending his hand. "I should be going."

"Going? But I've just got here, haven't I?"

"Yes, well..." Dan dropped the gesture and turned to leave. Victor spoke up almost immediately.

"You know, apparently they've discovered a body over by the lighthouse...murdered." Victor added the last word softly as he leaned into Dan's back.

He continued, "I'm off to see it all now. I've been home, in England, on holiday for the last couple of weeks and it would seem I've missed all the excitement one can imagine such a discovery would generate. I've just returned yesterday morning."

"Oh yeah?" Dan rotated and faced the man. "Well there's nothing to see now. The body's gone."

"Yes. I reckon it would be, wouldn't it?" Victor said, looking thoughtful.

"Nonetheless, apparently they suspect some writer visiting…goodness, is that you? Are you a deranged, murdering madman? Should I be frightened?" Victor asked, placing his right hand on his chest, visibly mocking Dan with his theatrics and, perhaps more clearly, not concerned in the least that Dan was any kind of a threat.

Dan reluctantly engaged Victor. "Who's saying this?"

"Well, I certainly don't owe you any sort of an explanation, do I?"

"But," the Brit looked left, then right, apparently wanting to ensure that his big reveal didn't leak beyond the two. "I was at Sun Dried Tees…you know, below the Sugar Shack, and I overheard Ronnie Anderson telling Ilsa all about the macabre discovery. Of course, when he saw me, he immediately called me over and filled me in about the horrific affair. Ronnie tells me everything, you see. I once gave him a copy of my book, and he's never forgotten. The island class. So simple, really. So easy to please."

He gazed into the distance.

"Anyway, he told me all about your little affair, you naughty boy, and how you smeared your DNA everywhere and ensured that it was impossible for them to know if your germs came from then or before, when the man died. He seemed quite bothered by that.

"Of course, I'm not so easily swayed. I doubt you did it…not that you couldn't. I can certainly see why he's threatened by you. You're quite strapping, aren't you?"

Dan glanced toward Cat's house.

"Ronnie Anderson. I say, he's threatened by you. I can certainly see why."

When Dan still didn't respond, Victor fanned himself with his hand and added, "I say, it's quite warm today, isn't it?"

Dan eyed him. "Why don't you take off your jacket?"

"You know, I was coming over on the ferry yesterday morning. I'd arrived the night before...from England. Did I tell you that?"

"Yes, you did."

Victor inhaled, then continued, "On holiday to see my family. I'm a bit of a local celebrity, as one can imagine. Nonetheless, I'd returned the day before and stayed the night in Marsh Harbour at the Abaco Club. I took the mid-morning ferry yesterday. I often meditate as I travel between the two islands, center myself as I return home." Victor closed his eyes and held his right hand to his chest, thumb and middle finger pressed together. He opened his eyes and continued.

"But, on this trip, I'd felt compelled to watch the water as I floated into my beloved Hope Town and I thought I saw something odd floating in the water in the direction of the lighthouse.

"Well, after what Ronnie confided in me, I feel quite certain I was the first to actually see the murdered man. Yes, quite certain. He was wearing a red t-shirt with some kind of a religious insignia. A cross, I think? I'm sure Ronnie will fill me in on the details, should I ask him, which I probably won't. I'm not one for idle gossip. So petty, isn't it?

"I gifted Ronnie a copy of my book once...signed, of course. He's never forgotten my kindness."

Victor turned his head to the left, then back to face Dan, tossing a dismissive, "Well, I'll be going now," into the trees, before he spun and continued on toward the lighthouse.

Dan watched Victor as he sauntered down the path. The man scratched his left arm with his right hand, then switched to do the same to his right arm, near his elbow, occasionally rubbing his left arm against his stomach as he hiked.

So, supposedly Victor had seen the dead man before he'd washed up on shore. Of course, he'd also said the man was wearing a red shirt (and with a cross), which Dan knew wasn't true. But why would the man invent a detail he had to know Dan would be able to confirm or, more likely given that level of detail, repudiate?

He pulled out his notepad, flipped to the page with *'Thomas'* and *'Dan'*, and, beneath their names, wrote *'Victor Bennett:'*, paused, then continued, adding *'desperate'*. Dan closed the pad and pushed the pen and paper into his pocket before he proceeded down the path.

True to form, dark clouds rushed to cover the island and a soft rain started to shower Dan, quickly turning into a downpour. The rushing water felt refreshing in the day's heat, and he stopped to stretch his face to the sky, remembering Cat after finding the dead man, before he sprinted down the soon to be muddy path toward Queen's Highway.

When Dan reached the librarian's house, he bounced up the steps to her front door, even raised a fist to knock. But he stopped and dropped his hand to his side when he noticed water dripping from his arm. He was soaked. Visions of Cat's pawing at the lighthouse instantly invaded his mind and he turned and stepped off her stoop. Filling her in on the day's events could wait. There was really nothing to report, anyway.

So, he continued on toward home. The coffee house was barely farther, though, and, rain or not, he decided to stop in; he'd just ask for his order to go. Dan had regretted skipping his French press that morning and, as his unintended nap had demonstrated, cravings were meant to be satisfied.

As he approached the coffee house, Dan saw a pair of golf carts parked haphazardly along the side of the road. Busy afternoon, he thought. Jamie, as usual, waited behind the counter and two, no three (the couple on the deck, huddled under an umbrella, weathering the dying rain) groups were sitting and eating pastries and sipping from mugs. One particularly boisterous party looked at Dan as he walked in and grew suddenly quiet.

"What happened to you?" Jamie laughed and reached under the counter for one of the clean cloths he used to wipe off the counters.

"Thanks." Dan pressed the rag against his face, then moved the cloth to the top of his head (this had to be one of the few times his lack of hair came in handy) before continuing on to quickly pretend-tousle the sides' closely cropped bristles and act out smoothing the hairs back into place with his hand. "Just exploring. I went out to the lighthouse and ended up getting caught in the rain."

Dan handed the wet cloth to Jamie, who swung around and tossed the rag toward a bin with other washables, missing the receptacle by about two and a half feet. He turned to Dan, looking embarrassed, and predicted, "French press?"

"Yes. Please. Thank you."

Jamie started the coffee, then returned to the counter to ring Dan up and asked, "So, is it true you were the one that found the murdered body over by the lighthouse?"

Dan dropped his head and chuckled. Small towns. He looked back at Jamie. "What? Do you guys have a nightly recap at the end of each day?"

"Yeah, pretty much." Jamie said, grinning. "So did you?"

"Yes. Cat and I did."

"Cat?" Jamie looked surprised.

"The librarian. You know her?"

"Not really." The barista glanced away and checked on Dan's French press. "Mostly that she's the librarian. I've seen her, I think. But, I don't know that I've ever met her." He paused. "So is it true then, what they're saying?"

Dan tilted his head and narrowed his eyes at Jamie, "Who's they and what are they saying?"

"You know, everybody." Dan resisted pointing out that *everybody* was just as vague as *they* and instead let the boy continue. "That you're having an affair with her."

Dan didn't say anything at first, just hung his head again, this time in resignation. Then, he looked up, indicating no. "No, no affair."

"Oh," Jamie looked to the side. Dan couldn't tell if the boy believed his denial or if Jamie thought, like Constable Anderson and, Dan was starting to think, the rest of the town, that Dan couldn't be trusted.

"Really, Jamie. I'm not. There's nothing going on."

Jamie spun back to face Dan. "Oh, yeah. I believe you. Too much sip sip in this town."

"Sip sip?" Dan asked, smirking.

"Sip sip. You know, gossip."

"Ah." Dan nodded. "Sip sip. Yes, too much sip sip."

Jamie smiled at Dan and the two stood silently for a few seconds. After a moment, the barista spoke up, "Your coffee's likely done now. I'll get it ready for you. Have a seat," and walked away.

"Jamie," Dan called out. "I'll take that coffee to go."

The boy returned with a mug and the French press, not yet pressed. "You sure? It's ready now. I was about to press it for you. I thought we could talk. You can tell me about your book." He waited, looking at Dan, obviously hoping he'd say yes.

Dan wanted to leave, to go home and escape these *sip-sippy* streets and pretend to be writing his next great novel. But, as he surveyed the shop, he noticed that the place had cleared out. Everybody had left, and Dan felt sure the patrons hadn't simply all finished their drinks at once and gone. Apparently, Victor wasn't the only person Constable Anderson had confided in. Maybe the man really did have more pull over what these people thought than Dan, or likely they, wanted to acknowledge. Was it possible that Anderson had started a whisper campaign, blaming Dan for a murder he couldn't possibly have committed? He was, after all (at least according to Constable Anderson) a serial adulterer. Wasn't murder the next logical rung in Dan's descent into purgatory?

A friend may not be something to reject so frivolously.

"Sure," Dan said. "Let's sit."

Jamie beamed and carried the empty mug and Dan's coffee, still in the press, around the counter to one of the tables. "How's this?" he asked, holding out Dan's cup.

"Perfect," Dan said, forcing a smile, tired and wanting to sit down and dive into the hot liquid waiting for him. He was starting to feel a bit of a chill, and didn't know whether it was the wet from the rain or the dawning realization that he was alone on an island where his only friends were Jamie, the barista, and Cat, the woman with whom he was, allegedly, having an affair.

Jamie sat, nodding and smiling, and pushed the plunger down to press the coffee. Dan sat in the seat opposite him. The young man filled Dan's mug and set the press to the side.

"Thanks." Dan looked across the table at Jamie. "Nothing for you?"

"Eh, no. Well, maybe I'll get some water." He started to get up.

"No," Dan stopped him. "Sit. I'll get it for you." He stood and walked behind the counter, crossing to the sink. "You have cold?"

"There's some Perrier in the fridge."

"Ooh. Fancy," Dan joked and smiled as he opened the door and got out a bottle. "You want ice?"

Dan looked over at Jamie, but the young man sat focused, texting on his phone and seemed not to have heard him. He looked in the freezer, but saw no trays. So he simply poured the sparkling water into a glass he found on a shelf and carried the cup and bottle back to the table.

"Anything else, Sir?" Dan asked as he set the drink down and stood at attention, like a server awaiting further instructions.

"No, thanks," Jamie chuckled and shifted, seeming unsure of exactly how to respond. Dan sat across from the barista and held up his mug.

"To sitting down."

"To sitting down," Jamie repeated, laughing, and extended his glass of Perrier. They each took a sip of their respective drinks and Dan pressed and held the hot mug lightly against his cheek.

"I needed this. I've had an interesting couple of days."

74

Jamie looked across at Dan and tittered, surprisingly muted as he sat across from the man he'd seemed so anxious to pin down. He set his drink on the table and looked as if he were ready with a question he was feeling reluctant to ask. Finally, they both spoke at once.

"So, are—what was—you dating—the body like?"

The two grinned. Dan answered first.

"So, you want to know what the body was like, huh? I thought you wanted to hear about my book. I can't win. I'm losing out to a dead man."

"No, it's not that." Jamie smiled, looking devious. "I just, well, I've never seen a dead body. I'm curious, I guess."

"Okay, but then I want to hear a little more about you," Dan said. "Okay. Let's see...It was a dark and stormy night."

"You went to the lighthouse at night?"

"No, I'm kidding. I...It's a line..." Dan started to explain, then abandoned his obviously failed attempt at comedy. "Never mind...so, I saw the body first. It was bloated and blue. Well, not really blue. Dead blue...you know, that pale, blue-white...more of a...."

"Enough, writer," the boy laughed out. "Blue will do."

"The man was blue." Dan smirked at Jamie, and added, "Light blue."

"And you think he was murdered?" Jamie asked as he took another drink. "Is that why you went back this morning?"

"Yes. And yes, I guess. Although, I'm not sure what I was hoping to find out."

"And you were with the librarian when you found the body?" Jamie sat back in his chair.

"Cat? Yes, I—"

"Did you know Cat before you came? Why *did* you come here?"

Dan smiled. "So many questions."

Jamie looked embarrassed. "Oh, sorry."

"No, no, that's fine. Okay, Cat. No. I didn't know her before. Actually, I'd just met her the day before we went to the lighthouse. I'd been here before with my wife about eight months ago. We both loved it here, but we never got out to the lighthouse."

"Where's your wife now?"

Dan fidgeted in his seat. "She stayed home. She's a lawyer, a partner at her firm. I came so I could get some writing done."

Jamie stared down at the table. "Sounds lonely."

He nodded. "Sometimes." His marriage was definitely not something Dan wanted to talk about. Time to change the subject.

"Ronnie said she's leaving you."

Dan's face flushed and he bristled out, "Anderson told you Susan was leaving me? What the...?"

"No, not me. Just people. They told me."

"I...I...No, she hasn't left me. I can't believe you people." Dan snorted and banged the side of his fist against the wall to his right, knocking loose a sliver of paint, which fell into his mug.

Jamie pushed away from the table. "No, I...I don't know what's really happening. That's just what I hear. People talk to me...I can't help it. I don't believe it. I didn't think it was true. I just..."

"Jamie, stop," Dan said, inhaling deeply through his nose. "It's okay. Listen, I should go anyway."

Jamie begged Dan, visibly shaken. "Dan, I believe you. I'm not one of them. I don't fit in here. You have no idea.

It's just...I only know what I hear. I...I'm sorry. I'll tell people it's not true. I can make sure they know."

Dan stood and started to take a final sip of his coffee but noticed the paint chip floating in the liquid. He pulled the cup away from his lips and set the drink down. "Thanks, Jamie. Don't bother. People are going to believe what they believe. I just...I need to go. My clothes are damp and I need to get out of them, take a hot shower. Be alone. Thanks for the coffee."

Dan stormed past the tables and out of the coffee house, slamming the door and knowing how the crash would affect Jamie, a flash of compassion rushing by but not stopping. He paused, closed his eyes and inhaled deeply. He glanced at the coffee house door then started back to his house, not caring that while they'd been talking, the storm had passed.

Eight

Dan set his wine to the side. He'd spent the last few days reading through Edward Hawkins' journals and had been able to forget, or at least avoid, his discovery from earlier. He'd progressed into the second volume when he found two pages that had been stuck together. He ran his finger along the outer edge of the sheets, feeling for a ridge he could manipulate to pry them apart. When he found the unevenness he was looking for, he massaged the tip of his finger between the pages, carefully separating the two surfaces. He was worried that the crisp and brittle paper would tear and the memories contained between them would be forever lost. He smoothed the pages once he'd pulled them completely apart. He caught his breath. Another drawing. The journals had included a number of sketches, but this time a sort of cobbled-together memorial sat at the head of a mound of disturbed dirt spread across both pages. A stone with some words scrawled across its surface had stopped him.

John Hawkins

December 1, 1848 - February 2, 1850

This had to be the man's...He flipped back through the entries until he found one of Edward's earlier sketches. Simple, hurried. The man had clearly spent more time shaping the drawing Dan had just discovered, developing the detail that would serve as, perhaps, the only memory of what was likely his own young son. Apparently, the boy was only fourteen months old when he'd died. In a flash, Dan felt a surge of gratitude for the nine years he'd had with his son. But, the sentiment evaporated just as quickly as he determined, with a shake of his head, that any time with a child was too short. Any memories were incomplete. Only a greater sense of loss had resulted from any extra minutes with Ryan. Time didn't exist when mourning the death of a child.

He wiped at his eye and returned to the drawing: precise, but devoid of color. Why? Maybe dyes were too difficult to procure in that period. Or, and this Dan could understand, perhaps using color would have been too indifferent. Too present. Too accepting.

He carried the book to the kitchen counter and returned for his wine.

Edward had written about his wife, Frances, and one child, a boy named Percy. Dan had thought Percy was their only child, but, evidently, Edward had had (at least) one other son. There'd been no mention of cholera, so his son's death was probably not caused by the disease. Dan had skipped ahead at one point and found that cholera did finally appear in the journals. At least in theory. At the end of the second volume, Edward had started writing about his concern that the plague attacking the world had finally reached Hope Town. The man had had a special connection to the disease. Apparently, when he was a child, his mother had received a letter from relatives in Exeter, England. She'd learned to read as a young girl and would gather the family around her any time correspondence arrived so they could hear the news together.

According to the journals, he'd never forgotten the sound of her whimpers as she read to them their relatives' impressions of the suffering they were witnessing or of his ever-present fear that he would be next to fall victim. As young as Edward had been at the time, he'd never really forgotten his own sense of dread.

Dan crossed to his laptop and sat down to try writing again. To say he'd written anything of substance since he and Cat had found the body would be kindly generous. In truth, he'd sit at his 'desk' and type, then delete, then type some more. Then delete. Then he'd pause to gaze out over the harbor to the lighthouse.

Because no matter how much he resisted, Dan always got dragged back to the beach, to his need to make sense of what he and Cat had found that day. And not just because he worried that he might someday need to prove his innocence. A life had ended. A man had been murdered. And whatever sins (or good deeds) may have led him to his death, that man had ended up as a nameless corpse snagged in a gnarl of mangrove on a beach. Decomposing and unknown.

And no one wanted to be unknown.

Unknown like the mass of bodies buried in the hill off Queen's Highway. The thought would push Dan back into his writing where he'd type and delete some more, always aware that at any moment a dead man's eyes could pull him back.

Or that a heavyset jailer might arrive unannounced at his door.

Although really, Constable Anderson's bluster was probably little more than a lonely man throwing his substantial weight around. Dan's own grilling by the lighthouse had certainly been nothing more than the policeman's pointless demonstration of bravado playing out to impress an uninterested woman. Anderson had to know, at least at some level, that there was no way Dan could have been involved in the man's murder. And certainly no more than the constable's beloved Cat. In the end, Anderson would have no choice but to accept Dan's innocence; though, to paraphrase Dylan Thomas, the policeman would likely go kicking and screaming into that good night. And all along the way Dan would likely be swatting away a certain feline.

Which brought him to Cat. Dan hadn't seen her either, which had surprised him, especially in light of her behavior on the one day they'd actually spent together. Of course, she had no idea where he lived. He'd reluctantly given her his number (she had her ways) but Dan realized that, even had she called, he'd never know. When he finally got a phone again, he'd likely spend the first day listening to (and summarily deleting) Cat's innuendo-filled and passive-aggressive pleadings.

And then there was Jamie. The young man was nowhere to be seen. He'd been missing from the coffee house since their 'casual' conversation. Dan was pretty sure the barista's absence had something to do with his own reaction to the rumors swirling around town. But, until he saw Jamie again, there was no way to know for sure and little he could do to soothe the situation, anyway.

And Susan. Dan hadn't talked to his wife since the night after he and Cat had found the body and she'd treated him like some kind of hostile witness. Like Cat, Susan had no way of reaching him. Of course, he'd not tried to call her, either. Jamie would no doubt have let him call from the coffee house, but the boy was MIA. Fortuitous? Yes.

Flimsy as an excuse? Maybe. According to Susan? Definitely.

He closed his laptop and walked into the bathroom. Maybe a shower would help.

After, Dan returned to the kitchen for a drink of water, wearing no more than a towel, when three quick raps sounded on the front door and Dan suddenly found himself face to face with the likelihood that he'd have a chance to call Susan after all, only from a police station. And for nothing more than to let her know he'd been arrested.

He tried to imagine how this call would go.

"Susan, this is Dan."

"Yes, you told me that."

"I've been arrested."

"Are you guilty?"

"What?"

"You must be guilty. Ryan thinks so too."

And then she'd hang up.

Probably better not to imagine.

So back to the door: Dan had just reached the refrigerator when he heard the sounds and glanced reluctantly toward the entrance. He strolled casually into the bedroom (no point in rushing to a jail cell) and tossed on a light-blue t-shirt and some jeans. After more banging started, Dan called out, "I'm coming," straightened the bed's already straight sheets, and returned to open the front door.

Cat stood leaning against the harbor-side wall of the home's front landing, running two of her right hand's fingers along the building's stucco, apparently doing her best to look flirtatious and pouty.

"Cat, how..."

82

"Dan, you cad. You seduce a girl and then don't bother to call or stop by."

Dan didn't answer at first, just crooked his head and gazed at Cat. Finally he said, "I didn't seduce you."

"Oh, I know that. No need to remind me."

"My phone's broken."

"Mmm hmm. Likely story. Anyways, aren't you going to invite me in?"

"Yes, of course. Sorry." Dan looked dutifully embarrassed and stepped back into the house, motioning gallantly with his entire body for her to come in. He had to admit, he was glad to see her. Her never-ending energy was infectious and, although Dan couldn't let Cat know, he'd even missed her incessant come-ons. "Please."

"Oh, I don't have time. I just stopped by to make sure you were alive."

Cat flipped around and began to slink away, leaving Dan in the doorway, shocked and opened-mouthed as he watched her go. He started to protest, but she spun suddenly and laughed out, "Just kidding, I could never be mad at you, silly," as she pushed past Dan and into his house.

"A kitchen and living room. A couch. Where's the bedroom?"

He grinned at her but didn't answer.

"A girl's gotta try."

She twirled and bounced to the doors leading to the deck. "Wow. What a view. This is almost as beautiful as from the lighthouse. Maybe more. This must have cost you a fortune."

"So," Dan said, changing the subject, "how'd you find me?"

She glanced over her shoulder, smirking. "Were you hiding?"

"No...I just mean...I never told you where I lived."

"Yes, you did, silly. Over by the lighthouse, before we found the dead man." She opened the doors and stepped onto the deck. "You said I could probably see your house. I just narrowed down which one was yours. It wasn't hard."

"Ah," Dan said nodding, wondering how Cat had actually been able to hear him or, for that matter, been listening as she'd danced above him that day. He continued, "You know, everyone thinks we're having an affair."

Cat whirled to face him, eyes wide and clearly struggling to suppress a grin, "Really? I wonder where they got that idea," she said, a little too coquettishly, and Dan started to think Ronnie wasn't the only source of the rumors.

"Well we're not," she went on.

"No, we're not. I'm married."

"Yes, I think we've established that."

"Happily."

"Then why are you here and she's there?"

She stopped and studied him, squinting. "Wherever there is."

Dan opened his mouth to respond, then walked into the kitchen instead.

"Can I get you a drink?"

"Sure. Some water would be good."

Dan got a plastic bottle out of the fridge (the water he'd meant for himself) and poured Cat a glass. He grabbed a goblet and started to pull the cork out of the open bottle of Zin he'd been sipping from earlier. But, as he lifted the wine, he could tell the container was mostly empty. So he simply turned and handed Cat her drink, keeping the bottle for himself.

Just then, they heard a knock. Dan's gut wrenched at the sound.

He lifted the wine to his lips, 'chugged' what turned out to be little more than a swallow, and threw the container into the recycling. He looked at Cat, who stared unaffectedly back at him, and crossed to the entrance to open the door.

Constable Anderson stood on the stoop, head down, fishing something out of his nose with his left index finger. He seemed to become suddenly aware that Dan had opened the door and straightened, dropping his hand to his side and wiping his fingers on the cloth of his pants.

"Mr. Harris," Constable Anderson began and stepped into the cottage without waiting for an invitation. "I thou..." He froze, eyes wide. "Oh...Cat. You're here."

"Hi, Ronnie."

Constable Anderson seemed to have lost his train of thought and fixated on Cat, scanning Dan's home, most likely trying to pinpoint the bedroom to inspect the state of the sheets. "I didn't expect to see you here. It's so early."

"Yes."

"She just stopped by. Got here just a few minutes before you," Dan said, stepping forward. "What can I help you with?"

"Well, I..." Constable Anderson looked at Dan, then back at Cat, and finally turned his focus away from Cat and back to Dan, "I...so, Mr. Harris, you said you'd never seen the dead man before."

"Right, never."

"So, if I told you he arrived on the same flight as you, Bahamian Airways," he consulted his note pad, "flight M41 to Marsh Harbour…" he said and looked up at Dan.

"Is that a question?"

Cat giggled and Constable Anderson glanced quickly at her sideways. He hissed out, "Just answer the question. Were you on that flight?"

"Could be. I don't know. I don't remember my flight number. I'd have to look."

"Yes. You never seem to know anything for sure, do you?" Constable Anderson said straightly. "But, I know. That was your flight. You and the dead man arrived together. Well, he wasn't dead when he arrived, but—"

"Yes, I think we get it."

Constable Anderson glared at Dan.

"That doesn't mean anything, Ronnie. So they arrived on the same flight. So what?" Cat said as she moved toward the constable.

"Those flights are small. Maybe 25, 30…maybe 40 seats. You sure you never saw him, Mr. Harris? It just doesn't seem possible that you didn't."

"No, never," Dan answered, quickly, sharply. "I never saw him."

Constable Anderson stood with his note pad, staring at Dan.

"I never did. I don't know who the man is," Dan continued, repeating his denial.

Cat stepped to the side, away from Dan, and Constable Anderson remained motionless, standing harshly. He studied Dan, glanced at his note pad, flipped through some pages, then looked back at Dan. This was a new, not-so-bumbling Constable Anderson. Something had changed. Dan broke first.

"I don't know what you expect me to say. I don't know him."

"But I'm thinking you saw him, which means you're lying. His name was Ed Wilson." Constable Anderson stood and waited for Dan to respond to the new information.

Finally, Cat spoke up, "Should that name mean something, Ronnie?"

"Maybe not. But, maybe. Just letting you know. Something to think about. Think it over, Mr. Harris."

"This man, what was his name? Ted Wilson?" Cat spoke again.

"*Ed.* Wilson." Constable Anderson repeated, his eyes fixed on Dan.

"Ed Wilson," she repeated, nodding. "Marsh Harbour's a landing point for a lot of the outer islands. This Ed Wilson could have been going to any one of them."

"We know he was coming here, to Hope Town."

"How?" Cat and Dan said in unison.

Constable Anderson looked at Cat and opened his mouth as if he were going to respond, but then he studied his notepad and said, "That's not important. But, we know he was headed to Hope Town. And now...now that we know he was coming here, Ed Wilson's death is definitely a local matter. *But*, his death is also a homicide. So I've called Nassau. An Inspector..." Constable Anderson peeked at his notes, "...Johnson will be arriving later today."

He looked at Dan. "I'd suggest you think hard about your story, Mr. Harris. There will be two of us looking at everything you say. If you've got nothing to hide, just admit you saw him. It's that easy. Then we can move forward with all the facts."

Dan held steady and focused on Anderson. "I never saw the man before Cat and I found him on the beach," he insisted. True, Dan thought. But, the truth was suddenly too prone to reality and he felt unstable. Maybe he *had* actually seen the man. Dan had to admit the scenario seemed possible, even likely. But, how did that matter? Even if he had, in fact, seen him, what did that prove? Just as likely, so had every other passenger on that flight.

"Okay, thanks for your time."

Suddenly Constable Anderson's businesslike demeanor melted away and he walked over to Cat to comfort her and tell her how sorry he was that she had to be mixed up in all of this. Anderson shifted back and held her shoulders, peering earnestly into her eyes. "If you need anything, or if this man is pressuring you in any way, just let me know."

Ahhh. There was the Constable Anderson Dan had gotten to know and loathe.

Cat leaned forward and hugged Ronnie before guiding him to the door and thanking him for stopping by, as if this were her house he'd visited. "Thanks, Ronnie. I'm sure there's some explanation for all this. There has to be." She watched him walk away. "We'll give you a ring if Dan thinks of anything."

Cat was taking control, making it seem as if she and Dan were somehow together, and Dan didn't like that at all. She turned to him and said, "So your phone is broken."

"Yes," he answered. "But, and I can't emphasize this enough, not really the issue."

"So, what is then?"

"Well..." Dan shook his head and crossed to the sofa. Cat followed. "I don't know. This thing doesn't seem to be going away. Maybe Constable Anderson is right. Maybe I did see this Ted..."

"Ed."

"Ed. Olson."

"Wilson." Cat smiled.

"Whatever." Dan dropped his head, then peeked over at Cat with a grin.

"Maybe I did see him. Or maybe I should just say I did. I'd like to see him make something of it. What's he going to do, arrest everyone on that flight, everyone at the airport...the pilot?"

"Well, maybe if they were coming to Hope Town."

Dan glared at Cat.

"I'm just sayin'." Cat shrugged.

"So I guess I need to get a new phone. Susan's probably wondering what happened to me."

"You can use my phone to call her."

"Uh," Dan thought briefly, very briefly, but quickly decided that he didn't want Cat having access to Susan's phone number. "No. Thanks. But could I call my carrier? Get them to send me a new phone?"

"Sure."

Cat pulled out her cell and passed the phone to Dan. He looked up his service provider's out-of-country number and called, walking into the bedroom to talk privately, and arranged to have a replacement sent. They'd send one right away—overnight, the attendant promised—but he'd likely be without communication for as long as a few days.

"Thanks." He handed the phone back to Cat.

She watched as Dan moved into the kitchen. "I'm sure you have nothing to worry about, Dan. This new inspector will get here and he'll be more sensible. He'll indulge Ronnie and then move on to the real investigating. Anyways, there's nothing we can do about it now. We just have to wait."

Dan didn't respond, just leaned against the counter and studied the kitchen floor. Cat crossed to him and reached out her hands to take his. He didn't pull away. He simply raised his eyes and peered into hers.

"Cat. I'm married. I—"

"Yes," she spit out and pushed his arms away from her. "But she's not here and I am."

"Cat."

"I think I'll go. Anyways, you don't want me here." Cat turned and started toward the front door.

"Cat. No. Stay. I'm sorry," Dan pleaded. She stopped and stood facing away from him. He imagined her grinning like the villain in some movie who stops and smiles deviously as she tricks the fool hero into falling into her insidious trap.

He said, "Let's get some food. My treat."

Cat spun at his concession and smiled. "Okay, how about the coffee house?"

"Really?"

"Yeah, they have food. Anyways, I could go for some tea."

"Okay, if that's what you want. Maybe Jamie will be back." Dan said as they headed out the door.

"Jamie?"

"I'll tell you later."

* * * *

A woman who looked to be in her late 40s, wearing cat-eye glasses (the same woman who'd been working the last few days) waited behind the counter when Cat and Dan arrived at the coffee house. This time, Dan gave in and asked her if Jamie was okay and when he'd be returning. She glared across at him and said, "You must be Dan."

"Yes, nice to meet you." When she didn't respond, he asked again, "Is Jamie okay?"

The woman ignored him, just turned to Cat and said, *à la* Jerry to Newman, "Hello, Cat."

"Hello, Jean." Cat tapped Dan's shoulder and looked into his eyes. She mumbled, "Let's go. I'm not hungry," before she turned and headed for the door.

Dan watched her go for a moment, confused, then threw an apology across the counter at Jean and followed Cat out the coffee house door. "Cat," he called out after her. "Cat, where are you going?"

Outside, Cat stopped and waited for him.

"Cat, what's going on?"

"Oh, nothing. I'm just not hungry anymore."

"I thought you wanted some tea," Dan pointed out, ignoring the silent altercation he'd just witnessed.

"No. Just trying to make you happy. You said you wanted to go to the coffee house."

"What?" Dan said, chuckling and shaking his head. "No I didn't."

"No? Well, then we're both happy." Cat smiled and started back to Dan's cottage, calling out over her shoulder. "Let's go sit out on your deck."

Dan didn't go after Cat at first, just watched as she pounced away from him, then bobbed his head and grinned. He followed her to the stoop of his house, where she stood, leaning *seductively* like she had when she'd first arrived that morning.

As he reached the landing, Dan leaned over and kissed her cheek.

She lifted her hand to her face. "What was that for? I mean, I'm not complaining. But what was that for?"

"Because life is never boring with you," he said and pivoted to put his key in the door he'd forgotten to lock when the two left.

Nine

Cat and Dan relaxed on the deck for the rest of the morning and into the afternoon, commenting occasionally on the day's lack of rain and clouds and simply being. The wooden slats stretched across the entire length of Dan's home and three deck chairs (a number that had always seemed odd to Dan) were just right for the two. One for Dan and two for Cat, who managed to make her overuse of the home's resources seem natural.

Occasionally, a ferry sped by and the boat's engine would interrupt the ocean-front silence. But mostly the only sounds the two heard were the lapping of the ever-so-slight waves against the posts of the platform and the occasional bird squawking overhead.

But, in the end, reality came knocking at the door. Cat had gotten up to explore the fridge for more snacks (they'd never ended up getting food) and was, to Dan's dismay, able to answer the door almost immediately. She stepped outside to let Dan know about the visitors.

"Constable Anderson and Inspector Johnson are here to see you, Sir," Cat said, officially, with a bit of a smirk.

Dan sat forward. The news didn't ruffle him—much; he knew they'd come knocking before too long, just not so soon—and certainly not today. But, after their relaxing morning and afternoon, he didn't feel ready for the interruption. He gazed out over the harbor, across the water to the lighthouse, pausing to absorb the view, and reminded himself that Inspector Johnson's arrival was a good thing. Any threat of arrest would certainly be gone (or at least a distant Andersonian dream) with the inspector leading the investigation.

Dan got up from his deck chair and stepped into the comparatively dim light of the living room where the two policemen, little more than silhouettes at this point, waited. Constable Anderson opened his mouth and stepped forward, but the other man placed his hand on Anderson's chest.

"Mr. Harris. I's Inspector Johnson, from Nassau. Nice to meet ye." Inspector Johnson was tall and slim, and more of the typical Bahamian. He extended his hand and smiled generously. His white teeth stood out against his dark skin, and his beaming grin, coupled with his strong Bahamian accent, disarmed Dan and made the policeman seem even more laid back and friendly. "I's hoping I could talk to ye."

"Of course." Dan nodded.

"Cat, why don't we go out to the deck?" Constable Anderson said and stretched his arm around Cat, who strained to look back at Dan as the constable escorted her out the still-open French doors. Anderson pulled the doors closed quietly behind them. Dan watched Cat go, feeling an unexpected rush of what he could only identify as abandonment as she left the room. He pivoted back to face Inspector Johnson.

"Can I get you something to drink?"

"No. Thank ye, Boss."

"I think I'll have some water," Dan said and crossed into the kitchen and opened the refrigerator. "I was expecting you to come, just not so soon."

"Yeah. Ferry just arrive, police station right there. Leave my bags and come here. Want to catch ye unprepared, so to speak."

Dan eyed the Inspector, who smiled back at him. Dan leaned forward and pressed his hand against the edge of the open door. Cold air leaked onto his face and he shoved his lips forward while he stood staring blindly into the enclosure. Finally, he shook his head and stood. "You sure I can't get you anything to drink?"

"No, thank ye, Boss. I's fine."

Dan grabbed some water and poured himself a glass before putting the bottle back on the shelf and closing the refrigerator. He forced a grin at Inspector Johnson. "You know, I'm really glad you're here."

"Oh yeah?" The policeman sniggered.

"Yes." Dan nodded and took a sip, stepping forward toward Johnson and pausing as he reached the table.

"This whole thing's been very unsettling," he continued. "I'm not sure what Constable Anderson's told you, but he's gotten it into his head that I could actually have something to do with this man's death."

"Murder."

"Yes, of course. Murder. That's what I kept saying."

The corners of Inspector Johnson's mouth twitched and he motioned to the couch. "Youse mind if I sits?"

"Yes...I mean...no, I don't mind. Please." Dan lifted his drink to his mouth.

"Ye too, Boss."

Dan jerked his glass forward, splashing water onto the floor and table. "Yes, of course. Sorry."

He licked his lips and stepped to the kitchen to grab a paper towel, then spun back instead and slid his hand along the table's smooth surface to squeegee the spilled liquid next to his computer. He wiped his palm across his jeans and crossed into the living room. The wrap-around end of the couch faced Inspector Johnson and Dan dropped into the cushions and grinned at the man. Johnson, though, only returned a blank stare (still grinning, of course). Dan pressed his hands nervously together then, after a moment, sat back and stretched his left arm across the rear cushions of the sofa before he shifted forward with his forearms on his knees then sank back again, tapping his leg the entire time while he waited for the interrogation to start. Finally, Dan leaned forward into his left knee, as if he were stretching. "Should I start?"

"Okay." Inspector Johnson nodded once, slowly.

"Well, Cat and I…" Dan glanced to his right at Cat and Constable Anderson on the deck. The two leaned against the patio's railing, talking and laughing. Cat pointed toward the center of town. Dan spoke without taking his eyes off them. "We…"

"She pretty."

"Who? Cat? Yes, she is," Dan said.

"Ye likes her?"

Dan spun his head to face Inspector Johnson, snickering. "No. Of course not. I'm married."

"Constable Anderson too. That—"

"Wait." Dan's grin evaporated. "Anderson's married?"

"Yeah. Ye not know that?"

"Eh, no. He doesn't wear a ring."

Dan stood. "And we didn't really spend a lot of time getting to know each other. But…."

He was about to point out that Constable Anderson was the worst kind of hypocrite, as if there could be degrees of hypocrisy. He really wanted to verbally bash this man, who, Dan would stress, didn't know him in the least, but who had decided that he'd seen enough to accuse Dan of being unfaithful to his wife, a woman who, Dan would later learn, at least according to this eagle-eyed investigator, had already left him. And then this arbiter of the law, this guardian of justice and truth, had gone around town broadcasting these lies to anyone within earshot and, apparently, Dan was learning, all in a misguided effort to divert attention from his own lascivious inclinations.

But instead, he merely lowered himself onto the couch again and nodded slowly, deliberately, before he pressed his mouth closed, pushed out his lips and added a top heavy, "Hmmm."

"Yeah, he a hypocrite." Inspector Johnson said, and a smug smile broke through Dan's controlled facade. "He talk non-stop about how youse after Cat and how youse an adulterer. Seem more concern with that than the murder he suppose to be solving."

Dan studied the inspector then stared at his own hands, his head bobbing subtly. There was no safe response in this situation. "Listen, do you mind if we just talk about the case?"

"The case?" Inspector Johnson guffawed. "Sure, Boss."

Johnson shoved a leg forward and reached into his pocket, suddenly serious. He pulled out a notepad. "So, youse a writer?"

"Yes." Dan relaxed into the cushions and exhaled. Evidently, the *case* could wait. "I am. And, before you ask, yes, I am working on something. That's why I'm here."

Dan pushed forward. "But, don't you already know all this? I would think Constable Anderson would have briefed you on all this."

"*Brief?*" Inspector Johnson chuckled. "Youse got all the words, Boss. Yeah. He *brief* me…brief." (He chuckled again.) "But, like to get to know ye first. May have to accuse ye of—"

"Accuse? But, you said Anderson…"

"Yeah, but…"

"No. No but. I'm innocent."

The inspector shrugged. "Maybe. But, innocent a loaded word, Boss."

"Loaded? What do y—"

"Yeah, loaded. Like a gun with the safety on."

Dan shot to his feet. "But, I didn't kill the man."

"Probably." Inspector Johnson watched Dan pace around the room.

"No, not probably. I didn't. I couldn't." He spun to face the policeman. "I didn't even know him."

"But, Constable Anderson say ye come together."

"No, we didn't."

"He say youse on the same flight and ye see him. That not true?"

"Well…yes, it is…sort of." Dan closed his eyes and shook his head. "I don't know. But, even if that were true, I don't remember seeing him and it certainly doesn't mean I had anything to do with his death."

"Murder."

"Yes. I get it. Murder." Dan pushed his face into his hands.

"Youse okay?"

Dan dropped his hands and squinted across at Inspector Johnson. "Yes. I just thought you'd be different."

"Different, eh?" Johnson set his notepad to the side. "No need to worry if youse innocent. And, beside, I believes ye. Not me saying all this. Anderson the one. He crazy, I thinks."

98

"Wait, what?" Dan let out a laugh. He eyed the inspector. "See, I don't get you."

"No need to get me, Boss."

Inspector Johnson reached to his side as if he were going to pick up his pad of paper, but held his hand over the notepad and studied Dan. "But ye has to help me. Who ye thinks kill the man?"

"Me? How would I know? I don't even know anyone here."

"Ye knows Cat."

"Well, yeah. I do. But she was with me when I found the body. I don't really know anyone else."

Johnson picked up his notes. He glanced at Dan.

Dan stopped.

Except for Victor Bennet.

Victor had insisted he'd actually seen the body. That was something. He'd even claimed to have seen a red t-shirt—a shirt Dan knew the dead man hadn't been wearing, or at least a shirt he hadn't had on by the time he and Cat had found him. What about that? Victor was odd, there was no getting around that. And, Dan didn't feel any loyalty to the man, didn't even like him, really.

But, Dan thought, more than likely, Victor was nothing more than a dried-up has-been, hoping to reclaim some of his former glory by inserting himself into the current island drama. For all he knew, Constable Anderson was the only acolyte Victor had left. And not even Victor deserved to lose everyone.

"Boss?"

Dan snapped his eyes toward the inspector. He shook his head. "No. Nothing. I was just going to say that I know Jamie, too…from the coffee house. That's all. But he had nothing to do with it."

"Sure?"

Dan shook his head. "Yeah, I'm sure. I know him, that's all."

Inspector Johnson nodded and sat back. "Okay. Don't think so. But want to ask."

The two men stared at each other. Johnson motioned with his lips. "Like to hear a theory?"

Dan shrugged.

"Here my thoughts. When Constable Anderson first talk to me, I think he crazy, like I says. But I's not so sure anymore. I thinks maybe ye hiding something.

Vertigo, in the form of an oh-no-not-again feeling, washed over Dan and his stomach tightened. He sunk onto the edge of the couch facing the harbor and peeked, empty, through the doors' windows at the sun falling behind the lighthouse. Suddenly he was back on the beach, having just vomited and swimming through accusations. He inhaled and turned his head to study Inspector Johnson.

"So why didn't you just say that before? Why all the games?"

The policeman shrugged. "Want to see if ye lie. And ye did."

"What? I didn't..."

"Constable Anderson say ye touch the body. That true?"

"Well," Dan stood and crossed to the wall to the right of the French doors. "Yes."

He spun. "But, I was just trying to see if the man had any ID on him. We didn't know who he was. Like I said, I'm not from here and Cat didn't recognize him."

"Yeah. Wouldn't think so. He not from Hope Town...not even from the Bahamas."

"Wait, you know where he's from? Where?"

100

Inspector Jonson stood. He studied Dan, then continued. "So, ye not find anything?"

"No. I just...where's he from?"

"Constable Anderson think ye just making sure yer DNA all over the body."

"That's ridiculous. I just..."

"It true, though?"

"No, of course not."

"But, ye touch the body?"

Dan shrugged, acquiesced.

"See. We be laid back here, but we still knows how to investigate a crime...maybe what ye think is that these incompetent Bahamians can't know what they doing. Must need my help. That it?"

"No, I..."

"Best ye leave the investigating to the real investigators, Boss."

Dan nodded. "Yes, of course. I just—"

"What ye find?"

Dan hesitated for a moment. Should he tell the inspector about the wallet? Unfortunately, he'd waited so long that at this point saying anything would probably just throw more suspicion in his direction. And there was already plenty of that flying around. The wallet had turned out to be empty anyway.

"Nothing. Just got a little sick from the smell."

"Constable Anderson say ye find some heroin."

"Oh. Yeah." Dan squeezed his eyes closed and shook his head, quickly. "That's right. Yes, sorry. I did find some drugs."

"There ye go. Ye lie again.

"They yer drugs? Constable Anderson think they yers."

"Of course not. Do you really think I'd give him my own drugs?" Dan shook his head and moved to the other side of the doors. "You people."

"Ye people?" Inspector Johnson bellowed. He smiled and chuckled again. "Ye people?....ye..."

He shook his head, then continued. "Didn't think so anyhow. I tells ye, Boss, that man crazy."

Johnson looked at Dan, as if waiting for him to respond. Finally, he continued, "So, no ID, nothing?"

"No, nothing."

Inspector Johnson frowned.

Dan shifted and glanced through the doors again onto the deck at Cat and Constable Anderson. The setting sun made details difficult to pick out, but Dan could see in their colored silhouettes that Cat studied a sheet of paper and Anderson leered at her side, certainly using whatever they were studying as an excuse to hover closer.

"Ye quite interested in what's going on out on your deck. Worried about what they saying?"

"No, just...just checking the light." Dan flipped the switch on the wall and returned to stand across from the inspector.

"No need to worry. Youse probably innocent, like I say before...Or maybe youse guilty."

Dan grinned. "See. Like I say before," Dan said, imitating Johnson. "I just can't figure you out."

"Well, like *I* say before. No need. That my job. Figure *ye* out"

Dan shook his head. "So, am I under arrest? 'Cause if not, I think we're done."

"Calm yeself. Youse not under arrest. And I says when we done."

102

Inspector Johnson crossed to the French doors and peered out. He spun to Dan.

"We almost done."

Dan inhaled deeply through his nose.

"But, first, I need yer passport."

Ten

"What?...No. Absolutely not. I won't"

Inspector Johnson shrugged. "I can arrest ye if ye prefer."

"That's ridiculous. I haven't done anything wrong."

"Maybe not. That's what we're looking into. But, while we do that...yer passport," Johnson said and pushed out his hand.

"Wait, you..."

Gone was the friendly façade of beginnings. Dan studied the inspector. Johnson looked less like a caricature than before and Dan instantly realized he'd fallen into a hubristic underestimation of the man. His speech was still loaded with a Bahamian accent. But the man's syntax, the grammar, everything had changed.

Dan shifted. "I'll call the US Embassy. I'm sure they won't like hearing that some small-time Bahamian inspector is bullying an American citizen."

Inspector Johnson chuckled and pressed in his eyes. "Small-time Bahami... youse insulting me? Just get me your passport, Chief. No more games."

When Dan didn't budge, Johnson added a pointed, "Okay. Then, you're under ar...."

"No. Wait."

Dan felt trapped. His eyes bumped around the room frenetically, searching for something to latch onto that might save him from the reality he'd been shoved into. He shook his head subconsciously.

"Ye saying no?

"No...I..." Dan stumbled forward and fell into one of the chairs at the table.

"Then, what's it going to be, Boss?"

Dan wanted to call Susan. She'd know what to do. She'd have a solution. She'd pause. Listen. Ask questions. She'd unravel the mystery and shift into lawyer mode. Likely, she'd jump on the first flight to the Bahamas and fly in to rescue him. She'd save him.

But...she'd save him.

And then he knew. A different kind of hubris spilled over him and he recognized that his only option waited in front of him in the form of a Bahamian policeman who studied him, looking puzzled, with his extended hand sinking by the second. Dan had no choice. Not really, anyway. Inspector Johnson at least seemed more pragmatic than Constable Anderson. And he could always call Susan later.

So Dan stood.

And nodded.

And breathed.

"Yes, of course. I'll get it for you. Just give me a few minutes, please." He stepped forward.

"I'll get it."

He spun around, his weight on one foot, almost stumbling, reassuring himself as he shifted that this wasn't anything to stress about. He would figure this out. The chaos would wind its way through the miasma of distrust and clarity would be waiting at the end.

Dan paused again, trapped in some sort of pizzicato while the implications of what he was about to do sunk in, surprised at how apocalyptic something as simple as the surrender of a small blue booklet could feel. He stepped deliberately, automatically toward the bedroom and pushed the door closed gently behind him.

Inspector Johnson and reality waited on the other side, but, for a few minutes at least, he was free. Dan surveyed his room. Nothing had changed since this morning. Although, what did he expect? Automated, sensing each step, he crossed to the bed and sank into the mattress, stretching his hands over his head and closing his eyes. This was...

Instantly he started and rolled to his side, bolting to the French doors that led to the deck from his bedroom. He peeked through the glass, on edge, searching to take in what had been effectively obscured from his view. His heart trembled.

Cat nuzzled Constable Anderson's ear and her arm snaked around his shoulders and back, seductive no doubt. She looked to be whispering something to him between pecks and Anderson reached for his own hair, certainly to brush the strands away from his ridiculous blushing face. Her hand rose to help him.

She spun the constable toward her, wiping her hands down his chest across his shirt, fussing with the collar and pressing on both shoulders with the palms of her hands, her mouth moving the entire time. She stumbled forward with her lips and grazed his mouth before sliding to his overtly plump and undoubtedly trembling cheek.

Dan found one of the door's handles, never letting his eyes wander off them, and leaned into the metal until he felt a quiet, pressured click. He waited briefly. Then he shifted back slowly until just a crack opened and ocean sounds rushed in. As he did, Cat jerked away from

106

Anderson and let out (what Dan thought was) an exaggerated cackle. He fixated on her lips as they moved, straining to interpret more than sounds. But, the words' empty meanings evaded him. All that was clear was her chortling and the movement of her body too close to the policeman's.

He nudged the door closed and slowly released the handle, stepping back so they couldn't see him. The red and white stripes of the lighthouse were still barely discernible and he gazed achingly, like he had earlier before the chaos, at the beam, still barely visible, that emanated from the top of the structure.

He plotted his escape. The deck. He could creep, careful not to alert Cat and Constable Anderson—who were probably too distracted by each other to notice anything, anyway—and lower himself over the far right side to the strip of land between his house and whatever stood next to the building (he felt a brief sense of embarrassment when he realized he had no idea; he'd have to remedy that—later) where he could sneak along the path to Front Street and then sprint to the post office dock to convince some boater to whisk him away to Marsh Harbour and the airport. And then he'd be free.

Or he could run past the town center, to Cat's, to her boat, and he could 'borrow' the vessel—she owed him (after what he'd just witnessed, more than ever) and jet away to freedom and back to Susan, who'd know he'd failed. She'd know. In the end, he'd have failed. And she'd know.

"Mr. Harris, everything okay?"

Dan spun toward the voice coming from the other room.

"Yes, Inspector, sorry, just a few minutes.

"Just..." he mumbled as he trudged across the room toward the dresser where he kept his valuables. He pulled open the top drawer just enough so the contents didn't fall out into the room and stared into the cubby. He absorbed the things he cared most about.

And this was what he saw. Smushed up against the back extreme of the drawer was a red t-shirt. From underneath, dark-blue poked out. He pushed both to the side. Underneath the passport was the photo. This was what he wanted. The last portrait his small family had taken.

At the time they were three. Susan must have changed Ryan's clothes and hair and shoes innumerable times, sending Dan to the store at one point to find a new outfit for their son, who had thrown a tantrum sadly appropriate for a nine-year-old boy and who, in the end, had been allowed to wear his favorite shorts and t-shirt and sandals after all. For all her toughness, Susan had only smiled at her son's burgeoning independence. So they'd sat for the portrait and, after almost no deliberation, Dan and Susan had selected only one 'pose' for printing. This one. Ryan sprawled across their laps, his hair static-clinging to Susan's sweater, laughing while Dan tickled his stomach. Susan beamed. She'd turned and was just pressing her lips against her husband's cheek. Soft. Dan stared into the photo.

Careful not to smudge the surface, Dan lifted the image closer to his face, at one point almost rubbing his small family against the skin of his cheek and willing, begging them to press back before he moved the portrait to the palm of his left hand and hovered over Ryan's smile with the fingers of his right.

And then he was there, standing at the door. Dan turned to face the boy. He jumped up and stomped to the doorway, pushing Ryan back, frustrated because his son was interrupting his writing. He breathed to him, "Go back to your show. Daddy's got a deadline." And Ryan wailed, "No!" and he threw his small body to the floor, forcing focus and pushing edges, and Dan insisted again, this time more forcefully "Ryan. Now. Go. I've got to work."

Ryan stood, refused to leave, started to cry.

And Dan shouted, "Ryan!"

And Dan yelled, "I don't have time for this. I've got to get this done."

And Dan screamed, "Go. Now!"

And Ryan slowed his crying and down-shifted his emotions and spoke between sobs, "Can I go outside?"

"Yes, I don't care what you do. Just don't bother me."

So Ryan sunk, whimpering, and rushed down the hall.

Dan had slammed the door. He'd held his hand against the surface and almost reconsidered and run after his son, but instead the anger and the frustration had won and all he'd thought and the only thing he could wish was *How do I get back to that space?* and...

"Mr. Harris?"

A tear fell from Dan's face and he dropped the photo and pivoted to face the voice, shaking.

He stared at the inspector in the doorway, a mist surrounding the why of what had brought him to his bedroom, until slowly the day came back to him and Dan reached into the drawer and pulled out his passport. "Yes. Sorry. The passport. It's right here. I'm coming."

Inspector Johnson stepped halfway out of the bedroom and waited while Dan straightened the items in the dresser and glanced one more time at the portrait, without covering the image of his smiling family, of Ryan's laugh. He wiped his eyes and felt a grin sneak across his face. Then, Dan slid the shirt across the photo and pushed the drawer closed before he moved to the doorway and joined Inspector Johnson.

The policeman moved to the side and reached out to take the booklet from Dan. "Worried ye were making a run for it, Boss," Inspector Johnson said and guffawed once more and Dan felt nauseated and angry at the man's insensitivity. The policeman threw the passport to Constable Anderson who, evidently, had come inside. Anderson fumbled and "*oh!*"ed and missed the tossed document and the blue book bounced across the floor. Dan watched it all happen, cloudy and distant and disconnected.

"Thank ye, Boss. I'm sure I'll be returning it to ye soon," said Inspector Johnson as he walked away from Dan.

Dan snapped. "Don't I get some kind of a receipt or confirmation...something that says I've given my passport to you?"

"Yes. We'll get ye something. In the meantime, Cat can act as your witness. Ye okay with that, Cat?" The inspector motioned to Cat who stood by the couch, silhouetted against the setting sun, blocking the lighthouse and the building's shadow.

Dan shot a look at Cat who glanced over at him.

"What? Yes. That's fine," she said. But she seemed detached and Dan wondered if, amid all her flirting, she was starting to doubt his innocence too.

"Good. We'll be going then," Inspector Johnson said. "Thank ye for your time, Mr. Harris."

"Cat, are you coming with us?" Anderson walked toward Cat, extending his hand to her.

"No, Ronnie, thanks. I'll stay here. Dan and I were going to get some dinner."

Anderson pulled back, looking shocked, and turned to Dan, discolored and straight faced.

He grimaced. "I hope you're starting to see how serious this really is. A reckoning is coming."

* * * *

Dan closed the door to the policemen.

"'A reckoning is coming?' What was that? That man's a fool."

Cat grinned, "Come on. You're just stressed, silly. Besides, that *fool* gave me some intel that might be important."

"Some intel? Really? Some intel?"

"Oh, shut up." Cat giggled. "Yes, some intel. Something that might help us a little."

"Okay." Dan motioned to the couch. Maybe she was still on his side. They sat beside each other. "Did you get it while you were kissing his neck?"

"You jealous? I like you jealous." She slid closer to his side. "How'd you see us anyways? And, yes, actually, I did. A girl's gotta do what a girl's gotta do to protect her man, right?"

"I..." Dan stopped. "You were saying?"

"Okay. The reason they know Ed Wilson was coming to Hope Town was that he said so on his customs form. You would have filled one out, too."

"That's right. And?"

"Look."

She pulled out a folded piece of paper. "See, here on the back. It looks like he was making a to-do list. Number one and two don't really matter, but number 3. See, he only got as far as to write *ride to Hope Town, call S-a-r,*" Cat pronounced the final letters individually. "It looks like he got interrupted."

"How'd you get this?" Dan said, grabbing the document from her. "And why would he make his list on this? He must have known he was going to turn it in."

"I don't know. How would I know that?"

She continued, "Anyways, I got it from Ronnie. He has no idea I have it. That's why I was snuggling with him…to distract him. You didn't think that was real, did you?" She shuddered. "Ew."

"Won't he miss it?"

"He won't even notice it's gone until later. And, when he does, well, he'll probably just figure he lost it and be too embarrassed to say anything until he finds it."

"Or he'll think I took it somehow. The man doesn't need any more ammunition."

"Okay." Cat snatched back the form. "I'll give it back to him. I'll just tell him he must have dropped it."

"Well…" Dan reached across and took back the paper. "No reason not to look at it first."

Dan grinned. "S-A-R…probably Sarah."

"Or Sarafina. Or Sariah," Cat said, in a bit of a singsong voice.

"No. It's Sarah. I feel it." Dan grinned and flipped over the paper.

"And look," he said, pointing to the section titled *Home Address*. "He's from Missouri."

"He is?" Cat sounded surprised and studied the paper. "Oh…I didn't see that."

Dan nodded, feeling optimistic for the first time in several days. He stood and started pacing in front of the French doors. "Sarah. Who do you know named Sarah?"

"I can only think of one woman. We could start with her, I guess. But, you know, the Sarah he was calling could live in Marsh Harbour."

"Maybe. But we have to start somewhere." Dan hurried across the room to where Cat was sitting. He leaned down and hugged her and kissed her cheek. "Oh! I feel so much better."

Dan handed the customs form back to her and returned to sit, this time across from her. "Make sure you get that back to Anderson. I don't want any other accusations coming at me."

Cat nodded.

Dan went on, "What are you doing tomorrow?"

"Are you asking me out?"

"What? No." Dan shifted. "I was just wondering if you'd have time to go talk to this Sarah you said you know."

"Oh." Cat sank into the couch. "Yeah, that works, I guess. We can go in the morning."

They decided on a time to leave, 9:30. Dan didn't bring up the dinner Cat had claimed they were having—no need to remind her. They planned to meet at her house, and he walked her to the front door. Cat, who apparently read romance into everything, moved forward with her eyes closed. But he'd already leaned in to give her a hug and her lips glanced off the side of his head instead. Her cheek brushed against his.

"Oh. Ow." Cat pulled away from him and half smiled, half grimaced. "I..."

For a moment the two stood awkwardly, neither saying a word until Cat flipped her head to the right and said, "What was that?"

"What was what?" Dan stretched and looked down Front Street, immediately recalling the old man that had been lurking around his house earlier in the week.

"I…" Cat started and then stopped and looked as if she was listening.

"I guess it's nothing," she announced and spun to slink away as she had that morning.

Dan called out after her, "I'll see you tomorrow," but she only waved her right hand without turning around to face him.

Eleven

Dan watched Cat go. She slid, unaware, shifting from side to side on Front Street, acting as if each extreme of the road held a unique and exciting something for her to study. A breeze swung her hair to the left and periodically she brushed her hand across her neck and over her shoulder, forcing rebellious strands back into place behind her ear. She strolled away from Dan and his house and the day's events and he leaned against the frame of the door, sliding his finger up and down the wood, recalling her arrival that morning when she'd done the same along the stucco of his house, skating her fingers seductively up and down, acting the seductive kitten with her lips and pushing her everything in his direction, clearly hoping he'd respond. He smiled. Soft. Blurred. The memory was enough to force away the rest of the day that had followed. But suddenly Constable Anderson was there, marshaling, pushing past Dan and into his house and then the once-affable Inspector Johnson was barging in and he would devolve too quickly into the man who would do worse than simply throw accusations his way, hoping they'd stick. He would steal Dan's identity.

His smile melted and a scowl fell hard into its place and Dan's eyes morphed into slits. His head slid unconsciously from side to side and suddenly his hand, the hand that had been caressing the slats of his entrance, formed a fist and crashed into the wall, glancing off the wood and grazing the building's exterior with enough force that the roughness of the plaster sliced into the skin of his knuckles and red blood trickled down the white side of his house. He shoved the back of his hand into his mouth with a muffled "aaah!" and he exhaled and inhaled so quickly that the two were almost one and he glared at Cat who was gone.

And all that remained was fury.

He hurried into his house, slamming the door with his shoulder, and rushed into the kitchen, to the sink, to knock the water on and throw his hand into the stream and drift as the colored liquid swirled around the drain and again he saw himself pass his freedom to Inspector Johnson's outstretched hand and he felt nauseated and weak.

Dan punched the faucet off with his fist. For a moment he did nothing, only stared into the empty basin at the droplets of blood and water that remained, joined by new drippings. He grabbed a strip of paper towels from the roll next to the sink and wrapped his hand while at the same time he twisted to face the living room and his laptop.

He stared across the room. Nothing to do now but go back to—

He spun.

Something.

A sound.

The bedroom?

He stopped breathing. Listened. Silence answered him and suddenly he felt the lights. Bursting. The living room, the kitchen (he!) blared into the surrounding night and whatever was out there could see him. But he couldn't see it.

So he crept. Slowly. Cognizant of the reality that sudden movements might alert a predator to his location.

His makeshift first-aid, stained with blood, fell off his hand. He glanced down. Froze. Heard.

Nothing. Only his own breathing.

He inhaled sharply through his nose and his mouth curved into a smile.

"What is happening to me?" Dan muttered to himself and then shifted back into the kitchen, reviewed his hand and saw that the bleeding had stopped. He opened the freezer for the vodka and poured himself a drink, adding a couple of cubes of ice to his drink proving, if only to himself, that he was cutting back. Then he crossed to sit at the table.

Whatever menace was out there would have to wait, he thought, pretending boldness. This, he determined, taking a sip of his drink, this was a night for progress. He set his vodka to the side, pushed the cup back slightly in a show of resolution, and lifted the cover to his laptop. He peeked at the journals resting on the counter. Edward and his family could wait. Time to write.

On the screen in front of him, he scanned to a few paragraphs before the end of what he'd finished up to that point. He closed his eyes. He needed to clear his mind. He cast himself—

Phht!

Dan flashed.

He scanned around him.

Listened…nothing. He pushed his seat back and started to rise.

A burst of light and a crash lit up his home. The windows vibrated. A storm had moved in and rested over his house. No predator. No villain. And, Dan realized, humiliated, no monster stalked him, about to attack. He grinned and dropped into his chair.

Back to his book. Dan closed his eyes again to the wail of the wind around him. He pictured the walkway to the lighthouse, littered this time with his book's characters and events and imaginings. There was William, the devoted town doctor, taken by surprise by the sudden plague as much as those he watched die around him; his wife, Jane, whose common-sounding name was a foil to her ambitious and social-climbing nature; and their son, Theodore, Teddy. Teddy was five. Atypical of the period, the boy was an only child.

Teddy would 'help' his poppa by tagging along when he visited the homes of his patients. While William attended to the suffering and their families, Teddy would play with any of the children of the household. But with cholera, all this had changed. The settlement had heard rumors of the plague circling the globe and fear of the epidemic was almost as debilitating as the reality of the disease. The conventional wisdom of the time dictated quarantine as the most effective solution to halt the spread of the suffering and William, as did many of the doctors of his time, agreed. As such, Teddy was no longer allowed on the outings and spent his days instead with his mother.

And that was as far as Dan had written. Or almost. Later, Jane would have an affair, and both she and her lover would contract cholera. William would be forced into the untenable position of ministering to a town that depended on him while he cared for his own son and fought to keep him safe. In addition, William would be faced with all the emotions dumped on him because of an adulterous wife, not to mention his having to care for both her and her paramour—a woman (no less) and the wife of the settlement's magistrate. Dan would be able to save Jane, but not Adelia, the other woman, which would raise accusations that his maltreatment of her was intentional. Even William would be confronted by the possibility. As mayor, Adelia's husband would rally the town against William, while he fought to save them.

Dan opened his eyes and started typing.

Adelia answered the door.

Bump!

Dan froze, his fingers stiff over his keyboard.

Phhht!

His eyes darted to the bedroom, to the kitchen, to the entry. The howl of the storm swarmed by him, but this sound was different. Pressured.

He saved his work.

Silently, he pushed the lid of his laptop down and stepped, cautious, toward the entrance of his home.

"Hello?"

He waited.

"Is someone there?"

No answer.

He wrapped his fingers around the door's handle and pressed his ear against the wooden surface, straining to pick out detail amidst the whine outside.

"Hello?"

Dan didn't wait. He yanked the door open. A gust blew against him and nearly knocked him to the floor. The inside handle slammed against the wall to his right. He threw himself against the door's surface and pulled-pushed until no more than a crack remained opened. He scanned the area outside. No one. He flipped around and pressed his back against the entrance to shove the door the rest of the way closed.

Black.

Instantly the house fell into darkness.

"Oh great!" he muttered. He could barely hear himself and his voice sounded distant and dangerous in the chaos.

Dan pivoted, spun, desperate for any light or glow, immediately losing his balance and crashing to the floor. He slid along the surface to the left until he found a wall and then stood and crept until he felt the door. The beam from the lighthouse rushed over the harbor and momentarily lit his living room and kitchen, drowning him in brightness and temporarily blinding him.

A flashlight. He needed a flashlight. The bedroom. There was one in the bedroom, in the bottom drawer—

Thptht!

His heart sunk. The flashlight and intruder were in the same room.

The lighthouse beam flew by again.

He waited in the dark and considered his situation. The French doors. Had he secured them earlier? He'd been distracted because of the demand for his passport and the revolting scene of Cat and Constable Anderson and her (he threw up a little in his mouth) flirting. With the storm, perhaps—

Scrape!

Not the doors. That was a bump against furniture. Someone was in the house.

Dan scanned the dark. A knife. The kitchen. A weapon. Something.

He scuttled his hand against the wall to the kitchen. In between pans from the lighthouse, he was drenched in dark with no way to see anything around him. Suddenly Cat's mention of kerosene made more sense. A gust outside rattled the doors leading to the deck.

He came to the drawers and began to pull open one, then another, pressing his hand against the contents of each to determine its makeup, until he found the silverware and he…

He stopped. Twisted. Nothing.

Outside the wind wailed, but inside only silence and lack of movement surrounded him.

He reached into the drawer and carefully pawed around, thankful that the sound of the storm drowned out the chaotic symphony just touching the utensils created. He pressed against what he was sure was a knife and grabbed gently at the handle. He ran his hand cautiously along the surface of the blade. His spirits sank. This was a knife in name only, meant for simple tasks like spreading butter or jam, not for defending one's life against the potential of a homicidal murderer.

He paused to consider the redundancy.

He crept out of the kitchen to the bedroom door, more confident in his movement at this point, and listened. Waited. Breathed. He tapped the door open with his foot.

"Hello?"

Silence.

Dan stepped slowly into the room. Out of habit, he fumbled for the light switch. Nothing. The beam from the lighthouse spun around and lit the bed enough that he hurried across the room to the nightstand, immediately bending and pulling at the bottom drawer and retrieving the flashlight. He pressed the on button. Nothing. He shook the flashlight and it flickered and emptied and flashed. Then fell dark again.

He froze, 'knife' in one hand, useless flashlight in the other.

The storm. Certainly the invader was nothing more than the weather and his too vivid imagination. That had to be it. The more he waited, unmoving, in the darkness, intermittent swings of light sweeping across him and the room, the more he was sure that he'd imagined everything. He stepped around the bed, turning too soon and bumping into the mattress to return to the living room. The beam panned around again and he stopped to gaze out across the black and white of the harbor. Rain began pelting the roof over his head and the wailing of the wind suddenly died. Dan grinned at the beauty around him. He turned to leave the room.

Immediately lightning sizzled and blasted the room with static. Hair all over Dan's body stood on end. In the doorway, two eyes stared menacingly back at him. He stumbled and raised his 'weapon' but the man had already rushed blockish into Dan, who spun. But too late. His knife flew out of his hand and across the room and skidded across the floor. Dan heard a knock against the doors leading to the deck. The two crashed to the floor smacking hard against the ground as thunder exploded. The flashlight ripped out of Dan's hand and flew spinning under the bed, suddenly working and frenetically mocking Dan in the process. His breath gushed out from the impact of the fall and lint and dust scurried in front of him. He sucked in air again and gagged as the debris came rushing back into his mouth.

He couldn't move. His hands, even his fingers were useless. Somehow his attacker had managed to pin them harshly against his own hips while the man lay atop him and held him immobile. Dan kicked his legs. Instantly another set of limbs locked around him. He bucked. Nothing. He shimmied like a snake instead and managed to

122

slide himself and his attacker to the left until they pressed hard against Dan's bed and he felt his assailant's grip loosen from the pressure. Dan shifted and pushed them both again, more forcefully, against the bed.

"What's your problem? Just calm down," the man said.

Dan kicked his feet. He writhed back, tried to force himself to his knees.

"I said calm down."

Dan felt himself squeezed back to the right, away from the bed.

He froze. He'd just play dead, quit fighting and give this man the impression that he'd won.

"That's better. Just stay still. I'm going to call Constable Anderson."

"You're going to call…?"

Dan tried to spin his head, confused. As he did, he felt the grip of one of the hands pinning him soften. Dan shoved back onto all fours and pushed to his feet. His assailant's hands wrapped immediately around Dan's chest and his legs lifted and snaked around Dan's middle, squeezing constrictor-like. Dan stumbled back until he heard a strike against the wall and a raspy *uhhh*. He leaned forward and shoved back again, repeating the movement several times until his attacker's hold finally released and Dan heard a crumple on the floor.

Dan jumped to his feet and spun. As he did, the lighthouse panned again and Dan saw his attacker spring to his knees and pull a cell out of his pocket. The phone flew out of the man's hands and soared across the room and Dan heard the phone crash against the dresser, pieces striking and skidding across the floor. Dan felt his assailant sideswipe his knees and Dan dove at him. But instead of meeting flesh he knocked hard against the edge of the dresser and let out his own *humph*. He threw his arms in the direction he'd felt the man move and found his legs. Dan latched onto them and pulled his attacker toward him, but the man kicked and squirmed and managed to free himself from Dan's grip. Dan heard him scrambling.

Suddenly the room glowed full of light. Dan saw his attacker immediately crash into the chest of drawers. The dresser shuddered. A clock crashed from the surface. The intruder smashed against the wall next to the door, gasping. Dan threw himself on top of the man, ignoring his attacker's wheezing and his labored pleas to *stop, please, I can't breathe*. Dan rose and pummeled down on him, shoving his elbow into the man's face and yelling into his mouth.

"Why are you here?…Tell me."

Dan forced his knee into the man's gut. He heard a whimper.

"What…" Dan started, then instantly pulled back, sensing suddenly that he'd lost control. He jumped to his feet, stepped back to the bed, kept his eyes on the intruder.

"Where's my phone?" Dan shouted, immediately realizing that he'd removed any possibility of a call for help a few nights ago.

"Where's my phone?" he repeated, now only for the benefit of his attacker. He sneered at the *man* crumpled on the floor.

"You're just a kid."

"I…" the boy wheezed. "I'm 25."

"What are you doing—?"

Dan stopped. "Why did you say you were going to call Constable Anderson? You broke into my house. You attacked me." He jumped off the bed as the anger flurried back. His attacker whimpered and flinched, and Dan burst out laughing, instantly falling silent, like a madman. He glared at the young man on the floor.

"I should be the one calling Anderson."

The jumble still seemed to be having trouble breathing, and Dan stretched out his hand and stepped toward him. The young man flinched.

"It's okay. I'm not going to hurt you. I just want to make sure you're okay."

Nothing at first. Then the young man gasped and let out a soft, "I didn't break in."

The boy rushed over to his broken phone and picked up one of the pieces. "And you broke my phone," he rasped as he threw the chunk at Dan.

Dan watched the plastic fly by him. He lost it this time.

"What are you laughing at?"

Dan wiped at his eyes.

"Don't laugh at me. You're the one in trouble here."

"Oh really?" Dan said, chuckling. "How do you figure that?"

"I heard you. The inspector. I heard it all. You'll be sorry. No wonder you tried to pin it on my dad."

"Your dad? What?" The last few days instantly congealed and the attack became clearer.

"Wait, are you Daniel?"

The boy didn't answer. Dan shook his head.

"And you heard what all exactly?"

"Ronnie. That inspector from Nassau. They took your passport. They think you killed that man. And you thought you could blame my dad."

"I didn't think I could blame your dad. But so what? What are you doing in my house?

Again nothing.

"Are you listening? I want to know what you're doing in my house." The adrenaline was wearing off and Dan wanted to sit down.

Daniel spoke up, "There's no way my dad could have anything do with a murder. Have you seen how frail he is? No way could he overpower someone else."

"Not sure I'd call him frail," Dan said, remembering the rather large boulder the man was carrying, not to mention the knife. "But I get your point."

Dan continued, "Regardless, answer my question. What are you doing in my house? How do you people even know where I live?" Hope Town was seeming more like Stepford every day, only a less sanitized version.

"Ronnie. He told me. He was just leaving your house. I wanted to talk to you. Just find out why you were bothering my dad. But you weren't here. I knocked, but the door pushed open on its own. What was I supposed to do?"

"Uh, not go in."

Daniel paused and gazed to Dan's right. "Anyway, when I saw that no one was here, I thought I'd look around. But then I heard you and Cat on the porch and I hid in the bedroom."

"Or maybe you saw us leave and figured you'd have a look around?" Dan glanced out at the lighthouse. "Okay. So what are you still doing here?"

"I left." He paused. "But I came back. I just wanted to talk to you. Really. I knocked this time, but no one answered. When I tried the door, it opened. So I went in."

Dan humphed.

"But then Cat let Ronnie and that inspector in and I was trapped."

He snarled at Dan, "I heard him. The inspector. He thinks you did it. And now you have no passport." Daniel looked pleased. "You're stuck here."

"I didn't kill anyone. And I didn't accuse your father either."

"Yeah, sure." Daniel glanced to the side.

"I didn't. I was just trying to figure out what happened. He started calling for you and I left."

"Yeah, well, he would have been calling for a long time. I wasn't home. He…" Daniel rubbed his side. "My dad gets confused."

Dan said. "Sorry to hear that."

The boy shrugged.

Dan continued, "So you know Cat?"

"What?"

"Cat. You said she let the police in. How do you know her?"

"Oh. I know her," Daniel said, snickering.

"What does that mean?"

Daniel peered out across the harbor toward what Dan realized was the boy's home. "Let's just say she stands out, even in a town full of tourists."

"So what about you?" Dan motioned to Daniel. "Did you see anything?"

The young man moved onto his knees and then his feet. He shook his head.

"Listen, Daniel. I didn't kill the man. I don't even live here. I'm just visiting."

Daniel glared at Dan. "Why would I believe you over Ronnie?"

"I don't know. But I didn't kill him."

The young man eyed Dan.

"Okay. I did see something I thought was strange at the time. I'm not saying I believe you, but…"

Dan nodded. "That's fair. What'd you see?"

"There's a writer on the island. Victor something."

"Victor Bennet."

"You know him?"

"Met him. Don't really know him."

"Well, I was getting back to the lighthouse one evening. I'd just come from shopping over at Maxwell's in Marsh Harbour and I was still at the dock. He came running up to the lighthouse from the other side, the outer side of the island. He didn't see me. At least I don't think he did. Maybe. But he stopped for a minute and then ran off into the trees on that new path they made that ends up at Queen's Highway. Didn't think much of it at the time. He looked a little freaked out, but that's Victor. Reckoned it had something to do with drugs."

"Drugs?"

"Yeah. That's the rumor anyway. Takes a lot of drugs. He's an odd guy anyway though. There's just something about him. He's a weird one, don't you think?"

Dan found himself feeling a little sorry for Victor. "We're all weird to someone."

Daniel shrugged. "I guess. So you're a writer?"

"Yes. I am"

The boy nodded. Apparently Daniel was done reporting what he'd seen. He stomped over to Dan. Tough. "Listen," he said, jabbing a finger in Dan's chest. "Leave my dad alone."

Dan didn't answer at first, just nodded. Time to let Daniel have a win.

"Could your dad have seen something but be holding back?"

"Doesn't matter."

Dan studied the boy and then motioned to his bedroom door. "Okay. Well. Thanks for stopping by."

Daniel strolled out of the bedroom, into the entryway of Dan's cottage. He pivoted to face Dan, "Watch your back. People here don't forget."

"I didn't kill the man. Really." Dan opened the door. Daniel glanced into the road outside and then twisted back to Dan.

"I know."

Dan looked surprised. "You do? What changed?"

But Daniel didn't answer. He stepped through the doorway and walked toward the town center. Dan watched him go, just as he'd done with Cat earlier that evening, but without the affection or nostalgia. He closed and locked the door.

"I need a drink," he announced to the room as he crossed to the table and picked up his cup from before. He took a sip, then grimaced and dumped the watery drink into the sink before he opened the freezer to get himself a fresh pour. He tossed the empty bottle in the recycling and put a new one in the freezer.

Twelve

Dan glanced around his room. People had been in his house.

He could only remember one visitor clearly, though. And mostly because he felt him. Or at least the repercussions of him. Daniel, the lighthouse keeper's son, had *stopped by* and as a result—Dan discovered as he sat forward—all of him ached.

Evidently (and at least) he'd made the trip to bed but hadn't managed to change into his preferred sleeping attire, skin. He was still wearing his clothes from yesterday. He pushed back to the day before. Daniel had shown up. And his visit had resulted in their impromptu wrestling match.

But before that, Anderson had come too. The constable had shoved his way past Dan and into his house and then the policeman had returned with some inspector from Nassau. And that man...Dan bolted forward (well, bolted was perhaps too strong a word; he shifted—he felt as if his bones had been dipped in concrete). The entire episode hadn't been a dream, after all. He'd surrendered his passport. The inspector—Johnson, the interrogation came rushing at him like a stampeding bull—had been quite insistent. And Dan had complied. And Cat had been flirting with Ronnie.

And Cat...*Cat*. Instantly the rest of the day came flooding over him. He and Cat had plans.

He slid off the bed and hobbled to the bathroom, biting off some toothpaste and swishing the minty gel around in his mouth (counting the action as a thorough brushing). He stripped out of his clothes and hurried into the shower where he paused and inhaled. He felt his eyes fall closed. The lukewarm water cascaded over his body, soothing his sore muscles and relaxing his mind. Exhausted, he leaned forward and rested his head against the wall under the shower head. He paused.

Reluctantly, Dan stumbled out of the shower and toweled off before tossing on some jeans, a t-shirt and some sneakers. Because uninvited visitors were starting to feel a bit too much like the norm in Hope Town, he reviewed all entrances and windows and double checked the front door on the way out.

At the coffee house, Jean still acted as shop girl and, in an apparent act of magnanimity, deigned the impertinence of his presence a nuisance she could overlook. She released a weighted sigh as she took his order and stared aggressively at him almost non-stop while his coffee steeped. At least he assumed she saw him. She wouldn't meet his eyes or return any of his several generous (he thought) smiles. In the end, she dropped the to-go cup on the counter without a word and Dan hurried toward Cat's. (Along the way, though, he eventually dumped the brown liquid onto the side of the road. Calling the drink coffee would be too generous. Jean, as one might conclude, was a horrible barista.)

Cat was pacing on the stoop when he arrived.

"You're late."

"Am I?" Dan reached into his pocket for his non-existent phone (the modern man's pocket watch), worried that she was actually frustrated and not just acting annoyed for effect.

"Yes," Cat spit out. "But I'll let it slide this time."

He went with effect and grinned at her. "That's big of you."

Suddenly she gasped, and spun and rushed into her house. Dan glanced around the area, not sure if she was expecting him to follow. He started up the steps of her deck.

"Cat?"

She barreled out her door, knocking into him. He grabbed the railing to stop himself from hitting the ground, which would have been catastrophic given the state of his body. As it was, he merely winced as he caught himself.

"Dan!" She yelled as a purse went flying by him. "What are you doing? You almost knocked me over."

He righted himself and hurried down the steps to retrieve the bag that had joined him as collateral damage, wondering at the purse, an accessory he had yet to see Cat carry. In fact, had she not been so consistent in her come-ons, he'd have thought she'd be more interested in Susan than in him. So far, she'd shown herself to be more of the quintessential tomboy.

The thing was, Cat's tomboyishness actually made her more attractive to him than if she'd been more of the typical girl, whatever that was. Strength and independence had always been attractive features to Dan. Those had been the traits that had initially drawn him to Susan. She'd embodied that seductive mix of a challenging intellect and looks that could catch the eye of every man (and woman for that matter) in any room she entered. But, he simply smiled at her and said nothing, recognizing that his surprise might come across as judgement. He handed her the purse and she looped her arm into his.

"Should we go?" She motioned to the south. "Sarah's house isn't terribly far from mine. Just a little farther out of town."

The two strolled, wordlessly, like some couple who'd been together for nearly a lifetime. But instead of feeling comforting, their silence left Dan feeling disjointed, as if their lack of conversation exposed how little they actually knew about each other. All he'd managed to glean so far was that she'd been in Hope Town for about ten years and that, at least according to Daniel, she stood out even among the tourists. Before long, they stepped up to a bright red house sitting back among hibiscus. Cat knocked.

"Does she know we're coming?"

Cat shook her head. "No. But she won't mind. At her age, she's just happy to have visitors."

"At her age?"

Cat didn't have time to respond. The door opened and a tall, slender, older woman stood in the opening. "Cat. What a nice surprise. So lovely to see you."

"Wally." Cat leaned forward and wrapped her arms around the woman. "How are you?"

"Oh, you know. Old." She scrunched her eyebrows and looked at Dan, smiling. "Now, who is this handsome young man?"

"This..." Cat pivoted and tapped Dan's back. "... is Dan. He's a writer." She leaned forward and added the last detail in a lower tone, as if she were the stereotypical Jewish mother pawning the new doctor in town to her single daughter.

"Well," Wally winked at Cat, at least she appeared to try. "Nice to meet you, Dan. Please, do come in."

Inside, Cat touched the older woman's arm. "I was just telling Dan about your delicious sun tea. I was hoping that you'd have some that he could try."

"Why yes. Of course. You two have a seat and I'll be right in."

Cat and Dan stepped into the room on their left. Once. The entrance for Wally's house fed into a hallway that opened immediately to the sitting room. Wally headed in the opposite direction.

Cat called after the older woman, "Wally, can I help?"

Wally paused and twisted around. "No, no. Thank you. Just make yourselves comfortable. I'll be right there."

A settee stood across from a rocking chair and side table with a book and a magnifying glass on top. As Cat sat on the sofa, bouncing, Dan studied the photos on the walls.

"You know," Dan said. "Wally might be a good source of information about life on the island, even as far back as the epidemic."

"She's not that old." Cat giggled.

"No, I know. Of course," Dan said. "But people may have talked or told stories or something. The epidemic was a pretty big deal in the town's psyche. I'm sure someone must have told stories about it at some point."

"You have more important things to worry about, silly. Anyways, come sit down."

Dan moved toward Cat, but instantly rushed to Wally's aid when the woman entered the room with a tray of filled tumblers. "Let me take that for you."

"Why thank you, Love. So kind." Wally handed the platter to Dan, then touched his hand and grinned at Cat. She crossed to the rocking chair. A lace doily draped down the back. Before she sat, she leaned forward and ran her hand down the covering.

134

"Bea made this for me. So beautiful."

Dan waited while she situated herself and then held out the tray so she could take one of the glasses. He rotated to Cat and waited while she debated between the remaining two cups, then he scanned the room for a place to set the empty carrier. There was no coffee table in the room and the only other surface was the table holding Wally's book.

"Just set it right there." Wally said, pointing at a spot on the floor next to the sofa.

Dan set the platter down and sat next to Cat with his drink.

"I was just walking past the entrance, returning to my reading when you knocked on the door. What a nice surprise. Oh my goodness.

"Well," Wally continued. "Truthfully, I was sleeping. But my book was on my lap, so…I'm reading Les Miserables. I read the book when I was a little girl. But now, I think I probably get more sleep in than actual reading."

Dan took a sip of his tea and then held the glass in front of his face to hide his grimace.

"Wally," Cat said. "You've outdone yourself with this tea. So good."

Wally beamed. "Yes. I added a bit of lime to it. That must be what you're tasting."

"Well, it's certainly very good, whatever you did," Cat said, smiling, and turned to Dan. "Isn't it?"

"What? Oh yes. Yes. Very good."

"Okay," said Wally, setting her drink on the table next to her book. "Enough of this ridiculous small talk. What are you here about? I may be old, but I've not forgotten what it's like to be in love. And it doesn't include spending time with some old lady drinking her tea." She glanced at

Dan, grinning. "And pretending to like it…are you two getting married?"

"No! Cat and I…we're not…"

Cat nudged him. "It's true, Wally, I was missing your tea and I always love to see you."

Cat took a sip of her tea and acted as though she'd just thought of something. "But, you know, now that I think of it, I do have a question. Do you know anyone named Ed Wilson?"

Wally glanced around at the pictures on her wall. "Why no, I don't think so. Should I?"

"Not necessarily. Just wondering."

"Do you have a photo of him?" Wally said, fingering the glasses around her neck.

"No," Cat removed the drink from her lips and swallowed, shaking her head. "No, we don't. And, if the name doesn't mean anything to you, you probably don't know him. He wasn't from here."

Dan sat forward. "Do you think Sarah knows him?"

Cat and Wally looked at him and Wally giggled. Cat rolled her eyes.

"Dan, this is Sarah. Sarah Wallace."

"Yes, dear, Wally's just a nickname."

"Oh." Dan lifted his glass to his lips, pretending to take a drink.

"You said he wasn't from here?"

"Yes, I'm afraid he's passed." Cat lowered her head.

Wally gasped and tsk tsked. "Dead people." She shook her head.

Dan glanced at Wally, a look of bemusement and humorous disbelief washing over his features. Cat continued.

"He was visiting the island and me and Dan are just trying to figure out if anyone here knew him. Apparently, he knew someone named Sarah. We're just trying to piece it all together."

"Well," she ran her hands down and across the folds of her dress. "I don't know him, thank goodness. Now, my brother-in-law's name was Edward. He's passed. Are you sure it's not Ed Wallace? He was old."

Dan twisted to Cat, grinning, pressing his cup to his lips.

"Yes," she said. "We're sure. Anyways, he wasn't from here."

"That's right. You said that." Wally glanced around the room again, as if the framed photos scattered across the walls might jog her memory.

"Well, my granddaughter's name is Sarah, too. You could ask her. She might know this man."

"Thanks." Cat handed Dan her unfinished tea who, not knowing what he was supposed to do with the drink, set the cup on the floor to his left. "We'll check with her. I don't think I know her. Where does she live?"

"Em, to the north. On the other side of town. Too far for me to walk anymore." Wally paused, looking nostalgic. "I don't get to see her as much as I'd like. Smart girl. Beautiful. She's married to Scott Patterson. You must know him. Now he's not dead, I'll tell you that much."

"No," Cat shook her head. "I'm afraid I don't know him. You say he's not dead?"

"No, he's quite tall," Wally said. "Their house is Ocean Breeze."

"Ocean Breeze?"

Dan considered the glass he was holding. He wanted to set the drink down, but worried that, based on where the conversation was heading, he might need the cup for cover.

"Yes. Just take Back Street, past the church where the road turns into Queen's Highway again. Go past the cemetery. It's on the right. If you reach Taylor's Park, you've gone too far."

"Perfect. Thanks so much." Cat stood. "And thank you for the tea."

"Going so soon?" Wally said. "I was going to make some cucumber sandwiches. Do stay, won't you?"

"Yes, Cat. Do stay." Dan motioned for her to sit back down. "We can leave in a few minutes. I wanted to ask Wally about the cholera outbreak."

"Oh, honey," Wally chuckled and straightened her dress. "Just how old do you think I am? That was well before my time."

"Yes, Dan. Just how old do you think she is?" Cat shifted to face him.

Dan flushed red and he scowled at Cat. He muttered, embarrassed, "No...I...yes, of course. Not you. I..."

"You know," Wally began, "I do remember walking by the cemetery each day on my way to school when I was a little girl and feeling a bit of, well...I don't know, almost a sort of longing, as if I'd actually lived during that time.

"I even wondered if I'd been one of the children who had died. And here I was so many years later, walking by, wondering about my own death." She chuckled, and peeked at Cat and Dan, shaking her head. "The imagination of a child, I guess. Sounds crazy now."

No one spoke for several seconds. Then Wally went on, "Do you ever wonder if the past never really happened?"

138

She didn't wait for an answer, just shook her head and reached to her side to pick up a lace blanket, which she laid over her lap. "Bea made this for me, too. Isn't it beautiful?" she said, running her hands across the tatting. "She's from somewhere in Spain. La Ara...La something..."

"La Orotava?" Dan interrupted.

"That's it. You've heard of it?" Wally said.

"Yes. It's famous for its lace. It's in the Canary Islands. Who's Bea? She's from Spain?"

Cat turned to face Dan, "You met her, silly. Remember? That day in the library. Mrs. Galson. You opened the door for her."

"Oh," Dan's said. "That's right. I do. Hmmm. I'll have to talk to her. My grandparents are from Spain."

"Oh, she'd love that. You know, when I met her...years ago...she hardly spoke any English. I so love Bea. Such a thoughtful woman."

"Yes." Dan grinned and Cat nudged him with her elbow.

"Oh, I almost forgot," Cat said, standing. She reached into her bag and pulled out a silver necklace with a single pearl as a pendant. "I brought this for you."

"Why, Cat, it's beautiful. Why..." Tears flooded Wally's eyes and she reached out to cup the pearl in the palm of her hand, trembling as she did. "My goodness. It's just beautiful."

Cat gave the woman a hug and a kiss on her left cheek, then handed her the necklace. "Thank you so much for the tea. It's always so nice to see you, but we really do need to get going."

Wally glanced up to acknowledge her and then returned to examine the pendant in her hands. "Yes, yes, of course.

"Oh, Cat," she continued. "Before you go, would you mind helping me? I'd like to put this on right away."

Cat took the necklace from Wally's hands and draped the chain around her neck. Wally leaned forward and Cat hooked the clasp. Dan gathered the group's cups and arranged them on the silver platter, which he started to carry out of the room to return to the kitchen.

"No!" Wally shouted and threw the lace to the side. Cat and Dan jerked.

"I mean, no. Thank you. I'll put all that away. No need for you to worry about it."

"Oh, we don't mind."

"No, really." Wally stood and pulled the tray from Dan. "I'll take it. Thank you."

Dan watched her struggle with the platter. Finally, he said, "Thank you. It really was very good tea," and bent forward to kiss Wally on the cheek.

"Oh," Wally said. "My goodness. You've certainly made an old woman's day, Daniel."

The trio stepped to the entrance and Wally continued down the hall, glancing in their direction, serving tray in hand.

After Dan closed the door, Cat muttered, "Okay. What a waste. Wally's certainly not reliable. She wonders if she could have been one of the children that died? Wow. Although, you know, it's always the crazy ones that are the last people you suspect. Maybe she did kill Ed."

"Well, she did call him 'dead people'," Dan said and motioned to the road. He smiled. "Or she's on to something. Maybe we're the ones confused about reality."

Cat *humphed* and Dan grabbed her hand as she stepped over a tree that had fallen across their path.

"So you're from Spain?" Cat asked him.

"No, my mother's parents. She was born in the States."

"Aha. That's why you're so sexy." Cat leaned in to Dan and he stepped out of the way but her momentum was enough that she almost fell and he dove forward to catch her, essentially negating his evasive maneuvering.

"Why, thank you, Sir," she said, in a southern drawl.

He nodded and pushed her back to standing, "You're welcome."

After a few seconds, he added, pronouncing each syllable, "Ma'am."

Cat grinned. "How about the Sugar Shack?"

"Sugar Shack?" Dan grimaced. "Kind of early for sweets, don't you think?"

"It's never too early for sweets, *muh dahling*," Cat said and started skipping.

* * * *

The Sugar Shack was the place to go for ice cream in Hope Town. The shop, a sort of partly-walled deck located above Sun Dried Tees, was the second floor of the first building visitors saw as they exited from the post office dock. Fran, the girl behind the counter, waited while Cat and Dan studied the menu on the wall above her. Well, Cat did. Dan already knew what he wanted: two scoops of vanilla bean, with a topping of hot fudge.

Fran began checking her phone and sighing, vociferously.

"I...don't...know," Cat muttered, as she tapped staccato on her lip with two fingers of her right hand. "Can I have a taste?"

(another sigh)

"Sure," Fran said, "what one ye wants?"

"One of each," Cat said, matter of factly.

"No."

"No?"

"No." Fran shook her head. "Cat, ye does this every time ye comes here. And youse always leaving with the same. A scoop butter pecan, a scoop bubble gum."

Dan grimaced when he heard the combination. Cat spun to him. "See? Do you see?"

She pivoted back to face Fran. "Fine."

Then, after a moment: "I'll have one scoop of butter pecan and one..." she stopped and pressed her fingers to her lips again.

"And one bubble gum."

She smirked and turned to face Dan. "At least I'm not boring."

Cat stomped away and Dan smiled apologetically at Fran. "I guess I'm buying." He pulled out a wad of cash and handed the money to the girl. "Keep the change. Thanks."

Fran grinned at Dan. "Just ye goes and sits down now. They's a nice view off the balcony of the harbor. I bring yer ice cream."

Dan joined Cat to peer over the harbor.

A few minutes later, Fran approached them with two bowls, one (Dan's) more generous than the other. As she walked away, Cat called out, "Hey Fran. Do you know anyone named Sarah?"

Fran stopped walking and rotated to face the two. At first she said nothing, then she winked at Dan. "Well, ye knows Sarah...Sarah...oh what her last name? She live north."

142

"Are you talking about Wally's Granddaughter?"

"Yeah. She the one."

Cat shrugged. "We already know about her."

"Mmmm. Youse going talk to her about the dead body they find at the lighthouse?"

Dan straightened. He wouldn't have been shocked to hear Fran connect them to finding Ed. At this point, someone's not doing so would be suspicious. But, her assuming they would be looking for this Sarah to ask her about Ed was a surprise.

"Why do you say that?"

Fran glanced at Cat, then spoke to Dan, "The airplane form. The dead man coming to see Sarah. No?"

Dan dropped his head.

Fran continued. "Nothing this exciting happen here in a long time. Not since the little boy shoots his mum's leg with the fishing crossbow. I hears that man all bloody and half eaten by sharks. Youse thinking Sarah kill the man? That girl not right. I knows she do something crazy eventually."

"Oh, yeah?" Cat set her ice cream down on the small eating surface around the deck.

"Yeah. Once she start fighting with her husband, right where youse is. They trying to keep quiet, but I hears everything. Keep saying sorry and youse a liar. Sorry. Hmmph. I's sorry for Scott. Cat know. People calls him the Gentle Giant because he so nice. She even hitting him. But, I thinks it all her and she just yellin' at him because she so guilty feeling. I thinks she having an affair.

"Not right," she added.

"Well, we'll see," Cat picked up her ice cream again. "We're going to see her as soon as we finish here. Anyone else? Someone local? Maybe from Marsh Harbour."

"Mmmm. Nah."

Fran winked at Dan once more and went back to the counter. Cat tilted toward Dan.

"That's why I wanted to come to the Sugar Shack," she whispered. "Fran's a total gossip and knows pretty much everyone in town...or of them. If there's another Sarah we should talk to, she'd know."

She smiled across the room at Fran, giving her a nod. "She's probably figuring out who she can tell about this right now. Only in her version, you'll have been flirting with her the entire time, and she'll have been the one that wouldn't give you the time of day. And it will be me that was sure it was Sarah that killed Ed and I'm only going to see her so I can confront her. Probably even hurt her. I probably even have a gun I smuggled in from the States when I first came."

Cat took Dan's bowl from him and threw the container into the trash. She scooped an oversized final spoonful of her own ice cream into her mouth and tossed the bowl into the same bin. She pressed her hands against her head.

"Oooh, ice cream headache."

Dan sneered in her direction. "Cat. I was eating that."

But she was already crossing the deck to the stairs. As Cat passed Fran, she leaned toward the girl, grabbed some napkins, and said, "Oh, by the way, Fran. We were the ones that found the body, and it was pretty much intact. No shark." Cat glanced at Dan and rolled her eyes. "Bloated. Knifed. But no blood."

She started down the steps. "And no sharks. None."

After a moment, Fran yelled after her, "I already knows that." She beamed at Dan as he rushed past her and after Cat.

144

Cat shouted from the stairs, "Whatever. If you think of anything or anyone else, let us know." Cat threw her purse over the counter. "And here. You can have my bag."

At the bottom of the steps, Cat waited for Dan, grinning. "There's nothing worse you can do to a gossip than to make sure their story's a boring one." She spun and headed north out of the town center. Dan ran behind her, feeling more like the annoying younger brother than her friend. He stayed quiet at first then grabbed Cat's arm and pulled her toward him. "Did something happen between you and Fran?"

"No. Why?"

"Just, uh, you just…"

"Oh my, Dan. That's just how we are. We like each other just fine."

"Does she know that?"

Cat started hiking again. She pointed at a white church building. "Probably. We go to the same church. Hey, you should come with me tomorrow."

Dan shook his head, "Uh, no. Thanks. I don't do church."

"Well, here you do. C'mon. Anyways, Preacher John is fun. He's not your typical preacher. He's nice. He used to do a ton of drugs. A lot. And he'd be the first to tell you that. He doesn't hide it."

"I don't know."

"I'll take that as a yes," Cat smiled. "Anyways, it's for the case."

"Mmmm." Dan grumbled.

"The *case*?" he said, mimicking Inspector Johnson's goading.

She stopped and poked him several times in the chest. "Don't you want to clear your name?"

"Fine, fine. Stop." He pushed her hand away. "I'll go. What time does the service start?"

Cat jumped a bit and clapped. She hugged Dan.

"9:00. I'll come by your place a few minutes before."

* * * *

Their piety (or lack thereof) established, Cat and Dan continued on toward Ocean Breeze. When they reached the cholera cemetery, Dan approached the fence surrounding the plot. Cat stood by his side. A sudden gust rushed by and whipped Cat's hair into her mouth and she spit and pulled at the strands, tucking her hair behind her ears.

"So, give me a name." Dan turned to Cat. "One name of someone who died and is buried here."

"How would I know that?"

"It doesn't have to be real. But, try. Feel it," he said mysteriously and pushed his eyes closed. "Just close your eyes. And toss out the first name that comes to you."

"You're crazy, Dan."

He felt Cat brush by him. He opened his eyes and called after her. "I bet there was a Sarah."

She spun and faced him, visibly annoyed. "What's your point, Dan?"

He motioned to her to come back. She tossed her eyes to the right, into nothing. Finally she stomped toward him, pouting, with her arms stretched to the ground at her sides. "Fine." She leaned against his chest and he wrapped one arm around her shoulders and hovered his fingers tight in front of her face.

He shut his eyes again. After a moment, he said, "I'm sticking with Sarah," and nudged her with his hip.

He heard her breathing, as if straining not to participate. After a moment her eyelashes brushed down against his hand. Finally, she whispered, "Tom."

Dan released her and she added, eyes still closed, "He was five."

"I don't…" she opened her eyes and rotated, staring into him. Slowly, she stretched her mouth to his and pressed her lips against his lips for several seconds. She pulled away, peering earnestly into him. "You ju…"

She whirled abruptly and started up the road again. "Silly, we don't have all day. Let's get going."

He watched her glide away, the gusty wind still tossing her hair messy around her head and he glanced one last time at the cemetery.

Tom, he thought. Tom.

The wind blew waves across the grass. He smiled. Then he followed after her.

Thirteen

Cat batted Dan's hand away from the door.

"What now?"

The two stood on the stoop of the Patterson home, Ocean Breeze. They'd spent the last several minutes going over their options for how to approach Sarah. Neither of them knew her and, although Cat had appeared immune to shyness around other people up to this point, in this case, she seemed hesitant. Apparently, Fran's sip sip about the conversation she'd overheard at the Sugar Shack had spooked Cat enough that, at least as far as she was concerned, *this* Sarah was far from innocent. Dan watched Cat bite her lip.

"Hold on. I just need a second to think," she said and studied the ground. Dan glanced around at the billowing Yellow Elder trees crowding the home's entrance. Finally she turned to him, "Okay."

He grinned. "You sure?"

"Yes, go ahead," she said, clearly impatient, as if he'd been the hold up. Immediately though, Cat banged on the door herself and stepped back. They waited silently for several minutes. Dan pivoted to Cat.

"Maybe…"

Just as he began, they heard scuffling from inside the house. Cat stepped forward and called out, "Sarah?"

"Yes. It's me. But, my gran called and warned me you'd be coming. I don't want to talk to you. Go away."

Cat ignored her. "It's Cat. I work at the library. Your grandmother told me to stop by…she said you might be able to help us."

"I know. I already told you, I know who you are. I don't want to talk to you. Now go away."

Dan shouted into the door, "Sarah, this is Dan Harris. I'm staying on the island for a few months. Nice to meet you. We were just hoping to ask you a few questions."

A gust of air rushed into Cat and she lost her balance. She muttered under her breath, "Oh, this is ridiculous," and grabbed at the locked handle. She shouted over the wind, "Did you know Ed Wilson? Were you having an affair with him?"

Dan whipped his head, eyes wide, and mouthed, "Cat!"

Sarah flung open the door and stepped outside, pulling the opening mostly closed behind her. She glanced back into the house. "What are you trying to do? I left all that behind."

Cat moved toward Sarah. "So, you were."

"No. I…it's none of your business. Scott and me, we worked everything out. More or less. Now just go. You shouldn't be here."

Dan stepped to Cat's side, "Listen, Sarah. We don't care what you may or may not have been up to. That's your business. We're just wondering if you knew this guy."

Cat interrupted, "Why did he write your name on his customs form?"

"What? He wrote my name?"

"You know, he's dead now. But I bet you already knew that."

Dan flashed at Cat, exasperated.

Sarah looked panicked. "I didn't kill him. I didn't even know him. What's this guy's name again?"

"Yeah, right." Cat smirked. "You didn't know him."

Dan spoke over her. "His name was Ed Wilson."

"Nope. Sorry. Don't know him. Now leave."

Sarah leaned back and peeked into the house again. As she extended her neck, Dan noticed a bruise reaching up from under her collar. Sarah faced them again and harrumphed. "We can't talk about this. It has nothing to do with me. Listen, if Scott sees you..."

"Maybe we could talk to him," Cat shouted as another rush of air hit her.

"NO! You can't. And...be...quiet," Sarah stage whispered. "Now leave." She stepped back and started to close the door. Dan shoved his foot into the opening.

"Listen, Sarah. We just want to ask you some questions." He whispered, "You can come with us. Is he hurting you?"

"What? No!" Sarah blurted out and rushed her right hand to her neck. "Of course not. And why would I go with you anyway? Just go. Please."

Cat rushed forward and reached out to grab Sarah's arm. Sarah twisted away from her and glared.

Dan held up his hands. "Okay, fine. We'll go. But Sarah, the police seem to think I knew this guy. But I didn't. I have no idea who he is. I really don't care what you did or how you know him."

Sarah began to protest, but Dan spoke over her. "I just need to know if you knew him or not. Please."

"What? So you can tell Ronnie? I don't think so. I said no." Sarah kicked Dan's foot out of the way and shoved the door the rest of the way closed.

Cat looked at Dan. "Great. So, what do we do now?"

"I don't know," Dan said. "She seems really scared of her husband."

Cat banged on the wood again. "Sarah, we just have some questions. That's all."

The door flew open and a tall, muscled man hovered over them in the opening. He paused briefly, then rushed at Dan and slammed the entrance closed behind him. He pushed his head down into Dan's face and yelled, "Stop harassing my wife. I'm not going to tell you twice. Get off my property. Now!"

Dan caught his breath, but remained calm. "Okay. Okay. But, we're not—"

"I don't care what you're doing here."

Scott shoved Dan and he tottered backwards and started to fall. Suddenly, Dan saw Cat fly by him. She leapt onto Scott and wrapped her right arm around his neck, scratching at his face with the fingers of her left hand. Small beads of blood started smearing across Scott's skin. Dan rushed forward and pried at her arms, but he only managed to pull half of her upper body loose. As she fell back, legs and right arm still wrapped around Scott, she dragged her fingernails across his cheek. Rivulets of red dripped from the broken skin left from her scratching. Scott, evidently having had enough, raised a muscly arm sharply and Cat flew back, slamming into one of the surrounding trees.

Scott raised his hand to his face and looked into his palm, which Dan could see was splashed with blood.

"What the hell?"

He hurried inside and slammed the door.

Dan leaned over to help Cat onto her feet, but she smacked away his hand and climbed up on her own. She stared overtly angry at the door and darted her eyes around

151

the house, seeming to search (Dan worried) for an alternate way into the home.

"Cat. Stop. What are you doing?"

She rushed to the entrance, raising her fists as if she were going to bang against the wood of the door with both hands. But she simply dropped her arms and spun to face him.

"It's her. I know it's her. She knew Ed and just won't fess up to it. Something's going on in there and the answer to everything is hiding behind that door."

"Like a coward," she yelled over her shoulder and into the house.

"I think you might be right," Dan said. "But, we're not going to beat it out of them."

He stretched a hand forward, hoping to calm her, and he noticed drops falling and splashing off his arm. "Come on. Let's go to the coffee house. It's starting to rain. We can get out of the storm. Have a cup of coffee. Decompress a little. You're probably thinking that I need to calm down." He grinned at her.

Dan reached forward and held her shoulders, ironically using the same comforting stance that Constable Anderson had taken to intercede against the danger that was he. "I'm worried about you. What's gotten into you, anyway? You scared me."

He smiled at Cat and nudged her playfully.

She threw her arms up, freeing herself from his grip, and pushed past him.

Fourteen

Cat stormed away from Dan.

The few random drops exploded immediately into a torrent, and Dan threw his arm around Cat and pulled her forward in an effort to both protect and hurry her. But she refused.

In fact, she stopped moving all together. Dan, counting on her to be at least somewhat more pliant, slid off her and stumbled head first into the puddles forming at their feet. He jumped up, annoyed, and pleaded with her while water cascaded around them both. Having had enough of her games (not to mention the rain) he spun and darted off alone, deciding to fend for himself.

But suddenly she bolted by him, down the street and into the coffee house, slamming the door closed behind her as he reached the entrance. He pulled the door open again and rushed in, ready to lay into her, but she simply wrapped her arm in his as if nothing had happened and declared that she'd just have a glass of water. Dear.

She glanced at Jean and the two women shared what Dan was beginning to think was their standard "Hello Jean," "Hello Cat" monotone exchange and Cat walked out to the deck, leaving Dan to deal with Jean. He shook his head and forced a grin at the woman.

"What do you want? I don't have all day," she said, tapping a pen on the counter.

Dan ordered, then waited while Jean got things together and crossed outside to the deck to find Cat leaning on the patio railing, watching him with a look of impatience as he struggled with the door.

"You know, they have an inside," he said, without stepping fully out.

"I know."

To the right of the door was a table, above which an overhang kept shop patrons and their refreshments dry. Dan motioned to the area. "How about we at least sit over here?"

Cat glanced at the corner and shook her head. "No. It's hardly raining anymore anyways. Just sit the drinks down and come over here."

Dan slowly rocked his head from side to side, consigned, and crossed to the table to set down her water and his coffee. She pivoted as he came closer and he instantly switched out his scowl for a smile.

"Look," she said and twisted away from him. "You can see your house. It's just right there."

"Yep." He nodded. "That's my house."

He continued, "So, what's going on, Cat? You're obviously upset."

She peeked over her shoulder at him and shrugged. "No I'm not."

"Okay. So what was that back at Patterson's? You kind of freaked me out."

"Nothing."

Dan inhaled sharply through his nose.

"Listen, Cat. This whole Ed thing is my problem. Not yours. I shouldn't have involved you in the first place. It wasn't fair. I think I just need to let things run their course. Trust in the system."

"No." She stretched her neck and peered over the edge of the railing. "It's fine. Really. I just don't like to be threatened."

"Are you talking about Scott?"

Cat nodded.

"He didn't threaten you. He threatened me. And besides, he didn't even really threaten me. He just pushed me."

"Exactly." She spun to face him. "That's more than a threat. But, anyways. I'm loyal. I watch out for my man," she said and batted her eyes.

"Regardless. I should just handle this myself. Thank you." He wrapped his arms around her and squeezed.

She pushed her arms out and shoved him off her. "No!"

Dan yelled, exasperated, "Cat! What's going on? Why are you—?"

"Listen. I know you're just trying to make me feel better, but don't. Really."

"I'm just—"

"Dan. Shut up."

"What did you just say?"

"So my dad was a preacher."

"What?"

"My dad was a preacher."

"Yeah, I heard you. But what are you talking about?"

She didn't say any more, didn't even look at him, just shifted away. Finally she mumbled, "I'm not from here."

After a moment of nothing else from her, Dan grinned. "Yes. I know. And, I hate to break it to you, but I think everyone else here knows too."

She snarled at him. "Ha ha. No, that's not it."

"Cat. I'm wet. Can't we at least go over to the table?"

155

"So," she ignored him. "I'm from this small town in Oregon called Davenport. Not Hope Town small, but small. My dad was the town preacher. Everybody loved him. I loved him. My mom loved him. My brother loved him. The…"

"I get it. Everybody loved him."

"Yes. *Everybody*. He made sure of it."

She stopped and moved even farther away from him, running her hand along the railing. "So, I'm out with my boyfriend, whose name happens to be Scott also, if you can believe it."

"Okay. I get it. So this Scott reminded you of him?"

"No! Dan, please. Stop trying to understand. Just listen."

She shook her head. "Maybe. I don't know. Anyways, I'm out with my boyfriend, Scott, like I told you. We go to some woods, you know Oregon. So we go to the woods, to a parking lot and we're getting a little frisky in his car. You know, had to live up to my name, preacher's daughter and all that. So we're getting frisky and out of nowhere my dad rips open the door to Scott's car and yanks him out and throws him to the ground. Poor Scott had his shirt off and my dad starts kicking him. And screaming at him. And kicking him."

Cat was trembling and she pleaded, "Don't make me do this."

Dan glanced around, confused. "I'm not m—"

"So, I'm running up and hitting my dad with my fists and he whips around and knocks me back and I fall to the ground and he yells at me to go get in the truck and I'm yelling at him and he starts kicking Scott again and I can hear Scott crying out—crying!—and I start hitting at my dad again and he stops and flips around and slaps my face

156

and grabs my arm and rushes me over to the truck and shoves me in and my shirt catches on something and rips and he slams the door. Then he turns and starts back to Scott. But at this point Scott's limping away into the trees like a wounded animal and my dad runs toward him like he's going to do something else to him and I'm jumping out of the truck and suddenly my dad turns back and knocks me to the ground and grabs my arm again and drags me back to the truck. I had shorts on and the dirt and rocks of the parking lot tore into my skin. I guess I'm just lucky it wasn't asphalt. And I'm back in the truck and my dad slams the door and runs around to the driver's side and we leave, and he's..."

Cat was sobbing at this point, her nose running as she rushed through the narrative punctuated by sniffs and breaks in composure and Dan stepped toward her to try to comfort her. But she shook her head and shoved out her hand and growled, "No."

She went on, "We just left Scott there. In the woods. He had a few broken ribs and some internal bleeding and his parents took my dad's side. Can you believe that? *They took my dad's side.*"

She struck out at the air. "Said he had every right to do what he did and said that he'd done right by stopping sin. Said *he* was the preacher and spoke for God."

She leaned over the railing. Cat pushed up suddenly and turned to face Dan.

"The thing is, I don't think my Dad was upset because we were fooling around. I think he was upset because I was cheating on him."

"What do you mean, cheating on him?"

"Just that. He was upset because I was cheating on him. He saw Scott as a threat."

"Oh, you mean, figuratively."

She rolled her eyes. "No, silly, literally. I'd been sleeping with my dad since I was, I don't know, since forever."

Dan froze. He reached his right hand out to grab the railing, suddenly feeling weak.

"Cat." He stopped. Inhaled. He had no idea what to say to her. "Cat. You don't sleep with your dad." He felt sick and leaned to the side of the deck, afraid he was going to vomit.

He faced her again. "You know that, don't you? That wasn't...he molested you."

She glared at him with tears in her eyes. She nodded once. "Don't judge me. You don't know what it was like with him. We were always so close. It felt so good to be so loved."

Dan moved closer to her. "That wasn't love. That's..."

But he stopped, unable to continue. Finally, she went on.

"I know. I guess. It's just..." She paused. "I mean, yes. I do, of course. Logically. That's why I'm here, in Hope Town. I ran away from all that."

"Did your mother know about all this?"

She sneered at him. "You just love to judge, don't you? She's dead, if you must know."

After a moment, she softened. "She was already dead. Cancer. Earlier, though. She might have known before. I don't know. Anyways, not long after the whole thing with Scott and the car, I threatened my dad. We were having a fight and I said 'I'll just tell Scott everything and we'll run away together.' That we were in love. How'd he like that? But he just laughed and said '*we'll see...*'

"A few days later, Scott disappeared. He left a note. *Supposedly*." Cat said the last word forcefully, staring directly into Dan's eyes.

"But, I'm pretty sure my dad did something. I'm not sure what, but I'm pretty sure he did something."

"Maybe. Or maybe Scott's parents sent him away," Dan suggested.

"Don't defend him." She shook her head violently. "You're just like everyone else."

He moved forward and started to protest but she cut him off.

"Anyways, so I came here. I just up and left and didn't tell my Dad. He never knew where I went. I'm almost sure. And now I live here. And now I'm a librarian."

"And now you're a librarian?" Dan chuckled.

"But, the weird thing is, I swear I saw him last week."

"Your dad?"

"Yes, my dad, stupid," Cat said. "I'm pretty sure Scott's dead."

Dan pulled his hand from the railing and pushed his fingers into his forehead. "Cat. I…Cat. This is…"

"See, I knew you wouldn't believe me." She stomped toward the door leading into the coffee house. Dan reached out and grabbed her arm. He spun her toward him.

"No, that's not it at all. Not at all. I don't know wh…this is just new. This is just new information."

They stood in the middle of the small patio. The rain had mostly stopped but gray clouds still hovered overhead and Dan poked his hand out, palm up, signaling to the table where their drinks waited, near the building. "Let's sit. You can tell me the rest."

Cat nodded.

Once they were seated, Dan reached out and took Cat's hand. "Alright, I'm listening."

She shrugged, suddenly unemotional. "That's kind of it. Scott disappeared. I came here. I think I saw my dad. I don't know how he could have found me. Maybe it wasn't even him. Who knows? But seeing him just kind of reminded me of everything I'd left behind, everything that happened. Then we meet another Scott, and he's a bully like my dad and…"

"And it all came rushing back," Dan said.

"Yeah. Kind of all at once."

"Cat." He squeezed her hand. "I'm sorry about all that. Really. I had no idea. That's horrible. No one should have to go through that."

"Yeah, well." She pulled back her hand. "So, what about you? You're married, but not really, but kind of and everyone should stay away, but you spend your Saturday with a beautiful librarian, anyways."

Dan smirked.

She grinned back, "But maybe you're not so married after all."

"Well that's about it. My wife, Susan, and I are trying to figure some things out. We were here after my book got published. To celebrate. We met this man, Richard, who owns the house I'm staying in. I saw the cholera cemetery and wanted to write a book about it. So Richard, who says he always leaves during the hurricane season anyway, offered me his place so I could get away and write."

"Why'd y'all separate?

"Y'all?" Dan said with a southern accent and laughed.

"Yeah," Cat said, pushing back her shoulders. "You got a problem with that?"

160

"No. Not at all. Just haven't heard you talk like that, that's all. Not very Oregonian."

"My mom was from the South. It's in my genes."

"I see."

Jean peaked her head out the door. "Oh. You're still here. Time to go. I'm closing up."

Dan leaned back and smiled. "Of course. Thanks for the coffee."

Jean frowned. She stepped onto the deck and took their untouched drinks, eyeing Dan's mug and shaking her head. "You didn't even drink it."

Dan ignored her. He stood and said to Cat, "Shall we head back to my place?"

"Why, sir, what are you suggesting?" Cat acted the southern belle, flashing her eyes and placing her hand on her chest.

"Nothing," Dan grinned. "Just talk. That's all."

"Oh. Then never mind."

Dan pulled her forward out of her seat and wrapped his arms around her. "Thanks for telling me about your dad. You know I'm always here."

She hugged him back. There was no exit from the deck so the two were forced to walk past Jean again. Dan thanked her and she raised her hand and rolled her eyes at them.

"I think you're growing on her," Cat whispered into Dan's ear.

Dan grinned and nodded. Outside he said, "Okay. So…"

"I think he did it," Cat announced.

"Who?"

"Scott, silly"

"Maybe."

Cat reached down and took Dan's hand. He glanced at her, but didn't say anything, just started walking.

"You might be right. He didn't do himself any favors by reacting the way he did."

At his house, Dan unlocked the door and moved to the side so Cat could step in. Just beyond the entry, she froze and he bumped against her.

"Cat," Dan laughed.

He raised his head and looked forward. A silhouetted woman stood from the sofa facing the harbor and the lighthouse.

Dan pushed Cat aside.

"Susan."

Fifteen

"Who's this?" Susan asked, tapping her foot and folding her arms across her chest. She lifted one finger and pointed at Cat.

"What are…how did you get into the house?"

"Well, hello to you, too, Dan. I have a key. Remember? Who's this?"

"Cat. What are—"

"She's a cat?" Susan raised her eyebrows, a condescending grin spreading across her face.

"No, her name is Cat. She's just showing me the island. What are you doing here?"

"Get her out of here."

Cat smiled. "Susan, it's so nice to finally meet you. Dan can't stop talking about you. He was just telling me how beautiful—"

"Dan. I said get her out of here."

"Susan, it's nothing. She just—"

"Get her out of here!" Susan yelled.

Dan glanced at Cat. "You should go. Thanks for all your help today."

"Susan, really," Cat said. "There's nothing going on. I'm the librarian here and I was just helping Dan with research for his book." She chuckled. "We didn't know going to the lighthouse would turn into such a—"

"Fine. I'll go." Susan stormed forward and Dan grabbed her by the arm and begged, "No. Please, Susan. Stay. Cat's going."

He jerked his head over his shoulder. "Go. Now. Please."

Cat opened her mouth, but Dan cut her off. "Just shut up and go. Seriously."

Susan smiled harshly in Cat's direction. "Yes, seriously. *Cat*. Just shut up and go."

Cat moved to the front door and started through the entrance. She peeked her head back in and opened her mouth.

"Go!" Dan and Susan both shouted.

Cat pulled the door closed and Susan shoved Dan. "What's she talking about, the lighthouse? Did you go to the lighthouse? That was something we were going to do together."

"I…"

"And what's this?" Susan stomped around the back of the sofa to the end table and snatched up a notecard. She read, *dead body think it's me—why?* 'think it's me'? 'dead body'? They think you killed somebody?" She whipped the card across the room.

Anger poured into Dan. "Were you going through my things?"

"No, it was just…oh, it doesn't really matter, Dan. Does it? Why did you write that? What does that mean? I come here, thinking I'd surprise you." She stepped forward and pointed at the entrance. "There's blood by the door outside. There's a bloody paper towel down there."

"Oh, that."

"Oh, that," Susan mimicked Dan in a baby voice.

She moved to him, "Yes, oh that. I come all this way. I find this cryptic note. Blood. I wait all day. Worried. You're nowhere to be seen."

"I—"

"And then you come waltzing through the front door with some tramp you've picked up here, that you're...what, dating?" Susan leaned against the back of the couch, shaking her head. "Really, Dan. What's going on? Are we over? I thought we were just getting some air."

"We were. We are." Dan crossed to Susan and fixed on her eyes. "Really. I barely know Cat."

"You know her well enough to go to the lighthouse."

"We never talk..." He paused, dropped his head. "Yes, you're right. I shouldn't have done that. She suggested going and telling me more about the island. And I went. I wasn't thinking. But it was just research. And I haven't called since we talked because my phone broke."

"Yes." She nodded and crossed the room to her bags, pulling out a package. "I know. Or I figured. They sent a replacement phone to the house."

She walked over and tossed the box onto the kitchen table.

"Oh, that's why."

"So, what's this about someone thinking it's you? A dead body?"

"I found a body. They think I killed someone"

"So that's really it?" Susan stumbled back. "When?"

"When Cat and I went to the lighthouse."

"Which was when, Dan? I wasn't there. Remember?"

"Just before the last time we spoke."

Susan nodded, a quick, harsh nod. "So this had already happened when we talked. Wow. Seems like something you'd tell your wife."

"You wouldn't listen to me, remember? *I just called to tell you to call Mike,*" Dan said, imitating a woman's voice.

"Really? Is that supposed to be me? Besides, be honest. You were just making conversation. Trying to keep me on the phone."

She shook her head and flicked the air in the direction of the door. "So, what's-her-name, the tramp. She was with you. Do they suspect her also?"

"No," Dan shook his head. "I guess the dead guy and I were on the same flight to Marsh Harbour."

Susan shrugged. "Not conclusive. So were a lot of other people."

Dan beamed. "That's exactly what I said."

"And..." Dan ran his finger along the surface of the telephone box, like a child about to confess to invading the cookie jar. "I might have touched the body."

"You touched the body?"

"I said *might...*"

Susan glared at him.

"...have." He swallowed.

"Yes," he went on. "I know. No need to lecture me. I was stupid."

"Stupid's an understatement. I'd suspect you, too."

Dan glanced across the living room, over the harbor to the lighthouse. He started toward the kitchen. "You want some wine?"

"Some things never change, do they?"

He stopped and stared at her.

After a moment, she said, "Yes. I do. A cab if you've got...oh, what am I thinking? Of course, you do."

"Ha ha." Dan crossed to the cupboard and pulled out two goblets, then opened a fresh bottle sitting on the counter. He poured them each a generous portion, and returned to the living room, handing Susan her glass and taking a sip from his own.

"Let's sit down. You must be exhausted from traveling and I've had a bit of an overwhelming day myself." Dan paused. He caressed Susan's shoulder and kissed her, peering into her eyes. "I'm glad you're here."

"I'm still deciding," she said and moved away from him, lowering herself onto the left end of the couch. She took a drink of her wine and set her glass on the end table. Dan moved to the middle of the sofa and waited for her to continue. When she said nothing, he began, "I—"

"How's the book coming?"

Dan rotated to face her, defensive. "I've had some other stuff going on, as you might recall. I wasn't expecting to find a body. And I certainly wasn't expecting to suddenly have to defend myself."

She bristled, then almost immediately dropped her shoulders. They sat in silence for what felt like several minutes.

"So, tell me about this body."

Dan filled her in on going to the library, meeting Cat, and their eventual fated trip to the lighthouse. "Anyway, that's when I found the body. Cat was pretty upset by the whole thing."

"Oh, poor Cat," Susan whined.

Suddenly she stared forward, fixated ahead at nothing, and pushed out her lips in a pout.

"Susan, are you okay?"

"Shush. I'm thinking."

After a few minutes, she said, "Okay, so," and reached to her left toward her wine. Her hand knocked the goblet off the table and the dark-red liquid soaked into the white throw rug to the side of the sofa.

Immediately Susan dropped her head and started sobbing. Dan rushed to her side and threw his arms around her. She folded into him and he stroked her chin with his thumb and raised her face to his, kissing her gently on the lips, tasting the salt from her tears as he pressed against her. She kissed him back and, for a moment, the chaos of the last few days faded away.

She shot up abruptly, wiping her lips with the back of her left hand.

"Dan. What are you doing?"

"Kissing my wife. Is that a problem?"

"Yes. No. Just not now. Oh," she exclaimed and rushed to her knees over the stain. "Do you have any salt?"

He hesitated. "I think…"

"How about wine. Do you have any white wine? Oh, what am I saying, of course—"

Dan spun and glared at her. "Yes, very funny. We already did that joke."

"Just…"

Dan hurried to the kitchen and opened the fridge.

"And some paper towels or a clean rag."

He returned with a bottle of pinot grigio and a cloth. She reached up and snatched the rag from his hand, pressing the cloth into the stain. She took the bottle from Dan.

"Another rag, this time wet."

Susan poured the pinot grigio over the red spot and glanced to the kitchen.

"Now, Dan," she barked.

Dan jogged across the room and handed the cloth to Susan, hovering while she blotted the stained area.

Then she softened and knelt back on her feet, gazing toward the lighthouse across the bay. The sun had fallen

168

low in the sky and cast a shadow around the building's outline. Susan dropped into a sitting position and Dan watched as one tear, then two streamed down her cheek. She opened her mouth and pressed her eyes closed and more tears fell into her.

Dan felt nauseated. He fumbled to the side of the sofa, not sitting, certain that the apprehension he felt was the last of the emotion leaving her body and squeezing into his. He waited, ready to collapse. She'd slid into this sort of loaded but controlled state of empty when she'd first declared that she'd had enough, before he'd been exiled to Hope Town. When she'd pronounced that their *not* being together was the only remaining salvo in their battle to stay together. Finally, she twisted to him.

"I think I'm just going to go back tomorrow morning."

Dan breathed. He opened and closed his mouth, searching to make sense of what her words meant. Slowly, he forced out, "But…you just got here."

"No," she snapped. "I got here this morning. I've been sitting here alone, wondering where you were, worried. And all this time you've been out with your girlfriend. Doing *research*."

Dan threw his arms in air. He yelled, "She's not my girlfriend. And we weren't doing research. We were trying to make sure I don't go to jail for the rest of my life. What should I do?"

He sank violently into the couch and threw out a petulant, "Why did you even come?"

And then, over the top of each other: "You don't seem to want to be here." "I don't know."

Neither said anything. Finally, Susan continued, "Yes, I do. I do. I want to be here. I wanted to come. I felt so bad after our last call. I know I was horrible to you. And then the phone came for you and I realized why you hadn't called again. It seemed like a sign. I could bring you the phone and surprise you. I just...after coming all this way, I thought you'd be happier to see me."

Her eyes sparked. "And I certainly didn't expect you to be out all day and finally show up here with some floozy."

"Floozy?" Dan laughed. "Floozy? 1920 called. They'd like their vocabulary back."

Susan let out a giggle. Then slowly her face fell and she became more serious. She stood and crossed to him on the sofa, lowering herself onto his lap and wrapping her arms around his neck. "Listen, it's going to be best if I go in the morning."

He started to protest and she pressed her lips against his, talking out of the side of her mouth. "It's okay. I'm not mad. It's just not going to be good if I stay. I..." She stopped and studied Dan's eyes. She stood.

"I want some food. Let's get some food. What's that place we always went to last time we were here?"

"Harbour's Edge?"

"That's it. Let's go eat. You can tell me more about what's been going on."

Susan reached out to Dan and he took her hand. After a moment, she chuckled, "I'm not holding your hand, Dan. I'm pulling you up."

He stood and she wrapped her arms around his chest and held onto him.

"I'm glad I came. Really. I don't want to admit it, but I really have missed you. So much."

Then she pulled away and studied the spot on the rug, shaking her head. "We just have to hope for the best at this point."

She started toward the door. "If the stain's still there when it's dry, we'll buy Richard a new rug."

She grinned back at him. "You can pay for it."

* * * *

"I still can't believe you thought it was a good idea to handle the body."

"I didn't think it was a good idea." Dan turned and stood in front of his wife.

The couple had just finished dinner at the Harbour's Edge, or the *Hedge* as locals called it, and were walking home. Frankly, he was surprised she'd waited as long as she had before bringing up the murder. That was, after all, her field. Or it was if one considered corporate law the same as criminal law. But she'd lasted through the entire meal without mentioning Ed or any of the fallout that had followed Dan's discovery of his body, or even asking any of the questions Dan had expected (or truthfully hoped) she might have. In fact, the closest she'd come to talking about anyone's death was to bring up Ryan. Or she'd tried. But Dan had simply muttered, "I don't want to talk about him," and she'd whisper-yelled, "But, we have to," and he'd ignored her and summoned the waitress for the bill.

"I didn't think it was a good idea," he repeated.

"And I didn't handle the body. I touched it. That's all. I just thought I'd see who the man was. I wanted to make some sense of what I'd just found."

"Haven't you seen, well, any crime show or movie? You don't touch the body. That's *Discovering a Dead Body 101*."

"I know." He nodded. "I get that. It wasn't a smart thing to do...but you weren't there. Can we move on, now? Please?"

171

Susan knocked Dan gently out of the way.

"Yes. So, who was he?"

"I don't know. All I know is that he was named Ed Wilson and they're saying we arrived together, at least on the same flight. I don't remember seeing him, but they keep insisting that I did and that I'm lying. I think I'll just tell them I saw him."

"Did you?"

"No. Not that I remember."

"You're innocent, right?"

"Of course," he said. He twisted to her. "You don't think I could have really done this, do you?"

She didn't answer at first, then quickly shook her head.

"No. Of course not. So don't say anything. Better to stick with the truth. Once you start lying, as inconsequential or well-meaning as you think it is, you have to start remembering what you said and it all snowballs."

"Good point. See, I knew I married you for some reason. It helps to have a lawyer in the family." Dan smirked.

Susan shoved him. "Well, I hope you're with me for more than just free legal advice."

Dan shrugged. After a moment, he grinned and kissed her cheek. "Yes. Of course."

They'd reached the house but Susan pulled him closer. "Let's keep walking. It's actually turning out to be a really beautiful night."

As they headed toward town, Dan filled her in on the customs form and the name Sarah and their investigations that day.

"Well, I hate to say it," Susan said. "And I'm only speaking as a lawyer now, but you should listen to Cat.

She's from here. She'd be a good source of information. As your wife, though, I just want to point out that that doesn't mean spending time with the tramp."

Dan smiled. "I don't think I've heard you ever say tramp, and now it's your favorite word...*tramp*."

He pulled his fingers out of Susan's hand and stretched his arm around her shoulders. "I wish you wouldn't go."

"You're not going to ask me to stay?"

"Would it matter?"

Susan sighed. "No. Probably not. But, it would be nice to be asked."

"Okay." Dan knelt in front of her and dripped out, "Darling, Won't you stay? Please. I've missed you so."

She yanked him up, giggling.

"Really, though." Dan turned serious. "I do miss you. I wish you'd stay. I have to admit I worry about you alone in that big house."

"It's hard. At least if Ryan..." A tear ran down her cheek.

Dan hugged her, fighting a sudden rush of emotion of his own. "I know."

He squeezed her, paralyzed other than his own desperate thoughts rushing around his head. Hope Town pressed around them and the beam from the lighthouse caressed the pair each time the light floated by. He pressed his lips to her cheek then pulled back and brushed away her hair. She nuzzled her head into the crook of his neck and sobbed into him, forcing her arms more tightly around his chest and soon he cried too. Finally, she pushed away from him and peered into his eyes.

"I don't know how to do this."

"Just come here, to Hope Town. We can be together here. You need a break, too. I can—"

"No, Dan!" She shoved him back.

"I have cases. I can't just get up and walk away. Besides…" She pivoted and stomped toward Dan's house. "We're separated. I don't think you get that."

He rushed after her. "Oh, I get that. Don't worry about me. I know very well how separated we are."

She spun to face him. "What's that supposed to mean?"

He froze, taken aback by her pointed question and not ready to face the answer. He breathed, harsh. "Nothing. You're right. We're separated."

He clomped past her.

"And you're right. It's better if you go tomorrow."

Sixteen

Dan had imagined a visit from Susan, but never one like this.

In his dreams, Susan would sneak into the house, dancing of course (he'd never understood why) and he, focused at the kitchen table, inspired by the tragedy buried in the mound of the cemetery, would be so absorbed inside the words and characters he'd created that he wouldn't notice her as she crept behind him and wrapped her fingers across his eyes like a child playing a game of *guess who*. But he'd know *who* immediately (this was his world after all), even though she'd throw out her best George Burns impression in a futile attempt to confuse and disorient him. But he'd sense her. Instantly. He'd jump to his feet without calling out her name and he'd spin to her and embrace her and she'd declare her love for him and she'd beg him to come home.

And then there was reality.

Actual events had turned out to be quite different. The evening had ended with their march in silence through the last of their after-dinner stroll before she'd pushed through the front door and crossed directly to the sofa, grabbing her cell and pressing the phone to her ear, leaving Dan to cringe as he watched her fingers tremble from across the room. He'd ached to find some way to comfort her. But he knew that, in truth, he was the cause of all her pain. He was the reason she shook. She'd spoken, then, to the attendant on the other end of the line, rearranging her scheduled flights and plans so she could leave the following day. And after, she'd dropped her hand to her lap and ended the call with a breath.

"It's done. I leave tomorrow at 1:00."

Dan nodded. He stared across the harbor as the lighthouse shot light into dark in never-ending circles. Then he crossed to her and held her in his eyes.

"I'm sorry."

He didn't wait for her response. He didn't really care what she said. But he didn't know how else to end their standoff and he couldn't bear the possibility that this tension might be her final memory of him. He pulled her into him and wrapped his body around hers.

"I understand," he whispered. Then he held her for a moment before he released her and crossed to the bedroom.

"Dan?"

He stopped and turned to face her.

"Do you mind if we just sit on the deck and watch the night?"

He smiled.

"No, I don't. I'd like that."

And so they did. And then they slept in Dan's bed with one lingering kiss before they fell asleep, each sequestered in his or her own half of the sheets.

The next morning arrived too quickly. They showered and prepped and decided they'd have time to stop for coffee before Susan had to leave to catch her flight home. As they left, Dan grabbed Ed's wallet and shoved the billfold into his pocket. At the coffee house, Jamie stood sweeping the floor behind the counter. Dan beamed.

"Jamie. You're back. I'm so glad. I've missed you."

"You did?" Jamie said, glancing at Susan.

"Yes, of course. That other lady never seemed to get my drink right."

"That's my mom. It's my family's shop."

"Oh…" Dan studied the counter.

"You're right, though," the young man said, grinning. "She's no good at making drinks."

Dan shrugged and smiled back. He'd wanted to apologize for the other day, to make sure there were no hard feelings and reassure Jamie that he knew the kid was on his side. But doing so during this visit would mean revisiting the rumors about him and Cat in front of Susan. The couple had ended their night in a sort of unspoken detente and Dan couldn't see any benefit to reminding Susan of why they'd fought in the first place. Jamie, though, saved him the trouble.

"I'm sorry about the other day. I—"

"Jamie," Dan interrupted him. "This is my wife, Susan."

"Nice to meet you," Jamie said with a straight face and nothing more than a quick peek in her direction.

He went on, "I really shouldn't have brought up all the sip sip. I guess it probably seemed like I thought the rumors were all true, but I—"

"What rumors?" Susan asked.

"You know," Jamie said. Dan flashed his eyes at the boy.

"Know what?" Susan spun Dan to face her.

"All the rumors around town about him and Cat," Jamie said, playing the innocent; although Dan had his doubts.

"What's he talking about?" Susan glared at Dan.

Dan stuttered, "That…"

177

"They think he killed a man," Jamie broke in. "Yeah. He didn't tell you? Everyone is talking about it. Him and Cat found a body."

He turned to Dan. "Do they still think you two were involved somehow?"

"It's just...who knows what they really think," Dan said. "Could we get a couple of French press coffees, please?"

Jamie stared at him. Finally, he mumbled, "Of course," then rang them up and took Dan's money.

"Keep the change, Jamie. Thanks." He twisted to Susan. "Let's sit outside. Jamie will bring us our drinks when they're ready."

"This is cute. Why didn't we ever come here before?"

Dan leaned into her. "We had other things on our minds."

Susan slapped his arm.

"Now I come here pretty much every morning. The shop will close soon for the off season. But for now it's great."

They sat at a table on the deck and Dan reached over to take his wife's hand, but she jumped up immediately and crossed to the edge of the deck, to the railing where Cat had stood the day before. She faced in the direction of the lighthouse. Dan joined her and pointed to the left.

"You can see Richard's house right down there. See?"

Susan nodded. Dan heard Jamie call out his name.

"That was quick," he muttered and stepped inside to find their coffees sitting on the counter. He threw a questioning look in Jamie's direction and picked up the mugs, but Jamie simply turned his back, and Dan returned to Susan back at her seat.

"That's strange. He usually brings me my drink."

"He's jealous. He likes you."

"Probably. What's not to like?" Dan said, grinning.

"No. I mean he *likes* you."

Dan blew on his coffee. He set his mug down and stared at Susan. "What? No. He's not gay."

"Mmmm, I don't know. I think he likes you."

She went on, "He's cute. You two'd make a cute couple."

Dan glanced toward the inside counter. "No, he's just friendly...at least, he usually is. But, so what if he is?"

"Nothing, of course. You know I don't care about that." Susan said. "I'm just saying. You have an admirer."

"Well, if you're right, I'm flattered. But, he's certainly not as cute as you." Dan winked.

"Really, Dan? You're not helping your case any with these tired lines."

Susan eyed him directly. "And I know those rumors about you and Cat aren't about finding the body. I'm not stupid."

"What are you talking about? Of course they are."

"Dan. Really? You and Cat?"

"They are. People here all think I did it. Cat just gets lumped in because—"

"So, you won't admit it?"

"Admit what?"

"Such a cliché." Susan shook her head.

"Me?"

"Is there anyone else at the table?"

"Well, that didn't take long." Dan tossed his drink down. Coffee splashed across the table.

"Hey. I'm not the one having an affair." Susan glared at him.

"Here we go again. Susan, I'm not having an affair. With Cat or anybody."

Dan nudged his cup to the side. "You really think I'm having an affair?"

Susan didn't respond at first. She took a sip of her drink.

"I don't know. I guess not. But, I know you. You're not happy unless everybody likes you. I'm sure you've at least been flirting with her."

"No, I haven't. I made it clear I was married. I told her all about you and I even said everything was mutual. I made sure she didn't think you were the bad guy. I didn't tell her about how you left me."

"Because I didn't."

"Well, kicked me out. Whatever."

Susan scanned the deck and pursed her lips.

"I never kicked you out, Dan. You left me the moment you killed our son."

Dan froze. For an instant, there was nothing. No sound. No thoughts. No Susan. Then, a backdraft rushed the world back into him and angry, frantic thoughts pulsed through his head. He stared at the table and sucked air in deep through his nose. He could hear the other patrons silent their conversations and shift and stretch their necks to hear her violent words. He couldn't look at her, couldn't even glance in her direction. Tears brimmed at the corners of his eyes. He wiped at his face and shook his head and slammed his fist on the table. More coffee splashed messy across the surface and Dan ripped at the napkin dispenser and swabbed at the spill.

He bolted up.

"You should go. You were right. It's not going to be good if you stay. I...You should go."

"Dan, we have to talk about this."

"Go. I mean it, Susan. I don't want you here anymore."

Susan stood and moved around the table. She reached out to Dan and he knocked her hand away. The other customers on the deck started snickering.

Dan spun and shouted, "You all happy? You got your drama for the day? Let's all pile on Dan."

Susan erupted and stormed off the deck and through the coffee shop. Dan pursued close behind to his house, then watched her as she gathered her things before they continued on to the post office dock to catch the ferry. Dan reached out and snatched her bag.

"Here. Let me take that."

She tried to steal her suitcase back from him—"I can take it!"—but he swung the bag away from her and kept trudging, silent and stormy.

At the dock, he dropped her bag and they waited for the ferry to arrive. Dan could see the boat stopping at the other docks around the harbor. The couple stared straight ahead at the water, neither uttering a sound until, at the last moment, Susan stepped in front of him, enunciating her words.

"Dan, I'm sorry. I don't know why I said that. It wasn't helpful."

He nodded but kept his eyes forward. The ferry chugged in their direction.

"Dan, here comes the ferry. Please don't let us finish like this."

He could hear her voice break.

He picked up her suitcase.

The boat floated into the dock and the few travelers began boarding. He passed Susan's bag to the man taking cargo. Dan stared over her. "Have a good trip."

181

"Dan...please."

He heard her gasp and he glanced at her and shook his head, then pivoted and walked away.

* * * *

Dan moved away from Susan and the ferry but stopped, suddenly nauseated and sick and aching to spin and call out to her and beg her for even one hour more. But he didn't.

Instead he ran for cover. To the right of the dock, a pergola sat hidden, obscured by growth, and Dan rushed in and leaned into one of the posts. He searched, desperate, through the mostly empty boat but couldn't locate his wife, even though he stretched and angled for a better view. But no matter how he contorted, he couldn't find her.

She wasn't there. Susan wasn't there. She'd never gotten on the...

Ecstatic, he twisted and darted his eyes around the dock and along Queen's Highway, even glancing at one point at his own feet. He stumbled out of the covering and ran up and down the roadway, jogging to the steps leading up to the Sugar Shack before he turned and peeked once more at the dock and the ferry, just now pulling out.

And then he saw her. His shoulders dropped and he stumbled forward, instantly weighted, feeling oddly like a voyeur as he watched his own wife locate a place to sit and lower herself onto one of the ferry's benches, unsteady and wiping at her eyes as she did. He shifted closer, feeling outside his body, and he noticed her lift her head and gaze in his direction, then raise a gentle hand and wave before she twisted away from him as the boat left the harbor. Suddenly, his need to re-litigate their morning and determine which of the two shouldered the majority of the blame melted away and he felt insignificant and

182

unnecessary. He dropped his head. All around him were loneliness and sadness and resentment and abandon—and guilt—hovering just within arm's reach, but for all he stabbed at the emotions, he couldn't bat them away. Finally, he turned, surrounded by irony and, after a moment, he trudged toward home. Listless.

He considered his next steps. Dan pulled his new phone out of his pocket and glanced at the display. Cat would be at the church. There was still time to meet up with her and he could get credit for having shown up without the boredom of actually sitting through an entire church service. So he continued on, past the barriers intended to keep cars and golf carts at bay, and veered to the right toward the Hope Town Methodist Church. As he approached, harmonic singing tumbled from the windows and somersaulted mist-like through the streets. The white building and spire cut strangled, but beautiful lines into the blue sky above and behind the tabernacle. The structure was stunning, not because of any remarkable architecture, but in spite of it. Immediately Dan felt softer.

He nudged the door open and slid inside. As he did, a man in robes stepped to the podium, pushing both hands in Dan's direction and, one by one, the organ and members of the congregation quieted their worship until one woman sang alone. The pastor spoke.

"Welcome, Br...Sister Mavis...Mavis....Sister." He motioned to the gentleman at the woman's side and the congregant poked the lone singer with his elbow. She spun to him, clearly frustrated, but flushed red and snapped her mouth closed. The preacher spoke again.

"Welcome."

The parishioners all turned their heads as one and looked toward the entrance, tossing their individual '*um-*

hum's and '*well, I*'s and '*you see*'s in his direction. One child leaned to his mother and Dan heard him ask, "Is that the man?" before she shushed the boy and pulled him closer. Cat motioned from the middle of one of the pews, shifting to her right and pushing the woman on her left away from her. He indicated no, but she kept insisting, stage-whispering "C'mon" and finally the pastor prayed, with a chuckle, "Please, Lord, inspire our visitor to feel welcome and join yer flock."

Dan mouthed *I'm sorry* to the room and excused his way down the aisle to sit at Cat's side. Once situated, he smiled toward the pulpit and nodded.

"Ready? Good," the preacher said and bowed his head. "Our Great and Bounteous Lord, we thank Thee. Amen." Then he gazed out across the chapel and commanded, "Now, brothers and sisters, go ye all and serve the Lord."

Dan twisted to Cat. "That was it?"

Cat nodded and jumped to her feet, grabbing Dan's hand and rushing down the narrow walkway, stepping over the feet of the other, apparently less anxiety-ridden worshippers still in their seats.

Cat darted to the front of the chapel. A circle of devotees had already snaked around the pastor, as if in anticipation of meeting some celebrity, and Cat tapped the shoulder of one of the acolytes. The woman turned, bumping her large hat against the face of the man at her side. Cat said, "Mary, I want our guest to meet Pastor John. Do you mind?"

Mary didn't respond. She grimaced at Dan and returned to the preacher, again knocking the man next to her with her hat.

Cat stamped her foot. "Well, I..."

She tapped Mary's shoulder repeatedly and, it would seem, each time more insistently because suddenly the woman whipped around (forcing her companion to stumble) and glared at Cat, raising her index finger to the sky and opening her mouth.

"Sister Cat," Dan heard a man say and he felt a swelling of gratitude for the interruption to any potential melee.

The voice continued, "How good of ye to bring a guest."

Mary sneered at Dan and Cat and spun her head once more, thumping the man yet again. At this point, Dan thought, he's just asking for the abuse. The mass of parishioners floated back.

"Brother. Sister. Welcome. God be with ye."

"Pastor John, this is Dan," Cat caressed Dan's shoulder with both of her hands. "He's a writer here working on a book."

"God be with ye, my son."

Dan extended his hand to the man who could only be his father if he'd been born seconds before him.

"Pastor, I was hoping we could have a word with you," Cat whispered and wrapped her arm into his elbow, guiding him away from the other congregants.

Pastor John glanced over his shoulder as Cat led him away from the group. Dan hurried behind them.

"...leave the rest of my flock," the preacher was saying as Dan moved to Cat's side.

"Yes, I understand. This will just take a moment."
"So," she began. "Did you know Ed…"

She closed her mouth and scanned the room.

"Pastor, do you still use drugs?"

"Cat!" Dan exclaimed, grabbing at her elbow.

She flipped her head toward Dan. "I'm not judging. I was just wondering. He could be the one."

"Brother Daniel," Pastor John said, chuckling. "No need. I knows Sister Cat well. She one to say her mind. And, I's not ashamed. But I serves the Lord now. So no, Cat. I doesn't. But, Cat. I's not the one. We all equal in the eye of the Lord."

"Not what I'm saying, but good to know. So Ed. You know him? Ed Wilson? The name mean anything to you?"

"Ed Wilson? He the one you find dead."

Dan burst out laughing. Cat and Pastor Johnson glanced at him.

"No, I...sorry. Just...How does everyone know all this? Are there no secrets in this town?"

"I..." the pastor began, then immediately shifted his eyes to the right and smiled. Constable Anderson strolled into the group.

"Brother Anderson. God be with ye."

Cat hurried to Dan's side, pushed her head toward his neck, and whispered, "Just act casual."

"Very nice service, Pastor." Anderson nodded. "Inspiring as always."

He pivoted to Dan. "So sorry to interrupt, but I'm really here to see Mr. Harris. See, I'm missing something."

"Oh yeah?" Dan said.

Cat singsonged through gritted teeth, "Casual."

"I was wondering if you knew anything about it."

"Don't know. Maybe some more detail would help," Dan said.

Constable Anderson frowned and moved his fingers to his forehead.

Cat spoke up, "Is this what you're looking for, Ronnie?"

She reached into her pocket. "You dropped it at Dan's and I picked it up. I think it's some kind of a form or something."

"Let me see this," he spit out and snatched at the paper.

"Well...what do you know?" He flipped the document over, then flashed at Cat and Dan. "Wasn't that lucky? Like you two had it planned all along."

Cat shrugged. Inspector Johnson joined the group.

"Seriously?" Dan breathed out, suddenly caught off guard by a torrent of bitterness. "It's like a comedy of errors in here."

The inspector grinned at him. "Why, Mr. Harris. Nice to see ye, too."

"Actually." Dan paused. "You know. I'm glad you're here. I thought of something and I need to talk to you.

"Okay." The inspector motioned to the side of the chapel. Cat and Constable Anderson followed them.

He turned to Dan and glanced at Cat. Dan spoke.

"Yes. So, during our interview, you asked who I thought killed Ed."

"Ye solve the case already, Chief?"

Constable Anderson snorted. "Harris. Stop wasting our—"

"No, no. Let him speak. I want to hear what he has to say." Johnson indicated to Dan. "Go ahead."

"It's just that..." Dan lowered his voice. "It's just that I think you should look at Victor Bennett."

"The writer?" Cat said.

"Ye do now? Why's that?"

"I...well, since you and I talked, I was talking to Daniel, the lighthouse keeper's son, and—"

Cat nudged Dan. "When did you talk to Daniel?"

"The other night. He came by." Dan said, not looking in her direction. "Anyway, I guess Victor was over by the lighthouse and acting kind of strange around the day Ed arrived."

"The day you arrived," Constable Anderson said and nodded his lips at Dan.

"Yes. Fine. The day I arrived too. But the important thing is that Daniel saw Victor run past the lighthouse, acting strange."

Cat smashed her arms down across her chest as if pouting. "You didn't tell me this."

Dan glanced at her. "I just thought of it."

"I see," said Inspector Johnson. "Well, we'll look into that." The policeman pivoted to Constable Anderson. "Ye know this Bennett?"

"Yes, good guy. I'm sure he didn't have anything to do with all this. He's British."

"Oh, he's British?" Dan rolled his eyes. "That's your big deduction?"

"I don't know, Ronnie." Cat stepped closer to Ronnie and rubbed the policeman's shoulder with her hand. "Dan may be onto something here. There's something just not right about that guy."

He shook her off. "Cat. You're playing games with me."

She stepped back. "What? No, I'm not, Ronnie. Anyways, h—"

"I just don't know whose side you're on anymore," Ronnie snapped.

Inspector Johnson cut in, "Thank ye, Mr. Harris. Anything else? Anyone else ye want to accuse?"

Dan shook his head.

"Well, then. We'll look into it. Thank ye. Anderson, come."

Anderson whipped his head in Johnson's direction. He jerked at Dan and sniggered before he padded off after the inspector.

Dan shouted after him, "What?"

Cat exhaled in a huff. "Oh, you guys are like children."

"What do you mean? I'm not doing anything. It's all him."

"Case in point," she said as she surveyed the chapel. "But you see? He's gone. Tell me that's not suspicious. He's hiding something."

"Anderson?"

"No!" She stomped her foot. "Pastor John, silly. Something's up. That man's hiding something."

"Cat." Dan sighed.

"What? I'm telling you. There's something there."

"Because he once used drugs?"

"Yes," Cat said. "Exactly."

Dan grinned. "Okay. Fine. Whatever. But I'm hungry. Let's get some lunch."

He started out of the church, cutting around the few remaining huddles of parishioners, ignoring the occasional leer. At the entrance of the church. Dan opened the door for Cat.

She stepped through the entrance and he let the door fall closed. She pivoted to face him.

"Listen."

And then she stopped. She glanced off toward Dan's house and took a step away from the building.

"It's about your wife."

"Susan? What about Susan?"

"I just…"

A scream sounded inside the church.

Seventeen

Cat and Dan froze.

"Anyways, like I—"

"Shhh." Dan pushed two fingers forward then spun and called out, "Stay here!" as he rushed back into the church. Cat grabbed at his shirt and pulled him toward her.

"No, Dan. Please. Don't leave me here. Besides, haven't you already caused enough problems in this town? Don't draw any more attention to yourself."

Dan twisted to face her.

"What? No. You'll be fine."

He pried her hand off him and pushed through the doorway. Inside he skidded to a stop. Nothing.

A few remaining congregants milled about, but everything looked pretty much the same as when they'd left only moments before. He shrugged and pivoted to return outside, even getting as far as to press his palm against the wood of the door when another, "Aaah!" screamed out. Dan whirled back around. To the right. He flashed to that side of the chapel before glancing back at the stragglers in their groupings. Only some seemed to have reacted to the sound, but those few were already turning their focus back to whatever pressing conversations they'd been in the middle of before.

Dan rushed to the aisle that ran along the side of the pews and tried the first door entering the chapel, then the second (wondering as he did why a church this size needed so many openings). When he pushed on the third exit, the door swung open and he stumbled through into a narrow hallway. A small crowd of churchgoers focused on the opposite end of the passage where two men wrestled on the floor. Sarah Patterson stood leaning over them whining, "Scott, stop. He didn't do anything. Please."

Dan shifted sideways to let the doorway fall closed behind him and stepped toward Sarah and the two men. She rushed toward him and he threw open his arms, ready to receive and console her. But when she reached him, she merely shoved him back against the door he'd just come through and yelled, "What are you doing here? Haven't you done enough?"

He opened his mouth to respond, but as soon as he did, the solid surface behind him slapped against his back and propelled him forward into Sarah and then directly on top of the grappling pair.

"Dan! What are you doing? Get off them. Oh! You never listen. I told you to stay out of it."

Dan rolled to the side. Cat hovered over him, wagging her finger at him like the villainess in some Disney movie orphanage. The two men he'd fallen on crawled to their feet, evidently having determined that his tumble justified a ceasefire, or, just as likely, that they now shared a common, more immediate, enemy, namely him. Scott, seemingly unfazed by it all, charged at Dan, hoisting him from the floor and slamming his back against a wall. He exhaled in Dan's face (his hot breath smelled surprisingly fresh and minty). Immediately, though, Scott flew back and Dan saw that the other man had leapt onto the gentle giant's back, his weight apparently enough to unbalance Scott, forcing him to stumble backward. The two crashed to the floor. Scott jumped up, apparently unaffected once again, and rushed again at Dan. Sarah screamed.

Suddenly, Dan heard Constable Anderson barrel out, "What's going on here?"

Scott continued his darting at Dan, ignoring the yelling and shoving past the constable, knocking the policeman to the side as he did. Sarah grabbed at her husband's arm as he ran by but all she snagged was air. Cat, who had apparently chosen this moment to take part in the festivities and join the fray, was there to *catch* Sarah when the woman lost her balance and crashed into her. Cat flew against the wall and slid to the floor, wailing, "Ow! My wrist."

As if voiced from the heavens (or rafters) above them, Constable Anderson bellowed, "Stop! This! Now!"

Everyone froze, then spun toward him in unison. He rushed to Cat's side and crouched, pressing his hand to the wall to keep from toppling over and shouted over his shoulder, "Look what you've all done to her."

"Cat, are you okay? What did Sarah do to you?"

He spun and glared at Dan. "This is all your fault."

"Mine? How is any of this my fault? I just came to see what was going on. I heard a scream." He motioned to Sarah. "She…"

Constable Anderson shook his head and returned to Cat. Dan heard him mumble, "Americans."

Dan continued, "I was just trying to help. This was all started before I even got here. Scott and this guy…" Dan pointed, then whirled around. Almost everyone, including the other participant, had disappeared.

"There was another guy here before. He and Scott were fighting."

"That true, Sarah? You scream?" Anderson tipped his head up to her.

She hesitated.

Anderson glared at Dan, "You're always trying to blame someone, anyone close to you. You're pathetic."

Cat spoke up. "Ronnie, Dan's right. It wasn't him. He wasn't even in here when it all started." Ronnie kept his attention on Dan and Cat squeezed her wrist and whined, "Ow. My arm."

Anderson hurried to console her.

"Fine," Sarah finally went on. "Scott thinks I'm cheating on him. But I'm not." She slunk toward her husband. "I'm not, baby, really. You have to believe me."

She pointed at Dan, then Cat. "It's their fault, though. They started all this when they showed up to the house going on about some guy named Ed. Said I was sleeping with him and that I knew he was dead. But, Ronnie, I don't even know who he is."

Anderson glowered at Dan and rose to his feet. He yelled, "What's all this?"

Scott stomped forward, pressing his hand to his cheek. "She did this to me. Look, Ronnie."

Dan glanced at Cat. He waited. When she said nothing, he began, "We just…"

"Oh, come on, Ronnie," Cat finally spoke up. "I felt sorry for Dan. He saw me looking at the paper you dropped and I let him look at it. What was I supposed to do?"

Ronnie leaned to Cat and motioned toward Scott. He said, gently, "That true, Cat? You do that to him?"

He didn't wait for an answer and continued, more loudly. "Did little old you hurt that big strong man?" He snickered.

194

Anderson leered at Dan (which elicited outstretched arms and a *what's your problem?* head shake from the writer), then he bent and wrapped his arm around Cat's torso. She struggled up, looking properly beset. He directed a stander-by to fetch a chair for her to rest on *in case she feels faint,* then pivoted to Sarah and Scott.

Scott stepped forward and said, "I'm really sorry, Ronnie. I didn't mean to bump into you. I was just trying to stop this guy from hurting my wife. You can understand that."

"Dan," Sarah spit out. "His name's Dan."

Scott flashed at her, then added, "Exactly. Dan."

He softened, "And, Cat. I'm so sorry to see that you're hurt. Are you okay? I'd feel just awful if I did anything that would cause you to suffer in any way."

Cat massaged her forearm. Finally she said, "I'll be fine, I guess."

The enclave focused on Constable Anderson.

"Well," the policeman began, brushing at his hair and staring at Dan. "I guess we'll just leave it at this. Just a warning. Dan, you're just lucky Cat didn't get really hurt."

* * * *

Dan waited while Cat fumbled with her shoe. She glanced at him. "Go ahead. I'll catch up to you."

He slid inside, but held the door open.

"I can wait."

From across the shop, Jamie called out, "Dan. You're back. Did Susan leave or is she still with you?"

Cat peeked her head in. "No, she's gone. She took the morning ferry."

"No," Dan repeated. "I'm here with Cat. You know her, right?"

195

"Sort of. Not really."

"Oh yes he does." Cat stepped over to the counter. "Hello Jamie. How's your dad?"

Jamie ignored her and smiled at Dan. "So, what can I get for you? Another French press?"

"No, thanks. We thought we'd get some food."

"Get the curried chicken and asparagus quiche," Cat spoke up. "That's really good."

"Sorry," Jamie pointed to a tray of sandwiches. "All we have on Sundays is egg and bacon sandwiches.

"Unless you want some couple-day-old chocolate, coconut and espresso cake," he added, motioning to his left with his lips.

"Ooh. I'll have that." Cat leaned toward the far end of the counter to reach the dessert.

She picked up the pastry and turned to Dan. "Will you get us some silverware? Thanks. I'll get us our usual seat."

After she'd gone, Dan smirked. "I honestly don't know where she's going. We don't have a usual seat."

He continued, "Listen, Jamie. I wanted to apologize for the other day. I didn't mean for you to stay away like that."

"Oh, it wasn't because of you." Jamie said and picked up a cloth sitting near the register. "I was out of town."

"Oh." Dan peeked down. "Good then."

"So, you want a sandwich?"

"Yes, thanks. I think I'll get a coffee after all, too. How much do I owe you?" Dan glanced at Cat, who was already halfway through her piece of cake, despite having no fork. "I guess we're getting the cake as well."

"Don't worry about it." Jamie twisted and reached a plate off of some shelves. He placed a sandwich and some napkins on top. "It's on the house."

"You sure?"

196

"Yes. I'm sure...I think—"

Suddenly Cat was at Dan's side, pushing her arm around his elbow and leaning against him. "Can I get some water, Jamie?"

He hesitated. "Sure."

Jamie reached a bottle off a shelf, then set a glass on the counter and poured Cat some water. He smiled at Dan. "I'll bring your coffee out as soon as it's ready. Go ahead and sit down."

At their table, Dan said, "Well, that was crazy."

Cat scowled and nodded toward the counter. "I know. I don't think he likes me."

"What?"

"Jamie. I don't think he likes me."

"Oh. I'm sure it's nothing. But, I was talking about at the church. That was kind of crazy."

"Yeah. Victor? You think he—"

"What?" Dan shook his head. "No. Cat. In the hall. Scott and Sarah."

"Oh, that. Happens all the time."

"It does?"

"Yeah. There's always some drama going on with those two."

"I thought you didn't know her. Or him."

"I don't. Not really."

"But you said—"

"I don't know what to tell you, Dan. It's a small island. We all kind of know each other, but we really don't. Anyway, Victor Bennet. What's this about Victor?"

Dan sighed. "I don't know. I guess he was over by the lighthouse around the night Ed arrived."

"So Daniel said this? Could he have done it?"

"Daniel? Kill Ed?"

"Yeah, or Thomas."

"Well, not Thomas. He's a little old, don't you think? Besides, motive, Cat."

"So what's Victor's motive?"

"I don't know. But, there's something up with that guy."

"Just because you don't like him, doesn't mean he killed somebody."

"I never said I didn't like him."

She quirked her head and raised her eyebrows.

"Well, okay. I don't," he continued. "He's so self-absorbed. He's so…Come on. Nobody does condescending like the British."

Dan eyed Cat, but she was staring over his shoulder. He glanced behind himself.

"Anyway, Daniel mentioned that Victor had been over at the lighthouse around that same time. Seemed like something to bring up."

"I guess so."

"Well…" he said. "So, I wanted to talk to you about something."

Cat yelled across the cafe. "Jamie, you never brought me a fork."

"Be nice." Dan nudged her with his foot.

Cat grinned and leaned forward, just as she had when they'd first met. "A question? Really? It's about time."

"What? No." Dan shook his head and reached into his pocket. He tossed Ed's wallet on the table. "About this."

"What's that?"

"I found it that day we found Ed. It's his wallet."

Cat shoved her hand over the billfold and darted her eyes around the shop. She whispered, "Don't just throw that out here."

"Well, except for the way you're acting, nobody would have any idea what it is. Besides, it's just us and Jamie."

Jamie approached the table and set a fork down. "Anything else, ma'am."

"No," Cat spit out and glared at Dan. "Ma'am? How old does he think I am?"

Dan glanced Jamie. He mouthed *sorry* and focused back on Cat. "Anyway. What do you think?"

"What do you mean?"

"I mean, you know Ronnie. Should I tell him I found this?"

"No." She shook her head. "Absolutely not. First, because you just called him Ronnie. And second, you didn't tell him when you found it, why bother now? What's it going to change? Is there anything in it?"

She picked up the billfold and shoved her hands under the table.

"No." Dan shook his head. "It's empty."

"Well, there you go." She tossed the wallet across the table. "It's just a wallet. Doesn't change anything."

Dan studied the billfold, then leaned back and pushed it in his pocket.

"Well, somebody cleaned everything out. Almost certainly the murderer. There could be DNA."

"Yeah, silly, but now yours, not to mention mine is on there, too."

Dan paused, then nodded. "Maybe you're right."

Jamie set a mug on the table. "Can I get you anything else, Dan?"

"No, thanks, Jamie," he said and smiled.

As the boy walked away, Cat mimicked him in a taunting voice, "Can I get you anything else," then, extra syrupy, "Dan?"

"Cat, come on. Don't be mean."

"What? He obviously has a crush on you. You should watch out."

"He's just nice, But, so what if he does?" Dan took a bite of his sandwich.

"That won't go over well here."

"Well, it doesn't matter to me."

"Maybe he was in the States for something and had just come back."

"Jamie?"

"Nooo," she hissed out, sounding annoyed. "Keep up, silly. We're done with him. You're obsessed."

Dan snickered, shaking his head, and picked up his coffee. "Then, who are we talking about?"

"Victor. Maybe he was in the States and met this Ed guy and they came back for a romantic getaway and had a fight and Victor ended up killing him. Or maybe...Victor lured him back to Hope Town, planning all the while to kill him. Oooh, that's better. I like that. He was stabbed so it was probably someone he trusted."

Dan didn't respond at first. Finally, he set his drink down. "Okay. You sound a bit conspiracy theorist with everything else, but you've got a good point about the stabbing. You might be on to something there."

"That's what Ronnie said." Cat pushed her finger into Dan's mug and licked the coffee off.

"Mmmm. That's good."

Dan pushed the drink to the side.

"You talked to Ronnie?"

"Co—"

"Constable Anderson. Whatever. But you talked to him about this?"

"Well, yeah. About my idea about the stabbing. But I was just trying to steer him away from you."

Dan looked thoughtful. "Well, I'm sure he was already thinking that…not that your observation's not brilliant," he added quickly. "But no wonder he's trying so hard to make it seem like I knew this guy. Maybe all this is that simple. We just have to show that I didn't know him."

"How do you do that?" she said.

"I don't know."

"Listen," he continued, standing and picking up the mug and the plate the cake was on. He crossed to the counter, then returned to the table and picked up his sandwich. He started to the exit, calling out, "Thanks, Jamie," and turned to Cat.

"Let's go. We should call it a day. I'm kind of tired."

Cat studied him, looking confused, then shrugged and followed him. Outside she said, "We could go sit out on your deck. That'd be a nice break."

"No. Thanks. Really. I think I'm just ready to chill on my own. Susan and I were up kind of late talking."

Cat rolled her eyes. "Fine."

She stopped. He kept walking, then rotated to face her.

She said, "That's what I wanted to talk to you about before. You know, I'm really sorry if I caused any trouble."

"No…" Dan glanced to the side. "It's not you…not really. It's complicated."

Then he motioned to the sky over Great Abaco to the west. "We should get going. Those clouds look kind of ominous. I'm pretty sure we're heading for a rough night."

"Okay," Cat said and started again. At his house, he hugged her and she walked away. She spun after a few feet. "And, don't dismiss Jamie as a possible suspect. I'm telling you. It's always the quiet, unassuming ones."

"Got it. Don't use logic."

He watched her stroll away. After a moment, he called after her.

"Really? That's it? You're not going to try even a little bit?"

She kept going. "Nope. Bye Dan."

Eighteen

Dan tossed his sandwich on the counter and scanned around his home.

He was completely alone. And solitude, after so much chaos, felt oddly invigorating.

Of course, he was also alone. Not as encouraging a thought.

He crossed to the deck and stepped outside, leaning against the railing to study the dark clouds in the distance as they drifted closer. A breeze brushed across his head. He returned inside, pulling the doors closed behind him, and strolled across the room to the table and lifted his laptop screen. He exhaled.

"Time to do some investigating."

He opened Safari and browsed to Google, then typed *Ed Wilson* and hit *Search*—338,000,000 results.

"Wow. 338 mi…" He stared at the number and peeked into the kitchen.

Next to the fridge, the bottle of white he'd handed Susan for her cleanup stood open with the cork sitting to the side. Dan stood and moved to the counter then ran a single finger delicately along the rim. He thought of Susan, of her smile. He chuckled at her uncharacteristic overuse of the word *tramp*. Then he saw her kneeling and defeated on the rug, crying, and instantly his smile melted and became a sneer. He snatched the wine and dumped what was left into the sink, bouncing the container to hurry whatever stubborn liquid remained. Certain the flask was completely empty, he spun and threw the bottle into the recycling bin, then gathered the bag and hauled the waste outside to discard it by the front door. He glared at the surrounding area.

Done.

He stomped back into the kitchen and opened a new bottle.

Back at the table, wine at the ready, he took a breath, and another, and studied the results on his screen. Too many. Google wasn't going to work. Facebook or (he smirked) Bing.

Dan typed facebook.com into the address bar and entered *Ed Wilson* in the search field, again staring at a long list of profiles. He'd clearly underestimated how difficult this would be.

Missouri. The customs form had said Ed was from Missouri.

Ed Wild...(backspace, backspace)...*lson, Missouri.*

The results loaded.

Okay, he thought, taking a sip from his glass, now we're getting somewhere.

This list fit on a single page. One by one, he hovered his mouse over each linked profile, reviewing the photos of the individual Eds. Then he saw him. He inhaled sharply and downed a 'sip'. This was the right Ed. He was almost sure. In a flash, Dan felt dragged back to that moment, to the beach, to staring eyes. The man in the photo had bleached blond hair, not the same color as the dead body had had, but...he clicked the name.

The profile didn't provide much more information. Only three friends. At least on Facebook, Ed had not been the most popular guy. There were no posts, except one—a self-evident *I'm on Facebook now* announcement from over 10 years ago. Dan clicked the *About* tab. Missouri. His home state. *Photos:* three, again.

Dan took a drink and reviewed the images. One was of Ed with a woman, probably his wife or girlfriend by the way he was grabbing at her chest. Classy. One was of him standing in front of a terrarium holding some kind of rather aggressive-looking snake. Though, really, for creatures with no limbs, most snakes seem rather sinister. In the last shot, he was alone.

He enlarged the final photo. Ed was shirtless. A large bird, maybe a hawk, perched on his outstretched arm. But more importantly, the same tattoo of the eagle with the snake stretched across his chest. This was definitely him.

Easy.

Dan saved the photo to his desktop. In another browser window, he entered *images.google.com,* and dragged the same image into the search bar. Dan had tried this tactic once before and the process had been pretty useless. He wasn't expecting much.

Instantly, though, two links popped into the window. Dan sat back in his seat and glanced toward the kitchen. This, he thought, deserves a drink. He eyed his glass on the table.

"And not wine," he said, crossing to the freezer and pouring himself some vodka. He returned to his *desk.* From the screen, he read the title of the first result: *Beloved Preacher Murdered.*

Murdered. He grimaced. Ed was tied to another murder?

The link led to an article in the Wilson Daily Gazette that featured the same photo from the Facebook page, cropped to show only Ed's face, along with a portrait of a

205

dour-looking man and woman. The story described the murder of said *much-beloved* preacher in Wilson, Missouri. Evidently, John Wilson, direct descendent of town-founder Pastor Isaiah Wilson, had been killed by his wife, Ruth. According to the story, these were Ed's parents. And, Dan cringed, he'd been the one to discover his father's body. Poor Ed. That would really mess anybody up, he thought.

Dan gazed out the French doors and across the harbor to the lighthouse. After a moment, he returned to the results page. The second link led to a general Gazette page that listed the same article.

He tried again. This time, he typed *John Wilson murder* into the search bar. Several articles, all with a heading that had something to do with Ed's father's death ran down the page. Dan chose the third result and followed the link.

> Ruth Wilson was found guilty Thursday of first-degree murder in the gruesome killing of her husband, John Wilson, Pastor at God's Church of Christ in Wilson, Missouri. Wilson will serve a life sentence at Richter Penitentiary...

Dan hit the back button and clicked a different link. A shorter article appeared, looking more like a corresponding aside than a news story. But this one was more recent.

> Ruth Wilson, serving a life sentence at Richter Penitentiary for the brutal slaying of her husband, John Wilson, has been diagnosed with stomach cancer. She will be transferred from the prison's general population to the penitentiary's medical ward.

A bolt of wind rushed past him and sent his note cards flittering around the room and to the floor. Dan felt moisture brush against the side of his face. He spun. The French doors had blown open. He scrambled out of his seat and slammed them closed. Within seconds, overpowering pings engulfed the roof above his head and he glanced out the doors to see that the harbor was inundated. Trees danced and rough waves gusted across the surface of the water. Dan stared, seduced by the violence, and leaned against the glass to watch the chaos. He pivoted and crossed back to continue his search.

He started to read again. He froze. Everything outside had at once fallen into silence. Surrounding him was calm. Stillness. He pushed up from his chair and moved to the French doors, lifting his hand and pressing his palm against the glass of one of the panes. He pulled the door open. Dark and ominous clouds hovered gently above his house and the harbor. He stepped onto the deck. Not even a light breeze rustled his clothes. In the distance, bright white lit the sky and outlined the column of the lighthouse. Dan felt a sudden chill.

He twisted and moved back inside, pushing the door closed and locking the handle. Goosebumps ran across his body.

A BANG cracked and he thought he heard breaking glass. His ears rang and a chaos of other sounds floated distant and muted. He smelled something metallic, something burning. His hand pressed subconsciously against his side and as he moved he felt a searing pain. He lifted his fingers and peeked under them to find red ooze plastered across his palm, seeping into his clothes. He felt dizzy and tipped forward, whipping his hands out in front of himself to break his fall. He rolled onto his back as soon as he hit the floor, grabbing at the cloth of his shirt and pulling.

"Aaagh!"

Suddenly a hand flew over his mouth and Dan flinched as a revolver moved past his eyes.

"Shut up. Really. You're just embarrassing yourself."

Scott Patterson crouched over him. He eyed the gun in his own hand. "Apparently these things go off at nothing."

Dan pressed his head into the ground and twisted.

"I said stop. You're squirming. Just stay still. You moron."

Scott pulled his hand away from Dan's mouth and shifted on the balls of his feet.

"Help!" Dan yelled. Immediately Scott shoved his palm onto Dan's mouth and squeezed. He pulled his hand away and swung at Dan's head with the back of his hand.

"Actually, scream all you want. I don't care. It's not like anyone can hear you. In fact…"

Scott shoved a finger into Dan's bloody side. Dan wailed.

"Is that where it—?"

"Ahhh!"

"How about there?" He poked again, laughing.

"Aaaah!" Dan started to feel light headed. The room around him rocked.

"This is actually kind of fun." Scott cackled.

"Scott, listen I don't—"

Scott stabbed forward again. Dan flinched and Scott teetered and tossed to the side, laughing. Dan jabbed forward with his fist, connecting with Scott's eye. Immediately, Scott jumped to his feet and kicked Dan in the ribs. Dan squealed, flushing with shame as he heard himself cry out.

"Really!" Scott said, blinking frantically, "I don't think you get who's in control here."

He thrust down and grabbed Dan's right arm and yanked.

"This ends now. *Now!*" He glanced to the side and motioned to the broken window with the revolver. "And look what you did. There's glass everywhere."

Scott stormed across the room toward the deck, dragging Dan, who pulled and twisted and fought and yelled, "Help!" again.

Scott shoved Dan back and Dan collapsed into the sofa. The supposedly gentle giant aimed the gun in Dan's direction as he leaned to picked up some of the shards of glass, then crossed to the white rug and rubbed them against the drippings Dan had just left there, tossing the newly bloodied pieces against the French doors. He focused back on Dan.

He tapped his foot then rushed forward toward the sofa. Dan sunk lower into the cushions.

"Give me your hand."

"Scott."

"Just give me your hand."

Scott spun and crushed back into Dan, forcing him against the couch. He felt Scott grab his left hand and wrench it out from under his body, stretching his arm out and spreading his fingers flat against the sofa's arm. Instantly Dan felt a sharp pain as something solid smashed against his fingers. Scott jumped to his feet.

"There. Now it all makes more sense," Scott said, shaking his head and making a tsk-tsking sound. "You and your temper."

Dan's hand throbbed.

"Hopefully that will bruise before they find your body. But, if not…" Scott shrugged.

Dan's eyes opened wide. "Scott," he pleaded. "You don—"

"You really should have left my wife alone. She's got nothing to do with this."

"Stand up." He continued, motioning with the gun. "We're leaving."

"Scott."

Scott bolted toward him and knocked the side of Dan's head. "*Now!*"

Dan stood. His mind panicked, running through elusive thoughts. He couldn't leave with the man. That wouldn't end well. He had to think of something. He hesitated. He stepped slowly around the couch and pressed his hand against his side.

Scott shifted behind him and pressed the gun to his head.

"Now."

Dan felt himself duck reflexively.

"Scott."

"You know," Scott said. "You've got nothing to worry about unless I cock the…"

Click.

"Now you should worry. Like I said, these things go off at nothing."

"Okay," Dan said. "Okay. Just let me think."

"You think I'm stupid? Now!" Scott slammed his foot against the ankles of Dan's feet.

"Okay. I'm moving." Dan took a step forward slowly, then another, until they were at the front door.

"Now open it."

"Scott."

Scott reached around him and pulled the door open, then shoved Dan through the opening.

"Left. Toward my house."

The respite had ended and rain and wind fell wild around them. Dan's eyes darted and scanned the roadway, realizing with a sinking feeling that Scott was right. The street was empty.

"Scott, you don't have to do this."

"Oh really? I don't have to do this? Why's that?"

"Sarah. We were..."

Dan started to rotate his head. Immediately, Scott swung at his face and struck him. Dan stumbled to the side but didn't fall.

"Eyes forward."

Dan stiffened.

"Scott. Please. Let's talk about this."

They reached Russell's Lane.

"Right."

"Scott."

"Go right. Now."

Dan turned right.

"Up here. Just keep going. We're going to turn just...just...here."

A dirt road led into the trees, toward the north in the center of the thin island. Dan froze. At least there was light on the main roads.

"Scott, please. It was nothing. We were just...." he gritted his teeth and inhaled, "...asking ques—"

Scott shoved Dan. "Shut up and walk!"

The dirt road was muddy and slippery and Dan lost his footing. He slid and crashed, hard, expelling a moan, into the ground. Dan heard Scott shifting and probably swinging, and then, apparently having lost his balance, Scott slammed heavy into Dan's side.

211

"Daaah!" Dan gushed out. He yelled, "Help! Somebody...help!"

He shifted. Rolled. Away from Scott. Scott slid himself up but immediately lost his balance and crashed on top of Dan again. Excruciating pain shot through him again as Scott's massive body plowed into his. Dan caught the glint of the revolver as the gun slid away from them. It must have flown out of Scott's hand as the man fell. Dan kicked and thrashed. If he could just hoist Scott off him. He could scurry through the wet dirt in the direction he'd seen the gun go. But Scott's size was too much and the man pinned Dan into the earth. All Dan managed was to cover himself more in mud.

Suddenly, he felt Scott cover his mouth, just as he'd done in the house but this time pinching his nose as well. Dan couldn't breathe. He fought for a breath, to gasp, to cry, anything. But nothing. Panic rushed in and he twisted his head and hoofed and wriggled and twisted more and pried, desperate, at Scott's arms and he shoved at Scott's chest and he started pounding against the man, but Scott just knocked Dan's hands away with his elbow and laughed. Dan's strikes fell weaker and the world felt dizzy and he strained to keep his eyes open. Suddenly he saw Susan, in the distance, strolling, floating peacefully through a meadow. He called to her, but she didn't seem to hear, didn't look in his direction, just kept walking. He should never have let her go. He, but this was good. If she were...Scott...his thoughts started to become wispy and evasive and the night that was already dark...what with rain and clouds and the wi...became blacker still and the void became thicker and less discernible and at once Dan was okay with the nothingness and the emptiness and the nothingness and the...and then the empty was there.

Nineteen

Heroin removed the need to understand.

Victor glanced around the room. His arm was prepped and he reached for the remote and pressed play.

Mozart's Symphony No. 25 in G Minor swarmed through the room and washed around him and he thought, the masses, those plebeians have no idea. They mock only because they can't understand. This was culture. This was why he mattered and they didn't. He was brilliant. He was…Victor paused and stroked the air, conductor in his own symphony.

He placed the syringe's needle against the skin of his forearm and pressed. He always cringed at this point, apprehensive of the moment, but what followed was imminently worth any short-term pain. Sunlight slid into his veins and his head rocked and his brain skipped and then accelerated and slowed without motion and softness engulfed him and he slid back and dropped his head and felt free and was light.

And the room around him was blue.

And time melted.

And then he felt movement over his head and a kind of clarity engulfed him. And then he thought, I can't breathe. And then he thought, I don't understand. And then he forced open his mouth and inhaled but a surface covered his tongue and he blew out and a wet heat splashed back against his face and he lifted his hand to find the mist and his arm rose slow and he pressed his fingers against his face and his skin felt false and waxy and lost and he inhaled and exhaled frenetically, biology taking over, and he shifted his hands down to his neck to find an edge to pry away and some fingers…he squinted to consider if the hand was his own or someone else's. He pressed against the presence and started to fall into sleep but he couldn't distinguish between consciousness and the shadowy vagueness that surrounded him and he floated un-needing and then there was everything and then there was nothing.

And then there was Mozart.

Twenty

Dan's eyes shot open. He scanned around him, unsure of his surroundings. A house. Candles. A bed. He tried to sit forward. Dull ache shot through his entire body.

"Just sit back."

"Wha—?"

"You'll be fine. Just breathe through the pain. This is going to sting."

Dan felt cold drip down his side and he gritted his teeth and inhaled sharply.

"Who…" He sucked in air. "…are you? Where am I? Where's my shirt?"

"Lots of blood. Not a deep wound, but lots of blood. Grazed your rib. Mud everywhere. Your shirt's over there." The man motioned toward a dark corner of the room.

Instantly, the night flooded back to Dan.

"I've been shot," he blurted out and rushed his fingers to his side. His caretaker shoved his hand away.

"Yes. You've been shot. Just a flesh wound, though. You'll live."

The man laid some gauze against Dan's ribs and pulled some surgical tape out of what looked like a first-aid kit sitting on a night stand.

Dan glanced down at the man caring for his wound.

"Who…? Wait. I know you. You were snooping around my house the other day. How…?"

"You're lucky I was on the cay tonight. That Scott Patterson's a foul man."

"Scott?" Dan fought to make sense of what had happened.

"Don't know what you did that set him off. Lucky I heard you. You'd be dead right now but for me."

Dan dropped his head back and the top of his scalp scraped against metal.

"Watch yourself. Bed's not made up. Already closed up the house. Would of gone back to Marsh Harbour, but for the storm."

"The house?"

"Yeah, Richard's. Heard you scream and went out to investigate. Saw you two there, wrestling. Realized right away it wasn't mutual." He grinned. "Grabbed a shovel and finished him off."

"What?" Dan tensed. "You killed Scott?"

The old man looked offended. "No. I didn't kill him. Who do you think I am? Just hit him over the head. Stunned him. He's fine, mostly. Lying in the mud and the rain, but fine. Probably bleeding too."

Dan glanced around the room.

"Is the power out? Why all the candles?"

"Like I said, already closed up the house. Richard's got two, this one and the one you're staying in. Usually he just boards them up, but he wanted to set you up in the other one after...well, after everything that happened. Told me to keep an eye on you. Make sure you're okay. Turns off the power during the off season, just in case. I was here checking things out when the storm moved in."

The man leaned back. "Done. Now you rest. Morning will be here fast. Here's something to cover yourself, should you want it."

He tossed a blanket onto the foot of the bed.

"Thanks," Dan said and leaned forward. Surprised at how much better he felt already. "But, I really should get back to my house."

"No. No. Gave you something for the pain. Won't feel so good before long. Besides, no sense in you getting *spryed* on. Not crazy out there like it was, but the storm hasn't moved on completely."

"No," Dan insisted. "Thanks. I need to go. I can't...my book...everything is on my computer. Can't risk losing it."

"You should back it up to the cloud."

Dan twisted and stared, surprised at the old man's techno-literacy. He grinned. "Yes. I'll make sure I do that."

"Okay." He crossed and returned with Dan's shirt. "Still wet. But, as you insist on going, at least let me walk you back to your house. Make sure you get there safe. Lock your doors. I doubt Scott will bother you again tonight but you never know with that man. He likes weakness."

Dan pulled his shirt over his head, careful of the bandage and squeezing his eyes closed as he did. The caretaker was right. Lots of blood. A surprising amount of blood. Dan felt weak and teetered on his feet. He felt a hand at his back and he flinched and lurched forward.

"You sure about this?"

"Yes, thanks. I need to go."

They stepped outside. The storm had mostly passed and all that was left behind was a misty wetness in the air. Dan scanned the area, surprised at how little distance he and Scott had actually covered. A gun was an intense strangler of perception.

At Dan's house, the old man instructed Dan to wait outside while he checked things out. He returned a few minutes later.

"Alright, go ahead and go in. Your computer's sitting on your kitchen table, so there's that. Now, make sure you lock your door behind me. Don't want to have to come running to save you another time. May not make it." He motioned toward the French doors. "I'll come replace your glass as soon as I can. Maybe replace all the panes to make sure they match. Maybe just install new doors." He paused.

"Take these." He handed Dan some pills. "Pain killers. They should help. You'll probably ache for a while."

"I will." Dan paused, searching for more to say. "And, thanks, again. Have a good night."

Dan pushed the door closed and leaned against the wall of his entry. The room felt breezy. He crossed to the French doors and studied the blown-out pane and the bloody shard laying at his feet. More pieces of glass lay haphazardly on the deck, somehow having weathered the storm. He knocked the rest of the glass from the window, lifting his foot and wincing at the discomfort in his side. The pain killer was already wearing off. That didn't take long, he thought.

Vodka might help. Besides, he still felt on edge and the ache in his side would probably keep him up anyway. He crossed to the table, grabbed his two drinks from earlier and dumped out the remaining liquid into the sink. He poured himself a fresh glass from the freezer, and stepped out onto the deck. Propping himself against the outer wall of his house, he brushed some of the glass from the shot-out window into the ocean. Then he repositioned the reclining deck chair with his hip and plopped down into the seat to stare up at the clouds hovering overhead.

He'd almost died.

He'd almost died, but strangely the night up until now felt distant and inaccessible and he pictured Wally wondering if the past ever really happened.

"Hmmm."

He took a sip of his vodka, and felt the numbness swirl around his body.

This was better. He fluttered his eyelids. This was better.

He lifted the plastic cup to his lips and poured the rest of the vodka into his mouth, brushing his hand across his chest and down his side as the liquid spilled over his chin and into the cloth of his t-shirt, stinging his side just a bit. He glanced at his fingers. Red.

He drifted.

* * * *

This was the dream that Dan slept in.

He stood anchored, in a field, a green expanse littered with pixels of red and purple and yellow. But his existence was split. Color below. Black above. And across the meadow was Ryan.

The boy turned in Dan's direction, but Dan couldn't see his son's face because Ryan stood too close to the horizon and the exaggerated perspective of this world pressed the boy's head and shoulders into the black. Dan rushed to him, ducking, then crawling as his reality became more limited and, finally, he reached his son and wrapped his arms around his life and squeezed and fought to pull Ryan's eyes down and out of the pixelated empty. He struggled.

But then the world dissolved and slid away and left with everything.

Twenty-One

Dan squinted. The sun. He threw his arm in front of his face and pulses of pain shot through his ribs. He grimaced and glared at his side. Dried blood soaked his shirt. He glanced around him. His empty cup lay tipped against one of the posts of the railing surrounding the patio. He'd fallen asleep on the recliner from the night before. He peeked again at his side. His shirt clung plastered against his ribs and he reached carefully and pried at the fabric, but the skin beneath started to pull and tear and he froze with his hand hovering over the gauze. He closed his eyes and sunk deeper into the chair.

That feeling, that knowing he was about to die flooded over him. That moment when he realized that he'd never feel love again, that he'd seen all the beauty he would ever see, that pleasure was ended for him. That instant when he accepted that that second would be his last. Although, in the midst of it all, the experience hadn't been as inundating as he'd expected it would be. The disappearing. In fact, he'd felt a kind of okayness with impending nothingness. Not so much a resignation to the inevitable as a recognition of what was. At a certain point, he'd not been able to come up with a convincing reason to fight anymore.

The ferry sped by and pulled Dan back to the present. He twisted his head and glanced behind himself. As the boat's wake had splashed into the posts of his house, he'd heard a thud sounding from below the deck. He slid off the deck chair and pressed his ear to the slats of the patio, straining to determine what direction the noise had come from. Definitely some kind of bumping. He lifted his head and glanced toward the wall of his house, to the north end of the deck. Wincing, he pushed himself off the recliner and hobbled to the edge, then leaned over the railing. Everything looked normal. The waves from the boat died down and the frequency of the knocking dissipated until the bumping grew quiet and he heard nothing. Only nature.

He crossed to the other side of the deck. A ladder dropped into the water and he opened the gate and lowered himself onto the steps. Ocean water splashed against his body as he descended and salt seeped into the gauze covering his wound, forcing several gasps out of him, breathless and pizzicato. His left hand flew to his side. He pressed into the ache, gritting his teeth and squeezing his eyes closed until the stinging melted away. He continued. As he dropped below the final rung of the ladder, his legs floated free and he pushed into the weightlessness, allowing his eyes to drift closed. He heard himself moan. A slow, releasing sound. Without pressure, the pain from the gunshot was almost non-existent, even (in a strange way) pleasurable. He hovered, suspended. The sun washed across his face and, after a moment, he let himself dip under the surface of the water before he returned to his search.

Dan scanned underneath the deck. Nothing seemed out of place; although, and he was finding this more and more, he wouldn't know what *in place* looked like. He propelled himself under the surface of the patio, thrusting out a hand against one of the posts to stop himself as he floated out of the sunlight. The harbor was more agitated under the rafters and waves splashed stinging water against the supports and into his eyes. He blinked, wiped at his face, but his hands were wet too and no matter how frantically he swabbed against his eyes, the irritation kept at him.

Something bumped him and he flashed forward, straining to focus. Eyes. A face. Someone knocked against him. He blinked, rapid, desperate as he fought to see. And then his heart seized. Victor Bennet bobbed, staring back at him, spinning, like the lantern in the lighthouse. Dan flailed and kicked and paddled. The water was chaotic and directionless and his scattered movements only pulled Victor closer and at one point the man's fingers butted against Dan's lips and brushed across his face. He shoved Victor's body away from him, spitting in disgust and wiping at his mouth.

He stopped struggling. But, without movement to keep him afloat, he plunged deep into the water, desperate for oxygen after his frenetic panicking. He thrust out a hand blindly to grab at any of the posts and pull himself above the surface and into the air. Instead, though, his fingers wrapped around something too thin, likely Victor's arm or leg and he retched in his mouth and kicked away and swam in the other direction. Finally, he felt something thick and kicked against it to force himself above the surface. He gasped. Then froze. Held still. This time pawing at a post for support. Finally, the frenzy settled, and he swam cautiously toward the ladder and his escape. He glanced back under the deck as he pulled himself up, then scurried up the rungs, ignoring the ache in his ribs. Safe, he crawled across the wood surface until he reached his recliner and he spun and collapsed in front of it. He sucked in fresh air. He shuddered and squeezed his eyes tight. He had no choice. He'd have to call Constable Anderson. He grimaced and the ache in his side pulsed.

"Dan."

He bolted forward and twisted, immediately regretting the movement. Cat had cut her boat's engine and coasted toward him and his house.

"Going for a swim? Why are you wearing a shirt? You're too sexy for that, silly. You know, you really shouldn't swim in the harbor."

Her face turned ashen.

"What happened to you? Is that a bruise on your face?"

He rushed his hand against his cheek. He'd not seen a mirror since he'd come back with...with...he creased his brow. He'd never gotten the name of Richard's caretaker.

"Dan? Can you hear me? What's going on?" She shouted as she tossed a rope up and over the railing and secured her boat, fumbling and unsteady as she did. "You look awful. Are you in pain? What are you doing out here? Why are you all wet?"

She jerked herself up and over the railing and onto the deck, rushing to his side and flinging her arms around him, almost bowling him over with the force of her body.

"Ow!"

"Ooh. Sorry." She pulled back. "What happened?

"Scott Patterson, that's what happened. I think you were right. He—"

"Scott was here? He did this to you?"

"Yes." He paused. "But...Victor...Victor Bennett is dead."

"What?"

Dan nodded. "He's under my deck."

Cat plopped back on her legs. "Are you sure?"

"Yes," Dan snapped. "Of course I'm sure. Why would I say something like that if it weren't true?"

223

"Okay, Grumpy. No need to be rude. Just trying to figure out what's going on."

"Sorry. I just...I hurt..."

"You're bleeding." Cat reached to his side.

"Yes. Scott Patterson. I told you."

Cat lifted his shirt. "We need to get this bandaged up."

"It's already...'" Dan glanced at his side. The dressing was gone. And, apparently, he'd reopened his wound. Blood covered the deck where he'd lain and dripped between the slats. "Oh. Well. There was a bandage. I guess, the water..."

"Do you have any hydrogen peroxide? The harbor's filthy."

"I don't know. Richard has a first-aid kit. There might be something in there."

Dan explained to Cat where the supplies were and she went into the house. After several minutes, Dan yelled, "Cat?"

He was about to get up and go help her when she returned carrying a white box.

"Turn onto your right side" she said.

Dan grimaced as he shifted and pulled up his shirt to expose the wound.

"Hold your breath." She poured the antiseptic, waited while the bubbles died down, then poured some more. She dabbed at the shallow wound, then bandaged his side.

"Here. Put this on." She reached behind her and tossed him a clean shirt. "I'll call Ronnie." She pulled out her cell and held the phone up to her ear. After a few moments, she spoke.

"Ronnie. Yes. It's me. Cat."

"Yes." She glanced at Dan. "Why?"

"Okay. We won't. Yeah, his house."

Dan looked at her.

"He knew I was here with you. He's coming over. I guess Scott Patterson claims you were at his house...threatening him."

"I was threatening Scott?"

"I know." Cat set the nursing equipment to the side and stood. She grabbed Dan by the shoulders, but he knocked her hands away and stood on his own.

"I can do it.

"He's just trying to get in the self-defense argument first," Dan continued.

Cat shrugged. She sat at his side and pointed to the French doors. "What happened there?"

"Scott. Again. You know, you really need to start paying attention."

She glared at him.

"I think Scott's bullet must have shattered the glass," he continued.

"Mmmm," Cat said and turned toward the harbor.

Neither said anything for a few minutes. They both stared blankly at the water.

Finally he said, "So, I did some digging last night before Scott showed up."

"Digging?" Cat turned her head to face him.

"Yes. Virtual. On the Internet. I checked out Facebook and then Google and it turns out that Ed..."

"Facebook?"

"Yeah. Facebook." He grinned. "Anyway. So, I found him. And get this. His mom killed his dad."

"Why?"

"Why?"

"Yeah. Why'd she kill him?"

Dan chuckled out, "I don't know."

225

"Well, I'm sure she had her reasons."

He squinted and smirked at her. "Okay. So, like I—"

A knock sounded from inside the house. Cat stood. "Oh, that's probably Ronnie. I'll get it."

He watched her walk away. After a moment, he heard mumbling and she returned to the deck. Constable Anderson, Inspector Johnson and Scott Patterson followed. Scott had a black eye in addition to the remnants of Cat's scratches from before. Dan burst out laughing.

"Something funny, Mr. Harris?" Constable Anderson said.

"No, I just…" He motioned to Scott. "He looks so…"

The policemen and Cat glanced at Scott.

"What?" Scott said.

"Yes…well…" Anderson brushed his hand over his hair and stepped toward Dan. "We've had a complaint about you."

Dan stood, suppressing a grin. "Let me guess, I punched Scott in the face."

"You threw a rock through my window." Scott yelled.

Dan sniggered. "Oh, it was a rock."

"Scott, quiet. I'll handle this," Anderson said over his shoulder.

The constable continued, "You threw a rock through his window."

"You've got to be kidding me."

Anderson stared at him, emotionless.

Dan went on, "You believe him? So, let me get this clear. I snuck over to his house, in the middle of a storm, and threw a rock threw his window. Are we twelve?"

Constable Anderson stomped into Dan's face. "This is no joke, Harris."

"And I hit him in the eye? Come on."

"No, you hit me in the back of the head." Scott spun and pointed to a large gash in his head.

"I fell into the coffee table and hit my eye," he went on.

"That's from—"

"Harris. Quiet. Just let Scott finish."

"But this is ridiculous."

"Listen, Harris. We know Scott. We don't know you. And we already know you lie. So, just shut your mouth and listen."

Scott stepped to Constable Anderson's side and whispered in his ear. Anderson faced Dan and said, "Okay, Scott...I think we've heard enough. Dan, what do you have to say for yourself? Where were you last night?"

"So you'll listen to me?"

Constable Anderson said nothing.

"I was here," Dan continued. "At least until Scott shot me and forced me away at gun point."

"So, you claim that Scott attacked you? Was this before or after you attacked Scott?"

"I never attacked Scott! Seriously, what's wrong with you people? Look." He lifted his shirt. "I have a gunshot wound."

He pointed at his door. "That window is blown out. Doesn't what I just said make a lot more sense than his ridiculous story about a rock?"

"Were ye alone?" Inspector Johnson asked.

"Well, obviously Scott would have been here."

"Scott doesn't count." Anderson pulled at his pants and motioned to Dan's cup from before, still leaning against the railing. "You been drinking?"

Scott snickered.

Dan directed himself to Inspector Johnson. "What do you think, Inspector? You must see that this is crazy."

227

Johnson hesitated. He glanced at Constable Anderson. "What I think doesn't matter. I'm only here for the murder. But, I do have a question for ye, if Constable Anderson doesn't mind."

Anderson shrugged and indicated no, barely. Or, more accurately, he shook his head and rolled his eyes.

"If ye were shot last night, why ye walking around?"

"Well, it turns out it was just a flesh wound. But, look at the rug inside. There's blood all over it. Ask Cat, she saw the wound. She just fixed my bandage."

Constable Anderson pivoted to Cat. "That true?"

Cat glanced at Dan. "Maybe."

"Maybe?" Dan spun to her.

She turned to face Ronnie, paused, whined, "I don't know. I couldn't really tell. Dan had just been swimming and it was all wet and I helped him disinfect the wound and then bandaged it up. There was definitely a wound. But..."

Anderson turned to Scott. "Did you shoot him?"

"Ronnie, I don't even own a gun, you know that. How would I shoot him?"

"It was a revolver. I think a Smith and Wesson," Dan said.

The group twisted to face him.

"Now how could you know that?" Constable Anderson smirked. "Kind of makes you seem guilty now, doesn't it?"

"Guilty of what?"

"Well, how would you know something like that?"

"I wrote a mystery once. I did some research."

"Show us."

Dan chuckled. "You want to read my story?"

Anderson stepped toward Dan. "I want to make sure you're telling the truth."

"About doing research? What exactly have I done wrong? This is—"

"I was at home with Sarah," Scott cut in. "All night. She'll confirm that. I've got nothing to hide, Ronnie."

"Alright," Constable Anderson said, massaging his scalp. "I've heard enough. Scott, do you want to press charges?"

"That's it? You've heard enough? You call this investigating?" Dan dropped into the recliner and rubbed his face with his hands.

"You criticizing…?"

Cat had moved to Constable Anderson's side and tapped him on the shoulder. He leaned to her and she whispered in his ear.

He twisted to Dan and shouted, "You killed Victor Bennett?"

Twenty-Two

"You killed Victor Bennet?"

Constable Anderson spoke, but everyone, including Cat, stared at Dan.

"No! I—"

"No..." Cat shook her head. "I just said he's dead. I don't know if Dan killed him."

Dan flashed to her.

She began, "I mean, Dan just found—"

"Why are you just telling us now?"

"You kept talking about Scott. But that's what I called you for. Victor's dead. His body is under the deck."

Scott smirked. "I bet Dan did kill him. That's probably what happened to the window. It'd explain the blood."

Constable Anderson turned to Scott. "Scott, we're going to have to figure this out later. Dan will pay for your window. You want to press charges?"

"No. Just have him fix my window. I trust the Lord will even out the rest."

Dan rolled his eyes. "Oh my... I'm not—"

"That's awfully kind of you, Scott. I doubt you'd get the same kindness in return." Constable Anderson glared at Dan, then nodded to Inspector Johnson. The inspector led Scott off the deck.

"Bye, Scott." Dan waved at him.

Constable Anderson crossed to the edge of the deck. He pulled out his cellphone and dialed.

"Yeah, Vern. It seems that American found another body. Yeah…" Constable Anderson eyed Dan and brushed a hand through his stringy and, Dan thought, particularly greasy-looking hair. "Yeah. I know. Something up with this guy. Anyway, I need you to bring the boat over here to his place.

"That's the one. Thanks."

The constable clicked his phone closed. Inspector Johnson stepped back onto the porch.

"So, Mr. Harris, ye find another body?"

Constable Anderson answered first, "Yes. And this time he's a local. Victor Bennett. Didn't deserve this."

"Bennett?" Johnson pivoted to Dan. "This the same guy ye were trying to blame for the other murder?"

Dan glanced at Cat, hoping to get some help. He pressed against his rib, just below the bandaging.

"Yes, it's him. But I wasn't trying to blame him for Ed's murder. Ju—"

"How'd you know the dead man's name?" Anderson smirked at Dan and then glanced and nodded at Cat.

"Because you told me."

"I did?" He squinted. The group stared at him.

Anderson looked thoughtful for a moment, then continued. "That's not important. So, you blame Victor. And what do you know? He turns up murdered."

Dan sighed. "I didn't blame him. And how do you know if Victor was murdered? Maybe he just drowned."

"Did he?" Johnson spoke up.

"How would I know? But I wouldn't kill him and then tell Cat."

"He has a point, Ronnie," Cat said. Dan looked at her, relieved she'd decided to start participating again.

"Maybe you caught him by surprise. Killed him in a drunken rage and weren't expecting anyone so soon."

"I don't know, Dan. He has a point." Cat said.

"That's not a...Besides, I already told you. Scott shot me. If it wasn't for...for Richard's caretaker...he'll back me up. He was with me until this morning."

"Who's this?" Inspector Johnson asked.

"Richard's caretaker."

"Who's Richard?"

"This is his house," Dan said. "He has a—"

"Ye know this Richard?" Inspector Johnson asked Constable Anderson.

"Yeah, but I don't know of any caretaker. What's his name?"

Dan hesitated. "Well, that's the...I'm not really sure."

Inspector Johnson stepped forward. "So, this man is your alibi, bu—"

"Wait. Why do I need an alibi? We don't even know if this death is a murder."

Dan tried to catch Cat's attention with his eyes, willing her to come to his defense. But she merely studied the water over the railing. Finally, he said, "Okay, listen. Forget everything that came before. I fell asleep on my deck. And, yes, I'd been drinking. But, I'd just been shot and—"

"We're forgetting what came before. Remember, Harris?" Ronnie said, leering at Cat and chuckling.

"Fine. I woke up on the deck and heard a noise and went to investigate. So, I climb into the water and look under the deck. That's when Cat saw me."

"No," Cat spoke up. "That's not true. You'd already gotten out of the water."

Dan spun his head toward Cat, wondering why she was suddenly so committed to accuracy. "Yes. That's right, I—"

"Yeah," Cat said. "You were laying on the deck, all wet and bleeding."

"That your blood?" Constable Anderson indicated with his lips to a puddle staining the wood of the deck. "Why were you bleeding?"

"I already told you. Scott shot me. He grazed my side, so...you know, blood."

"Cat, that a gunshot wound?" Constable Anderson asked.

She glanced back at Dan, looking distressed. "I don't know. I don't know what a bullet wound looks like."

"No need to worry. Ye see any burned flesh?" Inspector Johnson stepped toward Cat and spoke slowly.

Cat spun from Dan to Inspector Johnson. "No. I don't think so...a gash...a..."

Dan stepped forward. "There wouldn't be. Not anymore. Richard's caretaker cleaned the wound. He must have gotten it."

"That's convenient." Constable Anderson smirked. "He this caretaker you're claiming you were with?"

Inspector Johnson turned toward the broken pane in the door leading to Dan's house. "So, yer saying instead of ye going to Scott's, Scott came here. Attacked *ye*. Why?"

"We were..." Dan glanced at Cat. She vigorously indicated no.

"Cat, you all right?" Constable Anderson looked concerned.

"Yes, just a gnat or something. Really, can't we stop this. Victor's dead. I'm ups..." She started sniffing. "It's just so hard to believe."

233

Vern floated up to the house in what looked like the same boat they'd used to remove Ed from the beach at the lighthouse. Constable Anderson crossed to the edge of the deck and spoke to him.

"Can you see under the deck? There a body there?"

Vern ducked low in the boat. "Yeah, I see him."

"Then get him outta there."

"How'm I supposed to do that?"

"Just swim under and pull him out."

Vern's face twisted. "I'm not swimming under there. That's disgusting"

Constable Anderson crossed to the edge of the deck and leaned to Vern. He spoke under his breath, but loudly, sharply. "Just get him in the damn boat and stop complaining before I call your mother and tell her to have a talk with you."

Vern glared at Constable Anderson. The young man unbuttoned his shirt and started to strip off his clothes. Dan shook his head and turned back to the group, relieved Constable Anderson wasn't the one removing anything. He heard a splash and the constable rejoined the group.

"You touch this body? Make sure there's some reason your DNA's all over the man like before?"

Dan didn't answer. He glanced across the harbor.

"So," Constable Anderson continued. "Here's what I think. You yourself got drunk. You went over to Scott Patterson's house and caused a ruckus, threw a rock through his window, hit him in the back of the head. You yourself came back here, to your house, just as the storm was brewin' up and Victor was here, waiting for you. He heard about how you threw his name out there and tried to blame him for Ed's death. You invite him into your house...you know how he is...nothing to worry about, you

234

think—just told him you wanted to talk and sort things out...or maybe, maybe you're sick like he is and you were having a thing with him."

"You were sleeping with Victor?" Cat turned to him shocked.

He glanced at her. "What? No! This is—"

"You two argue. Victor puts up more of a fight than you're expecting. Maybe he has a knife and gets a slice in—that's where your injury comes from—and you two break the window in your door and you yourself knock him out, throw him over the edge."

"Wouldn't it make more sense if I strangled him? Or even better, maybe I got the knife away from him and stabbed him?" Dan said.

"Dan!" Cat shouted. "Take this serious. A man's dead." She burst into tears and Constable Anderson rushed to her side to comfort her.

Inspector Johnson spoke up. "Okay. All of ye calm down."

"Mr. Harris. Maybe that's what happened. Don't know. But..." He turned to include Cat and Constable Anderson in his pronouncement. "We got to slow this down a bit and look over the body first."

Vern suddenly yelled, "Ahhh!" and the group spun.

The boy swam out from under the deck, pulling one of Victor's fingers as he dragged the man's body closer to the boat. "This is so...so...so...disgusting. Now what?"

Constable Anderson turned to Inspector Johnson. "Inspector, why don't you drive the boat over to the post office dock. It's not far. Vern can hold on to the side and pull the body along. That work, Vern?"

Vern steamed. Finally he mumbled, "Yeah, guess so. Just go slow, though. This guy's all slimy. And I don't want none of this water splashing in my mouth."

Constable Anderson turned back to Inspector Johnson. "I can have my other boy meet you both there and him and Vern can get the body into the boat to take it to Marsh Harbour."

Inspector Johnson nodded.

Vern kicked the boat over to the deck gate, and Constable Anderson helped Inspector Johnson as he climbed down the ladder and into the driver's seat. Vern pulled himself, with Victor in tow, as far forward along the side of the boat as he could get, then nodded to Inspector Johnson. "Okay, go ahead. But, s...l...ow."

Cat and Dan stood and watched the activity. Dan tried multiple times to catch Cat's attention, but she remained intently focused and avoided his gaze. As the death ferry inched away, Anderson lumbered over to where Cat stood and spoke to Dan.

"We'll see what we find, but don't think you got away with this. We just got to look things over. Cat, you coming with me?"

Cat didn't say anything at first and then motioned to the water. "My boat. I came in my boat."

"Well, we can take it. I can accompany you back to your house."

She glanced at Dan. "Okay."

"Cat," Dan stepped toward her, but Constable Anderson jumped between them.

"She said, okay. She's going with me."

"Cat," he said again. "What...? Please don't go."

"I need to." She pivoted and headed toward her boat's line.

"Can we at least talk before you go."

Cat handed the rope to Constable Anderson. She nodded. Dan walked to the far side of the deck and signaled for Cat to follow.

She crossed to him. "What?"

"What? Are you...? You don't think I killed Victor, do you?"

Cat didn't answer. She peeked behind herself toward Ronnie and the boat.

Dan grabbed her arm but she immediately pulled away from him.

"Everything okay over there?" Anderson called out.

"Yes, it's fine," Dan snapped.

"Cat?" Anderson moved forward.

"I'm fine," she called out over her shoulder.

"Cat, what's going on? I don't know who you are right now."

"Well, that's just it, Dan. Isn't it? We hardly know each other."

She went on, "Anyways, what do you expect me to say? You told me before how much you hated Victor. Maybe..." Cat stopped.

"Maybe what? You can't think I actually killed him."

"I said I don't know. But, here's what I do know." She shoved her finger in his face. "I just met you. I just met you and right away we," she gestured air quotes, "*find* a body and then lo and behold another person turns up dead. Someone you said you hated. Someone you tried to blame for the first murder."

"I didn't try to blame him. And that's just it. Why would I kill someone I was telling the police to consider? I need him alive. This is no good for me. Why would I do this?"

237

Cat stayed quiet. Ronnie called out, "Cat, you ready?"

"Just a second, Ronnie. I'm coming." She took a breath and glared into Dan's eyes.

"I don't know why. But, I know someone's dead…my friend…and I can't be here. I don't feel safe. I have to go."

"Your friend? You never…"

Dan watched her walk away.

"You don't feel safe?"

She rushed the last few steps to Constable Anderson, who waited with his arms open. He leered in Dan's direction as he hugged her, obviously enjoying the scene as he hitched up his ever-unmoving pants before he rotated and lowered himself into the boat. He winked at Dan and he and Cat drove away into the harbor.

Twenty-Three

Dan remained on the deck, feeling disconnected and discombobulated. He watched Cat drift away, and with Constable Anderson no less. Then he stepped inside and plopped down on the sofa, ostensibly for nothing more than to relax and catch his breath. But suddenly he was gasping awake, having no idea how long he'd been asleep. Or even if he had been. He cast his eyes out over the harbor and leaned farther into the cushions. The sun sat lower in the sky, telling him that at least several hours had passed and it was currently late afternoon. He scanned around his home, pausing at the recently bloodstained rug. He had to get out, away from all this. He jumped and rushed into the bedroom, grabbing a book off the dresser, then marched out the front door to the coffee house. As he entered, he called out, "Hi, Jamie."

Jamie spun, then laughed.

"Oh! You scared me. I didn't hear you come in. I was just…" He stepped closer to Dan. "…what happened to you?"

"I'll tell you in a minute. But first. Do you know Richard, the man who owns the house I'm staying in?"

"Kind of. Not too good. You know, small town and all that. Why?"

"Do you know if he has someone who takes care of his houses?"

Jamie shrugged. "Houses? He has more than one?"

"Yes. I guess a couple."

"No. Sorry. I don't. Wish I did."

"That's okay. Just thought I'd ask."

An electric kettle sat on the counter and Jamie picked up the receptacle and filled the container with water. He pulled a French press from a shelf over his head.

"If that's for me. Thanks, but no. It's too late."

"You sure?"

"Yeah, thanks. I just wanted to bring you this."

Dan pushed a book across the counter toward Jamie.

"What's this?" He grinned as he picked up the hard back.

"That's my first book. You said you like to read."

"What?" he exclaimed and flipped open the pages until he reached the end and the author bio and photo. He held the image up next to Dan. "Yep. That's you."

"Wow," he went on. "Thanks. I can't wait to read it."

He set the book on the counter. "You know, we'll be closing soon for the off-season."

"Oh yeah?"

"Yeah, but if you want, I can come to your house and make you your French press there."

Dan smiled, bemused. Maybe Susan and Cat were right. Jamie may have misread his friendly gesture.

"No. Thanks." Dan smirked and chuckled and Jamie's entire persona shrunk. "I think I can manage a cup of coffee."

"Oh. Yeah. Of course, you can. I was just..."

Dan watched red flush over the boy's face. He added, "But, maybe on the weekends or a few days a week. That'd be nice. I'd miss our talks."

Jamie grinned and turned an even darker shade of red. "Yeah. That'd be great."

"Do you mind if I sit?" Dan moved toward the table he usually sat at. "I need to rest."

"Yes." The young man tittered. "I mean no. I don't mind. Yes you c…Let me get you some water. You don't look so good."

Dan watched as Jamie pulled down a glass and filled it with Perrier from the fridge. He stepped around the counter and set the cup in front of Dan.

"Only the best for you, Sir." He smiled, then sat opposite Dan, fanning the pages of the novel Dan had just given him. "You know I keep that in the refrigerator just for you. Most people just drink it room temperature."

"So," Dan began. "It's been quite a day."

He studied Jamie, debating how much to share with the boy. With Cat apparently rethinking her position as related to her views on his innocence, the barista may be the only friend he had left.

"So, do you know Scott Patterson?"

"Yes," the boy said. "Not the nicest guy. I think he beats his wife."

Apparently, Jamie was not immune from the lure of the town's sip sip.

Dan smiled. "Maybe. So, why do they call him the gentle giant?"

Jamie shrugged. "Irony?"

Dan smiled at the young man's astute observation. He doubted, though, that the town was so nuanced.

"Anyway, he attacked me last night."

"What?" Jamie dropped Dan's book and reached forward. "That's what all that is?"

Dan nodded. "Yeah, but he's trying to pin everything on me. Trying to say I attacked him instead of the other way around."

"But, that's crazy. Just look at him. Why would you attack him?"

Dan opened his mouth but stopped. Cat seemed to see Victor's death as casting doubt on Dan's innocence. What if Jamie reacted the same way?

Finally, he said, "And the weirdest part of it all is that Victor Bennett...you know Victor Bennett?"

Jamie nodded. Slow. His eyebrows twitched.

"Well, the weirdest part of everything is that Victor Bennett's body was floating under my house."

Jamie's gasped. "Victor's dead?"

Dan nodded and glanced down at his glass of water. "Yes. And his body..."

"Victor's dead?" Jamie whispered.

"...was under my house. How strange is that? Scott shows up and attacks me and suddenly a dead author is bumping against the rafters under my deck."

A couple strolled into the shop and called out from the counter, just as a group of teenagers pushed through the entrance and walked in. "Hey there, Jamie."

"I can't believe Victor's dead."

"Hey there, Jamie," the man repeated.

"Victor's..." Jamie seemed stuck in some kind of loop he couldn't escape.

"Jamie, can we get some help? We've got a bunch of hungry and thirsty kids with us."

The group erupted into rowdiness, and the woman spun to face the kids.

"Quiet, people. Jamie, sorry to interrupt, but they're not going to wait." She chuckled, but her face showed strain.

Dan nudged the boy, and Jamie snapped to attention. "It wasn't Scott that killed him. I think I know who did it."

"Jamie," the woman said, smiling, but her patience was clearly evaporating.

"Let me take care of these customers." He stood and started toward the counter. He returned to the table for his new book. "Thanks, so much. Can you wait? I think I can help."

Dan nodded. "Yes. Of course. Go attend to your customers."

Jamie tossed Dan's novel back on the table and stepped behind the counter. Dan could hear him say, "Sorry, Rick, Liz. Church group?"

"Yes."

After 30 minutes and several apologetic looks from Jamie, Dan stood and picked up the book. He crossed to the counter and pushed the novel to the opposite edge. "Jamie, I'm going to take off. But, you'll be here tomorrow, right? We can talk then?"

A harried Jamie glanced over at Dan, "Sorry. I really shouldn't be much longer," he said as the door opened and two more couples stepped in.

Dan smirked as he glanced at the entrance. "Really, it's okay. We'll talk more tomorrow."

Jamie nodded and turned back to setting plates, pausing to count the number he'd already set out.

Twenty-Four

Victor died not seeing.

Twenty-Five

Dan tossed his shirt across the living room and walked into the bedroom. He grabbed a new one and pulled it over his head.

Jamie had been characteristically vague so, of course, Dan had no idea what he meant when he said he knew who killed Victor. How could he possibly know something like that? He crossed to the kitchen and poured himself some cabernet, then poured the wine back into the bottle, got a new goblet and instead filled the glass with pinot grigio. He was in the mood for something a little lighter. He sat at the kitchen table and opened his laptop. The tabs with the results from the searches he'd done the night before were still open. He reviewed the links.

Before long, Dan realized he was reading the words on the screen while not comprehending any of what they said, so he stood and crossed to the French doors to survey the damage from the night before. He knocked a few of the hanger-on shards with the knuckles of his right hand, then pressed the ridges of his left against his chest, massaging his hand and surveying the damage. Should he cover the opening? He'd have to hire someone to come replace the glass at some point. Why not sooner rather than later? Or, he could just count on the no-name caretaker to fix it. Although—and this was another case where his lack of etiquette was proving rather problematic—having no name or number made that simple task difficult.

He picked up his cell phone and dialed Cat, listening to the phone ring...and ring...and ring. Finally, the line picked up and Dan heard, "Hello...I can't get to the phone right now. I'd like to say I'm sorry I missed your call but at this point I don't even know you've called so I can't really be sorry about it, now can I, silly? Just leave me whatever information you feel obliged to leave and if there's a number in there, or if you're Dan..."

Dan pulled the cell away from his head and looked at the receiver, then smashed the phone back against his ear. Silence. She'd finished her recording and it was his turn to leave *whatever information* he felt *obliged* to leave. He opened his mouth to speak, but hung the phone up quickly and glanced at his computer.

He picked up the phone again and dialed her number once more. Same thing. Ring...ring...ring, then "Hello...I" Dan flipped his right arm back, about to hurl the phone, but instead he dropped his hand to his side and stared at the ground. The same impetuous anger had gotten him nowhere last time. Why wouldn't she answer? He slammed his laptop shut, then panicked and lifted the cover to make sure computer was still working. The screen lit up immediately.

He inhaled deeply through his nose, drank the rest of the wine in his glass, refilled the goblet and sat down again in front of his computer. The phone rang. At first, he just stared at the device and at Cat's phone number splashed across the screen, suddenly feeling apprehensive and unsure. He considered not answering, ignoring her like she'd been ignoring him, as if they were two teenagers desperate for affection. But after two rings, he grabbed at the cell and answered.

"Hello, Cat?"

The line was silent. He peeked at the display to see if the call was actually connected. "Hello?"

Silence still. "Cat, can you hear me? I think..."

"Yes, I hear you. What do you want?"

She sounded annoyed. "I don't know. You called me," Dan said, chuckling half-heartedly,

"Fine," she said and hung up.

Dan stared at his phone, shocked, and tapped her number in the recent calls. She picked up immediately this time.

"How could you?"

"How could...?"

"You call me...TWICE...hang up without leaving a message and then act all like nothing happened when I *generously* call you back. When do you think about me and how I feel in all this?"

"I..." Dan stuttered.

"Did you kill him?"

"What? No, I told you. I just heard knocking under my deck and there he was."

"No, not him, stupid," she said. "Ed. Did you kill Ed?"

"No." He stopped. He couldn't believe she was asking him this. She'd been the one. She'd been the only one to stick by him no matter what. And suddenly...

"Of course I didn't," he continued. "You were there. You were there when we found him."

"Constable Anderson says they're close to arresting you."

"What?" Dan felt his entire body tense and a wave of dizziness washed over him.

"Yeah. He says this new murder pushes everything into a new light. Makes it all the more urgent. Can't have you running free and wreaking havoc around our cay. You're a menace."

"You think that?"

"I do." She sighed. "I don't…I don't know. Not really. Maybe. What *should* I think?" She rambled softly, more like she was trying to convince herself than opening up to Dan.

"I didn't kill anyone, Cat. I couldn't."

But Cat didn't say anything in response and the two listened to silence, unconnected. Dan glanced longingly at the lighthouse and the setting sun that didn't silhouette the structure, but instead cast the building in a sort of bas relief. He rocked his head and stared straight ahead of him at *Preacher's Wife Kills Husband* on the screen. What would his headlines be?

"Maybe," finally Cat spoke up. "But, I can't be with you until I figure this out. I don't really know you. I can't feel safe."

Dan waited. After several seconds he realized Cat was gone.

Twenty-Six

"What does she mean, she doesn't feel safe with me?" Dan stomped through the broken French doors to the deck and hurled his wine and goblet out over the water. The glass skidded across the surface before disappearing. "That's ridiculous."

He inhaled, almost gasping, and pressed four fingers against his ribs, gently massaging the area. His wound had been feeling better, but was pulsing now, so he spun and padded to the kitchen, pulling a bottle out of the fridge and pouring himself some water. He tossed one of the old man's pain pills into his mouth and drank. He poured the remaining liquid into the palm of his hand and brushed his fingers across his face. Then, he turned and leaned against the counter. He pushed himself forward.

Susan would be expecting a call. And, especially after everything new that had happened today, he really owed her some kind of an update. He pulled out his cell, but shoved the phone back in his pocket and crossed back to the refrigerator.

"A little vodka won't hurt," he said and pulled a clean glass out of the cupboard, opened the freezer, and poured himself a drink before he crossed back to the sofa and plopped into the cushions. He took a sip and paused, then pulled out his phone again and stroked his fingers across the device's surface before he pressed the *Home* button and dialed Susan. She answered in the middle of the first ring.

"Dan! I was just thinking about you."

"You were?" Dan sat forward, instantly feeling better. She sounded happy. He gazed through the broken pane at the lighthouse. "Me too."

"You were thinking about yourself?" she said. Dan heard his wife giggle.

"No, I mean..."

"I know what you mean. I'm just teasing you, silly."

"Don't call me that."

"What?"

"Silly. Don't call me that. You've never called me that before."

"I'm sure I have, Mr. Sensitive."

"No, it's not that. It's just...Cat always calls me that."

"Oh," she said, terse. "Then I won't. Definitely. How about Scatterbrain? Mmmm. Doesn't really work the same."

"No, I gue—"

"How about Love? Or Sweetheart? She better not be calling you those."

"No." He smiled. "That's perfect. And I'll call you *Tesoro*."

He set his vodka to the side, onto the end table Susan had set her wine on (the same wine she'd subsequently spilled). For the first time in too long, he felt as if he were talking to his wife again. This was Susan. Their conversation wasn't a loaded gun waiting to be cocked as it had been. He beamed.

Neither said a word. Finally, Dan said, "Susan?"

"I'm here. Oh, Dan. I should have stayed." She paused. "I really wish I'd stayed. I should be with you. With everything going on, I should be with you. I could have had my assistant shift some things around. That's what

250

assistants are for. I should…seeing you again just made me realize how much I miss you."

Dan didn't answer. He splayed his fingers in front of himself and studied the bruises on his hand. He missed hearing his wife sound so affectionate, so normal. He'd not heard her talk like this since Ryan...

"Dan, are you there?"

"Yes, sorry. Now it's my turn, I guess. I'm here. I can't tell you how good that makes me feel. Watching you go yesterday was like watching a part of me drift away." He dropped his head. "And, I feel like too much of me has left already."

Dan glanced at his cup, even reached for a sip, but then shook his head and returned to the conversation.

"I know." Susan's voice broke.

"But we have to stop feeling sorry for ourselves," she added.

"I..." Dan said. In a flash, he pictured Scott. "I…"

"Dan? What's wrong?"

"I just…this is going to sound strange now. But, maybe it's better that you're not here right now."

"What? Why?"

"Just trust me."

"But..."

This was where love got tricky. There were only two options. Protect her. Keep her safe. She'd feel confused and rejected, but she'd be safe. Or, let the danger in. Know that he'd allowed the menace close because he didn't stop the threat. Because he'd wanted to spare her feelings. Either way she'd suffer. And either way, he'd be the one to blame.

"Listen, it's not that I don't want you here. I do. So much. It's just...it's better that you aren't here right now."

251

"What does that mean? Dan? What's going on?" Susan's voice was getting louder and lower pitched. Many people grew more shrill when perturbed. Not Susan. She became a baritone. "Dan? Talk to me."

"I just..." He glanced at his hand again. "So...they might arrest me."

"What?"

Dan heard a muffled *phhht* that sounded as if she'd dropped her cell and the phone had landed on a soft surface. She must be sitting in the living room, he thought. On her favorite reading chair. He pictured her there and his stomach sank.

He heard more muffling and she said, "...rry. I'm here. So...what? They might arrest you? When I was there you talked like there was no case against you. What changed?"

"They found another body. Well, I found it." Dan reached for his drink and took a sip.

"Hey, did you know Richard had a caretaker?"

"Dan, don't change the subject. You what?"

"I'm not changing the subject. Just trust...Does he? Do you remember?"

"Yes. You know, you never pay attention to anything."

Dan moved forward to the French doors and leaned his forehead against them, gazing through the broken glass at the lighthouse. The sun was lowering in the horizon and dark clouds rushed across the sky. He could feel air blow through the broken pane.

"I know, I know, I never pay attention to anything. So, he did. I knew it. Nobody here seems to know who he is."

"Well, that kind of makes sense. He isn't from Hope Town. Not even Elbow Cay. He lives in Marsh Harbour. His name's John. John Simons."

Dan crossed back to the couch, a smile rolling across his entire body. He sat down. Leave it to Susan to remember details. "That's right. John Simons. Okay. That's good."

"Now, will you please tell me what's going on? Why do you want to know about John? And another body?"

"Yes, well. John helped me with something. That's all. I just never got his name. I want to thank him."

"Okay, so…the body? And no protecting me. I'm a big girl. Tell me everything."

"Do you know who Victor Bennet is?"

"The writer?"

"Yes. Well, he lives here. Lived…here. He's dead. I found his body under Richard's house."

"You found his body?"

"Yes…"

"Okay." She sounded completely non-emotional, as if she were merely processing the information. "Was he murdered?"

"I don't know. But, I think so."

"Do they think you killed him?"

Dan bobbed his head. "Yes. I think so. But it doesn't make any sense. All they're going on is my finding the body. There's nothing else. I think it's mostly coming from Constable Anderson. He's got it out for me. He has a crush on Cat and I think he's jealous. He's convinced himself something is going on between us."

"Well, is there? She sure seems to come up a lot."

"No, of course not." Dan downed his vodka and set the glass on the floor next to the couch. He coughed. "We already talked about this. It's all coming from her. But this guy's sure I'm having an affair with her."

"Well, are you?" He heard her take another deep breath. "Are you sleeping with that woman?"

Dan sighed. Loudly. "No. Susan, I just told you no. I..." He started feeling light-headed.

"Okay. I just..."

"Listen, Cat. I'm inn—"

"Susan."

"What?"

"My name is Susan," she said. "You just called me Cat."

"Oh, I did? Sorry." He paused. "Anyway, it's all coming from her. She won't take a hint. I keep telling her we're only friends, but—"

"You keep telling her? How much time do you spend with this woman?"

"I don't know." Dan shrugged. "I see her most days."

Susan didn't respond and Dan opened his mouth to continue. But she spoke up.

"So, do you love her?"

"Really, Susan? How do you make that leap?"

"Just answer the question."

"No, of course not! What kind of question is that?"

"Well, you just seem to spend a lot of time with that woman."

"Cat, I love—"

"Again, Dan? You just called me Cat again?"

"No." Dan panicked, instantly realizing what he'd just said. He pushed to his feet. "I said, Susan, I love—"

"No, you didn't. You called me Cat. Again. And you were talking about love."

"Sorry. But, we're getting way off subject. The body. Victor Bennet's body. I'm just...it's been a stressful day and I just got off the phone with Cat and…John gave me these pills."

"You're using drugs now?"

"What? No. Pain—"

"Dan," she breathed. "How could you?"

He could see her pacing, jumping up from her reading chair and zig-zagging caged-lioness-like around the living room of their house, fighting off tears that had already defeated her.

"You're sleeping with her. Oh…my…"

"No, Susan, I'm not. I promise."

"Spoken like a true philanderer."

"Well, what am I supposed to say?" He was yelling into the phone now, pacing between the sofa and the French doors. "I'm not sleeping with her. That's the truth. She wants to sleep with me, but I keep saying no."

"What? It's to the point where you have to say no? What are you saying? It's her fault? Don't be such a man. It's never the man's fault. Always the woman's."

"Susan..."

"I can't believe I'm going to say this."

Silence.

"I want a divorce."

Dan froze. "What?"

His legs gave out and he dropped to the floor, feeling a slight ache in his side, but not sensing anything at the same time. Too much, all at once. So much… "Susan, no. Please. You can't do this."

He added forcefully, "I won't let you."

"Oh, you won't let me? Then, never mind." She harrumphed. "Well, it's not up to you, is it, Dan? You gave up any rights you may have had when you cheated on me. By the time, I'm done with you..."

Dan's eyes felt moist, synchronized with a sudden downpour on his roof and across his deck. He crawled to his feet, to the sofa and lowered himself into the cushions. To his left was the rug and his blood mixed with the spilled wine stain from Susan's visit splashed into the white. He pushed out, "Susan, please. Let's talk about this."

"No. It's for the best. You clearly don't love me anymore and you and that tramp can finally..." She gasped. "Finally have a good life."

And that was it. Once again Dan listened to silence. He hit redial, but the phone simply rang and rang until her voicemail picked up and he hung up and hit redial again, repeating the process several times and begging into the nothing. But Susan never answered.

He pulled his arm back, about to revert to his recently acquired go-to coping mechanism, but instead he merely dropped the phone at his feet and fell back into the couch. He stared at the phone. He picked up the glass he'd set down earlier and threw the container vigorously, breaking another window in the same French door, but this time two panes up as if he were playing the world's most destructive game of tic-tac-toe. He dropped his head into his hands and started sobbing, emotion on emotion on emotion. Ryan. Dan stopped. He stomped to the kitchen and ripped out another cup, this time a plastic tumbler, dumping himself more vodka from the freezer and spilling on the floor as he did. He guzzled some of the liquid, then refilled his drink and poured some more. He stumbled back to the couch and picked up his phone and dialed Cat. No answer.

"I'll show her," he said, ripping his front door open. He stormed through the opening and into rushing rain and wind and headed south toward the town center.

Twenty-Seven

Dan leaned into the wind as he stumbled forward, spilling his vodka and slurring out the occasional "Susan," with nothing following her name, only disdain and repudiation.

At the post office dock, after a stroll that should have taken no more than five minutes, but which he managed to convert into a brisk walk of twenty, he veered to the right, toward the harbor and sat in the same pergola he'd spied on Susan from as she left him. Rain pelted him through the slats. Taking care not to spill, which he did anyway, he placed his half-empty vodka cup to the right at his feet and bent forward, forcing his head into his hands. He wailed— a drunken cry that was more exaggerated self pity than true sorrow, there at some level, but deep and unattainable at the moment. Brief periods of nothing, marked by wonderings of what had moved him to such overwhelming sadness in the first place, punctuated his cries. He even jerked awake a number of times, having no idea he'd drifted off in the first place.

He stumbled to his feet, and continued, past the barriers just north of the town center. He glanced to the right. The Hope Town Methodist church glowed in the night and he realized with a flourish and a spin that he was moving in the wrong direction. He giggled and moved on. When he finally reached his goal, Cat's house was smothered in darkness.

"Ohhhh," he whined in a sing-song, child-like voice. "Where...?"

"Cat!" Dan yelled over the screams of the storm. He started up the stairs, but tripped almost immediately and tumbled forward onto the wood planks of the porch. He was soaked. His head was dripping and, as he rotated to his back, he saw that his shirt stuck aggressively to his body. He brushed his hands across his chest.

"Just like Cat likes," he mumbled and grinned. "Susan never..." Dan gulped and strained to squint down his torso toward town and his cottage, feeling a rush of emotion trip over him. He began drifting, hovering above an impending dreamscape, when he heard a creaking sound and Cat's voice.

"Dan? Dan, what are you doing here?"

He raised his head. "Look at me. I'm soaked. I'm all wet. No wonder Susan hates me."

"Susan?" Cat stopped. Her friendly (if pitying) voice turned instantly sharp. "Dan, what are you doing here?"

When he didn't answer, she started to close the opening. "I'm going to call Ronnie."

"No!" Dan leapt up, his sudden spryness surprising him as much as his burst of energy clearly shocked Cat. She jumped back and grabbed at the side of the door.

"Don't call Ronnie."

"Why not?"

No answer from Dan.

"Dan, why not? What are you doing here?"

"I just...I just...Susan thinks we're having an affair."

Cat pulled her front door back a bit. "Well, tell her to join the club. But, as you like to remind me, repeatedly, we're not. And, you know what? That's good. I'm glad now. I don't know you. I thought I did, but I was wrong. Ronnie had it right. You charmed and seduced me."

Dan jerked forward and Cat hopped back, pushing the door almost closed in front of her, but he spun immediately and rushed toward the harbor, leaning over the edge of her railing. The mostly liquid contents of his stomach bubbled up and into the water and splashed against her house.

She nudged the door open again. "Oh, Dan!"

He smiled at her, looking undeniably like someone who'd just thrown up his dinner. All he needed now was hair to dishevel and the look would be complete.

"Dan…" Cat dropped her shoulders. "Come inside."

"Really?" He grinned and wiped his mouth with his forearm.

"Yes. You're clearly no threat to me in this state.

"Silly," she added, grinning. Then more serious, "But hurry, this weather's going to…"

He bumped past her and into her house.

"Okay…and now you're inside."

He plopped into one of her clothes-covered chairs. "Cat, I miss you."

"Really?" she said and shifted the laundry on her bed. "I doubt that." She apparently found what she was looking for and threw a towel toward him. "At least put this under you. You're soaked."

She went on. "And you can't miss me already, anyways. It hasn't even been a day. I just saw you this morning."

"That was this morning? Wow," Dan said. "It seems so long…"

After a moment, Cat said, "Yes…well…"

"Ago."

Cat grinned and seemed to suppress a chuckle. "Well, it was this morning."

"I called Cat, Susan." He tittered. "I mean, I called Susan, Cat."

Dan leaned forward, "She wasn't happy about that one bit." He giggled but quickly his face dropped and he became serious.

"First, Ryan. And now Susan."

"Who's Ryan?" Cat's face showed shock.

"My son," Dan said and stretched his eyelids up, batting them rapidly. "He died."

"You had a son? And he die—?"

"Wait," he burst to his feet. "Where's my vodka?"

"I don't know. You didn't have anything when you came in."

Dan spun around loosely, righted himself and moved toward the door.

"No. No. I think you've had enough already, silly," Cat grabbed his arm and pulled him back. "Besides, I didn't see a bottle on the porch. You probably left it at your house."

"Hmmm," he pressed his hands against his pockets. "Maybe...hey, I'm really wet."

"Yes you are," Cat laughed. "Let's get you out of those clothes. You can use my shower and get cleaned up."

"Wow. Susan's right. You *are* a tramp."

Cat looked shocked and at least pretended to be offended. Suddenly she laughed. "Maybe...I guess if me wanting to keep you from catching a cold makes me a tramp, then yes, I am."

She stepped toward him and started to take off his shirt. Dan leaned in and tried to kiss her.

"No, no. No, silly." She pushed him back. "None of that. Let's get you cleaned up first. You reek."

He pulled at his shirt and she moved her hands to the button on his jeans.

"No!" He knocked her away, stumbling to the side. "I'll do it."

Cat held up her hands and stepped back. "Okay. Fine. You're on your own. Bathroom's right there." She pointed to a door at the side of her bed. Dan undressed the rest of the way, struggling. Cat tried to help him a couple of times but each attempt met with a slap of his hand or an ill-attempted kiss. Finally, he walked into the bathroom, leaving his wet clothes in a lump on the floor.

He showered, sitting cross-legged on the tile flooring, watching the water cascade across his body. But before long (at least by his reckoning) he became bored, struggled to his feet and turned off the water. He grabbed a towel from a stack Cat had placed on the toilet and wrapped it around his waist, then spun a different towel turban-like on his head. He stepped into Cat's living area.

"See, if I don't wrap my head, my hair gets all tangled. You know how that is," he giggled.

She grinned, then motioned to the table and handed Dan a large tumbler.

"Drink."

He took a sip.

"Water?"

"Yes. And don't act so indignant. You're done for the night," Cat said as she sat at the table.

Dan shrug-nodded. He pulled a chair out opposite her and dropped onto the cushioned seat. "Okay. No more for tonight. At least for now." Dan threw her a snide look and picked up a sandwich from a plate in the center of the table.

"Thanks," Dan said and his smile melted and he turned serious. "Really, Cat. Thanks. You're so..." He paused, took a bite of his food, and glanced out the window.

Cat watched him chew.

He turned back to her. "I don't feel so good."

"Well, you're drunk. You should be feeling great." She pushed the plate toward him and stretched back to grab a paper towel from a roll sitting on the counter behind her. "Keep eating. This won't end well for you."

She continued, "And, don't take all this...the shower, me letting you in my house, letting you throw up on my porch." She grimaced and smiled in one flash of emotion. "Don't think everything's suddenly okay. It's not."

He saluted with the fist holding the sandwich. "Got it, *Comandanta*."

"Although, it takes a lot for me to stay mad at you. You jerk...silly." She smiled at him.

"Do you want some more?"

Dan shook his head. His makeshift turban tumbled off his head and he bent to pick the towel up. He sat back and moved his hand to his forehead. "Oh. I'm dizzy."

He jumped up and knocked over his chair as he sprinted to the bathroom. He tossed himself down in front of the toilet and clear liquid and bites of sandwich tumbled into the toilet. Dan rinsed his mouth and then returned to join Cat in the kitchen-bedroom-living area.

She raised her eyebrows. "Feel better?"

He didn't answer, only snatched off the towel wrapped around his waist, tossing the covering as hard as he could and only reaching less than a foot. He dropped face-first into her bed.

* * * *

Dan watched Cat slink out of bed and tiptoe to the bathroom. She was naked. He lifted the covers and peeked under them, then squeezed his eyes closed and moaned. He dropped his head back. What had he done? As if in response, his late-night adventures thundered through his mind and he remembered the storm and the phone call with Susan and her angry pronouncement that they were over, that she wanted a divorce.

"Good morning, sexy," Cat said. Dan jerked, immediately mindful of there having been more to his night than only a phone call.

"I'm just going to jump in the shower, then we can get some breakfast. How are you feeling?"

"Well…" he began. He wasn't sure how to answer that question.

"Then food will be good. There's water in the fridge. Help yourself. How's your side?"

"Actually, it's starting to feel a little better already." He shifted. "Sort of."

"Then good. Sort of." She grinned and closed the bathroom door. He heard the sink turn on.

Dan pushed himself up, massaging his stomach in a pointless effort to control his nausea. Then he searched the room for his clothes, not an easy task given the morass of Cat's dirty laundry scattered around the room. About to write his things off as a loss, he finally located them, hung to dry across the room in front of a window that opened to the harbor. The worst of the storm had passed, he noticed, but dark clouds still filled the edges of the sky in the distance. He released and dropped back into the pillow. His head was pounding. Some of the water Cat suggested would be good.

He slid to the foot of the bed and rose to his feet, or at least he tried. His body didn't cooperate and he lost his balance immediately (more likely, he'd never actually found it), tossing into a chair in front of Cat's desk and knocking against a keyboard and mouse as he fell. He pressed his head into his arms and *mmm'd* to wait out a fresh round of nausea. Then, he lifted his head and blinked several times. The screen had lit up and a Word document was open—a letter, likely one she'd been composing before he'd started wailing on her deck. He read:

Momma,

He paused. Momma? Her mother?

I'm sorry. I

He scrolled down, but there was nothing more. That's where the typing ended. He glanced at the bathroom. Didn't she say her mother was dead? Of course, he conceded, people talked to their deceased loved ones at graves all the time. That wasn't really an option for her, so perhaps this was just her version of that. All this death must have pushed her into reliving her mother's passing. She'd probably begun, then become overwhelmed and stopped.

He should buy her some flowers. There must be a flower shop somewhere in town. Or he could always just pick some. He eyed the desk. He should write himself a reminder. An uncapped pen lay next to the keyboard. Now something to write on. To the right of the monitor sat a paper with part of a coupon printed on it. He flipped the scrap over. An obituary.

May Smith died…

The text was smudged and hard to read, especially the beginning. through what he could make out. …*pastor's wife..devoted mother…liked to read.* Toward the end of the write-up, he slowed down and read more intently.

> …survived by her husband, Henry Smith, and her five children: Henry Jr., Catherine, Terry, James, and Thomas, all of Davenport.

Catherine. Cat's full name was Catherine. He smirked.

And this was her mother's death notice.

He heard the splash of falling water as the shower turned on. There was time. He grabbed the pen and pulled the middle drawer open, cringing as the wood squeaked. He didn't want her to think he was snooping.

Empty.

He pushed the center drawer closed and opened the right. A number of hanging files spread down the center. He stroked his fingers across them and peeked into each of the folders. No paper. In fact, no anything.

He pivoted to the left drawer and tugged. Apparently, this was where she threw all her junk. He searched through the mess, sliding the contents around and dipping his head to glance toward the back. A metal frame faced down. He paused.

"Oh well," he mumbled. He was officially snooping.

He slid the drawer out a bit farther and flipped over the frame, letting the photo rest on the mess inside. He flashed his eyes to the bathroom. Then back to the picture, his mind grasping at nothingness to understand what he looked at.

In the photo, falling snow floated frozen around Cat. She held a leash that led off the print's edge—whatever animal she was attached to stood somewhere out of shot. She posed, smiling, wearing a purple parka with a fur-lined hood. But none of that was important. Dan kept staring at the man standing next to her, looking smug, with his arm stretched around her shoulder.

Ed Wilson.

He shot his eyes at the bathroom door, then pulled the framed photo out of the drawer.

This was the same man he'd found on Facebook and seen at the beach, he was sure of it. Granted, the image was several years old. And the man's hair was different. If he could just see his chest. All those predators—his tattoo menagerie—that would confirm his identity for sure. Dan pulled the image closer. Cat's friend's jacket was open. And something poked out from under the collar of his shirt. The snake. It had to be the tail end of the serpent in the eagle's mouth drawing that he'd noticed on Ed's chest when he'd first found the man's body.

Dan listened. He heard the shower. He still had a few minutes. He set the pen back on the desk and twisted the frame around to pull at the cardboard on the back. There might be some other photos or perhaps even a description of the day written on the flip side of the image, something that could clarify what he was looking at. But nothing.

He studied the photo again. Ed held a baseball cap in his left hand. The hat was turned slightly, but...Dan yanked the picture closer. The Cardinals logo was imprinted above the bill. That meant...he felt light headed, exhaled. The wound on his side throbbed. He rushed his

266

hand to his ribs and pressed against his bones. He lifted his head and scanned around Cat's house. A sudden rush of saliva washed over his mouth and he swished his tongue around, tasting acid.

What did this mean? This man had to be Ed. And he was holding the same hat Cat had given him that first day they'd spent together. The same hat she'd forced onto his head the day they'd...

Dan cringed and dropped the picture frame. He swiped at his head with his right hand, then he snatched up the photo and stared at the pair again.

What was Cat doing with a dead man? And not just dead, murdered. And more than that, with a man she'd insisted she didn't know?

The shower squeaked off.

Twenty-Eight

Dan flashed to the bathroom.

He glanced once more at the image, then flipped the frame face down and slid the drawer closed as silently as he could. The screen. She'd see he'd been snooping. He patted around the monitor, suddenly frenetic, dashing his fingers along the front and bottom searching for some kind of switch. He stopped, took a breath. Sleep. He'd have to find a way to put her computer to sleep.

Inhaling and exhaling methodically, he studied the icons on the screen. Her system was Windows; he used a Mac. He wasn't even sure where to start. He clicked around, desperate to see some kind of reaction from the machine. Nothing happened. He could minimize the application. That would have to be enough. At least, his having seen the letter would be less obvious. He moused over the top of the screen until he saw what looked like controls. He clicked. The file disappeared. His eyes darted around the screen. Did the document minimize or close?

"I have no idea," he whispered.

Dan leaned his ear toward the bathroom, then took a breath and held it, listening. Silence. What was she doing inside? For all he knew, Cat could be finishing up at this moment and he'd have no idea until she came traipsing out of the bathroom, still wet and toweling herself off, asking him about what sounded good for breakfast.

He focused back on the desk. The plug. He'd have to cut power to the computer. He could claim he'd slipped and tripped over the cord and she'd just chalk up his clumsiness to his being hungover. He shoved his head between his knees and searched around. A cable connected to a socket on the far right, in a corner, under the desk. She'd never believe it. And, the plug itself was too far for him to reach. He shook his head. No choice. He had to buy himself some time.

He stretched, pushing himself as low and as forward as he could to access the cord. But the desk blocked his reach and he couldn't…quite…He pulled up, banging his head on the bottom of the middle drawer as he did. A small, rectangular paper flitted to the ground, landing face up. Dan's chest pulsed. At the top were some circles and the words Bahamian Airways, Beneath the logo and airline was the word NAME. And beneath that: WILSON/ED.

Ed's boarding pass. Dan stared at the stub.

His heart sounded in his ears.

He breathed out. Blinked. Over and over.

He pulled himself back and sat on the chair, fixated on the paper at his feet. He eyed the bathroom, shifted his eyes down, scanned his eyes back across the desk. This time he noticed a slight unevenness under the lower left side of the monitor. Finally! He slid his hand forward and pressed up. The screen flashed dark.

He darted his eyes back to the bathroom, then hurried across the room to his clothes. He froze after only a few steps. The boarding pass. He spun around. The stub was still under the desk. He glanced to the bathroom and moaned. Again, he had no choice. He sprinted forward, sliding onto his knees and bumping his forehead on the desk. He snatched up the paper with his left hand and ran the fingers of his right along the bottom of the drawer, from where he guessed it had fallen. How had the boarding pass been attached?

A metallic bump snapped his thinking and he rushed his head up and flashed to the bathroom. The tip of handle started to drop. He heard fumbling from behind the door. With the boarding pass still in his grip, he leapt to his feet and bolted across the room toward the open window and his clothes. He heard creaking behind him, certainly the door opening. His running felt stifled and humidity-laden and too slow until at last he reached his clothing. He shoved the boarding pass into his pants' pocket.

"What sounds good for breakfast?"

Dan spun. Cat patted at her hair with a towel draped over her head and across her face, another wrapped around her body, just under her arms. Dan grabbed his boxers and jumped into them, tipping to the left and hopping to keep himself from toppling over. His side screamed.

"Actually, I was thinking I should head out…get some writing done. Yesterday turned out to be too chaotic and I got nothing done. At all."

"Oh," Cat said, spinning the towel around her head. "Are you sure? I thought I could make you something or we could go over to the coffee house and get some pastries and espresso. Something."

Dan pushed his right arm through his t-shirt and straightened the fabric down as he strolled toward Cat. Calm. He forced his mind through different scenarios. He noticed the desk as he walked. The drawer with Ed's picture. Something had popped up and blocked the opening and left a crack. She might notice. He hurried to her.

She reached above her head and pulled her turban down, tossing the wrapping to the floor. Dan stepped closer and kissed her gently on the lips, fighting off the nausea that this time had nothing to do with alcohol. Divorce or not, he'd betrayed Susan. "I…"

"I get it. You got what you wanted. Now you're off." She pulled away from him and peered into his eyes, slinking.

She moved around him toward her desk. "But…" She pivoted to face him. "I did want to talk to you about something. Can't we at least have lunch? Or, maybe we can talk now? Before you go?"

Dan hesitated. At best, she'd lied. At worst…he shuddered.

"Sure," he said and sat down on the bed, patting the mattress. "Have a seat."

"I'll just stay here. Thanks. I need…" She dropped her head and started sobbing.

Dan sprang to his feet and rushed to her side. He wrapped his arm around her shoulders.

"Cat. Are you okay? What's wrong?"

"I'm sorry." She sniffed. "I just…yesterday was the anniversary of my mother's death. That's why I stopped by your house. I wanted to be with the man I loved."

Dan jerked away from her.

She snapped, "Oh, don't worry. I know you don't love me back. I'm just…"

"No, Cat. It's not that." And then he shocked himself by saying: "I do love you. It's just…"

"Yeah. I know. It's complicated."

She glared at him. Then she sighed and shook her head. "I'm sorry. I understand. I get it."

"And, thanks," she continued.

Dan grimaced. *Thanks?*

"Anyways, I stopped by your place yesterday because I was hoping you'd go spend the day with me in Marsh Harbour. Take our minds off things...take *my* mind off things. But then you were on your deck, hurt and bleeding, and Victor." She gasped. "His...and Scott...and then..."

Dan caught himself glancing around the room, wondering when she'd get to the point, or if this was, in fact, the point and—

"Am I boring you?"

"No, I just...I..."

She looked annoyed and shook her head.

"Anyways, after Ronnie took me home, I started to write the letter to my mom. I know, I know. I could just talk to the air, but that always seemed a little crazy to me. So, anyways, I started writing a letter to my mom. See it's right here."

Cat leaned over and clicked her mouse but, of course, nothing happened. "That's weird." She pressed again and again.

Dan asked, "Is the screen on?"

"Yes, I..." she said and reached under the monitor. The computer lit up. "Hmmm. That's strange. I didn't...anyways...where's my..." Cat clicked at the bottom of the screen. Nothing. She turned to Dan, paused, then continued.

"Well, I don't know. There's not much to show you, anyways...So, you know, it was harder than I thought. The letter. I do it every year, but this year was really hard in particular. Nothing felt right. I wanted to tell her about you. Tell her how amazing you are. But I was so confused after being at your house and Victor and...lots of writing and deleting and writing and deleting. But, you're a pro. You probably don't have to worry about that."

"You'd be surprised." Dan forced a grin.

"Well," Cat glanced down. "I…

"I…"

She pushed her lips out.

"So, there's something else I need to tell you."

"Okay…" Dan shifted.

"I knew that Ed guy. Well, not knew him, but I'd met him. I didn't recognize him at first. That's why I said I didn't know him. I didn't." She opened the drawer.

"Or, I didn't think I did." Cat pulled out the picture of Ed that he'd just found. "See. That's him."

"Anyways," she went on. "Like I said, I kind of knew him. But I didn't realize it until later and by then I was afraid to say anything because of how it would look, like I was hiding something. You know what I mean."

"Kind of like you and his wallet." She fixed on him.

Dan nodded, sharp. "And what about this?" He crossed to his jeans, still hanging by the window. As he moved, though, he reconsidered. Something was off. Her explanation didn't make sense. Not when he figured in the boarding pass. Why would she have something so obviously recent if she'd not seen him since whenever that picture was taken. No, there was more to her relationship with Ed.

He grabbed at his pants and shoved into one leg, then the other, as if getting dressed had been his plan all along, as if he were angry, which didn't take much.

"This."

"This what? My goodness. You're so dramatic," she said.

Dan slipped on his shoes, then buttoned his jeans as he stepped back toward her. He snatched the picture out of her hand and pointed to the cap Ed was holding. "This. Isn't that the hat you gave me that first day? You told me an old boyfriend gave it to you. Was Ed a boyfriend?"

"What? Are you jealous?"

"Just answer the question."

"No. He wasn't. Calm down." She grabbed the photo out of his hand and studied the image more closely. "Oh my goodness. You're right. That is the hat. I forgot he gave it to me. What a coincidence. It's like God wanted to return the hat to him and had me give it to you so you'd wear it when you found him."

Dan rolled his eyes.

She harrumphed. "C'mon. I didn't remember where I got it from. Guys give me things all the time. Look at me." She batted her eyes.

"I just thought it came from an old boyfriend. Now I remember, though," Cat looked coquettish. "He had a little bit of a crush on me. It was a group date and he wasn't my date, so you can imagine how that went. He was Lisa…Lisa…oh, Lisa something's. She was not happy one little bit, I can tell you that. Not one little bit."

She leaned in and whispered, "But she was kind of homely. Probably used to that sort of thing."

She rushed in, "Oh. But so nice."

Cat stopped talking and eyed Dan, apparently waiting for him to respond. But all he could think to say was, "Okay."

"That's it? Okay?"

He shrugged, "Yeah, okay. I get it."

The two stared at each for what felt like several minutes. Dan reached around her, suddenly feeling the need to reassure her. He kissed her.

"Let's get lunch," he said. "I'll head home now and get some writing done and then we can meet up later and go for some food. Does that sound good?"

Cat didn't respond at first. She pulled back from him and practically leered into his eyes. Finally, she crossed to her front entrance, opened the door and pivoted to face him, beaming.

"That sounds great. I'll come to your house and we can go from there."

Dan scanned the room. He didn't remember bringing anything with him last night, so he planted one last peck on Cat's cheek to convince her that all was, in fact, okay and he jogged down her stairs. He took a few steps, then twisted and glanced back over his shoulder. She'd moved outside and stood on her stoop, watching him. He forced a smile, waved, and continued to Queen's Highway and toward town.

* * * *

Dan strolled down Cat's street, nonchalant, glancing a couple of times over his shoulder and waving goodbye at the lingering Cat, acting as if he hated to go. He spun one final time before rounding the corner onto Queen's Highway, expecting to find her still hovering there. But she'd finally disappeared and closed the door. He began to sprint. When he felt confident that he'd put enough distance between them, he slowed, reached into his pocket, and pulled out the boarding pass.

WILSON/ED, FLIGHT M4, 6D

He circled, paced toward the town center and back, gazed in the direction of Cat's house, returned to the stub in his hand.

6D. Dan had been sitting…well, he was certain he'd been seated more toward the back of the plane, maybe row 12 or 13. On a plane that small, even with a seat like 6D, Ed would have been sitting toward the center of the aircraft. Dan knew he'd been given an aisle seat. But not much else. There'd been a woman sitting next to him. That he remembered (she was hard to forget). He'd caught her eying the runway, looking nervous, glancing between the tarmac and the queue of passengers as they filed onto the late-departing flight. At one point, the woman had stared straight ahead and mumbled (in a southern drawl) to the back of the seat in front of her, *declaring* that she didn't like flying one bit and particularly not on these small, *sure to go down in the middle of the ocean* puddle jumpers.

"Ma'am?" Dan had stretched forward. "Ma'am?"

She'd spun to him.

"Are you traveling alone, Ma'am?" Impending death or not, panic was contagious. But so was distraction.

"What? Oh. Yes. Yes. But I'm going to visit my daughter."

"How nice. It will be good—"

"Her name is Molly. She was going to school in Nassau. Why? Well…don't ask me. My opinion doesn't matter anymore now, does it? I mean there's lots of good schools right in North Carolina. But, you know Molly."

"No," Dan answered and grinned. "I don't."

"Oh." The woman shook her head and peeked down. "Of course not. How could you? What's wrong with me? I just hate these planes. I declare, I…" She cast her eyes out the window.

"Do you visit your daughter often?"

"What?"

"Your daughter? Do you visit often?"

276

She shook her head. "No. Sometimes. Not enough, you're thinking. And you'd be right. And, I won't be staying long this time neither. I already told you about her school in Nassau—don't get me started 'bout that kind of bad decision making. But now get this. She meets some Bahamian—a black, wouldn't you know," she whispered behind her fingers. "Guess he lives somewheres in the middle of nowhere. But, I don't judge. No Siree. Not me. She set on throwing her life away, I say more power to her. Not my life. I married a good ole' southern boy not some n'er do well."

Dan shifted in his seat, not sure of the protocol when you realize you'll be spending the next hour with a racist.

"Oh, don't get me wrong. I ain't no racist. Don't care one way t'or the other 'bout the color of a person's skin. They're just different, that's all I'm sayin'. Everyone knows that. Is there anything wrong with a mother wanting the best for her daughter?"

Dan opened his mouth.

"But, then, she goes and falls...you know, I never told you my name. I'm Bessy. Well, Lizbeth, but when I was a little girl, everyone called me Bessy and it just stuck, much to the chagrin of my highfalutin mother, never you mind. I think I kept it up mostly out of spite." She giggled. "That woman. She was..."

Dan stared toward the front of the plane, longing to see the door finally closing and the flight attendants, all one of them, prepping for takeoff.

"Course, Molly and me...we're close. So close she'd never do anything like that to me, let me tell you. But then she runs off to a place like the Bahamas and falls for one of them...*and* it turns out they went and got themselves hitched. What was she...? You know, I almost didn't come. Show her what she's in for. But...now they're moving to some place called Cooper's Town. Not Nassau. Not even Marsh Harbour. Cooper's Town. You'd think they'd have enough respect to at least settle down in Florida. But no. Do you think she once thought of her mother in all this? No, Siree. I've lost her, I tell you. I just know it. How can she—"

A crash in front of them snapped the two forward. On the plane, once Bessy had gotten her wits together, Dan had returned his focus to continue the woman's *nonjudgmental* assessment of her daughter's selfishness. But, instead, her panic had returned in full force and she'd grilled him about what the sound was and what that could mean for them, if he thought it was a sign that she...

However, back on Queen's Highway, that moment on the plane hovered frozen as if he could reach out and touch the face of the man who'd caused all the ruckus, as Bessie would say. Dan realized that in the midst of a woman's fevered and racist rambling he had, as it turned out, seen Ed, as the soon-to-be dead man had bent to retrieve his bag and another passenger had pressed his hand to his own head and insisted everything was alright. That things happen.

But that meant Constable Anderson was on to something. Dan *had* seen Ed alive. And then he'd forgotten. Maybe Cat, too, had innocently overlooked that she'd met Ed so long ago.

He stared down at the paper in his hand. He shook his head. He had no choice. He had to tell the policemen about what he'd discovered. Of course, they'd want to know how he'd actually stumbled upon the boarding pass in the first place. He'd insist he'd been at Cat's, but they would almost certainly not believe him. Or, if by some miracle they actually took him at his word, Dan would be forced to suffer through Constable Anderson's jealous gloating about how he'd been right all along about Dan's lack of morals. Of course, all this assumed they wouldn't just conclude that he'd had the pass the entire time and arrest him right there. They'd ask Cat about his story but she'd deny she'd had the document in the first place. And they'd believe her. And...

He gazed toward the town center and the police station. He continued to home.

There was no rush.

Twenty-Nine

Dan shoved the boarding pass into his pocket. But he took only one step before he yanked the stub out again and stared at the words on the document. He twisted and squinted in the direction of Cat's house.

The picture in her drawer, that could be explained away. The hat, even her ridiculous explanation about God wanting to return Ed's cap to him...well, no (he shook his head—vigorously); God wasn't a part of this. But, Dan had to admit that not remembering exactly where she'd gotten the hat was certainly plausible. Memories could be fickle, as he'd just discovered. The boarding pass, though. There was no way she could explain that away. No matter what justification she came up with, her having Ed's boarding pass could only mean she'd seen him after he landed. And, if she'd seen him after he landed, she'd have remembered him. And if she'd remembered him and then lied about having done so, there was no denying that...he whipped his head and stomped off. He should have confronted her right there, forced a reaction from her. But, what would that reaction have entailed? Could he have been in danger? Was he still?

He reached his house and pushed open the doors, rushing directly to the table and sliding the boarding pass under his laptop. He stepped around the chairs and into the living area, panning over the harbor to the beach. This had all started there. Beneath the lighthouse. He noticed that the surface of the water was getting choppy. He glanced up at the sky, then rushed back around the table, made sure the stub wasn't visible, and walked out the front door.

In less than 24 hours, the world had made clear to him that he was nothing more than an interloper. At best he was not wanted: cue the citizens of Hope Town. At worst, he was reviled: Constable Anderson and, at least for the foreseeable future, Susan. He inhaled bluntly through his nose and shook away the thought.

But there was always Jamie. Crush or not, a visit to the coffee house was sure to be stress free. Divorce would never be raised as an option. And any possible ambiguity about their relationship would (almost certainly) not result in anyone's murder.

He bounded into the cafe and rushed forward, ready to have his ego stroked, but pulled back and stared around the room. The shop was empty. No patrons hushed their conversations, struggling to avoid looking in his direction. No one. There was no Jamie (not even Jean) waiting behind the counter, smiling as he entered (or in her case, not), ready to take his order. The room was silent. Almost eerily so. And stifling. He found himself pushing his hands into the air in front of himself for nothing more than to verify that he, in fact, still could. He chuckled to himself. This was what discovering that you've likely been palling around with a murderer for a week must do to you. Even the most innocuous situations become, well, nocuous. He crossed to the counter and leaned over.

"Hey, Jamie."

He swallowed, grimaced. "Jean?…Anyone here?"

He stepped out to the deck. Also empty.

He shrugged and trekked across the room to his recently established usual table, kicking out one of the chairs with his foot and dropping onto the seat. He studied his hands, glanced around the shop again. Then he lowered his head onto the table and rested.

"Oh hey, Dan."

He tossed his body up too quickly, throwing his hand to his forehead and wavering from one side to the other. Jamie strolled in from a back room behind the counter, wiping his hands on a towel.

"Everything okay?"

Jamie scrutinized him, "Are you drunk?"

"No. I just…could I just get some water? Please?"

"I could heat up a croissant for you, too."

"Sure. That'd be good. Thanks. Where is everybody?"

Jamie shrugged. "Just slow. That time of year."

He set a pastry on the rack of the toaster oven. "So, Mr. Writer. What's new?"

"What isn't?" Dan said.

Jamie twisted toward him and he added, "It can wait."

When the oven dinged, Jamie took out the croissant and tossed it on a plate. He added the roll to some Perrier and glasses already on a tray, then crossed to Dan and set the refreshments on the table. He grinned at Dan and twisted.

"Watch this. I've been practicing."

He leaned forward and tossed the platter toward the counter. It landed firmly on the flat surface with a metallic clang. He spun and beamed at Dan, looking pleased with himself.

"See."

"You should go pro." Dan smiled and poured the sparkling water into the glasses. Jamie sat across from him.

"So," the boy began and picked up his drink.

"I slept with Cat."

282

"What?"

Jamie set down the glass he'd just picked up. He fixated on Dan with a bewildered look. Finally, he continued, "Why are you telling me this?"

He paused. "Actually, I don't know…I…I have no idea." He shook his head. "It was a…Susan wants a divorce. I guess I should have led with that."

"Okay. That's too bad. But I still don't get why you're telling me this."

Dan shook his head, but otherwise didn't respond.

"So you've been lying to me this whole time? You are having an affair with her. You're just like—"

"No," Dan said. "I am not having an affair with her. I didn't lie before. It was once. Last night. After you and I talked before. And it was a huge mistake. It will never…ever…happen again."

"Yeah, right," Jamie said. Dan could see that he was gritting his teeth.

"That woman ruins everyone. She…"

The young man pushed back from the table and moved to the counter. He spun to Dan, his features flush, and inhaled bull-like through his nose. "Cat slept with my dad. Did you know that? My parents almost got a divorce because of her. Why do you think my mom hates her so much?"

"But Cat said she didn't know your dad was married."

"You knew?"

"Only re…she just told me."

"Mmm hmm. Well, she lied to you. She always knew."

"I'm sorry, Jamie. I really am. But I had no idea. Susan had just told me she wanted a divorce. And this whole murder thing." He slammed his palm on the table. "I'm not superhuman. It's really stressful to wake up every day knowing you could go to jail for a murder you didn't commit. And in a foreign country on top of that."

Jamie seemed unmoved. Dan studied him, then nodded and added, "But, you're right….I hate her."

Jamie humphed and the two stared across at each other for what seemed like several minutes. Finally, Dan said, "Well, there's more. Get this. I think—"

"Cat killed that man."

"What?" Dan said. "How do you know?"

"I saw it."

"You saw what, Jamie?"

Jamie rolled his eyes. "I saw her kill him."

Dan dropped his food. He stared at the surface in front of him, instantly swirling and blurred and angry. He pressed his hand against the wall, opened and closed and opened his lips again like a dying fish.

"What?

"Me and Victor…we were…we were on the outer side of the island, facing Marsh Harbour. Me and him…we saw, well I saw it all. Victor wasn't looking. She was on a boat. Only I didn't know it was her at first. She was facing away from us and she had a hoodie on. I could see the other man, though. At least his silhouette…kind of his face. But I didn't know him. They were arguing."

Jamie's voice started trembling. "And then she pushes a knife into the man's head. All of a sudden…I mean, I think she had it out first…she must have….but then…"

Dan watched Jamie drone on, not hearing him, not listening, not caring. He'd known. The kid had known. That was all that mattered. He shifted his eyes around the shop, dropped them to the side and down. His vision dimmed. Two friends…he'd had two friends on this island. Or he thought he had. Really, though, one was a killer and

284

the other one had known but had kept it secret. And Jamie could have stopped everything. He straightened his eyes and glared across the room. He shook his head.

"We're not friends anymore."

"What?"

"You heard me. We're not friends anymore."

Dan shoved back and bolted out of his seat. He stormed to the exit, flailing his arms up and to the side and feeling his lips move uncontrollably. He spun and darted back to Jamie, shoving his palms against the boy's shoulders. Jamie stumbled back. Dan shifted into him, hovered over him, forcing Jamie into submission and pinning him between Dan and the counter. Dan slid back and slammed his fist against Jamie's chest. The boy collapsed to the ground, heaving. Dan angled and hoisted Jamie up, slamming the kid down against the surface of the counter. Jamie gushed out as his back struck the hard wood, sounding like an old man gasping for his final breath.

"Dan."

Dan yelled into him, "You knew!"

He yanked Jamie up and forward, rammed him to his feet. He pushed into the boy, compressing him against the edge another time and squeezing his hands around Jamie's throat. After several seconds, he released and Jamie crumpled again to the floor, wheezing. He pressed his hands against the wall of the counter.

Dan leaned into Jamie's face and shouted.

"How could you, Jamie? Do you realize what you've done? My wife…Susan is leaving me."

He whipped his hands through the air.

"These people all think I killed someone, which makes no logical sense, but hey, he's the foreigner. And now two people are dead. And all this time you could have…" He stepped back and shrugged. "Victor's dead and that's on you."

Jamie's eyes flashed and his lips started quivering. He started blinking sporadically.

"I—"

Dan grabbed the boy's arm and jerked him forward off the floor. Jamie struggled to stand but his momentum propelled him forward and he tossed onto the floor and landed splayed across the tile.

"Let's go," Dan snapped. "Now. We're going to the police."

Jamie begged. "No, Dan. Please. We can't. Not yet…you don't understand. Victor and I—"

"Let me guess. You were, what? Dating?"

"No. I mean, not really…just…"

Dan flipped his head back. "C'mon, Jamie. Grow up. This is the 21st century."

Jamie hesitated. "But you don't know what it's like here."

"Jamie, seriously. Drop it. None of that matters. You have no excuse. Unbelievable!"

"But, you don't understand."

"No, you don't understand!"

Dan grabbed Jamie's wrist and thrust his face into the kid. He spit into him, "My life is falling apart!"

He twisted the boy's arm and dragged him toward the door.

"Ow. Dan, please. You're hurting me."

Dan flicked the boy's arm away. Jamie's hand slapped against the floor. "You think I care?

"Fine," he went on. "Get up. You can walk on your own. But we're going to the police now. You're going to tell them everything."

"But my parents don't know."

"So, your parents don't know. Big deal. This is my life we're talking about here."

"But they don't know that I'm...that—"

"That you're gay. Yeah, got it. Seriously Jamie. Do you really think anyone even thinks about that? You're nothing."

Jamie flinched. He crawled to his feet.

"Okay. But here they do. Here they definitely care." He squeezed his eyes closed and shook his head. "They'll...they'll probably throw me out and I...but, maybe if I tell them first. And they don't hear it from the town, they'll just send me away. If they don't hear the sip sip first, I...I just..."

Dan hung his head.

"Jamie." He stared into the young man's eyes. "You're, what...25? It's time to grow up. Because of you, they think I killed someone. Don't you get that? They took my passport. My wife...Seriously. You think I care about all that. You're a coward. Stop being such a coward."

"I'll go now." Jamie begged. "I'll tell them now and then we can go to the police. An hour. I promise."

Dan felt lightheaded. He moved to one of the tables and fell into one of the seats. He let his head rock back against the wall. After a moment, he pulled himself forward and glared at Jamie.

Then he spoke slowly, exhausted, "Susan's dad is gay. It took a while, but she finally learned to accept it. Your—"

"No." Jamie shook his head. "Not here. They never will."

Dan dropped back again and slid his head against the hard wall, relishing the discomfort he felt as the grooves butted against his scalp. He shifted up.

"Alright."

"Alright?" Jamie beamed.

"But you'll tell them tonight. No excuses."

Jamie nodded. "I'll tell them now. We can go now."

"No. Tonight's fine. Nothing's going to change between now and then. We can go to the police tomorrow. In the morning." Dan stood and started toward the door. He turned. "First thing, though. And if you don't tell them, too bad. We're going anyway."

Jamie moved to Dan. Dan threw his hand out.

"Don't." He stared at Jamie. Vacant. "We're not friends anymore. All this. My wife. My life fell apart...*still*...is falling apart. And you sat back and did nothing while..." He shook his head. "That's not what friends do, Jamie. We're not friends."

"But..."

"I don't want to hear it. Tomorrow. First thing. Then it's like we never met."

Jamie sunk to the floor.

Dan pivoted and pried the door open, sliding through the exit and trudging toward home, listless and defeated. About halfway down the street, he stopped. Wind whipped his shirt around his torso and he pressed his hands down, lost in the fabric. Ahead he could see his house. He shifted. The lighthouse jutted into the clouds across the bay. He dropped his head, then raised his eyes and shouted into the sky.

"Aaaah!"

He plodded back to the coffee house and threw the door open. He poked his head in.

Jamie hadn't moved. He sat on the floor in the center of the cafe. The boy's head was sunk into his chest and his shoulders trembled. A barely discernible moan floated across the room. Wet had soaked into the boy's pants. Dan watched him.

Then he let the door fall closed and walked away.

* * * *

Dan blew through the front door of his house and stormed straight into the kitchen.

On the counter stood an open bottle of red. He grabbed it, swirled the liquid around and sniffed, inhaled, rested his eyes closed. Then he dumped what remained of the wine into the sink. He spun and tossed the empty container into the recycling bin. He returned to the counter. A row of bottles lined the backsplash. All wine. All reds. He stared at them, started counting them. Susan's voice broke in. Her dismissive, "You said that," and her too void of emotion, "I want a divorce." He pictured Cat slinking out of bed and into the bathroom and purring out her un-fettered, "Good morning, sexy."

And he felt revulsion.

He ripped open a drawer and knocked the utensils around until he found a corkscrew. He snatched it. One by one, he opened the remaining bottles (seven), then dumped each of them into the sink, struggling to ignore the seductive perfume of the alcohol, wafting stronger with each pour. He reconsidered. He could skip the sink, if only for a moment, rest his lips against the rim of one of the bottles and tip, even a few drops of the nectar into his mouth. One or two (or three) last glasses of wine before he swore off any alcohol forever. Or at least for a while. Or at least until tomorrow.

He bumped the faucet on with his fist and watched the red soften and drift into the drain, ushering away, or so he hoped, the incessant yearning for just a moment more with his friends. The wine would stain the basin. He shrugged. So what? By the time, he was done with Hope Town (or, more likely, Hope Town was done with him), everything would be in ruins anyway. Buying Richard a new house would be the least of his worries.

He twisted to the refrigerator and pulled out the three bottles of white, dumping them into the sink. He flung open the freezer door and pulled out the two bottles of vodka. They'd only been intended as backup anyway (to replace the backup bottles from before). He set the containers on the counter, pausing, re-evaluating. All this might be nothing more than his own extreme petulance. He could be overreacting. He'd come to regret his rashness.

But then a sudden wave of longing for Susan washed over him. And a second, this time fury, stone-like and smothering, knocked against him. His *wife* had never even bothered to return his calls or thought (at the very least) to check in on him to make sure he was okay after her marriage-ending pronouncement. He could be dead for all she knew. He'd lay into her. He'd let her know just how uncaring she was. And this time, she'd have to listen to him. He reached for his phone.

One of the vodka bottles sat too close to the edge of the counter and he bumped, just tapped really, the outside of the container and it started to rock and tilt. He rushed out his hand to stop the movement, but somewhere, lost in the day, he managed instead to nudge the bottle back and the top bounced against the other and tumbled forward into the nothing and hurried to the floor. He jutted out his hand, tried to grab the falling bottle, but only accomplished following the bottle's descent, as if ushering the container closer to its demise had been his intent all along. The glass exploded and liquid shot out and wet his pants, soaking them in alcohol. One of the shards from the bottle rebounded back and sliced across his outstretched palm. He yanked his arm into himself and lifted his hand in front of his face. He fixated on his palm, how the blood dripped across his skin and down his forearm and melted into the chaos he'd been so instrumental in creating. He thought of Ed, picturing the boat, and felt his life leaking into nothing and he shuddered.

In an instant Dan cried out and rushed the fingers of his other hand against the river running across his palm, pressing them hard against the cut (which he'd discovered was actually quite small, but painful) in order to stanch the blood. He sucked in. Vodka permeated the air around him. He gasped again, inhaling, not knowing what to feel as he longed for the burn of the alcohol and needed desperately to attend to his suffering. His eyes darted around the kitchen to the paper towels. He jerked at the roll, needing only a section or two to act as a bandage. But as he pulled at it, the bolt flew off the counter and started to unwind across the kitchen floor and into the living room. He followed the strip, much like he'd pursued the vodka, and when the towels finally ended their escape, he tore several end sections and wrapped them around his palm, holding the makeshift bandage in place with his fingers of the same hand.

He gathered up the rest of the white and pushed the loose strip of towels onto the counter, against the backsplash. Then he located the hand broom and dust pan and cleaned up as much of the broken glass as he could see. He grabbed the remaining towels, soaked up the liquid and placed the cleanup in the trash. He glanced at his hand. The wrap would have to last.

He leaned against the counter and fiddled with the first-aid around his hand. He imagined Susan. She caressed him, her dirty blond strands brushing teasingly against his cheek and neck as she kissed him. Gentle. Longing. She whispered in his ear and goosebumps erupted across his arms and neck.

But then a knock broke in and she was gone. He spun his head to the foyer and dropped his shoulders. He paused. Another knock sounded. He studied the wet/dry floor in front of him, then crossed to the foyer and tossed one last, lingering look back. She was never there.

He pulled open the door. Constable Anderson and Inspector Johnson stood on the stoop. Cat hovered behind Anderson. Her eyes were bloodshot. She'd been crying.

Thirty

"Cat! What…?"

Instinct flooded Dan and he rushed at Constable Anderson.

Dan towered over the policeman by almost a foot, but Anderson was solid, aka fat, and the man outweighed him, Dan guessed, by close to 100 pounds. In spite of his mass, the constable moved surprisingly fast, and without warning Dan found himself pinned tight against one of the walls of the landing outside his house. Constable Anderson's forearm pressed painfully against Dan's Adam's apple.

He rasped out, "Cat, are you okay?"

Anderson leaned up and forward, using his heft to smash against Dan's neck. Breathing was impossible. Dan gasped. He pried at the man's forearm, dug his fingers into the policeman's skin, tried to jump up and knock himself loose. All useless. The constable only guffawed and pressed harder. Then, all of a sudden, the policeman jerked and pulled back, wiping his arm across his stomach, which was, conveniently for him, not a long trip.

"What the…did you cut me?"

Cat cried out and leapt to Inspector Johnson's side, then dashed behind the larger and more bulbous hulk that was Constable Anderson. Dan watched their movements. Understanding washed across his face.

"Is this…? Is she saying I did something to her?"

Constable Anderson twisted his arms in front of himself, then flashed his eyes to Dan's hands.

"You're bleeding."

Dan glanced at himself. The paper towel had fallen off into a corner and blood dripped from his hand.

"Yes, I…"

He spun and bolted into his house, to the kitchen, knocking the door closed with the side of his foot. He rushed his eyes around the room. All the paper towels now filled the trash bin. Soaked. Wet with alcohol. He shook his head and grabbed some of the strips on top and swaddled the dressing around his hand, hissing between his teeth and squinting as the vodka-soaked bandage pressed into his wound. He squeezed his eyes closed and breathed. He searched through his junk drawer and found some tape, this time fastening the paper towels more securely. As he finished fixing the wrap, he heard shifting behind him and twisted to see Constable Anderson and Inspector Johnson filing in. Anderson pivoted and extended his hand.

"C'mon, Cat. You can come in. You're safe with us. We won't let him hurt you."

Cat stepped through the door and the constable turned back into the house. He scrunched up his nose. "I thought I smelled alcohol. It reeks in here. You been drinking?"

"Again," he added and smirked. Dan saw the constable peek at Cat, probably for reassurance that she found him as hilarious as he found himself. Dan returned to the entrance. Anderson motioned to the woman.

"Cat told us everything."

Dan focused on Cat. "She did?"

She shifted her eyes away from him.

"What did she—"

294

"What kind of man hits a helpless woman," Constable Anderson said, and immediately Cat burst into tears and threw her arms around Ronnie.

"What? I didn't do anything."

"There, Cat, there," the constable said, stroking her hair. "You're safe now. He can't hurt you anymore. We're going to make sure of that." He pushed her back and gazed into her eyes. "But, first, you've got to show me where these things are."

Cat paused, then nodded and rotated to face Dan's bedroom. "In here."

Constable Anderson followed.

"Wait a minute. You can't just go traipsing around my house. Don't you have to have some kind of a warrant or writ? Something?

"You don't have my permission," he called after them.

"Actually, Mr. Harris," Constable Anderson said. He turned and hitched up his pants. "By your own admission, this is Richard's house. You could be a trespasser, for all we know. Plus, we called him.""

"And he said you could just go through my things?"

Constable Anderson didn't answer. He continued into the bedroom, following Cat.

"Ye fixed yer glass."

Dan spun to Inspector Johnson.

"What?"

"I said, ye fixed yer glass." The inspector motioned toward the deck with his lips.

"My...?" Dan peeked behind him. The broken panes had been cleaned and repaired, as if the entire previous couple of days and nights had been nothing more than a dangerous dream. "Oh...I was out. The caretaker must have..."

Constable Anderson and Cat returned. Anderson held Ed's wallet and (Dan had only recently discovered) the dead man's hat. A sudden wave of vertigo washed over him. He sensed himself teetering and he felt nauseated. He glared at Cat.

"Like to explain these, Mr. Harris?"

"Nothing to explain. That's my wallet." He nodded to the cap. "And my hat."

"They belonged to Ed Wilson."

"I don't think so." Dan shook his head. "Those are mine."

Constable Anderson stepped forward and pulled back one of the flaps of the billfold. "What about this?"

Dan peeked inside. A laminated card with the words PROPERTY OF EDWARD GERALD WILSON rested against the policeman's finger. He grabbed at the wallet.

"Let me see that."

Constable Anderson snapped the billfold out of his reach.

"Uh-uh," Anderson said. "No touching."

Dan turned to Cat, but she stared into a corner of his kitchen.

"She put that there. She had to have. It wasn't in there before."

"Who's she?"

"Cat. She—"

"Before what?" Inspector Johnson asked.

This was the end. The spiral was beginning to open and this was the time to bail while he could still see the edge and hope to grab reality. "I...okay...here's the truth, I took the wallet that first day, when I was looking over the body, right after we found it." Dan eyed Cat. "But, like I told you then, I was just trying to help."

296

"By contaminating the crime scene and kidnapping the evidence?" Constable Anderson said.

"Kidnapping?" Dan chuckled.

Cat shifted toward him and shouted, "Stop insulting him. He's just doing his job." She burst into tears. "Have some respect."

"Oh…my…Listen, I wanted to give it to you. I did," Dan turned and squinted at the lighthouse through the newly repaired French doors. "I just forgot about it at first. And then there was never a good time."

"The church? That first day? Any day between then and now?" Anderson shook his head. "Don't see it, Boss. There were many good times."

"I even showed it to Cat. But she said not to say anything," He stepped toward her. "We looked at it together and there was nothing in it, and she said, don't…she saw, there was nothing in it."

"Cat, that true?" Ronnie asked her.

She shook her head. "Ronnie, I really don't know what he's talking about. I wish I did. It kills me to think that Dan could have had anything to do with this. I trusted him." Her shoulders started trembling and Ronnie rushed to her and scooped her into him, glaring at Dan, or at least at the ceiling. Twisting was clearly a challenge for him.

"Just look what you're doing to her. She doesn't deserve this," he yelled at the kitchen.

Dan stared at Cat in Ronnie's arms. She sobbed and swayed as if she were feeling weak and overcome. Then she lifted her face to Dan and winked.

"Did you see that?" Dan pointed and spun to face Inspector Johnson.

She nudged Ronnie forward.

"Show him the picture."

"You sure. This can wait if you're feeling like it's too much."

"No, let's get this over with. I just want it to all go away." She sniffed and at least pretended as if she might break down again any minute. "Breaks my heart."

Constable Anderson patted her shoulder and stomped forward, displaying a photo. It was the same print Dan had discovered in Cat's drawer.

"Look, don't touch. Cat brought this to me. She felt horrible for saying that she didn't know Ed, but how could she have remembered something like that? It was an upsetting day for all of us."

Dan rolled his eyes.

"I feel so bad," Cat sobbed out.

The constable tripped his way to Cat's side. He brushed his hair across his forehead and caressed her shoulder. "Cat, really. There's nothing to feel bad about. You did nothing wrong here." He swung back to Dan. "She'd just forgotten that she'd met Ed a long time ago. It happens."

"I don't see what that proves. If anything, it just shows she knew him and lied."

"I'll tell you why it matters," Constable Anderson said. "Because then she saw the hat at your place and it all came back to her. It matters because she immediately came to me. You didn't."

Anderson pointed at the photo, at the hat in Ed's hand. He shoved the baseball cap in Dan's face. "See. Same hat."

"Cat gave me that hat," Dan said, monotone, recognizing as he spoke the words that there was no point.

"That true?" Inspector Johnson asked Cat.

She twisted her face as if she were reluctant. "Um…no. Dan, I'm sorry. I just can't lie anymore. You've already

298

asked me to do so much. You know I'd do almost anything for you. Still. I still would. But…"

Dan stared at the French doors.

"The caretaker. His name is John S…" Dan paused. He bit his lip. "John something. I…my wife would—"

"Didn't she leave you?" Cat said.

"She left you?" Constable Anderson smirked. "Did she finally find out about your obsession with Cat?"

"Yes." Cat rocked on her feet. "Yes, she—"

"No!" Dan threw up his hands.

"She didn't leave you?" Anderson eyed Dan.

"Again? Really? You want to talk about my wife?…It's complicated. Now, and I really can't believe I'm saying this, but can we please get back to the murder and your crazy theory? I had nothing to do with any of this. I'm being framed."

"That's ridiculous." Constable Anderson burst out laughing and shook his head. "I—"

"Who do ye think is framing ye, Boss?" Inspector Johnson said.

"Cat."

The inspector nodded. "Hmmm."

Suddenly the front door flew open and Daniel burst into the room.

Dan darted to the entrance, immediately feeling besieged by all the stress and emotion wrapped around being falsely accused. Again. He screamed, "Don't you ever knock?"

"I went to the station. Fran at the Sugar Shack…she said you all were here."

"Fran knows…?" Dan started, then immediately closed his mouth. He stared at Daniel. The kid's face was flushed and streaked with tears and blood. Dan edged forward.

"Daniel. What…?"

"My dad." Daniel gasped. His mouth began trembling. "He's dead."

Thirty-One

Dan felt paralyzed. Instantly his eyes began to water and he stumbled back. Daniel sunk to the floor and pressed his head into his hands. Inspector Johnson moved toward the young man and sat at his side. The inspector glanced at Dan.

Dan said, "Daniel. I'm so…"

"Daniel," Inspector Johnson said. He massaged the boy's shoulder. "Can ye answer some questions?"

Daniel nodded.

"When did this happen?"

The young man sniffed and raised his head. He pressed his hands against his eyes. "Uh…I don't know. I…"

He inhaled sharply through his nose. "I went to Marsh Harbour this morning to get some supplies. He was fine when I left. But…" He gasped. "…when I came back he was lying at the foot of the lighthouse. His head was bloody. He was…"

He wiped across his face and stared forward. "He wasn't…there was…"

"It's okay," Inspector Johnson said. "So he fell?"

Daniel indicated no. "I don't think so. He goes up the lighthouse all the time. And there are those trees. And bushes. He wouldn't…plus, I found this." He pushed out his hand. In his palm rested a cell phone. "It wasn't too far from him. It's not his, though. I don't know whose it is. Someone else must have been there."

Cat rushed to Daniel's side and hugged him. "You poor thing."

She snatched the cell out of his hand.

"Dan, this is just like your phone," she said.

Dan ran his hands over his pockets. He gritted his teeth.

"Well, well." Constable Anderson brushed his bangs to the side. "Where's your phone, Chief?"

Dan scanned his eyes around his house. "Uh, let me think. It's here somewhere."

Constable Anderson reached into his pocket and pulled out a handkerchief. He stretched the cloth across his palms, then extended his hand to Cat. "Do you mind?"

Constable Anderson lifted the cell between the folds, suddenly behaving like a policeman. He studied the device. Then he looked at Cat. "Do you have Dan's number?"

"Yes."

"Call it."

"Please," Cat said, batting her eyes.

The constable blushed. "Please."

Cat got out her own cell and started poking around the screen. She lifted her phone to her ear. Nothing happened. Dan sighed. He inhaled. Given how the visit had gone, he was certain the cell would ring and somehow his phone would have been left on the scene. By Cat.

Then he noticed the phone in Anderson's hand had lit up and was buzzing. The constable pressed the cell to his ear.

"Hello."

Cat dropped her hand. "Dan. How could you?"

Thirty-Two

"You know you'll never get rid of Ronnie, now."

"Oh, Dan. Are you jealous? That's so sad." She shrugged. "But, why do you assume I want to be rid of him? Anyways, he doesn't like it when you call him Ronnie. You should show him a little more respect. Your life is kind of in his hands now."

Cat hovered across from Dan. He sat, secured to a chair with chains that wrapped around the legs of a long, solid-wood work table in front of him. Constable Anderson had finally allowed Cat to be alone with Dan (after some serious flirting by her), but only if the policeman handcuffed Dan and the table separated the two.

At the house, Dan had watched what resolution remained in Daniel's face melt away as the phone in Constable Anderson's hand had sprung to life. The young man had stared at Dan, looking lost.

"You?"

Dan hadn't been able to answer at first. What could he say? He didn't do it? That excuse had become property of the guilty long ago. He'd wanted to point out that he couldn't have been across the harbor killing Thomas. He was with Jamie. Jamie would vouch for him. But, he'd glanced at Cat. If Dan was going to jail—as was starting to look more likely—he wouldn't be around to protect the young man. She'd proven with Victor what could be the result of her feeling cornered. There was no decision to be made. He indicated no. "I promise, Daniel. I didn't hurt your dad. I have no idea how my phone got..."

Before he could finish, though, Constable Anderson had knocked behind him, yanking his arms aggressively and whisper-yelling into his ear. "Shut up. You're under arrest for suspicion of murder. You make me sick."

Dan had pivoted to Inspector Johnson. He'd even begun to speak. But Johnson had simply shaken his head and looked away. "Sorry. Anderson's right. Yer under arrest."

"I'll just call over to Marsh Harbour and tell them we're bringing over a prisoner."

"No, Constable," the inspector had cut in. "We keep him here. At least 'till we put together more."

Anderson had objected and the two had migrated to the entry for a private, if animated, conversation. In the end, the policemen had returned, Inspector Johnson apparently having prevailed, and Constable Anderson mumbled that Dan would be held in the Hope Town Police Station. He'd added, "It just makes more sense," as if that had been his plan all along.

"Don't you have to read me my..." But he'd stopped when he considered Daniel. That and he hadn't really been sure what the procedure for arrest was in the Bahamas. He'd stumbled.

"What's that, Chief?" Anderson had asked.

Dan had only shaken his head and muttered out, "No."

On the way out, the constable had paused and leaned to Daniel. He'd whispered, "Sorry for your loss, Chief."

Cat had rushed to Ronnie and Dan. She'd massaged the constable, nuzzled him. "Can I go? Please?"

Anderson had grinned and giggled, rocked his head. Even his neck had blushed. He'd nodded.

"Of course. Yes. Just bring the evidence, okay?"

Instantly, Dan had flashed to his laptop. The boarding pass. He'd slid the stub underneath earlier. If they found it… If he said anything, they'd… If…

"I can't leave my laptop out there. All my writing is on it. It's too valuable. Can I at least move it in my room?"

Anderson had started to respond, but Johnson had interrupted him. "Yes, ye can, Boss. Make it quick."

"You're going to let him do this? We should at least take that computer into custody."

"Why, Constable?" Johnson had tilted his head and motioned to Dan. "Go ahead."

Dan had crossed to the table and lifted his laptop, placing his hand over the side where the boarding pass jutted out. He lifted the computer, pinning the paper in place with his fingers and walking into his bedroom. He set them both on his dresser, making sure that the document wasn't visible. Then he stepped back into his living room.

"Can I call my wife?"

Constable Anderson had exhaled, loudly, and spun Dan to face him. "Listen, Boss. No more requests. You're a prisoner now. You'll get to call when I say you get to call."

"Anderson!" Inspector Johnson had yelled. Abrupt. Then he'd directed himself to Dan, "You can call from the station."

But at the station, Anderson had simply shoved Dan harshly into what looked like a break room, shackled him to a chair, and, after some rather annoying giggling and hair-straightening, left to get some ice cream for Cat. And now, strapped in place, prisoner to her gloating, he listened to her declare her supposed devotion to Constable Anderson.

"But, alas…"

"Alas?"

She shrugged, sighed. "Alas, he's married. I can never have him."

"Well, isn't that convenient for you?"

"What? You didn't think me and you were going to end up together, did you Dan?"

"Well," she continued, leaning into him. "I must admit, for a while there I hoped that might happen. But, that bitch Susan wouldn't leave you alone."

Dan recoiled. He doubted he would ever lose the instinct to protect his...to protect Susan.

"You'll be sorry you ever picked that woman over me, Dan. You had your chance."

"She's my wife."

"Oh really, Dan?" she spit out. "You're not fooling anybody. That didn't stop you last night when it really mattered. Besides, she's not your wife any more. Or were you just lying about that to get me into bed?"

Cat stared at him. A grin spread across her face. He remained stoic. After a moment, he smirked.

"You really are crazy, aren't you?"

"Maybe." She shrugged. "Of course, they say the crazy never know they're crazy. So, if you think you might be, does that automatically mean that you're not?

"Good question," she went on, responding to herself. "But, I'm not the one in cuffs, am I?"

"Speaking of crazy, though," she continued again, having seemingly abandoned the pretense of two-way conversation. She crossed to a window in the door and peeked out. "You should use that as a defense. What do they call it? Innocent by reason of insanity? Your love couldn't be contained and just, well, it just got out of control. Ed was making all kinds of threats. He even said he was going to spill everything to your beautiful wife. You lost it. Went crazy. It happens."

"I see. So I'm having an affair with a man in your scenario?"

"You know, she really is beautiful. You guys make...oh, sorry..." She tilted her head, raised an eyebrow. "MADE...such a perfect couple."

"You won't get away with this."

Cat snickered. "Said every wrongfully accused, innocent sap in every book and every movie. You're so cliché, Dan. Did anyone ever tell you that? No good for a writer to be so cliché. And, anyways, look around, silly. I'm already getting away with it."

"Ronnie's probably listening to us right now."

"Stop calling him that!" Cat yelled.

"That-is-so-dis-re-spect-ful," she said, slapping her palm on the table with each syllable. "He's Constable Anderson to you. You should start remembering that. It couldn't hurt to play up the repentant criminal and get him to hate you less. He really hates you.

"And, anyways, he's not listening. He went to Sun Dried Tees downstairs. Then, he's going to Sugar Shack for an ice cream for me. Ilsa. Then Fran. Gotta love 'em. Two biggest gossips in Hope Town. He'll be a while."

"Maybe he's recording us."

"Oh, that's so cute. You think this isn't Hope Town. You're lucky they even found a room to put you in.

"You know what your problem is, Dan? You're too reserved. You probably could have stopped all this if you'd just been more aggressive. But, you're weak. I like strong men. Like Ronnie."

"Don't you mean fat?"

She conducted the air and sang, "Respect, Dan."

"So, was any of it real?"

"Dan." She stomped her right foot. "We already went over this. You've got to stop being such a cliché. It's hard to watch. You're making me wonder what I ever saw in you. Really. Did you think we had some grand romance or something?"

She flicked the air. "Oh, but of course, it was real. I had no idea we'd find Ed's body, though. That was…my goodness, that was just kismet. Could that have ended more perfect?

"And just so you know. You know, to perk you up a little bit." She pushed the back of her hand to her lips and talked through her fingers. "Because I know you're having kind of a rough day.

"I did fall for you. My goodness. I fell hard. You're so handsome. I might have done anything for you. But, that's just how manipulative you are, isn't Dan? You played me. And, I fell for you. Smoldering. That's what you are. Why…" Cat pressed her hands against her chest and spoke in a southern drawl. "Muh heart, it did go pitter-patter when y'all walked through those doors and into muh li-bary and into muh life.

"And then I find out you're Spanish. Rrrrr," she purred.

"Half Spanish."

She slapped him.

"Don't ruin this for me! Dan! My goodness. You ruin everything. What is wrong with you? Just let me have this one fantasy.

"You know, though." She paced in front of him. "I really hated hurting Thomas. I don't know why you did that. I guess you just figured it was time to get this thing going. People were starting to talk."

She shrugged.

308

"Oh well. He's just an old…oh, sorry…*was*…just an old man. He'd have been dead soon anyway."

Dan squeezed his eyes closed and shook his head. He opened his eyes and sneered at her. "You're sick, Cat."

"Why, thank you." She curtsied.

"Really, though. Listen. I don't want you to worry about getting a hold of Susan." She scrunched up her nose. "She probably wouldn't answer your call anyways.

"But, don't worry. I'll take care of all that."

"Cat."

"I'll even pick her up in Marsh Harbour."

Dan sprung to his feet. Or tried. The chains tightened and flung him back against the seat. He stood again as much as he could force.

"Cat. Seriously." He shook his head and fixed his eyes on her. "You don't go near her. You don't call her. You…"

Cat slapped him. She grabbed his face with both hands and pressed in against his cheeks. He could see her gritting her teeth. She shouted:

"Listen! You don't talk to me like that. Ever! You show me the respect I deserve. You clearly underestimate the situation. I won. You lost."

She shoved his head.

"You're nothing, Dan…Oh, but you get me. You really get me. Are you sure we can't make this work?"

He glared.

She waited, then: "Oh, lighten up, silly. You're freaking out over nothing. I'll get her and bring her to you. Well, hopefully. Those waters between Marsh Harbour and Hope Town…they can be really treacherous."

She slipped into innocent coquettishness. "She may not make it."

Dan lost control. He shoved up, held his stance. He thrust forward, pulling his arms tight against the chains. His biceps bulged. Veins popped out on his neck. "Stay away from my wife!" he yelled.

The table inched away from him. He flashed his eyes down and threw a foot forward to gain leverage. Then he leaned into the table and it slowly squeaked away from the wall.

"Dan? What are you doing? You're going to—"

All at once he jumped and yanked his hands up. The table flipped, taking him with it. He crashed against the far wall, moaning. Most of his restraints slid up and over the legs of the table and he bounced up and darted at Cat. She screamed and ran to the door. But he flipped back, losing his balance and almost crashing to the floor. He flashed his eyes back. The chains connected to the handcuffs on his left wrist hadn't come completely loose and had snagged around the edge of one of the table's lags. He whip-snapped them loose and spun and rushed at her again.

She scurried through the door and slammed the opening closed. Dan heard metal sliding against metal. She laughed. "Dan! Stop! You're scaring me. You better behave or you'll—"

Dan lurched forward and banged against the door. She screamed and shifted back. He pressed his hand against the ache in his side and sucked in air. Her face appeared in the window again.

"Dan? Do you hurt? You have no one to blame but yourself.

"Listen. silly," she continued. "I'm going to leave now. I know. I know. I'd love to stay too. So sorry. But I've really got to go. Best of luck with everything. So, just so I'm clear, should I tell Susan about us or did you want to?

"You know what?" she added, quickly, shaking her head. "Never mind. I'll take care of it. You have enough to worry about."

Thirty-Three

Susan blew out.

A framed photo of her family rested on a side table to her left and she picked up the image and dropped it face up into her lap. She dabbed at her eyes with a Kleenex. Her phone also sat to her side and she shifted her eyes to the left, glancing at the display through her peripheral vision. Dark. She scowled. She jabbed her hand to the phone and flipped the cell face down, then focused back on the photo. Ryan. His little body. His laugh. His...Her eyes moistened again and she felt a grin creeping across her face. His staticky hair. She raised her hand to her mouth and pressed her fingers to her lips. She tilted her head.

Leave it to her husband to have had the foresight to know that they'd be forever thankful they'd had the portrait printed. She chuckled. So old school. One would think he was an old man the way he held on to outdated ways of doing things. No one bothered with anything physical anymore. Virtual was in. Actual hands-on photos were becoming rarer every day. But Dan—she whimpered— he'd insisted. And now it was as if she could still caress her son.

She peeked across the room at her desk, at her supposed good intentions. She'd had her assistant, Josh, reshuffle her appointments so she could stay home and research her latest stack of contracts and broken agreements—another case that amounted to nothing more than the inevitable consequences of one person's blind greed or, according to some (and, more each day, according to her) corruption. She'd spent the last couple of days studying and organizing. And she'd made some pretty solid progress. At least she had until her conversation with Dan. That had stopped everything. He'd called several times after they talked but she'd ignored the ringing, even left the room to silence him. She'd returned, but he hadn't. She'd tried him, tapping her foot, then rising to pace and fidget. But no answer. She refused to try again, to be the one that folded. And still—still!—nothing from him.

She bolted from her seat and halted, briefly paralyzed, staring across the room at her work. In an instant, she dashed forward and swung her arms and torso like a madwoman across the surface of her desk. Stacks exploded into disparate sheets that scattered and flitted around the room. She watched, mesmerized. The room drifted, as if in slow motion, circling and taunting her. The documents descended one by one to create the world's most boring mosaic on the floor around her.

The phone buzzed and rang, breaking into her trance. She spun, hesitated, and lurched forward—all at once. But she skidded on the traction-less papers scattered across the floor and tumbled, crashing hard with an "mmmph" onto her side. She crawled the rest of the way and grabbed at the cell.

"Hello."

Silence.

"Hello?"

She pulled the phone away from her face and glanced at the screen.

Dan
Missed Call

"Damn."

She tossed the phone back on the table and struggled to her seat, sucking in any air unlucky enough to be within striking distance. She waited. And waited. Then she snatched the cell off the table and palmed the device between her legs, alternating between obscuring and revealing the display, willing the phone to vibrate. Finally, she flipped her cell face up and hit redial. She exhaled intently, expelling the imprisoned oxygen (now carbon dioxide) from her lungs. She darted her eyes from side to side.

She waited.

"Hello."

A woman's voice answered. Susan slid the phone away from her face, just as she had seconds ago, and peeked at the screen. She pressed the device back against her cheek.

"Cat?"

"You remember. See, I knew we had a connection. I told Dan just that. But, he kept saying, 'No, she'll be jealous.' Men. I think they want us to fight, don't you? Boosts their egos."

"What do you want, Cat?"

"Well, I would point out that you actually called me." She paused. Susan could hear her breathing. "But I can tell you're really not in the mood. You should watch your anger issues, Susan. You and Dan both. Blood pressure, dear."

"Cat. Shut up. What do you want?"

"I'm going to let that slide, too," Cat said. "I know it can be stressful to have a loved one in jail."

The room blurred and tilted and threatened to spin. Susan bit her lip. She edged forward and slid with a bump to the floor.

"Jail? Is Dan in jail?"

"Yes. Susan. You didn't know? Oh my goodness. I'm so sorry. I wouldn't have said anything if I'd realized. You'd think he'd call you right away. First, really. I'm telling you, men are so frustrating sometimes. You know what I'm talking about. I must say I don't blame him, though. You can be a wee bit judgmental, my dear. But, I want you to know, I'm here for you."

Susan stared across the room at an outside window. A breeze knocked a branch chaotically against the glass. Finally, she spoke.

"Cat, I don't want or need you to be here for me. I don't know why you have Dan's phone and I don't care right now."

"I just—"

"I don't care, Cat. Is there a number I can reach him at?"

"Who? Dan?"

After a moment, she realized the questions weren't rhetorical. "Yes. Of course, Dan. Who else am I going to ask about?"

"Temper," Cat singsonged.

"But, no," she went on. "I'm afraid not. Dan wanted me to take care of everything personally and let you know."

"I thought you just said you thought he'd called."

"Whoops. I guess I did…caught me. But don't worry. He wanted me to make sure of everything. I can pick you up in Marsh Harbour. He wanted me—"

"Cat. I have no intention of having anything to do with you. And I most certainly don't want you to pick me up. I'll be fine. Just make sure Dan knows I'm coming and not

315

to say anything to anybody about anything until I get there. I'll act as his representation."

Susan heard nothing for several seconds. Finally, Cat said, soft, "Susan. That hurts my feelings."

"But," Cat continued, apparently having recovered. "I know you're upset. And like I said, I'm going to let you off the hook. But, are you sure you don't want me to pick you up? I think you'll be glad I did." Cat's voice melted into melody again. "I have some things to tell you about."

Then in a pointed voice: "You'll want to hear them before you see Dan."

"No, I..."

"Susan, please...Wait a minute." Cat breathed. "Did he already tell you we're together? He was supposed to wait so we could do it together. He figured that was best."

Susan gritted her teeth.

"But, really, Susan. Not another word. I'll pick you up. You'll want to hear what I have to tell you. Trust me."

"I told you no."

Susan hung up, sorry only that current technology made slamming a receiver down impossible—this disconnection felt too passive. She needed the aggression. She reached above her and banged the phone several times on the side table. Pressing against the chair for leverage, she stood and crossed to her recently cleared desk and retrieved her laptop then returned to her chair and flipped up the screen. She searched for flights and found a red-eye to Ft. Lauderdale and a morning Bahamian Airways departure to Marsh Harbour. She'd arrive late the following morning.

For too long, she fixated ahead at emptiness. The room swarmed around her and melted into a Salvador Dali dreamscape. She pushed herself to her feet and walked somnambulist-like to the kitchen where she gulped a glass of water, before dragging herself back into the office. She glared at the floor, at the array of documents covering the carpet. She regretted having behaved so rashly before. But only because she'd used up her one dramatic-yet-pointless sweep for the foreseeable future. This was the moment the fury might really have done her some good. She kicked through the papers and pushed as many flying about the room as she could.

Then she dropped into her chair, hung her head, and sobbed.

She called Josh and explained to him that a family emergency had come up and she wasn't sure how long she'd be away. Hard to say with these things. She apologized for causing so much chaos, again. As any good assistant would, he assured her that everything would be taken care of and not to worry, to let him know if there was anything he could do. The firm seemed to have learned to adapt to her unpredictability since Ryan's death, but their patience wouldn't last much longer. She plucked a paper off the floor, glanced at the title to make sure the sheet was nothing important, then tore off a scrap and crossed to her desk. She grabbed a pen out of a drawer and scribbled, '*Take firm to thank you dinner,*' then tossed both onto the desktop. But, she immediately swept the pen and paper onto the floor with the rest of the refuse. She paused, dropped to her knees and lifted the note back onto the surface of her desk. She'd want to make sure she saw that later.

Susan paced for a few minutes. She sat, stood, sat again, tossed the phone over in her hands several times. She gazed out the window and reviewed her office. The room was a mess. She closed her eyes and inhaled deeply.

Then, without lifting the phone from her lap, she hit redial. After a moment, she held the phone to her ear and waited for Cat to answer.

"Hello."

"Okay."

Thirty-Four

"Sir. There's no answer. Would ye like to try a different number?"

"Shhh."

"Excuse me?"

"Please. Just…I…"

On the other end of the line, Dan could hear Susan's outgoing message. "…next flight. I'll get there tomorrow morning. Cat called. She offered to pick me up in Marsh Harbour…so I said—"

"Sir, would you like to try a different number? Yes or no?"

Dan glanced across the room at Constable Anderson. He stalled, waited, but there was no more of Susan's voice.

"Please try the same number again."

"Sir, we tried it three times. Is there another number ye like to call?"

"Can you just call it one more time? Please."

"No, Sir. Ye can try again in 15 minutes."

He nodded and replaced the receiver, then grabbed at the handset again and banged it several times against the cradle. The phone gushed out a ring each time like a man exhaling a wheeze with every blow to his chest. Constable Anderson jumped up from his desk and stormed across the main room of the police station.

"Hey! Stop that now."

Dan tossed the receiver and stepped forward, thrusting his arms onto his waist and recognizing immediately that he looked like some kind of lunatic superhero. He chuckled and dropped his head. The corded handset swung over the side of the desk.

The policeman skidded to a stop and spun to Inspector Johnson. "A little help here."

Johnson wrote at a table in a corner. He didn't look up. "Mr. Harris. Constable Anderson like ye to stop."

Anderson huffed out a loud sigh. He pivoted back to Dan. The constable rubbed his eyes with his fists. "Oh, poor me. I'm just a rich writer that does nothing all day."

Dan laughed. "I don't know what that is you're doing, but keep it up. I've been getting bored in here."

Constable Anderson dropped his arms and glared. "Except kill innocent people."

"So, and please correct me if I've got this wrong, if they weren't innocent, you'd be okay with—"

"Mr. Harris." Inspector Johnson stood and crossed to the two. "Like to ask ye some questions."

The inspector motioned to the room the policemen had been holding Dan in and the three walked inside. Dan had managed to stand the table upright again before they'd returned this morning. He'd even succeeded in (after a surprising bit of effort) recreating the policemen's 'elaborate' chaining system. As far as they knew, he'd waited placidly for their return. In fact, they'd found him sleeping on the table he'd been secured to.

As Dan passed Constable Anderson, he whispered, "And it's who, not that."

"What?" Anderson stopped.

The inspector directed Dan to the chair he'd been in before, with Cat. The two officers sat opposite him.

"Now. Thomas…" Johnson began and scrutinized some notes.

"Listen," Dan said. "I've got to get a hold of my wife. I heard her message. It said tomorrow, but I don't know what that means. Is today tomorrow, or is tomorrow…tomorrow?" He glared at Constable Anderson. "This is all your fault. It's already after noon. If you'd just come back yesterday and let me call like you promised."

The constable shrugged. "I saw Cat. She said you needed some time alone. They were your own words."

"No, they weren't. They were hers. Don't you see? She's setting me up."

"Setting ye up?" Johnson asked.

Dan nodded. "Yeah, framing me."

"Ye said that before. Ye have any proof?"

Constable Anderson harrumphed. "Proof."

"We all know Cat knew Ed and lied about it. Ed's mother killed his father. There's got to be something there. Look into it."

"Not sure I see a connection, Boss," Johnson said.

"I thought you said you didn't know him." Anderson leaned back in his chair, grinning.

"I don't. I just did some…Wow. You must be really bad at your job." He focused back on the inspector. "Listen, you don't have to believe me now. But my wife. I have to get a hold of her. It's urgent."

"Forget your wife." Constable Anderson slid his hair to the side—apparently the move wasn't just for Cat's benefit. "You didn't seem to care about her the other night. Besides, your wife doesn't want to have anything to do with you. That's what she told Cat."

Dan flashed at Anderson.

321

"Yeah," the constable continued. "She's done with you. Cat told her everything. How you took advantage of her. How you were drunk. Two nights in a row. You have a problem, Boss?"

Dan shifted to Inspector Johnson. The inspector glanced down and pulled out his cell. He studied the screen.

"One minute," he said, standing and facing away from the table. He spoke softly into the phone.

While he talked, Constable Anderson smirked at Dan, at one point giggling and making faces at him. Dan smiled at Anderson.

"Yes. I was ten once, too. Don't worry. You'll grow out of it."

Constable Anderson leapt out of his chair and pulled his arm back. Inspector Johnson grabbed his elbow.

"What the...what do ye think yer doing?"

He tossed Anderson's arm away and pivoted to Dan.

"I need to go," Johnson said. "We can continue this later."

"But, my wife. I—"

"Anderson will make sure you get another chance to call."

Constable Anderson threw out his arms and started to protest. Inspector Johnson's eyes grew wide and he motioned to the door. The two walked out. Dan could hear them arguing. Finally, Inspector Johnson poked his head into the room.

"Dan?"

Dan stood.

"Ye can make yer call now. I'll be back in an hour or so."

He heard the inspector say, "Constable, let him try his wife again. Now."

After a moment, Anderson responded. "Fine. But only once. This isn't a hotel."

The constable appeared in the doorway and curtsied.

"Thanks?" Dan quirked his head. "I think. You know, curtsies are for women. Men bow."

Constable Anderson's face flashed into a scowl and he slammed the door.

"Anderson!" Dan heard Inspector Johnson yell.

"What?"

"Open that door now and let him make his call."

"But he—"

"Now."

The door squeaked open and Inspector Johnson motioned to Dan. The inspector stormed out of the police station, mumbling, "Now, I's going to be late."

Anderson glowered at Dan. He gestured to the phone. "Go ahead."

Dan picked up the receiver and rotated away. He spoke to the operator and explained that he needed to place a collect call and gave the woman Susan's number.

"One moment, S—"

The line went silent.

"Hello?" Dan waited. "Hello?"

He twisted and glanced behind him. Constable Anderson had pressed a finger on one of the phone's plungers. The policeman smirked.

"No more calls. You're done. I don't care what Johnson says. This is my island. My phone. My rules."

Dan exhaled. "Please. I know you don't like me. I get that. But, I have to get a hold of my wife. I…" He stopped talking and studied Constable Anderson. The man would never listen.

Anderson seemed to interpret Dan's silence as weakness. The policeman shoved into his face and yelled, "My island! My rules!"

Dan paused and took a breath. "Sorry. I really have to talk to my wife."

He swung the receiver at Constable Anderson's head, knocking him hard enough that the man lost his balance and stumbled to the side.

"What the…?"

Dan tossed the handset away. The receiver skidded across the surface of the desk and crashed onto the floor with a smack, bouncing into the air as the spirals stretched tight. Shards exploded and splintered across the tile. Dan rushed forward and shoved into Anderson's chest with both hands. This time, though, the man hardly moved.

The policeman squinted his eyes and breathed into Dan's face, "You've done it now, Boss."

Anderson punched forward and hit Dan squarely in the chest. Dan stumbled back and knocked against the desk, shoving the workstation squealing into the wall with a thud. The phone sat near a corner and the base shifted, but didn't fall, merely balanced precariously on the edge of the desktop, jutting out into nothing. Dan scurried in the opposite direction of Constable Anderson, scooping up the broken receiver as he ran and yanking the coils toward him. The device tumbled from the surface, and Dan dove and caught the phone in his hands. He skidded and smacked against the desk.

He sprung to his feet and rushed toward Anderson, but the cable connecting the phone to the wall pulled taut and jerked him back. He glanced behind him and pulled again.

And again. The desk had pinned the cord, and therefore the phone, against the wall.

Constable Anderson darted after Dan, who scrambled around the station and slid to the ground, feeling along the base of the phone as he did, searching for where the cable connected into the device. He felt the port, under the base, but the cord wound around pins designed to minimize any loose wiring. He had two choices. Unwind the extra cable to get to the plug or pull the desk out enough that he could yank out the cord from the wall. Only one of those options was realistic.

A flash came from out of nowhere and knocked the phone out of Dan's hands. The device shot up but froze in mid-air and banged to the ground as the wiring reached its limit. Dan pried at the legs of the desk and managed to wrench the furnishing away from the wall. Immediately, though, the desk shifted back, slamming Dan's fingers into the open space he'd just managed to create. He jerked back. And again. He finally extricated his hand. A pen, paper, ruler, scissors…glitter…all tumbled off the surface of what was apparently an arts and crafts worktable. Dan grabbed at the scissors. He bounced to his feet. Anderson shifted back.

"You better think hard about this, Mr. Harris. Anything happens to me…you hurt me even a little bit, you'll never leave this country."

Dan glanced at his hand. "They're only scissors. Don't be so melodramatic. I just want to talk to my wife. Just let me call Susan. Cat's a madwoman."

"Not going to happen, Boss."

"Well, then…"

Dan shrugged. He stepped toward the phone and grabbed the device just below the cradle, extending it out in front of him. He snipped the outgoing cable. Constable Anderson grinned.

"Well, now you've done it, Boss. Now you'll never get to call."

"I'll find another way...Sorry about this. But I really need to talk to my wife."

Dan lunged forward and swung one last time with as much force as he could muster. The phone connected with a clap against the side of the constable's head. Plastic scattered around the room. Anderson collapsed to the ground, silent. His eyes fluttered and his head rocked to the side. He slumped.

Dan panicked. He rushed to the man, crouching over him and pressing his fingers against the constable's neck, fishing through the excess flesh to find a vein. He felt a pulse. He exhaled, squeezed his eyes closed, and sunk back onto his feet, pressing his head into his hands.

A phone. He needed a phone. Otherwise, all this would have been for nothing. Somewhere lost in the morass of man laid out on the floor before him was exactly what Dan needed. He just had to find it. So he went digging, so to speak, and after an unsettling and inappropriately grueling struggle to massage the constable's bulky stomach out of the way, he managed to pull Anderson's cell out of the holder hidden under his belly. Dan flipped the case open. The screen lit up with a photo of Cat on the display. Dan eyed the man on the floor. He shook his head.

"You have a wife. And a kid. Kids!"

The cell was passcode protected. He'd seen the constable make calls before, and the man had never entered a code. At least Dan had never noticed him doing so. The device had to have fingerprint protection. One by one, he smashed the tips of Constable Anderson's fingers against the home button. The phone turned on each time but never unlocked. He repeated the process. Still no access.

Dan scanned the police station. A door stood slightly open. Dan had noticed Inspector Johnson standing in the doorway before, returning with a notepad. Must be a supply closet. He scampered over and scanned inside the storage area. The room was a mess (it must have been decorated by Cat). He slid several items to the side. Then some more. Finally, he discovered what he'd hoped to find. A rope. He hurried over to Constable Anderson on the floor.

"I'm really sorry about this," Dan said to the unconscious constable as he secured the ties around the man's arms and legs. "But you left me no other options."

He tugged on the restraints. Secure. Constable Anderson wasn't going anywhere. Dan hadn't been able to find any kind of a cloth he could use to gag the man so he grabbed the scissors and cut around the bottom of his t-shirt. He'd look ridiculous, but that was a small price to pay. If anyone saw him, they'd just assume he was a wannabe muscle-head and shake their heads at the American's crazy sense of fashion. They already thought he was a murderer; he'd just be a killer with a bad sense of style.

Gag in place, he set Anderson's cell across the room on a high shelf and laid the scissors to the side. Dan returned to the constable. He bent and nudged him. Nothing. He shook him a little harder. Slowly, Constable Anderson opened his eyes and blinked. He jerked, darting at his ties.

"Wdthhldyuthkyd-g."

"Your cell phone is right over there." Dan pointed across the room. "There's a pair of scissors too. You'll be able to free yourself and call for help once you can get to it. I'm really sorry. But you left me no choice. My wife needs me. Inspector Johnson should be back soon, so there's also that. I just need a bit of head start."

Constable Anderson grunted and screamed anger at Dan out of his eyes.

Dan stood and crossed to the door. He turned.

"I'm really sorry."

Thirty-Five

Dan cracked the door and peeked out. The air outside felt muted and oppressive, and Dan could hear rumbling in the distance—a drawn-out, saddened bubbling that lingered for what felt like several minutes and left him feeling inexplicably as if the yearning had ended too soon. A storm was imminent. And he was free. He slid a foot forward.

The police station rested above the post office in the building that butted up to the north side of the Sugar Shack and Sun Dried Tees. Unlike the entries of that structure, however, the doorway to these offices opened to a solid but exposed stairway that jutted out perpendicular to the building and descended to a small courtyard and side street, away from the town center. Good. Mostly. Unfortunately, that also meant he couldn't know for sure who might be lurking close by. He paused, listened. Adrenaline pulsed through his body and he had to shove his fists into his pockets to keep from fidgeting as Victor had on…

He stopped, pulled out his hands.

No time for caution, he thought. Any dilly dallying would only risk Johnson's return or, even worse, Anderson's somehow getting loose and surprising him still strategizing on the landing. He bounced down the steps in twos and stopped again. Listened. He rushed to a corner and spied around the buildings onto Queen's Highway.

"Act casual, act casual," he mumbled to himself as he stepped...

He jumped back.

Inspector Johnson.

He edged forward and peeked around the corner again.

The inspector was strolling out of Sun Dried Tees with a woman who looked just like Heidi, if the girl had aged about 40 years (and set up shop in the Bahamas). Ilsa, he assumed (he'd never actually met the woman), tagged close behind Johnson, caressing his shoulder as she brushed by, then sliding her hand down his arm to lead him by the elbow. She twisted and pulled him closer. He, almost imperceptibly, shifted at the same moment and moved gently away from her. She either didn't notice or didn't care because she continued resting her everything against his forearm, lingering.

Suddenly she pulled away abruptly and focused, pointing in Dan's direction.

He jerked his head behind the wall. Excess adrenaline came rushing back at him like a rabid bull. (Do bulls get rabies? He'd have to look that up—later.) He glanced at his hand to make sure his most-recent wound hadn't started bleeding again. He waited motionless for several seconds, then tiptoed toward the stairway and paused, focused like Ilsa, straining to sense any footsteps that might be coming toward him. He darted his eyes around the courtyard. There was nowhere to go. He couldn't return to the office. Anderson was there, restrained and, perhaps more importantly, awake. Certainly angry—strike that, definitely furious. There was the space on the opposite side of the stairwell. He could hide there. But, cowering wasn't an option. This was a time for action. He had to stop Cat. He had to warn Susan.

He crept over to the courtyard entrance. As he did, a tall silhouette crossed into the opening and Dan inched back, fighting to blend in with the nearest wall (an effort that didn't go well). But no one came through the walkway. He scooted to the edge and peeked out.

Inspector Johnson was no more than ten feet from the alley, but heading north, away from the station and no longer facing Dan. He gazed toward Sun Dried Teas. Ilsa was also gone. He followed the policeman with his eyes until the inspector was past the barriers and had turned to head toward the Methodist church, then he slipped into the town center, moving south, determined to make up any time he'd lost and doing his best to look as calm and inconspicuous as he could. As long as he acted as normally as any other local strolling down Queen's Highway, no one would jump to the conclusion that he'd just attacked and hogtied their constable. So he took steady, deliberate breaths as he walked, stopping at one point to pretend to study the horizon and smiling and waving at any passersby he encountered—only two.

When he reached the wooded roadway that led away from Hope Town's version of a main drag, he twisted and scanned the area before speed-walking the rest of the way until he reached the small street that led to Cat's house. He disappeared into the trees surrounding her home.

The building appeared to be deserted. Though, really, how else would her house look in the middle of the day? He crept to a side window and peered in, then tapped on the glass and ducked. He waited a moment before slowly straightening and scanning through the room. Empty. He rushed around to the front and bounced up the steps to the deck and her front entrance.

He knocked.

No answer.

He knocked again.

Still no answer.

She was gone. He was too late. He spun and fell back against the door.

"Think," he whispered to himself.

There'd been a phone. He'd noticed a phone the last time he was in her house. A landline. That was why it had stood out to him. Who has a landline anymore? A paned window was set to the right of the door and he peeked in once more to make sure Cat wasn't home and to search for the phone. He didn't see either.

He pulled back, ready to punch his way through the glass. He froze. The last thing he needed was to bleed to death. His losing blood was starting to become an issue. He ripped off his shoe and paused, then banged it against the glass. The rubber sole ricocheted out of his hand and the sneaker flew across her deck and rolled into the harbor with a *plop*, as if the shoe were nothing more than a flying fish.

"aaaAAHH!" he yelled.

He glanced at his feet.

"Oh well."

He pulled off his other shoe and squished his fist inside. He wasn't taking any chances this time. He faced the window and steeled himself. Instead of the glass itself, he eyed the wood bar separating the two panes and slammed against the divider with all his strength. He thought. The wood splintered, but nothing more.

"You have got to be kidding," he muttered, glancing at his hand. "I don't have time for this."

He slipped the shoe back onto his foot, made a fist and punched his knuckles against the wood.

A thick split spread across the bar. The wood cracked. It didn't break, but he felt weakness. He tapped against the splintered divider, intending only to test its strength. But instead the upper sheet dropped almost instantly and he had to jump back to keep his toes from being severed by the falling glass. The pane shattered across the deck. Shards splashed into the water. He grinned. He leaned away from the window, lifted his socked foot behind the knee of his other leg, and pressed a finger against the inside of the top of the bottom pane. He covered his eyes, flicked the glass (then again, more firmly) and sprung back. The pane tumbled out and somehow didn't explode against the deck, just bounced with a dead sound a few times before the sheet stopped moving.

He reviewed the area to make sure no one had heard the sound (as one does when engaging in criminal activity), then he hopped forward on his shoed foot and shoved his arm through the new opening. He stretched to the lock and twisted, pushed on the handle. The door wouldn't give. The knob was still locked. Or, he sighed, realizing the more likely scenario, maybe her house had never been locked in the first place. He twisted the lever back and tried again. The door opened.

He chuckled. None of this had been necessary. He kicked the door and jumped inside.

He hurried to the sofa, dropped to the cushions, tore off his remaining shoe and both socks, and bolted back up—all in one fluid, seemingly choreographed movement. He scanned the room. No phone. At least not one visible. Although, one could miss a semi-truck in all that chaos. He squeezed his eyes tight. Where had the phone been?

He realized far too quickly that thinking wouldn't do him any good. At least not now. So he flipped open his eyes and darted around the room, throwing piles of clothes into the air and kicking at the random knickknacks flung across the floor. Nothing. At least nothing he could fashion into a communication device.

He forced himself back to slow and methodical. He paused...breathed in...closed his eyes. After a moment, he drifted his eyes open again, gentle, ready to receive. He glanced toward the kitchen. There, on the counter, as if bathed in rays of sun and accompanied by the harmonious voices of angels, rested the afternoon's holy grail.

He scrambled across the house, bouncing his butt on the bed, and snatched the telephone handset out of its cradle. He hovered his fingers over the square of numbers on the face and waited to hear the dial tone.

Silence. He played pizzicato on the phone's plungers. Nothing.

Again—tap, tap, tap, tap.

Nothing.

He hurled the receiver across the room. The cord yanked the base and the rest of the phone pitched off the counter after, clanging against the cupboard doors with a half-hearted ring. Thunder erupted in the distance as if a grand conductor had cued the cymbals. He squeezed his eyes closed and threw his head toward the storm.

"Aaaah!"

Sucking in a deep breath, he let his eyes fall closed. He exhaled. Inhaled. Exhaled. Slow. Sustained. Calming...Voided. He slid into a sort of meditation. What next? Focus. This was it. Susan was depending on him. He'd learned on his and Cat's first outing together that the librarian barely tolerated anyone with the gall to leave their cell phone unattended. She'd certainly have taken her phone, but...he scanned the room.

Well, this would definitely be a waste of time. On the plus side, the house looked pretty much the same as it had before. She'd never even know he'd been here, apart from the hard-to-miss evidence of his initial (and, as had turned out, unnecessary) breaking and entering.

He returned to the rush.

Jamie. The young man might be at the coffee house. He'd definitely let Dan make a call. Of course, he'd have to make the trek across town, which could be risky. But he...oh, and one more thing...he hadn't exactly left the boy on the best of terms the last time. But, Jamie must have told his parents and they could go together to the police. That would convince them to take him seriously. Regardless, his options were dwindling.

So Dan ran out the door, jumping over the broken glass and past the oddly intact pane to the stairs leading from the deck. He sprinted up Cat's dirt entrance, with the occasional *ow* and *oh* (he was, after all, barefoot). But, as he rounded the roadway to Queen's Highway, he barreled into an elderly couple. He threw out his arm to catch the woman by the elbow as she was about to topple over.

"Oh my," she exclaimed.

"I'm so sorry, Ma'am."

"Young man! You—" the man began.

"Oh Harry. I'm fine." The woman twisted and focused on Dan.

"My husband gets so protective of me. I'm just glad you have such good reflexes, dear. Quite the sportsman, aren't you? I'd be flat on my...well, I wouldn't be standing here talking to you, now would I? That's for certain."

She smiled and pushed her arm out to greet him. "I'm Mildred. The thorny one is my husband Harry."

Dan shook her hand, then pivoted to her husband. "Nice to meet you both."

He whipped around and dashed off again down the 'highway.' He stopped abruptly and spun back to them.

"I'm sorry to be so blunt. But I'm in the middle of a bit of a crisis. You wouldn't happen to have a cell phone I could use, would you? I'd be happy to pay you."

"Just...one...sec..." Mildred fumbled in her purse. "Ah. Here you go. And don't be silly. No nee—"

"Of course you can't use our phone," Harry said, snatching the cell out of his wife's hand. "You practically bowl us over and knock us to the ground. Why, you could have broken Mildred's hip. Some nerve you have. What—"

"Harry, give him that phone."

"I'm not giving him our phone. He's probably one of those hoodlums that will just take it and run off with it. Just look at him. That shirt. He's not even wearing shoes. He's probably homeless."

"Harry, you're being ridiculous. He most certainly isn't homeless, he's...what's your name, dear?"

"Dan."

"Dan is clearly not a threat to us. Why, he helped me."

"Mildred," Harry began.

"Give him the phone."

"Mildred, I am not going to just hand our lives over to him."

"Harry!" She slapped her hip. "Give him the phone."

"I will n—"

"Yes or no?" Dan snapped. The couple stopped talking.

"I'm sorry. I don't mean to be rude, but I really need to place this call. Now. My wife..." His voice began trembling. Too much stress. Too much fear. Too much

336

arguing. He glanced toward the sound of drums. Too much thunder.

"Harry!" Mildred yelled. "Give the man the phone. Can't you see he's upset?"

Harry rocked his head, mumbling incomprehensible gibberish as he did. He gritted his teeth and shoved out his hand. "Just make it quick."

"Harry!" The woman shifted to Dan, resting her hand on his extended arm. "Take all the time you need, dear. We'll just be right over here…give you some privacy. And this is our honeymoon, if you can believe it."

She bellowed to the sky, "But it may be a short marriage if this keeps up."

Dan thanked the woman and jogged to the side of the road. He had to concentrate a little to remember his wife's number—he never had to actually dial the sequence—but it came to him in a rush and he punched it in. The phone rang and rang…and rang. He cast his eyes to Mildred and Harry, attempted an awkward half-smile. Finally, he heard a confused Susan.

"Hello?"

"Susan!" he gushed out. "Susan. It's me. I'm using someone else's phone. Listen to me. Cat—"

"How…? Did they arrest you? Cat said you…"

Dan heard Cat's voice in the distance.

"Is that Dan?"

"Yes, he…what? No. Of course not…NO!"

"Susan, what's going on? She's—"

"Cat wants me to give her my phone, but…no….no…"

"Susan, don't give her the phone."

"No…"

Dan could hear muffled, blunt voices, as if Susan were covering the mouthpiece and arguing with Cat. After a moment, he heard a scuffle and a static sound and Susan's voice in the background.

"Give me my phone…

"Dan," he heard his wife shout. "I want to talk to you when Cat's done. Don't let her disconnect."

"Dan?" Cat's voice came on the line, clear.

He could hear her grinning.

"Hold on just a minute," she said. "Yes, you're right. I know. I told her."

Dan waited for her to finish.

"I'm talking to you, silly."

"What?" Dan said.

"Yes. Fine. I'll tell her. One minute.

"Susan, Dan was wondering if you'd get him some bottles of water. He said they don't have enough in the police station and he's really thirsty."

"Let me talk to him."

"Hold on."

Then louder: "She wants to talk to you."

"Well, put her on." Dan glanced at Harry and Myrtle. He forced through a grin at them and held up two fingers. Myrtle blew him a kiss. He tried to smile, not sure how to respond, but was sure his look came across as more bemusement than anything.

Cat was gibbering on about something. "…I'll tell her, but I don't think she'll like it…Susan, he says get some water first. He wants to talk to me…yes, I don't know…I know!…men, right? Yes, right over there."

He'd been repeating Cat's name throughout her invented report. Though, he could have been trying to entice an actual cat over for all the good it did. She spoke again, sharp this time.

"You think you can warn her against me? Is that what you're doing?"

"Cat, I told you. Leave her alone."

"Oh…Okay.

"Sheesh," she went on, hardly pausing. "You must think I'm really stupid. Did you honestly think it would be that easy?"

Dan heard thunder and twisted toward Marsh Harbour. And the lighthouse. And Susan.

"Cat, you really haven't thought this through, have you?"

"What are you talking about, Dan? What haven't I thought through?"

"If anything happens to her…"

"Wait. Are you going to tell me that if anything happens to her, they'll know you're innocent?"

He nodded, threw out his free hand, jerked.

"But, you escaped," she continued.

He froze.

"What? How…?"

"Ronnie called. Yeah. Couldn't have been more than 30 seconds ago, well, was 30 seconds ago. Now maybe more like a couple of minutes. Yeah. He's free. And really perturbed. I mean really. They're probably scouring that enormous city for you right now. Not a lot of places to hide. Naturally, he was worried about my safety. Says you called me a madwoman. Not sure how I feel about that. I mean, I'm flattered, but…

"You know," she went on. "Some might even say that if anything happens to Susan now, it's kind of your…well, you get it, silly. Who's to say? But, then again, they're probably right. I know I kind of agree."

Dan pressed his fingers against his forehead. Suddenly, the ache in his side was back and he dropped his hand and massaged his thumb into his ribs.

"So quiet now," Cat said. "If I'd realized it was that easy to shut…"

Dan felt what he thought was a sprinkle on his cheek. He glanced up. The sky was still clear, but dark clouds were floating closer from the distance.

"I can prove it was you. I have a witness."

"Dan. You're being cute again. Look how desperate you are. If only…my goodness, if only things were different and—"

"You're not even listening to me. I said I have a witness."

"Oh, I heard you. I just don't care. You're talking about Jamie, right? I already took care of that, silly."

Dan's chest pulsed in and he started blinking. His eyes watered.

Harry called out, "Son, wrap it up." Mildred nudged him, but barely. Time to hang up. He turned to the couple and held up one finger this time.

"I'll confess," Dan said. "I'll confess. But only if Susan gets here safe and unharmed. I'll confess."

"Hmmm. Well, not sure I need you to do that. But, thanks. I'll keep that in mind."

Cat stopped. It sounded as if she were rubbing the phone against her shirt or somehow fumbling with the device. Her voice was distant. "Ahhh…there…"

"So, anyway," she said, loud again. "I was just saying, nice of you to think of me, but…oh, here comes Susan. That was quick. Time to…"

"Yes. Here she is…what?…"

"Cat."

340

"Oh. Okay. Are you sure?"

"Cat."

"Well, alright. But she'll be so disappointed."

"Cat."

"Dan, really. You shouldn't talk about your wife like that…"

"Cat!" he shouted into the phone.

"…telling you, she won't like it. But, if you insist. I'll tell her. Bye, love."

The phone went silent.

"Cat!

"Cat!"

Immediately, Dan redialed, waited, started pacing. Ring after ring after ring and Harry was walking toward him and saying something about time and jutting out his palm and Mildred was slapping her husband's shoulder and there was no answer and he hit redial and he felt like he would stumble and he did and he hit redial again and Harry was saying *now* and yelling at Mildred to *shut up* and Dan twisted away, tried to evade him. But too soon Harry was snatching the phone from his hand and he heard himself mumble *thank you* and he moved toward Hope Town and…

The world snapped back, and he spun and rushed to Mildred and Harry.

"Please. My name is Daniel Harris. Just remember that you saw me."

He started on his way again, then swung back and begged once more.

"And please. This number." He reached for the cell, but Harry drew away from him. Myrtle touched Dan's arm.

"What is it, dear?"

"Just hit redial. Keep trying the number I just called. Please. Susan. My wife is Susan. Tell her to stay in Marsh Harbour...get on a plane if she has to...anywhere away from Cat."

He spun again, tripping on his own feet, and stumbled toward the town center.

He could hear Harry and Mildred arguing behind him.

Thirty-Six

He ran.

Dan sprinted down Queen's Highway, dipping where the road fell and jumping where the earth bumped up. The roadway had never seemed as long as it did at this moment but, finally, he reached the town, scanning the center as he moved, watching for Constable Anderson or Inspector Johnson. This time, though, he hoped desperately to see them. Granted, he'd prefer Inspector Johnson, but at this point…

At the narrow street that led to the police station, he turned and hurried up the stairs. He threw open the door and scanned the office. The remains of his tussle with Anderson were everywhere, still strewn across the floor, joined this time by lengths of rope and the scrap from his shirt. But, other than the residual debris, the room was empty. He darted into his 'holding cell.' No one. He rushed out the front door.

Dan paused on the landing and considered his next steps. Warning the policemen, it would seem, was officially out of the question. Jamie was—he inhaled, sharp. Or was he? Cat could have been lying. Not like this would be the first time. She could have been fishing. Testing his reaction. The boy could be fine. And, if so…Dan skipped down the stairs. He froze, sliding off the edge of the step he'd pulled back on and cringing as he

343

thudded onto the next. The accented voice of a woman floated into the small courtyard.

"Inspector Johnson. Sir. Good day."

"Well, hello. Mrs. Galson, isn't it? So nice to see ye."

Close. They were too close. Dan hesitated, deliberated. Johnson might actually help him, he could…not worth the risk. The inspector might just as easily re-imprison Dan. And then no one would be helped. At least at the coffee house there'd be a phone, and he could try Susan again. Dan pivoted and started back up the stairs. He stopped. He'd be trapped if he continued. He spun and rushed toward the bottom. He could hide, duck into the opening between the stairs and the building's back wall.

He'd almost reached the courtyard floor when he caught the edge of Inspector Johnson coming through the small alleyway. He jumped over the railing to his right and backed against the staircase.

"Inspector," Dan heard the woman's voice call out. "Inspector. I was hoping I might speak with you."

Dan peeked over the edge of the steps. Johnson came strolling into the courtyard with Mrs. Galson.

"Of course. What can I do for ye?"

"You're from Nassau, no?"

Dan crouched. He could hear them droning on as their conversation resonated through the area, sounding as if they were ever-so-slowly creeping closer. He fought the impulse to look, to verify he was safe. Or not. But he couldn't risk glancing over the side again.

"…in my home country…"

A bee began circling Dan. He froze, then slid down and shifted back, eyeing the insect as he moved. He waved his hand in the pest's direction. Mrs. Galson and Inspector Johnson stopped talking. The bee flew off.

344

"Did you hear that?" the inspector said.

Pause.

"One minute, Ma'am."

Footsteps moved in Dan's direction.

"Bea…Oh. Hello, Inspector."

A third voice. Another woman.

"Wally," he heard Mrs. Galson say and he thought he caught the faint sound of kisses.

"Mrs. Wallace." The footfalls paused, shifted in the opposite direction. Dan heard a slide in the dirt. Mrs. Galson's back side poked into Dan's line of sight.

"Bea, one minute you're there and I'm talking to you, then I ask you a question and when you don't answer, I turn and you're not there anymore. People must think I'm senile."

"I just—"

"You can be so frustrating sometimes."

"*¡Mi madre! Eres una pesada.*"

"Hey. I understood that."

"Inspector, you know Mrs. Wallace? Wally?"

"Why yes. Hello Ma'am. We were at her house the other day to ask some questions. Offered us some sun tea."

"Yes, that's true. My best batch."

"Ye said then Mr. Harris came by to see ye."

"Well, yes. He did. So nice," Wally said. "He and Cat came by. You know, I'm really not sure what to think of that pairing. She's an odd one."

A pause rested over the group.

"Yes. Well, ye see, I had some more questions for Mr. Harris and I was just wondering if ye'd seen him since we spoke."

"No. Just the one time. Why?"

"Just want to ask him some questions."

345

He spoke again, "Mrs. Galson, ye interested in Nassau?"

"Oh Bea. Didn't you once live there?"

"Yes, but so long ago. It was just after I came from Spain, Inspector. My husband worked for First Bahamas National. You know the bank, Sir?"

"Of course. My mother…"

Dan sunk to the ground. They were going to be a while.

Suddenly, Dan heard screams and shuffling, frantic shuffling. Inspector Johnson said, "Just stay still. No…"

The women kept crying out, calling each other's names. Mrs. Galson stumbled back into plain view of Dan, waving her hands in front of her face, ducking and weaving. She twisted and froze, fixated in Dan's direction. Dan's eyes grew wide and he felt himself sinking, or at least trying to, farther into the dirt. But, the woman didn't move. She didn't react. Dan flicked his head, willing her to stop staring and return to the conversation, to at least move closer to the stairs so the inspector wouldn't, well, inspect the area. Dan raised his index finger to his mouth and pressed. He mouthed, "Shhhh."

Then he heard footsteps coming closer. Wally appeared in the opening and caressed Mrs. Galson's shoulder.

"Bea? Is everything okay, Bea? You look rather bewitched."

"Mrs. Galson?"

Wally turned and gasped. "Oh, my."

"Is everything all right, Ma'am?"

"Yes. Fine," Wally said. She eyed Dan quizzically and quickly shifted forward toward the stairs, out of Dan's sight.

"Excuse me. Inspector, why were you wondering about Dan? Mr. Harris?"

"Ye see him?"

Dan heard movement.

"No, no. I didn't see him. Just wondering about him. You don't think he could have been involved in that awful murder, do you?"

"Don't know that, Ma'am," the inspector said. "We're trying to figure all that out."

There was a lull. He spoke again.

"Ye sure ye didn't see him?"

Wally didn't respond. At least not at first. Dan braced, wondering what non-verbal conversation they might be having. Then he heard her mutter, "Well…no…no, I haven't."

"If ye see him, please tell him I'm looking for him. Need to clarify some things."

"Bea?" Wally's voice resounded in the square. "You've not seen him either, right?"

Mrs. Galson, though, simply continued her staring at Dan as he crouched down, smashed as far into the corner between the building and the stairs as he could force himself. He pleaded again with his eyes, entreating her to look away…why wasn't she looking away? Or even giving him up? Anything. Even being turned in would be better than this oppressive nothing that currently surrounded him. He motioned with his head once more. Turn. Walk. React. But she remained motionless and unflappable, as if her programming had simply malfunctioned.

Moisture beaded on his forehead. Sweat. Or rain. He glanced to the sky. Sweat.

"I," she finally said.

She paused, silent. Expressionless.

"Bea?" Wally said. "What is wrong with you? My land."

"Mrs. Galson, have ye seen him?"

Then he thought he caught a gentle grin and she stepped forward.

"Yes," Mrs. Galson continued. "Yes. I'm fine. So sorry. No, I've not seen the man. Just…all this talk of Nassau and the bank." Dan heard a sniff. "I just miss my Robert so much sometimes. *Que en paz descanse.*"

"Oh, Bea." Dan picked up footsteps approaching again. "We all miss—"

"Inspector," Mrs. Galson said and slid forward. Dan saw someone else pop into view and Bea's arm reached around them and guided them away. "Would you mind? I need to sit down. I feel a bit overcome."

"Yes, of course." More steps, shifting, the sound of dirt possibly morphing into the sounds of capture.

"Ye can sit on the step."

Dan saw a leg peek into the void.

"Ohh!" he heard her cry out, high-pitched.

"Bea, are you okay?"

"Yes, I…Inspector, I thought we could go up to your office. Be inside."

"Yes," Wally said. "Yes. That would be lovely."

"Ye don't want to climb those stairs, Ma'am. How about—"

"Please, Inspector. Some water, too."

She repeated, "I would like some water, also. Please."

There was no response from anyone for a moment. Finally, Inspector Johnson answered, "Certainly, Ma'am. Yes. Yes, of course."

Dan rose and pressed himself rigid against the corner of the staircase and building wall. He could see Johnson's head towering above the railing out of the corner of his eye, and he resisted the urge to turn and peek, to move. At least he tried. The instinct to survive won out, though, and he found himself shifting slightly and glancing in their direction. The inspector faced forward, but to the right, away from Dan, focused on someone else, probably Mrs. Galson. Several seconds passed, and Dan heard the door at the top of the stairs open and, after what seemed like an unnecessarily long pause, he caught the click as the entry closed.

At once, he shoved against the stairway and bolted forward. As he rounded the stairs, though, he stopped and squinted. A thin walkway led away from the square at the far end, presumably to Back Street. He shifted and stared a moment at the opening at the opposite end, exiting to Queen's Highway and the town center. Too many unknowns lay in that direction. He'd be less likely to be surprised by Constable Anderson's sudden return if he took the new route.

So he hurried to the split, sneaking a peek back one last time to make sure he was alone as he scrambled between the buildings. With each step, the structures pressed closer together and his escape path between them became more and more snug until, when he at last reached the end of the passage, he had to force out all his breath in order to squeeze through the thin gap to the trees on the other side.

He scanned the area around him. Forest. Bushes and dirt and rocks. But no road. He moved away from the buildings, slipping and teetering on the moist surfaces until, after perhaps ten feet, Dan could finally make out what looked like asphalt. He scurried through the last of the trees, tumbling once and springing back almost prematurely, as if he and the ground were metals oppositely magnetized to each other. He brushed himself off and stumbled onto the road.

The Methodist church stood ahead to the north on the right side. That meant he was, as he thought, on Back Street, not far from where the road ceased to exist in name and merged into Queen's Highway. The cholera cemetery would be just beyond that point, also on the right. He ran down the roadway, slowing slightly as he passed the memorial (out of respect), then speeding up again once he reached the other side. He planned to go west at Russell's Lane and head to the coffee house.

Suddenly, though, Dan froze. Scott Patterson strolled toward him down Queen's Highway from the direction of the Patterson home, Breezy Summer. He glanced up. Immediately the man pulled back and his face morphed into a scowl. He squinted.

Dan spun, about to return to town. But he stopped mid-turn and pivoted instead to face Scott head on. There was nowhere to go. The path he was currently on led to Susan. And that's where he needed to be. As ambiguous and undefined as his end game was, forward was his only option.

Suddenly and without warning (other than his presence), Scott darted forward. Dan crouched, steeling himself, ready for the *gentle giant* to slug into him and pummel him to the ground, holding him prisoner as he summoned Constable Anderson or the inspector. But, instead, he skidded to a stop with about two feet to spare. Dan could smell vodka on the man's breath.

Scott grinned/smirked/grimaced—Dan wasn't really sure what to call the man's expression. Finally, he burbled out:

"You're not going anywhere."

Dan shifted. "Why?"

"Why?"

"Yeah. Why am I not going anywhere?"

"Cause I'm h...what do you mean, 'why are you not going anywhere'?"

"Just tell me why I'm not going anywhere. Maybe it'll make sense and I'll listen to you. Change my mind. Could be you're just that persuasive."

Scott opened his mouth and pushed his lips out slightly. He shifted his eyes to left.

"What?"

Now it was Dan's turn to grin/smirk/grimace. "Well, Scott. I can see you've got a lot to think about. And, as much as I'm enjoying this...this...well, this, whatever this is we're doing...and I am. I really am. I'm in a bit of a hurry. You keep working on your thinking. Maybe I can swing back later and we can continue our conversation when you've had more time to develop your response."

Dan moved forward and brushed into Scott as he tried to push around him. Neither of them moved. Scott burped. This time Dan's face definitely sunk into a grimace.

"Oh, Scott. What...? Did you just eat clams?"

Scott said nothing, merely shoved Dan stumbling back. Dan flung his hands out behind him as he fell into the grass on the side of the road. He jumped to his feet.

"Scott," he said. "Let's talk about this."

Scott, though, seemed to have no interest in further discussion. He lunged at Dan, and the two tumbled together onto the roadside. Scott landed with a "Hmmph" on top of Dan. "I'm going to call Ronnie. He's..." Scott burped again. Dan's eyes stung.

Dan kicked and punched and rolled, anything to resist this hour's attacker, but nothing seemed to have any effect on Scott. He considered head-butting the man, picturing the key point of just about every movie fight set in a bar he'd ever seen. But he'd never really understood why that strategy wouldn't be just as damaging to the buttor as to the buttee. Plus, Scott's head was almost certainly very hard and extremely solid. If there was any logic behind the move, it would have to be that the instigator's skull would, by necessity, be the more stone-like of the two. This, he conceded, was no time to test his theory. He squirmed some more instead.

Immediately, Scott's face morphed into anger and hatred and...and nausea? He shoved Dan to the side and shifted slightly, displaying an uncharacteristic level of etiquette, and threw up into the space Dan had just occupied.

Scott burped out, "Oh...what..." He wiped his lips and started spitting and sliding his tongue around in his mouth with a scowl. Then he pressed his palm against the grass, certainly intending to push himself to his feet. Instead, though, his palms glided across the sick-slick blades (he had no one to thank but himself) and he thudded squarely onto his side and into the mess.

"Oh...what..."

Dan didn't bother waiting to find out what *oh...what...* was, despite *what*'s clear importance in this situation. He spun and darted toward Russell's Lane, then pivoted left and headed west to Front Street. He grinned. Finally, things seemed to be going his way. He cast his eyes to the sky. Even the clouds seemed less ominous. At Front Street, he jogged north to the coffee house and bounced up to the entrance. A sign hung in the small window peeking out. He paused and read:

closed for the season
see you in January

Until now.

He slumped.

He scanned around the area, struggling to weave his mind through all his visits with Jamie. Had the young man ever mentioned where he lived? Dan shook his head and wiped his forehead. All of this, everything had been for nothing. Really the only thing he'd accomplished at this point was to anger Cat more and place Susan in perhaps greater danger. Constable Anderson would now despise him to an even more ridiculous and absolute extent, if that was possible. And—and even Dan couldn't dispute this fact—the man finally had a hard-to-argue-with reason. The constable's hostility would no longer be just about jealousy. And what about Jamie? There was no way to know if the boy was okay. Or if Cat had already gotten to him. Or if Cat hadn't hurt him yet and the young man was fine and Dan would have been able to do something to save him. If only…

He kicked the air and yelled into the nothing. He glanced at his feet and spun, hurling himself back against the door.

Angry.

He tumbled inside.

The shop was unlocked. Maybe…Dan leapt to his feet. He sucked in a breath and scanned the room.

But something was off. He stumbled forward and a muddled look washed over his face. The shop was a mess. But, not a mess, sort of. Not a mess in the actual *mess*

353

sense of the word. Everything was in place—a little confusing, given the sign. But maybe the...he realized he had no idea of Jamie's last name...maybe the young man's family left the coffee house intact during the off-season. There was more, though. Something wasn't right. The energy was off.

"Jamie?"

He shifted to the side.

"Is anyone here?"

He crossed to one of the tables and scooted a chair, listening as the scrape of the leg reverberated across the tile and through the empty shop. He glanced across at the cash register, Jamie's usual post. Untouched. His breathing felt weighted. A sense of despair flooded over him.

He moved across the room to the counter and studied the empty cupboards and shelves. He peeked back over his shoulder at the sign in the door. He called out Jamie's name again. Soft. Questioning. Trepidatious.

And then he knew, in a flash, just like the blue he'd seen on the beach before finding Ed. He stretched and leaned forward over the counter, yelling Jamie's name.

"Jamie!"

He froze.

* * * *

Scott fell back onto his knees. He scrunched up his nose and a sneer smashed across his face. He sniffed the air around him. Everything. Everything (he repeated to himself) reeked. But, he nodded his head, he actually felt better. Maybe the clams had gone bad after all.

He glanced to his right. Dan was nowhere.

He could follow, head down Queen's Highway and track Dan like the animal he was. The man definitely didn't deserve much better. But then he thought, do I really have any idea where he's going? No. I don't. Going after him could take a lot of effort and that wasn't really…better to let the professionals handle it.

He peeked down at his own body, fanned out his fingers and twisted his hands around. Disgusting. He pushed to his feet, sliding his hands through any clean blades of grass he could find in the process. As soon as he stood, though, he tossed himself back to the ground, scowling as he rolled dog-like through the dirt and weeds around him, shifting forward as unsoiled surfaces became harder to find. He paused briefly when the spinning forced another wave of nausea, exhaling and inhaling, and exhaling and inhaling. Then he squirmed some more until he felt sufficiently clean. Or at least *cleanish*. At least he no longer stank. He'd just tell everyone he'd just finished playing a game of rugby.

He smirked.

So on to the police station. He stopped when he reached the town center and glanced up at the deck of the Sugar Shack. No Fran. He frowned. He should probably go see if she was up there. He'd always fancied her. She was certainly fit. And she would definitely go for him. Of course, she would. Who wouldn't? He scanned the dock area, straightened his clothes and brushed himself off.

But then Dan…he scowled…that guy ruined everything. Scott braced himself (and his expression) and made sure he looked as harried as he could as he ducked into the courtyard and trudged up the stairs to the station. He paused, then barreled through the door.

That inspector, Bea Galson and Wally sat in a small triangle. The three spun and stared at him.

The inspector looked bored. Or lazy. Hard to tell.

355

Bea Galson let out a small scream, pressing her hand to her heart and exclaiming, *"Jolín, mi niño. Me ha asustado."* All he understood was *boy*. He squinted at her. Suspicious.

And then there was Wally. The woman simply regarded him, seemingly unaffected by his over-the-top entrance, as if people barging in on her life was part of her everyday existence.

"Mr. Patterson, ye all right?" the inspector asked.

"I...is Ronnie in the office?"

"Ye drunk? Kind of early to be drunk."

He eyed the inspector. No. I'm not, he thought. Not really. And that certainly was none of the man's business anyway.

"Nah." He shook his whole body, sniffed. "Rugby. Ronnie around?"

"No." Inspector Johnson stood. "He's out. Something I can help ye with?"

"When do you think he'll be here?"

"Not sure."

"What's he doing?"

Johnson seemed to hesitate, blinked. "Well, Mr. Patterson, that's a police matter."

"Is it about that guy, Dan?"

"Mr. Harris?"

"Yeah, sure...Mr. Harris. Whatever."

"Did ye see him?"

Scott stalled, paced around the office, surveyed a swept up pile of plastic, topped with a strip of fabric. That must be from whatever Ronnie was talking about. He shook his head and returned to the group.

"Listen. I just really need to talk to Ronnie. No offense, but this is a local issue."

"Well," the inspector said, standing. "I don't think—"

The door slid open and Ronnie sauntered in. He had an ice cream in his hand. "I can't find him anywhe—Scott? What are you doing here?"

Anderson nodded to the women. "Hello Bea. Hello Wally."

"Ronnie." Scott rushed at him and the constable pulled back. Scott said, "Glad you're here."

"What happened to you?"

"Dan. I saw… he attacked me again. I don't know what happened. I told him you were looking for him and he just went berserk, knocked me back into a ditch and then just ran off…like a coward. Look at me."

"I thought ye said ye were playing rugby," Inspector Johnson said.

"Before. I was playing rugby before." Scott snickered and pointed a thumb at Inspector Johnson. "What's with this guy?"

Constable Anderson ignored him. He sniffed. "Was he eating clams? You reek."

Scott lifted his arm and smelled under his armpit. Apparently smells were relative. "You know, you're right. He got sick. Threw up all over me. I hadn't realized how much I stunk. All I could think of was warning you. He's a menace."

"Now yer saying he threw up on ye?"

"Yes. What did I just tell you? What do you think this smell is?"

Scott rolled his eyes.

Constable Anderson pivoted. "Let's go, Scott. Show me where you saw him."

The inspector twisted to Bea and Wally. "Mrs. Galson, Mrs. Wallace, so nice to see ye both. There's more water if

357

ye want any. Just close the door when ye ladies go out. Turn the lock on the handle, too, if ye wouldn't mind."

Constable Anderson grabbed Scott by the arm and swung toward the door. The two rushed out, followed by Johnson. Scott waited at the bottom of the stairs and watched as Ronnie and, by default, Inspector Johnson descended snail-like down the steps. Finally, all three stood together at the bottom. Scott glared at Ronnie. Ronnie threw his ice cream into the open space by the stairs.

"What?"

They ran (-ish in Ronnie's case) toward where Scott had wrestled with Dan. Scott spun several times along the way and yelled for Ronnie to pick it up.

"Now that inspector's going to get there first. Really, Ronnie. You could do with a little exercise."

When they reached the strip of road where Scott had seen Dan, they stopped. Scott signaled to the north.

"He went that-a-way."

"What about there?" Inspector Johnson indicated Russell's Lane. "What's down there?"

"Not much. Some houses, the coffee house. Go the other way and there's his house. There's a dock. Of course, that's back the first way. He could be trying to leave the island." Scott slapped his leg. "Or Sarah! He could be going for Sarah. He's going to hurt her."

Scott twisted to Ronnie.

"This is all your fault. You had him and you let him go. If anything happens to Sarah…"

"My fault? What was I supposed to do?"

"Not let him go, you moron."

"Hey! Watch your language. Besides, I only called you because I thought you could help. Not so you could tell me how to do my job."

"You—"

"Stop. Now, ye two. Doesn't matter the fault. Here's what we do. Ye two go look at Scott's house. Make sure about Sarah."

He indicated Russel's Lane. "I'll head down that way. Check that out."

Scott and Ronnie 'hurried' north. Ronnie shoved Scott's shoulder, and Scott did the same to Ronnie. The constable stumbled and almost fell onto the side of the road. Scott glanced back at Inspector Johnson, smirking. But the inspector wasn't watching. He was already making his way down toward Front Street.

Thirty-Seven

Dan stared over the counter. He couldn't move. He could barely breathe. The air in the room felt thick and syrupy and he had to force out, "Ryan."

He leaned forward.

"Ryan."

Silence.

"Jamie."

Red and legs and jeans. All poked out. And shoes. And blood. Too much blood. Pooled blood, seeping into asphalt.

He didn't hesitate.

He sprinted down the steps and along the cement path and dropped to his knees and threw his eyes to the distance. To the sound. The squeal. The tires. The car. Speeding away. Around the corner. D. He knew a D. And a J? Or I. And 7. 4. 2? And blue. A blue car. A blue car that moved too fast. And he lumbered along too slow. He fought to commit to memory a vision that would never get away.

Before. In his office. In his space. He'd jumped out of his chair when he'd heard the crash and a screech and he'd run from the room, cursing his impatience, condemning his intractability. Something wasn't right. He'd known it. But cars...they made noises all the time. So he'd run. And at the end of the hall he'd fumbled. The door. The handle. It was locked. Nothing moved. For the briefest of moments, he'd felt hope, he'd grinned, even chuckled, pivoted, considered the possibility that his son was still in the house. Ryan never remembered to lock the door. Never. Why now? This door, though? Instead Dan had palmed at the lock and twisted the lever and flung the door back and banged the knob against the wall, and the sun had blinded him briefly, so bright, and he cast his eyes ahead and saw the blood and saw Ryan sprawled, and a trash can. And a lid. And Ryan's bike, the new bike, his birthday bike spun mangled above the boy's head.

And all around him was blood.

He rushed forward to his son and dropped from his feet, to his knees, ahh, didn't cringe. And he touched Ryan's head, remembered all the inane counsel not to move an injured body. He ripped out his cell and his phone juggled into the muck and he snatched it out and struggled to dial 911. And blood. He managed 9 before he heard Ryan gasp and he tossed the phone to the side and slid his hands under his son's head and chanted over and over:

"It's okay. It's okay. It's…"

He caressed Ryan's forehead and he stroked his son's hair and he kissed his boy's cheek. And blood seeped from Ryan's ear.

"It's…" Dan's voice broke. He gasped. "It's going to be okay."

no no no no no

"Everything will be fine."

Because no one ever thinks, *today will end with the death of my son.*

And he twisted for the phone, stretched for it, just out of reach, shifted with the boy careful in the blood and Ryan huffed out a breath and a moan and Dan cried out for help and yelled for anyone close and Ryan began trembling and Dan screamed

"No!" and he yelled,

"Please help, somebody!"

as he spun his eyes and then Ryan tensed and twisted motionless and Dan begged out again "Help Someone Help!" and he was angry and he sniffed and he saw that his tears were falling and melting into the blood that was everywhere and he heard Susan's voice, calling out too, and he shifted to see her car advancing, rolling into the house. He heard a crunch. She was sprinting and dialing as she moved, pressing the phone to her ear and as she came closer he could hear her giving their address and pleading,

"Please hurry, please...hurry."

And she was wailing and begging "what? what? Dan? What happened?"

And Dan was fighting to speak but every time he opened his mouth a sob leaked out instead and he couldn't talk and Susan was reaching into his arms and prying and Dan managed to say,

"A car...speeding away...blue..."

And he heard sirens in the distance, so many. He'd never heard so many. And Susan pulled her son toward her and they held his body together, across their laps, and Susan was crying and Dan was crying and he was repeating, "I'm sorry. I'm so sorry," and she said, "Why? Why?" and finally the ambulance arrived and the paramedics hurried to them and started working on Ryan and they kept insisting, "Back please," and Dan kept yelling, "But this is my SON," and one of them motioned to Susan's car and said "Is that the car that hit him?" and Dan bled out "No," and Susan stood, surely to give the paramedics more room as she stumbled back and dropped onto the grass. Dan kept holding Ryan, refusing to give him up, and Susan folded into herself and whimpered softly and finally she answered and said, "No that's my car. I got here after." And the medics pleaded with Dan to let go for the boy's sake and Dan kept mumbling, over and over, "But he's gone already," and suddenly Dan pushed up and rushed to his wife and they held each other and sobbed. And Susan dripped out "what happened?" and Dan explained, the sound, the rushing, the sun, the loss. The Anger. The loss. And she'd said, "You couldn't have stopped it. It's not your fault."

And then, like a flash, he thought there must be something. Still. He slithered around the counter to Jamie slumped on the floor, blood leaking from his side, into his clothes, onto the tile. And the boy was motionless. Dan dropped to him, calling his name, "Jamie, Jamie, Jamie." And he ripped off his own shirt and bunched the fabric and pressed the wad hard against Jamie's side, to the wound, to stanch it. And with his free hand, he pulled at his belt, loosened and yanked it out through the loops, and the leather slapped against his arm at the end.

He wrapped the band around Jamie's torso and pulled tight against the boy's chest. He paused. He panicked. Should he have moved him? Should he have removed Jamie's shirt first? Don't know. What about infection? And hunger? Too late. He shook his head. Too late. He snaked his arm behind the boy's neck, around the young man's head, and shifted him forward, gently. He pressed the tips of his fingers against Jamie's skin, desperate for a pulse.

He yelled, "Help! Someone help!"

And he patted his own pockets. He didn't have his phone, he knew, but maybe, just maybe, somehow he did and he could call. Find help. No pulse. He rushed his palm to in front of Jamie's mouth. No movement. No breath. No moistness. No breath. He wasn't breathing.

"No no no no. Not again."

Dan heard wavering in his own voice and he shifted his hand back to Jamie's neck, kneading again. Hoping. Pleading.

"Jamie...Jamie...come on. Please."

Dan fell back against the doorless cupboards of the counter. This was it. Cat had...she was dead. He'd make sure of it. She'd gone too far. He yelled again, "Help!" but heartless this time because calling out was pointless anymore. He dropped his head.

Then he heard movement behind him. He shouted.

"Hello? Is someone there? Hello?"

"Mr. Harris?"

The voice was Inspector Johnson's.

Dan froze for a moment, adjusted, stretched to see Jamie's face. Considered. Knew. Then:

"Inspector. I'm over here. Behind the counter."

Dan heard rushing and Johnson shuttled into view. The inspector glanced around the shop. He said nothing at first, only studied Dan, seemed to absorb the situation, pulled out a gun and crossed deeper into the kitchen, then returned, stepping around the blood circling Jamie's body.

"Is he dead?"

Dan peeked away for a moment, shook his head. He nodded. "I think so."

"What do ye mean, ye think?"

"I just...yes...he is..." He squeezed his eyes closed, sniffed, realized he was crying. "I think..."

"Ye kill him?"

Dan didn't answer at first, just wiped at his eyes with his free hand and turned away. He gritted his teeth. He could have stopped everything. He could have changed it all if he'd just insisted on Jamie's going right then to the police.

And he despised Jamie's parents.

"Cat did this."

Inspector Johnson motioned to Dan.

"I need ye to set the boy down, come across to me. Ye have a weapon?"

Dan grinned, angry.

"No. It was Cat. I'd nev—"

"Okay. We'll figure this all out later. But first, move away from the boy."

The inspector put his gun away.

Dan gazed down at Jamie. He scanned his own body, took in his bare chest and pants soaked in the boy's blood. Then he pressed his hand gently against Jamie's shoulder and slid the boy off his own arm, letting Jamie fall to the side, but tender, cradling the young man's head to shield him from the wood shelving of the counter. He moved out from under Jamie's body and pressed against the floor to stand, suddenly feeling fatigued and spent and trembling. He crossed the kitchen.

"I didn't do this."

Inspector Johnson shrugged, nodded at the same time. Then he reached into his pocket and pulled out his phone, dialing and smashing the cell against his ear. After a moment, he shook his head and closed his eyes. He spoke.

"Constable, I need ye. Call me."

The inspector dropped his hand to the side.

"Well, we have to wait until he calls. Anderson. Why don't ye tell me what happened."

Dan recounted the constable's refusal to let him call his wife, his desperation, his escape (omitting certain, more

365

incriminating details), his finally talking to Susan, Cat's claim that she'd...he paused, swallowed, and inhaled, dark...that she'd already taken care of Jamie. Her words. He stopped, breathed...How he'd found the boy. About the blood. And so much blood.

"So yer saying ye didn't do this?"

Dan yelled, "What did I just say? And why would I do this? How would I..." He rocked his head.

"How would I do this? I don't even have a weapon. I don't...I tried to save him. My shirt's tied against his side. Why do you think I'm not wearing a shirt?"

"Or shoes." Inspector Johnson motioned to the ground. The edges of Dan's feet were stained red from the blood. He'd forgotten he was barefoot.

"Yeah. I lost my...it's a long story."

"All of this is a long story," Inspector Johnson said.

"What does that mean?"

The inspector didn't answer. They both stood silent for several minutes and stared at Jamie's body. Johnson pulled out his phone a number of times and glanced at the display.

"Where did ye..."

Jamie's foot twitched.

Dan jerked forward and pointed.

"Did you see that? He moved."

The two men studied the boy for several seconds, but there was no more from Jamie.

Dan felt his head and being sink. "I guess—"

"There." Johnson shoved Dan's shoulder. "Again. He..."

Dan rushed toward Jamie and dropped to his side. He hovered his fingers against the skin of Jamie's neck, but gently this time, barely resting the tips there to be sure he'd let any pressure through. And then he felt a flutter, soft and weak, but something. It had to be a heartbeat. He spun to Johnson.

"He's alive."

Dan shoved his arms under the boy and scooped him into his arms.

"We have to get help."

Dan struggled to stand, then hustled across the kitchen again toward Inspector Johnson, who had pulled out his phone and dialed again.

"Go." He motioned. Dan heard him speak.

"Yes, we're coming right over. We have a casualty, possible fatality. I think a stabbing victim."

"Yes," Dan called out over his shoulder. "A stabbing. But he's—"

"Yes, we're pretty sure it's a stabbing. We'll be there as soon as we can. We're in Hope Town. Just have to get to a boat."

Dan fumbled at the door, cradling Jamie and doing his best to keep his movements from jostling the boy. Inspector Johnson shoved his phone into his pocket and rushed to the exit. He pulled back the opening and the two stumbled outside to muted sun. Jamie hung in Dan's arms. Blood covered Dan.

Constable Anderson and Scott came toward them down Front Street.

They stopped. Anderson stepped forward.

"What's going on here?"

Inspector Johnson shifted forward and stood in front of Dan. "Where's the dock ye mentioned before?"

"Hold on a minute." Anderson moved closer to them. "What's going on here? You hurt him?"

"Where's the dock?" Dan shouted.

Scott shoved the constable to the side. "Ronnie. Seriously. What's wrong with you? Not far. He alive?"

Dan nodded, then shrugged. "Sort of. But he needs help. Now."

Scott motioned up the road, north of the coffee house.

"The dock's right up that way. Closer than in town. We'll need a boat. You both go ahead and meet me there. Ronnie, you go. too. I'll run into town and get us some transportation. We have to leave out that way anyway."

"Now wait a minute. He's not going anywhere," Constable Anderson said, motioning to Dan. "He's under arrest. He's going back to the police station."

But no one paid any attention to Ronnie. Scott had already darted off toward town before the constable had even started talking. And Dan and Inspector Johnson simply ignored him. Dan headed up Front Street, speed-walking, allowing his arms to act as shocks to cushion Jamie as he moved. Inspector Johnson jogged by his side. Johnson twisted and shouted.

"Come on, Constable. We'll deal with all that later."

They reached a break in the trees, the same pathway the old man, the caretaker, had snuck off on before. Dan stopped and pivoted. He called out to Anderson, who was only slightly farther along the road than when they'd started.

"This it?"

Constable Anderson ignored him.

Inspector Johnson snapped, "Anderson, is this where we turn?"

The constable didn't respond, at least not verbally. He nodded and flapped his left arm toward the trees with a scowl. Dan and Inspector Johnson ducked into the wooded area and continued until they reached the dock, less than twenty feet from the road. They waited. Dan tapped his foot and dropped his head. At last he heard the sound of a motor speeding toward them and he glanced in the direction of town to see Scott barreling toward him and the inspector. And Jamie. Vern was with Scott. As they pulled closer, Dan could see that there were blankets spread out across one of the benches. He climbed in the boat and laid Jamie on the covered side seating, resting his fingers on the boy's neck. He twisted and nodded.

"He's still alive. But we have to hurry. Let's go."

"No. Sorry." Inspector Johnson shook his head. "This is as far as ye go. Yer coming back to the station with me."

Constable Anderson had finally caught up with them (probably just worried he'd be left out of the excitement) and stepped onto the boat. He shoved Dan back toward land. The water surrounding them splashed and scattered.

"Go. Now."

Dan wanted to protest. Jamie was his friend. But there was no time. The boy was alive. Barely. But he was still breathing. And that had to be enough. He climbed out of the boat and twisted around to watch the group pull out in their makeshift ambulance and jet toward Marsh Harbour. Dan scanned the sky. Cloudy. And windy. The sun sat low above the horizon and cast an orange glow onto the boaters. Johnson shifted to the side and motioned an open palm to Dan.

"Go ahead, Boss."

He went.

At the road, they continued toward town on Front Street. Inspector Johnson seemed to fixate on Dan as they walked.

"Ye probably want a shower."

Dan nodded.

"We'll make sure that happens. Right now, though, ye need to go back to the police station. I need to get to the coffee house and look everything over. Secure the scene. Notify..." He paused, peeked to the left and rocked his head. "I need to notify the boy's parents."

"I can help. I don't—"

"No." Inspector Johnson glanced at Dan. "Yer going back to the police station."

Dan shrugged. "You know. I could just refuse. You nev—"

"We can stop at yer house and ye can get yerself a shirt and change yer trousers. At least rinse yerself off."

"Get ye some shoes." The inspector tilted his head at Dan's feet.

He continued, "Did ye ever get to talk to yer wife?"

"Not really."

He reached into his pocket and handed Dan his cell phone.

"Go ahead."

Thirty-Eight

Cat watched Susan. The woman scanned the sky, shifted, stepped backward and forward. Through it all she gnawed endlessly on her bottom lip. She couldn't have looked more out of place if she were...well, exactly what she was—an uptight prude standing on a soon-to-be stormy dock in the Bahamas contemplating her own certain demise.

Cat guessed.

She smirked. "You shouldn't chew your lip like that. It's going to start bleeding."

Susan shook her head.

"I just don't feel right about this, Cat. It's so windy. And it's going to start raining any minute. I'm sure of it. I'm just going to stay in Marsh Harbour tonight and catch the ferry in the morning. Dan will understand."

"What about me?" Cat feigned indignant shock.

"What about you?"

"You think it's so dangerous, but you're fine with me going?"

"Yep."

"Well, that's rude."

"You think I'm being rude, Cat? You stole my phone and wouldn't let me talk to my husband. What'd you expect? We'd be best friends? I have zero interest in having anything more to do with you. Zero."

Cat mumbled, "You think I do?"

"What?"

"Just agreeing." Cat sighed. "You're right. I'm a horrible person. I should have let you talk to him first. Really, though, I thought we'd have more time. How was I supposed to know? He was the one that said he had to go."

Susan gazed across the water toward Hope Town.

Cat went on. "Fine. I'm sorry you didn't get to talk to Dan. Happy now? Can we go? Please? We should head out before it gets too late."

"Why is there nobody else out there?"

"Because they're smarter than we are. They know better than to wait until the storm's already here like we're about to do. Really, Susan. We don't have time for this."

Susan paused, bit her bottom lip (again! thought Cat). Then she quickly and repeatedly bobbed her head. "Okay."

"Finally!"

Cat grabbed the day's shopping in one hand and Susan's purse and suitcase in the other, then boarded the boat and placed their bags along one of the sides. She turned and hoisted herself back onto the deck. Susan glanced around. She twisted and hovered in the direction of Marsh Harbour. Cat was done with Susan's stalling. She reached out and grabbed the woman's elbow.

Susan ripped away from her. "What are you doing? Get your hands off me."

"What now?" Cat flipped her palms in the air, then immediately clasped her hands to keep from slapping the woman and pulling her by the hair onto the boat.

"My goodness, Susan. It's always something with you. What's your problem? I'm just trying to help. You're so angry all the time. No wonder Dan got tired of you. I haven't even spent a day with you and I'm alre—"

"That's it! I'm not going. Give me back my things."

"I'm not getting the bags, Susan. They're already loaded. Let's just get going."

"Give me my stuff back."

"Susan, you're being ridiculous. Just get in the boat."

"I'm not going."

"Get in."

They both stood, implacable and silent, stormy like the weather Susan was so afraid of. Cat watched Susan as she rocked her head slowly back and forth, opening wide and squinting her eyes. The woman sucked in her lips, slid them from side to side, most likely projecting whatever inner dialogue had taken over, and definitely broadcasting far more than she realized. Cat slid forward, seductive.

"You're right, Susan. I'm sorry. I misbehaved. I was out of line and I'm sorry. But, really, if you hope to salvage anything with Dan, we should get going now so you can try to see him tonight."

Susan flashed at Cat.

"Am I seriously supposed to believe you're on my side in all this?

"Sides, Susan? Really?" Cat sneered. "There are no sides. We're not in high school. I guess it just comes down to who loves Dan more. I just want him to be happy. I'm just looking out for him. If that means I lose him, I'm mature enough to accept that. You could learn a lot about true love, my dear."

"Yes. I'll be sure to check in with you later about class times."

Cat rolled her eyes and exhaled. She stared at Susan for a moment then twisted and stared into the distance. Time to change directions. She exhaled.

"I just don't know how Dan could have done this."

"He didn't."

"Oh, of course." She spun back to Susan. "Of course, he didn't...probably. But, you know, we both have to face that it's entirely possible that he did."

"No, I don't. It's not. He didn't do anything. I know him."

"So do I."

The two women convened another stare off. All of a sudden, Cat jumped in the boat and pivoted to face Susan. She held out her hand.

"Please. Susan. Can we talk about this on the way? We really should get going. We'll be fine, I promise. But, not if we don't set off."

Susan hesitated and eyed the ocean and horizon one more time. She inhaled and closed her eyes, then opened them and shifted forward, slapping Cat's hand out of the way. She climbed into the boat, attempting to grip the surface of the dock for support. Cat watched Susan struggle, suppressing a chortle. She waited until the woman had managed to spread herself somewhat precariously over the water between the boat and the dock. Then she stretched out her arm and nudged one of the posts just enough that the boat drifted out ever-so-slightly, ever-so-unnoticeably. Susan cried out and jumped the last bit, landing on the floor of the vessel.

"Oh!"

"See." Cat grinned. "That wasn't so hard now, was it?"

Susan didn't answer. She crawled to her feet and moved to the rear to one of two chairs set to either side of the boat. Cat caught her eying a plastic bottle of bleach sitting in a corner in the stern of the boat.

"For fishing," Cat said.

"What?"

"For fishing." She nodded to the container. "I saw you looking at the bleach. I like to go fishing. But, boy, the boat can get stinky and gross. All those innards splashed out all over the floor. Sometimes you have to club the fish to get them to die. Did you know that? Otherwise, they just keep drawing out the inevitable. Anyways, that's why I have all this open space in the center. Supplies. And killing. They have to go somewhere after you catch them."

"You don't just put them in a bucket or something?" Susan asked and eyed the space.

"Good idea. I'm sure no one's ever thought of that. You should patent it."

"Alright," Cat went on quickly before Susan could respond. She snapped the dock ties loose and initiated the engine. "Let's go. Won't take us long. Maybe ten, fifteen, twenty minutes," Cat said.

"Twenty five," she added.

"What? I can't hear you." Susan flicked her ear with her fingers.

Cat smirked and returned to guiding the boat out of the marina. She glanced down. Her knife, her favorite knife, lay jumbled along with a smattering of fishing supplies on a shelf just under the steering column. Gloves. Extra line. A club for killing. She focused ahead at the water, rough from the gusts that knocked against the surface.

They sped along, the stormy weather driving nearly constant swells splashing and dipping around them as they moved. Cat steered into the waves, giggling to herself as she heard the high-pitched 'oh's and 'well, that's just's coming from behind her. She noticed one particularly high surge ahead and directed the bow directly into the roll, twisting her torso and watching Susan as they careened through the tumultuous water so she could get a good laugh as the woman bounced from her seat and slammed into first one, then the other side of the chair. She looked so foolishly uncoordinated. Cat burst into a bellowing cackle.

"Sorry. Oh, Susan. I'm so sorry. This water is just so choppy right now. I guess that's what we get for waiting. That's your fault, my dear. I'm trying to miss the worst of it. But..."

Susan raised a finger to the sky and moved her lips, likely trying to convey, "I can't hear you."

Cat snickered.

"Perfect," she yelled and pivoted to focus on driving again.

At about the half-way point between the two islands, Cat cut the engine and the boat floated to a stop. As if timed by God, the blowing dissipated and the ocean melted into calm, gentle undulations that Cat hoped accomplished little more than to rock Susan into complacency, like a mother soothing a baby into a sense of well-being. The air around them fell silent. Only the lapping of the shifting ocean as water splashed against the hull of the boat sounded in the background. The atmosphere felt almost serene. Peaceful. Ironic. Cat leered. Susan twisted and scanned the open space surrounding them. She faced Cat.

"Is something wrong? Why'd we stop?"

"No reason. I just thought we could talk for a few minutes. You were having a hard time hearing me."

Susan indicated no. Aggressively. "No. We can talk later. Just take me ho—" She seemed to catch herself. "To Dan's."

"Oh, you're right." Cat smirked. "I guess that's not really your house anymore is it?"

Susan stood. "It was never my house. It's not really Dan's either. It's Richard Jensen's. Dan's just using it. Now take me there."

Cat smiled her best sparkly smile. "Yes. Well."

"Cat, why did you even bother to pick me up? This is ridiculous. You obviously don't like me. And I have no reason to like you either. You're the reason..." She glanced to the side.

"You were saying?"

"Nothing. Let's just go. Please."

Susan sunk back into her seat. (The fabric made a whooshing sound as she dropped.) Cat gazed at the sky and at the water, then reached into the shelf with the fishing supplies and rested her hand above the knife. She gripped the handle and released, gripped the handle...and released. She stood from the control area.

"Don't you want to hear what I have to tell you. I mean, that's the real reason you agreed to this, isn't it?"

Susan shook her head. "Nope. Not at all. Just—"

"Okay. Deny all you want," Cat said and spun, snatching her knife from the fishing supplies and blocking the blade with her body. "Your loss. But you'll wish you'd said yes."

Cat searched the sky for any sun she could harness for a beam to glint off the knife and make this experience all the more dramatic. She heard Susan say, "Cat, I really don't care about whatever you might have to say. I want all this to be over and go see my husband. Please take me to Hope Town. Now."

Cat spun and directed herself toward Susan. She paused (this was all rushing by too quickly) then raised her hand high and in front of herself, eyeing the knife between her fingers. Susan jerked back and clawed at the sides of the chair.

Cat struggled to suppress a chuckle. She'd not even given the woman a real reason to worry yet.

"You sure you don't want to hear?" she asked.

Susan didn't answer. Cat could see the woman's chest rising and falling and her hands shifting forward and back and sideways, frenetic, on the arms of the chair.

"Cat…"

Cat smiled. She stepped forward, moving directly toward Susan, and paused again. She squinted. Then she diverted to the right to some excess rope that dangled over the side of the boat, pulled the tie taught and sawed through the twine. The strand fell into the water with a subtle plop and Cat leaned over the edge and watched as the snippet floated away. She spun back to face Susan, a grin smeared across her face. She acted surprised.

"Oh. Susan." She giggled. "Susan, what were you thinking? Did you actually think this was for you?"

She hurried back to the front of the boat and tossed the knife in with the other supplies.

"Your mind sure goes to dark places, my dear. Did you seriously think I would hurt you? Why would I hurt you? I couldn't ever hurt anyone. No matter how much I know you despise me. Who do you think I am? Dan?"

Susan scowled. She stood and pointed in the direction of Elbow Cay. "Take me home now, Cat."

"You mean to Dan's pretend—"

"Seriously, Cat. Never again. I swear. Take me to Hope Town. Now. I should never have agreed to this. What Dan ever saw in you, I'll never understand."

Cat scowled.

"Well, apparently he saw enough to leave you."

Cat studied the water surface around them. The ocean was still too calm. She needed more wind at the least. This would be better if Susan's death looked like an accident, as if she'd just lost her balance from all the rocking and fell overboard. She focused on the woman again.

"So, Brian."

"Who?"

"Brian. Your son."

Susan glared. "Ryan."

"Really? Dan always called him Brian. Well, that kind of makes sense. Okay. So, Ryan."

Susan flashed up her eyes and shook her head.

"Why are you bringing up Ryan, Cat?"

"You need to know what kind of man Dan is, Susan. You may not want to hear it, but I'm looking out for you. Sometimes friends are the only ones that can see what's right in front of your face. It's for your own good."

"Cat." Susan shook her head and dropped her face into her hands. "Please. Just—"

"Your son? Isn't he dead?"

Susan shot forward. Her eyes sharpened and she inhaled roughly through her nose. Her nostrils shoved out, then in and she gritted her teeth. Cat grinned.

"Testy. Anyways, I'm sure you know already that Dan and me are kind of an item."

Susan started laughing.

"What? We are. Are you making fun of me? You think you're better than me?"

Susan grinned. All this laughing, her grinning. She had to be feeling cornered, sensing what was coming. That was the only reason she'd be acting so irrationally. But then the woman said, "You really are desperate, aren't you Cat?"

"So you don't care that Dan hated Brian."

"Ryan."

"Whatever."

Susan twisted behind her and glanced toward Hope Town. She pivoted back to Cat. "How would you even know? Let me guess. He confessed this to you. In a moment of passion."

"Yes. Exactly," Cat said.

"Dan told you he hated Ryan?"

"Yeah. Only he called him Brian. But whatever. Yeah. He told me one night. Late. Remember? I told you we were an item?"

"Yeah, sure Cat."

"He did. Really. It was after a nice moonlit stroll and we were talking about how we both hated kids. And then he said how Bri...sorry, RYAN...kind of ruined everything after he was born. He made everything so complicated."

"Yeah, kids do that. Crazy, huh?"

Cat yelled. "Stop thinking you're better than me! Why do you think I'm telling you this? I'm trying to look out for you. You should want to know what a despicable man you were married to. Us women have to stick together."

"So you're making up some crazy story about how Dan...seriously, Cat. Just take me home."

Cat glared at Susan. She noticed that the tips of Susan's long, pretentious hair had begun to sway from side to side. Cat scanned the water. The wind was returning. The corners of her mouth twitched upward.

"It's true. He was relieved. When the boy died, Dan was relieved. I mean, I probably would have been too. But that was his kid. What kind of man is happy his own son is dead? Even I was I a little like...wow, that's harsh."

Cat watched Susan. She was silent. She'd gotten to the woman and she would die thinking how despicable the man she'd married was. Cat continued, "Don't you have anything to say?"

"Nope. Just waiting for you to finish so we can finally go."

"So, you don't care that your soon-to-be-ex husband hated your son?"

"No."

"What if he killed him?"

Susan looked annoyed. "Dan didn't kill Ryan, Cat."

"You don't know that."

"Yes. I do."

"Oh, believe me. It's all true. He hated that kid."

"Because, supposedly, Dan told you this?"

Cat grinned. "Yeah. After we spent the night together."

"I thought you said...you know what? Never mind." She shrugged. "Okay."

"That's it?"

"Yeah. Okay. You told me. Now can we go?"

"What kind of person are you? Okay?"

Susan cast her eyes to Marsh Harbour, seemed to study Cat.

"Did Dan ever show you the last family portrait we ever took? The last one before Ryan...before the accident."

Cat didn't respond.

"No," Susan went on. "I suppose he wouldn't. That would have been too important to him."

She took a couple of steps toward Cat. The wind had finally started to blow more consistently and the boat bucked and rocked. Susan walked with a wide stance and flung her arms out a few times in an effort to stabilize herself. Cat chuckled. The woman looked ridiculous.

"Did he ever at least tell you about it?"

Cat stared into Susan. A flat crack of a smile smashed across her face. The storm was starting to settle in. It wouldn't be long now. She tilted her head to the side. "The times, they are a-changin', my dear."

Susan eyed her.

"Okay. I have no idea what you mean there. Regardless, I'm guessing this is the first you're hearing about the picture. You're probably just now realizing that he doesn't care about you like you seem to think he does."

She took another step until she stood about a foot in front of Cat. Cat shifted back. Susan stared into her eyes. A large swell splashed across the boat and both women stumbled to the side. Susan began speaking more loudly.

"Well, that day...the day of the portrait...we were supposed to sit for the photographer at 1:30. Do you have any kids, Cat?"

The boat began to seesaw.

Susan scanned the ocean. "Maybe we should just go."

"No," Cat said. "Please. Make your point. Live in denial."

Susan shook her head. She sighed.

"Well, basically, you have to get ready and get cleaned up and make sure you get some lunch or you won't be getting *anything* ready on time.

"So, the plan was to get everything set in the morning and then take our time eating. Ryan's birthday was coming up and we were determined to draw it out for him, have some fun outings. So that day, we started early. Maybe too early for Ryan because suddenly everything was unacceptable to him. None of the clothes we'd chosen— and I say 'we' because Ryan and I went..." She stopped, caught her breath.

"Ryan and I went shopping together and he'd picked them out himself the week before….but none of them were any good anymore. He started throwing a tantrum. I mean a real tantrum. Screaming and crying and stomping his feet. He'd never acted out like that before. Never did ag…"

She glanced to the side into the distance. Cat noticed a tear trembling along the edge of her eye.

"I still don't know why he was so out of control. But, Dan…"

Her face turned saccharine and she pressed her lips together. She gently shifted her head from side to side.

"Dan was so patient with him. He did everything he could think of to make sure Ryan was happy. Everything. But, nothing would convince that kid that our outfits were the least bit better than his orange shorts and blue t-shirt. And sandals. I honestly don't know why Dan just didn't make Ryan wear our clothes. Or I didn't. Then. I was worried about precedence, naturally. I'm an attorney. I'm a pragmatist. I think about that sort of issue. If we give in now, what about the next time? That sort of thing. But Dan just wrapped his arms around me and brushed my hair away from my ear and whispered that we only had so much time. We could deal with everything else later."

"I know. Sounds a little condescending when I say it now. Like the man swooping in to save the day. But it wasn't. Just logic. We didn't—"

She pushed her head down, seemed to focus on her feet. Cat heard her sucking air in through her nose. Pathetic. Susan lifted her eyes and stared forward into Cat.

"We just didn't realize at the time how true that was."

"So Dan…" she continued, her voice wavering and dropping away. She started batting her eyes and looked like she was gazing directly into the sun. Cat found herself looking away to the right to avoid seeing her.

"Dan knelt down in front of Ryan and hugged him, like he'd just hugged me. But this time he just held on to him. Then he moved Ryan's little body back and told him that all that mattered was that Ryan was there, that he could wear whatever he wanted.

"And that he loved him."

Susan was silent for a moment. She wiped at the side of her face. Cat pivoted back and glared at her. Susan shrugged.

"Sorry, Cat. You should have picked something else to try. Dan loved Ryan. More than anything. That I know. He would have done anything for that boy."

She smiled, looking way too serene. Annoying. Smug.

Cat said, "I have no idea why you just told me all that."

Susan nodded. "I'm sure you don't...I just don't care." She inhaled sharply.

"Now take me to Dan's."

She rotated and moved to the back of the boat.

Cat grimaced. Angry. She darted to the steering area of the boat and grabbed her club and barreled toward Susan. She threw her hand into the air and started to bring the weapon down onto the woman's head. Time stopped. She relished the moment, seeing the end, feeling the pleasure of knowing she'd won. Knowing that Dan had lost. Again.

But, then Susan twisted her head and Cat heard another engine wailing from the direction of Hope Town. She whipped the club to the side and flung her eyes forward at Susan, then to the left at the boat bouncing in their direction. Vern was driving. Ronnie and Scott Patterson sat toward the center. Ronnie pressed up and waved with one hand while he held his hair with the other.

"Hey there, Cat," he yelled as they jetted close by.

Scott shouted, "Hello pretty lady," and waved and pointed at Susan.

Cat glowered at Dan's wife. The wake from Ronnie's boat rocked them even harder than the windy ocean had and Susan stumbled against her seat and looked about to topple over. She laughed and waved hesitantly, looking confused. She pivoted to Cat.

"Who was that?"

Cat ignored her. She rushed back to the steering wheel, lamenting the loss of her club that she could still sense tossing in the waves to their side. Sprinkles started to splash onto the surface of the boat and against their skin.

"Nobody."

She flipped on the engine and slammed her fist against the throttle. The boat lurched forward and they headed toward Elbow Cay.

Thirty-Nine

Susan stared at the paper in her hands.

WILSON/ED. Wilson/Ed. Ed Wilson. The name sounded familiar. She flipped the stub over. Why did Dan have this man's boarding pass? And why had he obscured the document under his computer?

She let her hand drop and glanced around the room. What had Dan been up to? There was blood on Richard's rug. Blood! She'd recognized it right off. Even dried, the then brownish-red stuff had a distinctive look. She'd taken on a case once, begrudgingly, that had involved representing one of her firm's most important clients in a drunk driving defense. She'd insisted that she wasn't the right person, that this kind of case wasn't even within her specialty—she was a corporate law attorney after all. But, this client had insisted (she'd found out later he had other, less family-friendly motives). He'd apparently always been confident regardless that his wealth and nearly limitless resources would deliver him an acquittal. But he'd caused an accident, after consuming more alcohol than most college students drink in a month. And in the accident a young girl had died. During the trial, Susan had been ordered to insert some rather salacious opposition research into the defense's narrative and, as a result and not surprisingly, the trial wasn't looking good for the prosecution. As a last ditch (and ultimately ineffective) play, they'd brought in some of the blood-stained seat the child had died on as an exhibit. And then Ryan...tears (and guilt) came crushing down on her. She folded to the floor.

So there'd been blood on Richard's rug. And then there'd been the still-wet, red-stained jeans. When she'd picked them up and felt the moistness, she'd immediately flipped them away and dashed into the bathroom to vomit into the toilet. Which was when she'd noticed the footprints in the mirror behind her (as she'd struggled to rinse away the taste of bile). There were rose-colored footprints in the shower and on the rug in front of it. And now this. What did this paper mean?

She shifted to her feet. A knock sounded at the door and she spun toward the entrance, rolled her eyes, wished away whoever was there. Only Cat even knew she was here. She shouted, "If you're Cat, go away."

"Mrs. Harris?" A man's voice. She hurried to the foyer and spoke through the door.

"Hello. Can I help you?"

"Mrs. Harris?"

"Yes. Who is this?" She noticed that she was still holding the stub she'd found and rushed to the counter and dropped the paper there. As she returned to the door, she heard:

"...Johnson, of the Royal Bahamas Police Force."

Susan flung open the door.

"Why have you arrested my husband? What evidence do you have?"

He hesitated, seeming taken aback by her lack of enthusiasm at his arrival. "May I come in, Ma'am?"

She stepped aside. Frowned.

"So, tell me. Why have you arrested Dan? Do you have evidence that ties him to this man? What's the victim's name?"

"Ed Wilson."

"Oh." She glanced down, bit her lip.

"You know him?"

"No." She shook her head. Her heart raced. "I just…I remember now that Dan had mentioned his name. You were trying to tie them together just because they arrived on the same flight. Right? But you couldn't. Has something changed?"

"Ma'am." He smiled. "I know yer concerned. I promise to review everything we have. Right now, though—"

"Is Dan okay? Why are there bloody jeans in his bedroom?"

The inspector took a breath. "That's what I would like to explain to ye. We just…Dan and me…we just came from finding the barista boy's body."

"Jamie?" Susan stumbled back. She crossed the room and fumbled for one of the kitchen chairs. She dropped into the seat. "Are you talking about Jamie?"

"Yes. Ye know him."

"I…he's dead?" Susan twisted her head to the side. She wiped at her eyes.

"No, Ma'am. Well, he wasn't. But, close. Might be now. Dan—"

"No." She leapt to her feet. "There's no way he hurt that boy."

The inspector didn't answer.

"No way."

"I was going to say that Dan found him. Stabbed. That's why his pants were bloody. He was helping him."

"Oh." Susan nodded and sat down again. "That sounds more like him. Where is he now? I want to see him."

"Jamie?"

"No! Of course not." She huffed. "My husband."

"He's been calling ye. Why don't ye answer?"

"What?"

Susan rushed into the bedroom to her purse and pulled out her cell. She checked the phone as she walked. "I have 9 missed calls...how is that possible? I must not have heard it ring."

Johnson crossed to the counter. "Do ye mind if I get myself some water?"

She didn't answer at first, fixated instead on the *Missed Calls* list. She lifted her head and motioned with her hand. "No, I don't. Go ahead."

"Can I get ye—"

"No." She dropped into one of the seats at the table. She glanced up at the inspector. "Thank you...Yes. Please."

He opened and closed several cupboards, then seemed to find what he was looking for and pulled a couple of glasses down from a shelf, then filled the cups with some water from the fridge. He handed one of the drinks to her. Susan took the glass and set the cup on the table. She pressed the last of the missed calls to call the number back. Inspector Johnson's phone rang. He reached into his pocket and pulled out his cell.

"He was using my phone."

She hung up and studied the inspector.

"I want to see him now."

"We can do that later."

"No. I want to see him now."

"Ma'am. I just came from finding the boy and getting him help. Then returning Mr. Harris to the station. We came here on the way."

"The bloody jeans." Susan bobbed her head.

"Ma'am?"

389

"I just…the jeans. Was Dan hurt?"

"No," the inspector said. "Just stained from helping the boy. But, as I was saying, I have to get back to the coffee house. I know ye'd like to see yer husband, but there's no time now. I've got to notify the boy's parents."

"I—"

"I'm sorry, Ma'am. But these people may have just lost their son."

Susan glanced down. She nodded.

"You're right. Of course you're right." She picked up her drink and pressed the cup against her lips. She could feel emotion forcing its way up her gullet and she suddenly felt close to vomiting the refuse out again. She opened her mouth wide and sucked in deeply until the nausea passed. Then, she waited while Inspector Johnson finished his water and opened the door and let him out.

"I'll come back here after I notify them. Or I'll make sure Dan calls again. I promise ye."

She nodded. She watched him head up Front Street and closed the entrance.

Ed Wilson. She patted her pants and crossed back into the bedroom. What had she done with the boarding pass?

She tried to run through different scenarios that might explain why her husband would be in possession of something so incriminating. He'd…or he'd…or…But that's where each had stopped. There was no logical reason other than…She felt herself inhaling and exhaling, quick, too quick. She started feeling light headed and shoved her hand out to her side into nothing. She inhaled once more, deep and desperate, and leaned her eyes back and to the ceiling, closing them to what was obvious. She stumbled into the bed and tilted back onto the mattress. She felt herself fall. Tears broke across her face and slid into her ears. She bounced to her feet. Had Cat been right after all? Which was worse? Cat being right? Or Dan being a murderer? Or…a knock interrupted her thinking and she whipped her head toward the living area and wiped at her face.

"Susan?"

Cat's voice. Susan spun, realized she was hovering and staring into nothing in the bedroom. She noticed Dan's bloodied jeans still crumpled near the bathroom.

"Susan?"

Susan rushed across the bed and snatched, well pricked up, the jeans between the thumb and forefinger of one hand, then sprinted the few steps into the bathroom, in front of the shower, and tossed the pants angrily onto the tile bottom. She slammed the door and breathed, then walked as calmly as her anxiety would allow into the entry.

"What do you want, Cat?"

At first there was silence. Then: "It's me, Cat."

"Yes. I know it's you. What do you want?"

"I just wanted to make sure you got settled. See if you needed anything."

"I'm fine. Thanks for stopping by."

Susan started back to the bedroom.

"Susan?"

She stopped. Cat didn't say more. Susan crept closer to the door and pressed her ear against the wood, jerking back as the pounding began again, reverberating throughout her body.

"Susan. Will you open the door? I want to give you something."

Susan glanced at the doorknob, then spun and gazed out at the harbor, at the lighthouse and the storm clouds suspended over the column. The sun pressed through them

391

and gave their misty mid-darkness a strange quality, a sort of smothered glow.

"Susan?" Cat continued. "Did you talk to Dan? Did he say something to you? You know he really doesn't want us to talk. Why do you think that is?"

"I don't know, Cat. And I don't care."

"Well, I promise. I just want to give you something."

"Cat," Susan said emphatically. "Inspector Johnson was just here and I really need to be alone, do some research. Another time perhaps."

"Oh, Inspector Johnson was just here?"

"Yes. And I don't have time for more visitors."

"What did he want?"

Susan dropped her head and eyed the door handle.

"I don't know, Cat. Something about Jamie, the barista kid. I'm getting back to my research. I'll talk to you later."

"Susan, I had no idea you still cared about Dan. Really. But, he pursued me. I kept trying to fight him off but he—"

Susan flipped the door open and blurted out, "What do you want, Cat? I'm really not focused on that right now."

Cat held out a cell phone.

"Just...this is Dan's. I forgot to give it to you before. He left it...well, he left it at my house."

Susan reached across and snatched the phone out of Cat's hand.

"Thanks." Susan shoved the door forward. Cat shifted her foot and blocked the opening."

"You're welcome.

"Susan," she went on, acting hurt. "I thought we left things in a good place. I don't understand what could have changed in such a short period of time. Can't I just come in? We can chat."

"Cat. This is exactly why I didn't want to open the door in the first place. I don't have time for you to just hang out and chat. No interest, either. Move your foot."

Cat didn't budge. She stared back at Susan, her eyes sinking tighter as they waited and finally her stare was nothing but a scowl. Cat pulled back her lips.

"Cat," Susan said. "Now. I'm not kidding."

Cat slowly pulled her leg back.

"You'll be—"

Susan slammed the door the rest of the way closed and whip-locked the bolt. She spun and stomped into the bedroom, pressing back against the wall and sliding down the surface. Her heart was pounding. She rushed her hand to her neck and massaged her fingers against the skin and artery. Lightning flashed behind the lighthouse. She wished the storm would move in faster. The sound of rain splashing in the water and plunking onto the windows and against the roof would wrap around her world—tight. She needed that sense of swaddling.

She glanced at Dan's cell in her hand and hurled it sliding across the floor, under the bed, willing the phone to crash into a wall. But instead the device slowed too soon and skidded to a stop precisely where Dan's bloody jeans had been, probably impeded by the left-over and (hopefully) dried blood. She pressed back against the wall and forced herself up with her legs. Then she walked into the living room and collapsed onto the sofa. Forget trying to see Dan tonight. She needed time. She had new information to process. The boarding pass—

She stopped. She should get her cell and bring the phone into the living room. Dan might call and she might (only might, she emphasized) want to talk to him after all. More lighting silhouetted the lighthouse and thunder broke almost immediately close behind. As the sound died down, she realized someone was knocking at the door. She rushed across the room.

"Cat," she yelled. "I'm not letting you in. I'm tired and I have no, absolutely no, interest in talking to you."

There was no response from the other side of the door. Then a timid: "We're not Cat. We're Wally. And Bea."

"Who?"

"Wally and…"

Susan heard whispering, disparate and rapid. She pulled open the door. Two older women stood on the landing on the other side.

"Mrs. Harris?" One said, the shorter of the two, dressed in black. Susan noted an accent—*Hah-rese* instead of *Harris.*

"Sorry, Ladies." Susan shook her head. "I thought you were someone else."

"Cat?"

"Yes. Do you know her?"

Both women remained silent. Finally, the taller of the two said, slow, "Yes."

Susan grinned.

The taller continued, "My name is Sarah Wallace. Everyone calls me Wally. And this is Mrs. Beatrice Galson. You may call her Bea."

"Nice to meet you both."

No one said more for several seconds. Susan watched as they, apparently, waited for her to continue the conversation. Finally, she stepped back.

"Would you like to come in?"

"Why, thank you. Yes. Of course." They moved into the entry. Wally indicated out the French doors.

"Oh, Bea. Look. How beautiful."

Susan twisted. "I know. Isn't it? I love the view. A little ominous looking right now, but...so, what brings you ladies by this evening? If you're looking for Dan, he's not here."

"We know," said one of the women. "Or we reckoned that might be the case. But we thought we'd try. Then we saw you talking to Cat."

"I..." Susan started, then stopped and inhaled. She shifted her eyes toward the bedroom and to the soft cushions of the couch. She continued, "You know, I was just going to sit down for a rest. I've been traveling all day and I'm exhausted."

"Oh, of course." Wally said, high pitched. "Sorry. That was so inconsiderate of us to inter—"

"No," Susan said. "I...I just. I was actually going to ask if you would mind if we sat down. We can talk some more. Right over here."

Both women smiled. Wally spoke again. "Why, yes. That would be lovely."

The two women followed her and the three sat on the sofa. Susan positioned herself on the wrap-around end, and the two visitors sat opposite her.

"So," Susan began. "Bea. I note an accent. Where are you from?"

"She's from Spain." Wally cut in.

"Wally!" Bea said. "*Deja ya.*" She pushed the back of her hand in Wally's direction, then focused back on Susan. "Yes, I'm from Spain."

"Oh." Susan jumped up from the sofa. "Mrs. Galson. You're Mrs. Galson. Dan had me...I have a gift for you."

As she crossed to her bag, Bea stood. "You have a gift for me?"

"Yes. I…" Susan opened her bag and started shifting around her clothes and belongings. "Dan had me…where?"

She let the suitcase fall closed and spun around. "Well, there was a gift for you. I don't know what happened to it. It was right on top. I stuck it in at the last moment. Or I thought I did…"

She returned to the case and lifted the lid and shuffled through her things again.

"I know I packed it. I don't….It was a book. Something in Spanish. So—"

"*Los Amores de Ana*?"

"Yes. That was it. *Los Amores de Ana,*" she repeated.

"He asked you to…" Bea dropped her hands into her lap and turned to Wally. "That's *The Loves of Ana*. It's by José María Santana Rodríguez. He's from Cádiz. That's the book I've been bothering Cat to get for the library. But the original. He must have…" She spun to Susan.

"He asked you to get it for me?"

"Yes. But, I'm so sorry. I'm almost certain I packed it. I…" She bit her lip. "I don't know what happened. We'll get you another."

"No. Certainly not." Bea shook her head. "It's not necessary ¡*Mi madre*¡ He's so…Mrs. Harris—"

"Susan, please. But, really, we'll get another. He was so insistent that I find it. It was almost like he was more interested in my getting the book than in seeing me on my last visit."

Susan paused. "Can I get you ladies some water?"

"Oh, yes please." Wally said and stood. "But you sit. As you said, you've been traveling all day. I'll get it. Do you mind?"

"No, I don't. Thank you." Susan rested back and pointed toward the kitchen. "The glasses are in that cupboard right there. On the left. There's water in the fridge."

She twisted to Bea and whispered, "Dan wanted me to get some for him at the jail, but I didn't because I figured there'd be some here." She grinned. "Hope I wasn't wrong."

Susan glanced over at Wally. She seemed to be reading something on the counter. "Wally? Is everything okay."

"Mrs. Har—Susan. Who is Edward Wilson?"

* * * *

Cat crept closer to the coffee house door, slow.

She peeked inside. Inspector Johnson stood, facing the back of the kitchen, resting his arm on what she assumed was a mop, likely cleaning up the blood and mess that Jamie had left behind. She wanted to rush in to him, to insist that this was not his job, that Jean should be in there, scrubbing and struggling to rid herself and her family of the stain that was Jamie. But she couldn't take the risk. No one could be trusted.

She refocused on the inspector. He wasn't moving, just staring into the back area of the kitchen, toward the door going out. Then he snatched up the wood pole and leaned it against one of the counters (from this angle she could see for sure—he'd been carrying a mop). He rinsed his hands in the sink and dried them, then crossed to the rear exit. He pulled a handkerchief out of his back pocket and wrapped the cloth around the doorknob, opening the door and stepping out and glancing around outside. He moved back inside and leaned into the door to push it closed. She sneered.

Did he really think it mattered which door Dan had come through? The boy was dead. Nothing would change that. And now Dan looked even more guilty. She grinned.

Inspector Johnson turned and pressed his back against the wood, then stepped deliberately, mouthing what Cat guessed were numbers until he reached the spot where she'd stabbed Jamie and he'd resisted but then died surprisingly fast. Suddenly. She'd dropped him and run out when she'd thought she heard someone coming, but—she would always wonder if she'd overreacted—she was pretty sure shortly after that all she heard was rumblings from the distant storm.

She focused back on the investigation at hand. Her heart froze. She ducked. Inspector Johnson had been staring directly in her direction. She sprinted down the road and into some bushes at the side, clutching at her chest, at her thumping heart, laughing, almost cackling at the rush she felt. The edge. That's what made life so good.

And then she watched.

And waited.

* * * *

Susan flashed her eyes at Bea. She bolted from the sofa and rushed across the room, thrusting her hand forward to snatch the paper Wally was staring at, but the woman grabbed the boarding pass and stepped back.

"Get out!" Susan said.

"Isn't Edward Wilson the name of the man that was killed? Why do you have his boarding pass?"

"Just give me the paper and get out!" She spun to face Bea and motioned to her. "Both of you. Out."

"I think you should explain," Wally said.

"Why?" Susan shook her head. "I don't owe you any kind of an explanation. I just met you."

"Did you kill that man?"

"Of course not. I wasn't even here in Hope Town."

"Did Dan?"

Susan didn't respond. She marched across to the living room to her cell sitting on the sofa. She grabbed the phone and dialed. "I want you both to go. Set the paper on the table and—"

A phone in the bedroom started ringing. Susan flashed her eyes to the room and dropped her hand to the side. She sunk to the floor, blinking away any indication of what she was feeling. This was too much. She let the phone fall into her lap and started whimpering.

Bea scooted closer to Susan on the sofa and tried to comfort her, but only her fingertips reached the woman and instead the Spaniard ended up mostly comforting Susan's shoulder. Wally moved to the table and dragged one of the chairs around the end of the sofa. She placed the chair next to Susan and sat at her side.

"Love." Wally leaned into her. "Don't cry. Please. We're not accusing you of anything. Just wondering. Why do you have Edward Wilson's boarding pass?"

Susan inhaled and wiped at her face. She breathed out, tilted her head back. "I just need you to go."

"But…" Wally stopped. "Love. Your phone."

"What?"

Susan glanced down at the cell in her hands. The screen had lit up and *Unknown* had popped up on the display.

"Oh." She grabbed the phone and pressed it against her ear but dropped it again into her lap. She snatched the cell, fumbling, and slammed it against her ear.

"Hello?"

"Susan." It was Dan. "I've been call—"

"Why do you have Ed Wilson's boarding pass?"

At first the phone was silent.

"You found it. Good."

"Yes. Of course I found it. And why would that be good? That's not good. Why do you have it? Did you kill that man?"

Susan heard Bea gasp. Wally started pacing at Susan's side. Dan sighed.

"No."

"That's it? No."

"I took it from Cat's."

"From Cat's?"

Wally stopped her pacing and shifted closer to Susan.

"Yes. I didn't mean to, but she was going to catch me and I had to shove it in my pocket."

Susan paused. She glanced at Wally and Bea while struggling to her feet with one hand. Wally reached out and tried to help at one point, but Susan merely knocked the woman's hand out of her sight and scowled. She rushed across the room to the bedroom, leaning away from the women and resting against the door jamb. She spoke softly. "Dan, you have to tell me the truth. I'm not just your wife here. I'm your attorney. If I'm going—"

"Susan," Dan said. "I promise. I took it from Cat's. I didn't kill anybody...Cat did. She's dangerous."

"She just came by and brought me your phone."

"Oh."

"Why did she have your phone, Dan?"

"I told you, I was at her house. I must left it there."

"So how are you calling me now?"

"I found another cord."

"What?"

"I found...nothing. From the police station."

"Oh. So you left your phone at Cat's. Where was she?"

"What?"

"Where was Cat when you were doing all this alleged snooping? I assume she knew you were there. Or are we adding breaking and entering to your rap sheet?" Susan shrugged. "Why wasn't she able to see you in the first place?"

"She..." Dan paused and Susan could hear him breathing on the other end.

"Never mind," Susan said. "I don't want to know. So you're at the police station. Inspector Johnson told me he'd arrested you."

"You saw him?"

"Yes. He came by the house. He told me about Jamie." She dropped her head and pressed her fingers against her lips. She shook her head. "I'm really sorry, Dan. I can't... how are you with all that?"

"I'm okay...worried, of course. But okay. Inspector Johnson came by? Does that mean you're at the house now?"

"Yes."

"I'm coming there."

"They don't have you locked up?"

"No." He chuckled. "They don't even really have a jail here."

"Stay there."

"What? Why? There's no place for you to sleep here. You won't be comfortable."

"I'm not coming there, Dan. I'm just...it will be worse for you if you leave. Wally and Bea are here. They—"

401

"Wow. You're making friends faster than I ever did." She could picture his smile as he teased her and her heart sunk. She missed him.

"Seriously, though. I'm coming there. It's too dangerous. Those two aren't going to be much help to you."

"No, Dan. Stay. You need to be as cooperative as possible. We need them to stop seeing you as antagonistic."

"I'm not antagonistic." (Susan rolled her eyes.) "And it doesn't really matter to me what they think if it means Cat can get to you."

"It matters to me. I'm your lawyer. And I'm telling you, don't come here."

The line was silent. Too long. Susan even peeked at the display at one point to make sure they were still connected. Finally, she said, "Dan?"

"I'm here…Okay. But lock everything. Windows, doors. Everything."

"Yes, Sir." Susan smiled.

"And what's going on? I've been calling and calling and you don't ever answer. I've been freaking out here."

"Yeah." She glanced around for her phone, then realized she was talking on it. She rushed the cell back against her cheek. "For some reason my phone isn't ringing. I have it turned all the way up too."

"Restart the phone."

"Really, Genius? You think I should restart the phone? If only I'd thought of that." She paused, wiped at her left, then her right eye.

"Okay, thanks for the advice," she went on. "I better get back to my new friends." She cringed. "I think I just kicked them out. I'll have to apologize and ask them to stay."

She bit her lip, hesitating, then continued, "I love you."

"Love you more."

Susan hung up the phone and pivoted. Wally and Bea scurried away from her as she turned. She grinned.

"Well, hello ladies."

Wally started to say something, then shrugged. "You were talking too soft. It was hard to hear you."

"Well," Susan said. "You probably heard then. I'd like you to stay. I'm sorry. I feel so much better now that I've talked to Dan. I'd really like you to stay."

"So, did he kill that man?"

"Bea!" Wally nudged her.

"No, he didn't," Susan said. "And it's okay. That's a fair question. But, I really can't share any details about this with either of you. I hope you understand."

"Of course, we do." Wally stepped forward and wrapped her arms around Susan. "But for what it's worth, I don't think he did anything they're accusing him of, either. Even all these rumors about Cat are ridiculous. Just look at you."

Susan smiled. "Please. Come sit down, both of you. Are you hungry?" She stared toward the fridge. "I'm not sure what Dan has but I can look and see."

"No, thank you. We really need to get going. It's going to be too stormy soon."

Bea had started toward the living area but had stopped and stood, focused on something on the table.

"This date."

"What date?" Susan asked her.

"On the boarding pass. The date."

Susan nodded. "What about it?"

403

"That's our anniversary. Of my Robert and me. We always ate at the Abaco Club to celebrate. I still go alone, now that he's no longer with us. *Que en paz descanse.*" She paused.

"That's so nice. What a beautiful tradition."

"Yes, but...what I mean..." Bea picked up the stub and pointed at the date. "...is that I was in Marsh Harbour that day. I saw Cat."

Bea paused and stared at Susan. Susan spoke again: "I'm not sure I understand what your point is."

"I saw her at the dock just outside of Marsh Harbour. I had just arrived on the last ferry. There were no more that day...I always stay the night...she has her own boat, so I don't know if she was coming or going. But she was with some man that I'd never seen before."

Susan shifted forward.

"Could the man have been Ed Wilson?"

"I don't know. I've never seen him. But he wasn't from Hope Town. That I know."

"Dan said he found the boarding pass at her house. He must..." She glanced at Bea and Wally. "Did you see Dan, too?"

"No," Bea said. "Just Cat."

Susan dropped into one of the chairs at the table and plunged her head into her hands. She broke down again. Wally rushed to her side.

"Love, are you okay? Is something wrong?"

Susan raised her head. "No, nothing's wrong. Thank you. That just answers so many questions for me."

Bea stepped closer to her. "We could go by Cat's to say hello and drop the boarding pass back there. That would—"

404

"No." Susan stood. "Absolutely not. It's too dangerous."

Wally placed her hand on Susan's forearm. "But, she'd never suspect us."

"No." Susan shook her head. "That's not happening. We'll figure something out. Dan would say the same thing. It's too dangerous."

"But," Wally said. "What Bea said proves he didn't kill the man."

Susan shook her head. "No. I'm afraid it doesn't. I wish it did. It helps. But without a picture of this man—or at least your knowing him by sight—this information really isn't as incriminating as it all might seem. It's only anecdotal. And there's always that chance that we're wrong, that there's some kind of explanation."

The two women nodded, but looked confused.

"Well, we really should be going," Wally said. "The storm will be here soon and we don't want to be caught in it. My house is all the way across town."

"Of course." Susan nodded. She motioned to their drinks. "Are you both done?"

"Yes, thank you."

Susan picked up their glasses and crossed to the counter. She set them in the sink, then she returned and showed the two women to the door. At the entrance, Wally twisted and said, "Will you take my phone number and call me if you need anything? Please? I can write it down for you."

She smiled and pivoted toward Bea. "I have a cell phone now. My daughter gave it to me."

"Yes." Bea didn't look amused. "She's very proud of it."

"As well she should be." Susan smiled. "And thank you. Both. It's so nice to have met you."

Susan found a pen and some paper and Wally wrote down her number. She handed Susan the scrap and moved toward the door again. She turned.

"Anything."

"Thank you."

Susan opened the door and walked out with them. She hugged them.

"Thanks again. Have a good night."

* * * *

Cat realized quickly, very quickly…after squashing a bug that seemed to think it was appropriate to crawl across her shoe…she realized very quickly sequestered, as it were, in the overgrown side of the road, that she really had nothing to worry about. Inspector Johnson wasn't looking for her. He was after Dan. Dan's escape had only given her more sure-fire cover for her latest indiscretion. As far as he knew, she was just some curious passerby. But still, she kept a distance between them.

When he, at last, stepped out of the coffee house, Cat studied his movements from the safety of the forest. He pushed the coffee house door closed, then pulled again at the opening, certainly to ensure that it was locked securely. He stepped back. He unwound some crime scene tape and stretched the plastic ribbon across the doorway. He paused and stared straight ahead. Then he worked the tape into the waist of his pants, rotated and started down Front Street.

She ducked farther into the trees as he passed. He stopped when he'd only gone a few feet beyond her and pulled out his phone, started dialing, then shook his head and pushed the cell back into his pocket. She grinned, lascivious. Awww, she thought. He has yet to inform the Fergusons about their son's death and he just doesn't know how he'll do it. So pathetic. Blunt. That was how you handled something like this. Just let the parents start their wailing and be done with it. Really, it's just more compassionate that way. The sooner you ruin their world, the sooner they'll be able to try to forget.

He began again, reaching the area in front of Dan's house. That was when she slipped onto the road and tagged along behind him. As she followed him down the street, though, Dan's front door opened and she darted back into the trees. She watched. Bea and Wally, then Susan stepped out. Susan hugged both women, smiling, looking annoying and glowing and perfect. Susan smiled as the women strolled away from her toward the center of town. Then she surveyed the area outside the house, nodded, smiled (again!) and went back inside. She closed the door. Cat leered.

Susan was alone.

Forty

Susan leaned into the door as she closed the opening and locked it. She pulled out her cell, studied it, flipped the phone over in her hand. She checked the volume. Again. Max—for good measure she bumped the top lever over and over. She opened the device's settings and clicked on *Sounds*. Both vibrate and ring were turned off. She sighed and gritted her teeth and darted her eyes across the room. She squeezed her eyes closed.

Dan had never needed water. That had been nothing more than a ploy to keep her away longer, to allow Cat more time to turn everything off. She adjusted the volume up again—all the way—and switched on *Vibrate* to be sure she wouldn't miss any more calls. Then she glanced around the empty house, even more desolate after the departure of Wally and Bea and her new knowledge that Cat wasn't just odd. And unpleasant. She was potentially dangerous.

"Maybe some food."

She grinned. She really was lonely, announcing her intentions to an unoccupied room.

"Now I'm walking to the refrigerator," she declared. "Nothing in the fridge. Maybe the cupboards."

She laughed.

She pulled out a can of tomato bisque and heated up the soup, then poured her dinner into a bowl and placed the meal on a tray. She crossed to the couch. She wanted to watch the storm and, she hoped, see the lighthouse break into the clouds and begin the beam's circling as the day sunk into dark. She opened the French doors so she could feel the breeze inside, then sat back on the couch and placed the tray on her lap.

She glanced at her phone. No call from Dan yet. It turned out that she didn't like being in this house alone after all. Especially not after what Dan had said about Cat. Could the woman really be a killer? Could she have killed this man Ed? And Jamie? Her eyes teared and she wiped at the sides of her face with her fingers. She exhaled.

She lifted a spoonful to her lips. The soup was still too hot. She lowered the spoon and set it back in the bowl.

Did Jamie's parents know, yet? Maybe they still hadn't found out and they were acting out their evening, frustrated that, yet again, Jamie had decided not to answer his phone, or at least called and told them he'd be late. Or even acknowledged what it was to be a parent and worry and fret about the evil that hovered everywhere in this world. Senseless. Or maybe they're angry at him for being so inconsiderate. And then when they did find out, they would always know that their last thoughts of him before they learned the truth had been of their own inconvenience.

She set her tray to the side and rushed into the bedroom to look for some tissues. Dan, being the man that he was, didn't have a box of Kleenex anywhere in sight, so she hurried into the bathroom and grabbed a roll of toilet paper. She returned to her dinner, tearing off a few squares and dabbing at her eyes and touching at her nose as she moved.

* * * *

Cat ducked into a small strip of land on the north side of the Dan's house. She blinked. The clouds were still dropping nothing more than sprinkles. But, along the home's outer wall under the boughs of the surrounding trees, although the drops fell less frequently, they landed with more force—the extra wait time produced larger bundles of water that sometimes crashed directly into one of her eyes and made seeing more difficult. Thus, the blinking.

She snuck up to below a window and stood on her tiptoes to peek in. She knew (from her snooping—Dan could be so naive) that this opening led into the bathroom, which led to the bedroom, which led to the rest of the house. Susan was somewhere along that trajectory. She pulled back. Listened. There was always the chance that she'd end up looking directly at Susan and neither she nor Susan (she felt confident predicting) wanted that to happen.

She heard nothing, so she stretched up and pressed her hand against the outside of the glass. She shifted her arm. The window slid. Silent. That was good. Good enough for the moment. She pushed the opening closed again.

She needed to know exactly where Susan was in the house before she ventured into the building. So she returned to Front Street, leering as she saw that night was finally descending on them. She strolled across the street and turned and peeked through the trees. The sun was indeed setting behind the lighthouse. So seductive.

She flinched. Out of the corner of her eye, she noticed Mark Rollie strolling toward her. No time to run back to the alley she'd just come from. But no one, and she meant no one, could see her tonight. She crouched facing away from Mark and the house and pretended to be studying a flower, no a rock. She waited as the man came closer and then slowed in front of Dan's house and stopped. What was he doing? Her breathing accelerated. She focused, inhaling and exhaling. She should have brought her knife. She'd not wanted to be tempted to use the blade on Susan, though. She still needed the woman's death to be ruled an accident. But this...She strained to glance over her shoulder, or better, she realized, to the side. She could keep an eye on him through her peripheral vision. She scanned the earth in front of her for a larger boulder. Just in case.

She found one and leaned forward, catching clearer sight of him as she bent. She was safe. He'd merely approached Dan's kitchen window. That snake. He was spying on Susan. And he wasn't leaving, only twisting and adjusting, certainly trying to find a better view. Maybe she'd have to kill him anyway, just so he wouldn't interrupt her plans and because it turned out that he was just another typical man. But then, all at once, he started on his way again and headed north on Front Street.

Cat exhaled. She pushed to her feet, then spun and started across the street. She froze, flustered again. The door knob to Dan's front door jiggled. She panicked. There was no time. She darted her eyes up and down the street, lunging forward, then back. She'd never manage to duck and inspect rocks again before the opening swung open. But then again, she thought, Susan would be the one walking out. She shifted forward instead, confident, ready. But the entry had fallen silent again. She waited. Then she glanced in both directions down the street and sidled up to the kitchen window. She stretched and twisted and massaged her hand against her neck, as if she were only trying to soothe sore muscles. Even if she'd not noticed and there was, in fact, someone hurrying home, anticipating a storm, they'd hardly remember seeing anything as she peeked in at the clueless woman. She spied.

Susan sat on the sofa, facing the deck and the lighthouse, staring straight ahead, dabbing at her face with what looked like a tissue, then lifting and lowering her hand in front of her. Eating. She must be eating. And she was beautiful. Even the back of her head was aggravating. Cat flared her nostrils and gritted her teeth. She hated her.

She ripped herself away from the window and stomped back to the strip of land, storming up to the window and sliding the glass completely to the side, not focusing any more on stealth. She wrapped her fingers around the ledge and tried to pull herself up. Too high. She surveyed the area. Someone had thrown some trash down the side, and among the debris was a crate. That would give her the extra height she needed. She kicked the box over to below the window (she wasn't about to touch the thing). Then she climbed on and stretched up.

The wind brushed by her and all at once Cat could hear angry rain splashing into the street to her left and pelting the layers of tree and cover above her. Lightning lit the island and almost instantaneously a crash broke out and surrounded the town. Perfect. Even if Susan were to hear anything, the storm would give her cover.

Time to get out of the rain.

She pulled herself up and crawled through the opening.

* * * *

Susan stepped out of the bedroom and crossed to the couch, but she flinched suddenly and spun. She inched forward. She'd seen a face in the kitchen window, she was sure of it. She held motionless and listened, then rushed across to the front door and verified that the handle was, in fact, securely locked. She pivoted and glanced to the French doors. Was she vulnerable? Should she close the doors? Secure them? Hole herself up in the bathroom and wait out the night?

She took in a deep breath through her nose. No. Not yet. She was just being paranoid. She returned to the sofa and set the roll of toilet paper at her feet, keeping a few squares in her hand. She smushed into the cushions and repositioned herself and her dinner platter. Then she dabbed again at her eyes and nose, and set the tissue to her side. She continued her dinner.

If she only had Jamie's parents' phone number. She'd call them, tell them that she could never know exactly what they were going through but that she too, just eight months ago—eight months, one week, and four days ago—had lost a child. She had survived through what they were living, even though too many times she didn't think she would. But—she whipped her head—no. Every grieving mother deserves to have her grief all to herself. She shouldn't have to share with some well-meaning American.

She glanced out the French doors over the harbor. Suddenly, torrents of wet splashed into the harbor. The sun was dropping out of sight behind the lighthouse and now the beacon circled, attempting to reassure those within its radius. She'd missed the change. The peace had started without her.

She ate a few more spoonfuls of her dinner (blowing was no longer necessary), then she set the spoon in the bowl and gazed out at the lighthouse. Breathtaking. She loved being here. How lucky they'd been to meet Richard on their last visit—

She spun her head to the right. What...?

Air rushed across the deck and through the French doors and a whine squealed by Susan. She felt a bolt of cold and her skin pimpled up and she cast her eyes to the

413

doors, then back toward the bedroom. She inhaled, deep. Then she grinned. She was being ridiculous. First she sees a face in the window, lurking, then every sound is a chaotic warning of imminent danger. She stared into her lap at the bisque and frowned. She didn't want the soup anymore, so she carried the tray to the kitchen and set her dinner on the counter, then returned to the couch.

She sat back down and stared out the doors to the storm. Her book was on the end table and she stretched for it and tabbed through the pages to find where she'd stopped reading, sliding toward one end of the sofa as she did so she could recline.

Immediately, she spun her head and sat forward. Her hair flipped into her mouth and she spit and grabbed at the strands. Her heart pounded. She clutched at her chest and felt like whimpering. *How do you know?* she wanted to yell! How can a person tell what's inside and what's outside in this kind of weather?

She focused. Breathed. She stood from the couch, crept slowly to the kitchen and filled a glass with some water from the fridge. She guzzled the drink, then closed her eyes and inhaled, exhaled. She refilled the cup, picked up her soup and returned to the living room, setting the water on the side table and the bowl on the floor next to the toilet paper. Maybe she'd want some more in a few minutes. Then she sat back and opened her book.

Rushing sounded behind her (she jerked, but too late) and something, something clear stretched over her head. Hands wrapped around her neck. Susan flailed over her head with her book but almost instantly one of the hands left her neck and the novel ripped out of her fingers. Her hand pulled away reflexively as one of the pages sliced across her thumb. She heard paper flutter and a thud against a wall to her right. The hand flashed back to her neck. She gasped but only plastic whipped in and spread tight against the ridge of her mouth and her teeth. She pried at the fingers wrapped around her, panicked, then pulled her hands forward and started jabbing with her nails.

"Ow. Ow. Stop that."

Cat. The voice was Cat's.

What felt like a fist slammed against the side of her head. She stretched to the side, to her water glass that she'd just filled, but she heard, "No, no. I see that. Don't even try it. I can finish this right now if I have to."

Susan blew out, creating a bubble and scratched at the plastic with her fingers until she caught some traction and ripped at what was certainly just a bag. Air rushed against her lips. She sucked in.

Cat yanked her head back and to the side and, amidst the chaos, Susan sank down into the cushions until Cat's grip was too weak and her hands flew loose. She ripped the plastic off her head, still gasping. Susan spun and faced Cat.

Cat glared at her. "Oh, you think you're so great. You got free of a bag."

Cat bent forward and tossed the sofa section forward. Tomato soup splashed across the tile. Susan tried to run, but slipped instead on the newly wet floor. Cat crashed on top of her and Susan's breath gushed out. Cat pummeled into her left side. She fought to flip herself over and managed to force her body through Cat's grip enough that the two women fought mostly face to face. Susan kicked and squirmed and punched (sort of) and managed to thrust Cat back and the woman stumbled up and skidded without traction until she crashed on the bisque-covered floor.

Susan heard Cat release a moan. She leapt to her feet and darted toward the front door of the house. Storm or not, she could at least run to town, run to Dan at the police station. But suddenly a weight crashed onto her back and fingers pressed against her eyes and blinded her. She began to spin, hoping to dislodge Cat and send her flying. She had height on her. But Cat was tenacious. And strong.

A wall. She could back into a wall and body slam the woman until she was forced to let go. She rushed backward. And backward...and backward. She must be headed toward the wall before the deck. She felt rain. Or, she breathed in, they had just barreled past the doors. She struggled to change direction but instead lost her balance and no longer moved back intentionally but fell back, chaotic and clumsy.

Suddenly they hit a barrier, low, clearly the railing. Susan pulled forward as soon as she realized what they'd hit, but too late and they tumbled together off the deck and splashed into the harbor. Cat immediately released, whether for self-preservation or because of shock at the sudden wetness. She began to thrash and kick Susan.

Susan felt Cat press down on her shoulders, bouncing herself out of the water while pressing Susan's head lower and beneath the surface. Cat's hands moved from Susan's shoulders to her head and Susan realized with panic that Cat was forcing her even lower. She swung her own hands forward, hitting into Cat's side, but recognized as she did that the strikes were useless because of the thickness of the water. She stopped struggling. Cat might believe she was suddenly unconscious and beaten and release her. But nothing. Cat continued to hold her in place underwater. So instead Susan dove lower and lower, too long without oxygen, and she swam, desperate, in the opposite direction of where Cat had been. Her head finally bobbed above the surface and she gasped for air.

Susan heard a splash. Then something yanked her and she started gliding back toward the house. She started swinging and hitting and kicking and above the flailing she heard, "Susan. Stop. It's me."

The hands pushed her toward the ladder of the dock and guided her hands to the rungs.

"Climb."

And then he swam off into the harbor and the storm and the tempest.

"Dan!" Susan yelled. "Dan!"

Lightning flashed and she caught him swimming and his silhouette reached a mass and she saw him raise his fist and swing down and he shoved up from the water and thrust again and the mass bobbed. But then the light was gone and all she could hear was splashing and wind and thunder and she screamed out again, "Dan! I need you!"

In flashes, she could see intermittent struggling and only barely discern the constant splashing and then suddenly the movement stopped and there was calm, except for the storm. She ran from one end of the deck to the other, searching through the darkness and the racket of water hitting water. She screamed into the wind and storm, "Dan!" and again, "Dan!" and then she fell silent and paused. She shifted along the deck, more slowly this time, straining to verify anything or even to know that either continued alive before her. She needed lightning. But only black. All she saw and heard was wind. And rain. Finally, she caught a figure out of the corner of her eye ascending the ladder. She flipped and raised a fist, ready to fight off her assailant. But then the light swung by and she saw him.

She rushed to him and reached for him and pulled him into her. She cried. She held him, grasping and squeezing. He nudged her forward and motioned. "In the house."

Susan spun, "But Cat."

Dan shook his head.

"You drowned her? Dan—"

"No." He looked emotionless. "I don't know. I'm just saying I don't know. She just stopped being there. I have no idea what happened. So, in the house."

Susan twisted and scanned the black. She hurried inside and he secured the doors, glancing quickly, looking perplexed, at the tomato bisque splattered across the tile. They gripped each other, silent, gasping and feeling their hearts race against each other's chests. Finally, she pulled away.

"What are you doing here?"

"Well, hello to you too," he breathed.

She grinned. "Very funny. I see what you're doing. You've made your point. Now, what are you doing here?"

"Inspector Johnson came back from the Fergusons...those are Jamie's parents. He said he'd seen you at the house and I told him I knew and that I was worried and he just interrupted me and said to go. Right then. So I did."

His face flushed. "And I'm so glad I did. I couldn't have..."

Susan peered into his eyes, then hugged him. "Me too."

Forty-One

Wally paced. She huffed and spun and darted her eyes at her watch, then twisted to peek through the trees, straining to catch sight of the day's first rays as they bounced across the harbor. The sun was rising behind her, and Bea was late. She stomped her foot and hovered at the beginning of the street that led to Cat's house, releasing an exaggerated sigh for no one's benefit but her own. Spaniards. Was a little punctuality too much to ask? Wally was nervous enough. She didn't need this extra aggra—

"Bea. There you are. Finally."

Bea slowed, stepping deliberately, clearly taking her time, and most certainly intending only to add to Wally's apprehension. Wally noted hints of a grin that Bea seemed intent on suppressing. As she came closer, Wally said, "My land, Bea. We don't have time for this."

And then she mumbled in a low voice, "You have the boarding pass?"

"Yes, for course. Let's go."

Bea continued, finally walking more briskly and pivoting onto Cat's street, motioning to Wally as she passed. "Well, come on. We don't have all day."

"Bea…Bea…" Wally caught up to her. She grabbed the woman's shoulder. "What's the plan?"

"Plan? There is no plan. We're just on a visit. If I have to, I'll just drop the paper on the sofa and we'll go."

Wally pursed her lips. After a moment, she whipped her head back and forth and muttered, "Fine. Let's go." But the reality was, she simply didn't have a better idea. Strategies weren't something she'd ever been particularly good at. Mostly, she merely went along with whatever was happening around her.

The two women paused on Cat's deck. Two panes were broken in the window on the side of her front door.

"Well!" Bea exclaimed and harrumphed. Apparently, that was enough to pass judgement and communicate her disapproval. Bea rapped on the entrance. They waited several seconds, then she knocked again.

Wally spoke through the empty panes. "Cat? Are you home?"

Bea knocked again, this time pounding on the door with the flat side of her fist. The door nudged open.

Wally called out again, "Cat?" and slid forward, grabbing the handle and almost pulling the opening closed. Bea knocked her hand away.

"Wally, *tonta*."

"Bea, don't be rude."

"Well, she's not home. Obviously. And, look, the door's open."

"I know that. I was trying to close it when you accosted me. We'll just have to come back later."

"Why would we do that?" Bea said, prodding the door in with her foot. "There's no reason we can't just go in now."

She twisted and grinned at Wally, then moved through the opening. Wally followed her.

"Bea, we can't. This is so…" She glanced around the room and her expression immediately dropped into a grimace. She pressed her hand against her stomach.

"Wally." Bea twirled to face her and motioned to the air. "She's a murderer. And that man you like so much is getting blamed for it. I'm just going to put this…" She held up the scrap and crossed the room. "…on her desk over here and then we can go."

"We don't know that for sure. And, besides, you like him too."

"That's not the point," she said. "We're doing the right thing. Just be a good girl and do as I say."

Wally scowled. She moved closer to Bea and nudged her friend's shoulder, motioning to the stub Bea had just placed on the desk. "At least put it in a drawer so it's less noticeable. But hurry. We don't want her coming home while we're still inside."

Bea pulled open the left side drawer and swept the boarding pass into the opening. There was a brown-paper package on the desk. She picked up the parcel.

"Wally, look. It has my name on it."

"Cat got you a present? I thought you said she hated you."

"She does. It's a book. Look at it. This is the book Susan was trying to find. I'm certain."

"Bea, now you're just being ridiculous. You don't know that. And how would Cat get the package, anyway?"

"I don't know. But I'm taking it."

Bea tucked the package under her arm and started snooping through the desk.

"And now you're a thief." Wally flicked her fingers at Bea and raised her eyebrows.

Bea shrugged. She opened the file drawer and started to finger through the hanging folders. Then she shoved the drawer closed and crossed to the kitchen. She started pulling out kitchen drawers and opening cupboards. She spoke forcefully as she went.

"*¡Qué guarra, esta mujer!*

"Bea, stop snooping. You're such a snoop! And speak English. Let's go. We already did what we came to do."

Bea grabbed a crusty butter knife and held it up. "See. *Guarra.*"

She set the present on the counter and ran the blade along the side at the top. She pulled back the paper.

"Look," she said, holding up a book. "I knew it. '*Los Amores de Ana.*' *Te lo dije.* What did I tell you?"

"Fine. Bea. You were right. Now let's go."

Bea tossed the knife toward the sink. The metal utensil bounced off the counter and fell onto the floor. She shrugged and hurried across to Wally.

"I'm taking the book."

Wally rolled her eyes and opened the door.

"Fine. May we go now?"

"*Lista.*" Bea grinned.

Wally moved outside and started down the steps. Suddenly, she spun around and scurried back toward Bea. She scanned the area, then grabbed the woman by the shoulders and pulled her into the house. She pushed the door closed with her back.

"It's her. She's coming down the street. There's a boy walking with her carrying grocery bags. I guess she was just shopping."

Bea darted around Cat's house, muttering, "We have to hide. We have to hide." She twisted and pointed toward the front entrance.

"The door. It was open before. You closed it. *Tonta.* We should leave it like it was. She'll know."

Wally spun and reached to open the door.

"No!" Bea shouted and Wally twisted to face her.

Bea went on, softly this time, "Yes, okay. But hurry...No! Stop. It's too late. Just leave it."

"Bea, I don't know what you expect me to do."

"Leave it." Bea whispered and rushed into the bathroom, motioning for Wally to follow her. She pushed the door gently closed.

"Great," Wally whispered. "Now we're trapped. And in the dark."

"*Mujer, no seas—*"

"Shhh!"

"Well, it's not that—"

"Bea!" Wally whisper-shouted.

They heard the front door open and the sound of rustling plastic. "Thank you." Pause.

"Yer welcome. And, thank ye, Ma'am."

Wally whispered, "I don't feel very well. This is all your fault."

"My fault? *¿Cómo es que yo—*"

"Shhh. She'll hear us."

Outside the bathroom they could hear shifting and moving and footfalls leading out of the house, growing quieter, then after a moment, becoming louder again and sounding closer, inside the house. The noises repeated their sequence. During one of the pauses, Bea pivoted to Wally.

"Maybe she'll just leave and we'll be okay. We can just—"

The steps returned. Wally's phone started ringing. They both began whispering frantically.

"Turn it off, Wally. Turn it off."

Ring.

"I'm trying, Bea."

Ring.

423

"I don't know how. What do I do?"

Ring.

"How would I know? It's your phone."

Ring.

"Bea."

Ring.

"Just answer it. But don't say—"

Ri—

"Hello?"

The door to the bathroom shoved open, knocking both women down and against the wall. They struggled back to their cowering.

"Hello, Ladies."

Forty-Two

Dan kissed Susan's cheek and slipped out of bed. He headed into the bathroom. At the doorway, he spun and peeked back at his wife.

"Do you mind if I jump in the shower first? I'll be quick." He tilted his head and grinned. "Or you could just join me if you want."

"Tempting...but no. Thanks. Besides, we just did that last night. I think I'm going to call Wally, thank her for stopping by, make sure they know how nice it was to meet them."

Dan shrugged and closed the door. She heard him say, "My loss."

She smiled and crossed the room to the dresser. She grabbed her cell, then reached her hand into each of her pockets, pulling the contents out and spreading the items out across the surface of the chest of drawers. She located what she'd been looking for: the scrap of paper Wally had written her phone number on. She dialed. The phone rang several times. She waited, surprised that the voice mail never picked up. She was about to disconnect when she heard a timid voice say:

"Hello?" Raspy, slow, whispered.

"Wally?"

At first she heard nothing in return. Then a scuffling sound and a distant, "Hello, Ladies." The voice was Cat's.

She stumbled back and bumped against the bed. "Wally! Wally! Can you hear me?"

Then: distant, accented. Bea. "We can explain. We jus—"

"Who are you talking to?"

"Yes."

"Wally," Susan said. "You can hear me?"

"Yes."

She heard Cat yell, "I said who are you talking to?"

Susan pushed off the mattress and paced into the living room and across to the French doors. She peeked out. Another storm was moving in. So early. She pulled back the doors and stepped onto the deck.

"Wally, are you okay?"

"No."

"Give me that phone."

"Please," she heard Wally say. "It's just Dan's wife. The phone was a gift from my daughter. I live alone and she was—"

"If you don't give me that phone now, you won't live long enough to need it."

Susan rushed back into the house and toward the bathroom and shower. Dan.

Cat came on the line.

"Susan. I've missed you. How have you been?"

Susan froze.

"Cat, leave them alone."

"Oh," Cat said. "I don't care about them. I just want you."

"Done."

"Really? Done?"

Susan started toward Dan again.

"Stop!"

426

Susan flashed her eyes around the house. How…?

"So, here's what we're going to do. Where are you?"

"At home."

"Where at home, dear?"

Susan considered for a moment. Did the room matter? "I'm in the living room."

"Walk out of the house."

"Okay, but I'm not wearing any shoes. Give me a minute."

"No. You'll be fine. Is Dan anywhere near you?"

Susan scanned around herself and glanced longingly toward the bathroom. "He's right here. Should I put him on?"

"Yes. Why don't you do that."

She started toward the shower.

"Are you going to get him, dear?"

"He's right here…just a second."

"Stop walking now!" Cat yelled into the phone.

Susan's skin instantly popped and she felt tears breaking into her eyes. She spun, then spun again, feeling lost and overwhelmed and panicked.

"Just don't hurt Wally," she said.

"Or Bea, dear."

She stopped, headed immediately for the door. "If anything happens to them…"

"Oh my goodness…you two need to work on your clichés. So boring."

"I'm outside. What now?"

"Come to my house."

"I don't know where you live, Cat."

"I KNOW THAT!" Cat shouted into the phone. "You think I'm stupid? I know that!"

She huffed. "I'll walk you in. Head toward the town center and go past it. But walk fast, dear. I may get impatient and just do away with one of these sweet ladies."

Susan heard whimpers.

"Cat."

"No talking, dear. Just walking. And by the way, if I hear you say anything to anyone on the way, you won't need to bother coming here. I've already killed one old man. What's two old women?"

Susan picked up her pace. She rushed past the post office dock and onto Queen's Highway.

"Okay," she said. "I've left town. Where do I go?"

"Keep walking. After no more than a football field, you'll see a small road on the right. There's a bird of paradise plant just past it. Take that. It leads to my house. You're still alone?"

She nodded and started running.

"I can't hear you," Cat singsonged.

"Yes! Just…"

When she reached the turn that Cat described, she spun right and hurried down the road and onto the deck of the house. She didn't knock. No point. She just barged in. Bea and Wally sat holding each other's hands on the couch. Cat stood in front of them, pointing a gun in their direction. She held a phone to her ear.

As Susan stepped in, Cat pressed the cell directly against her lips and said, "Hello, Susan."

She tossed the phone to the side, then motioned with the gun toward the sofa.

"Sit next to the old women."

"Are you ladies okay?"

"Yes," Wally said.

Susan pivoted to Bea. "You're okay?"

428

Bea nodded.

Susan twisted back to face Cat.

"I'm here, Cat. Just let them go."

She shook her head. "Why? So they can go tell Ronnie or that goody-two-shoes inspector? I don't think so."

"Cat, we had a deal."

Cat sneered. "No we didn't. I said come and you came. There was no deal."

Susan glanced across the room to Cat's bed. She tipped her chin.

"You're leaving?"

"Yeah." Cat looked wistful. "Boat's all loaded. Just waiting for my last package to arrive. And now you're here. I think I've gotten all I can get out of Hope Town. Time for me to move on."

"Good. Then there's no reason to hold Wally and Bea. Just let them leave."

"Cat," Wally began.

Cat spun and pointed the gun at her. "Yes?"

Wally dropped her eyes and shook her head. "Nothing."

"Cat. You're terrorizing these women. Stop." She glanced over her shoulder and shifted toward the couch. She motioned her hand behind her. "Wally, Bea. Leave."

Cat shifted forward and lifted the gun. "They're not going anywhere. You think you're in charge here?"

Susan twisted her entire upper body and moved in front of Cat's gun. "Ladies, go."

Bea and Wally jumped off the couch and 'rushed' behind Susan to the open door. Cat swung the pistol, hitting Susan on the side of the face and knocking her to the left, forcing her to lose her balance. As Susan fell, she yelled, "GO!"

Bea and Wally hesitated, then scrambled, certainly their version of hurrying, and squeezed past the door. Cat started after them and Susan dived at Cat's legs as she went by but missed. She heard Cat yell, "Stop. Or I'll shoot."

Talk about clichés, Susan thought. She leapt to her feet and rushed out the door. The women were off the porch, but they had stopped moving and were holding their hands in the air. Susan sprung toward Cat, knocking the woman to the deck. The gun went off. Susan shouted again, "Go, run, go!" and motioned with her hands. She watched the women disappear down the street. Cat sprung to her feet, surprisingly spry, and Susan lunged into the bottom of her legs. Cat shifted but didn't fall. Susan glanced up at Cat and saw the barrel of a pistol pointing at her.

"Get! Up! Now!"

Susan crawled to her feet, feigning aching and near immobility, which didn't take much. Cat watched her move.

"Oh, hurry it up, woman. You're being a baby."

"All right." Susan rushed forward and knocked against the hand Cat held the gun in. Another shot sounded. Susan heard ringing. They wrestled and another shot exploded and Susan watched as the gun skidded across the deck. Cat bounded for the pistol, screaming out as she did, but the gun slid over the edge of the deck and fell with a strangely silent plunk into the harbor. Cat sprung to her feet, her nostrils flaring. She rushed at Susan, kicked her.

"That gun was a gift from my father!" she said through clenched teeth, sliding her head slowly, almost imperceptibly from side to side.

"You have no idea who you're dealing with, do you?"

She grabbed Susan by the hair and pulled her toward her boat.

"We'll just have to get going now. That shot is sure to get some attention and now you've sent those women out into who knows what." She leered at Susan. "All you've managed to do is rush your own death."

Cat reached into the boat, still gripping Susan's hair. As she struggled to her feet again, Susan saw that Cat had a club in her hand.

"And dear."

Cat swung the weapon and whacked Susan across the head. The world went black.

* * * *

Dan panicked. Sudden. Angry. Pulsing.

Sharp.

She was gone.

He knew.

He slammed off the water and leapt out of the shower, reached for a towel, didn't find one but ran anyway through the house calling out her name, calling out "Susan" and hearing nothing back. He yanked at the French doors and rushed onto the deck, realized he was naked, didn't care, sprinted to the railing to peek over the edge, resisting the dread, resisting the recognition.

Just resisting.

He darted his eyes as far under the planks of the patio as he could, to the support beams. Too long. Longer than he knew he should, squinting, verifying. He pulled back and spun, then shoved back through the doors that had swung closed without him, shouting, "Ahhhhh!" as he moved. He threw on pants and a shirt and shoes—forgot socks—and hurried out the front door.

Cat.

She must have…He ran down Front Street and into Hope Town center, shaking his head, struggling to understand. He thought to go directly to Cat's. Or to the police station. Or Cat's. She'd be at Cat's. Not the police station. But help.

Cat's. He rushed past the dock and onto Queen's Highway, remembering Harry and Mildred and their footsteps and then he glanced forward when he heard an alarmed woman's voice and he saw Bea and Wally scurrying toward him. His first thought was to ignore them, to not engage. They'd only want to chat and there was no time. But they waved and called for him and suddenly they were in front of him. And Bea was crying.

Wally said, "I think she shot her."

"Bea?"

"No. Susan."

Dan's world started spinning and he stumbled and the two women stepped forward to stop him and he said, "Wha…?" couldn't finish, just left the words hanging between them and Wally massaged his shoulder and she broke and sobbed out, "She told us to leave and we did. There was…there was another shot…behind us at the house. She'd shot at us…before. Cat…This was different. But Susan said to go. So we did.

"And then there was another shot. And another. And we—"

Dan knocked past them and sprinted forward. They called out behind him, "Don't go. She has a gun."

He pivoted at the turn to Cat's house, tripped over his own feet, sprung back again and at the front of the house, the door was open so he scrambled inside, then out. But she was gone. They were gone. Spots of blood stained the edge of the deck and his legs gave and he stumbled and

432

searched to sit but he stood. He sniffed, gas, and he twisted behind him and saw a boat and a motor and Cat. She was leaving and something or somebody—had to be Susan—was a lump slouched over one of the seats.

He yelled, "Cat!"

And lightning exploded across the already bright sky, in the distance, faint under the shine of the sun but brilliant against the backdrop of grey. He scanned his eyes around the deck, searching for something that he could use to hurl out his distress and fury but nothing. So instead he spun and rushed back and punched the final unbroken pane in the window to the right of her door. The glass shattered. He pulled his fist toward him and saw blood and he wiped the red across his brow before he threw himself off the landing and headed back toward town.

He searched through the trees as he ran and, finally, he pinpointed them and saw that Cat's boat seemed to be slowing. She was slowing. So he slid to a stop and watched as she directed them toward the lighthouse, toward the beach where they'd first found Ed. Cat stood from her steering wheel and moved toward the back of her boat and slapped the bump on her seat. Then again. And again. And finally he saw Susan raise her head and Cat kicked with her foot and Susan stood and he felt a rush of fury and relief and hatred. And Cat grabbed Susan, shoved her to the edge of the hull, and they paused while the boat slid toward land.

Instantly, Dan flipped around and bolted south on Queen's highway past Cat's drive to the path in the trees that led to the lighthouse. He jumped over the edge of the street and continued down the trail, sprinting and grimacing then feeling a grin seep in as he at last noticed the building's weather vane rise into his line of sight. He hurried on until he reached the edge of the trees at the opening of the path and he cast his eyes to the right and saw that they were heading toward him on the path. Cat gripped Susan and held her close. Susan's arms and legs were bound. She was barefoot. Cat held a knife close to his wife's throat. Too close. He almost darted forward, almost rushed them and pummeled Cat, but then he paused and inhaled and breathed and calmed. The blade was too present. The blood. Her life. But her face was focused. Intent. He wanted to catch her eyes, but if she reacted...that could. He ducked into the jungle and listened, strained to hear when they walked by. Then Cat's voice at last saying:

"...you never thought of me.

"Did you?

"Never once...

"Are you listening to me?"

Susan never answered. He never heard her voice. The talking stopped and he crept to the edge and peeked out in time to catch Cat as she pressed her mouth toward Susan's ear and seemed to whisper something, then she pulled back and licked Susan's face and Dan cringed and imagined at the filth Susan was enduring. They headed toward the buildings, Cat and her prisoner, toward the houses. He thought of Daniel. If the kid was home. What would happen? Would Susan be in more danger? Or less. Could he get Cat from behind? Pull her loose from Susan. Cat might stab him, but so what? If Susan could escape, it'd be worth it. But at least Susan could run, get free. Not with her feet tied the way they were, though. She couldn't run away.

He slunk silent up the path...There was blood! He followed a line of red, thin, that ran down the planks and off toward the boat and then up again toward where they'd retreated, toward the lighthouse and houses. He paused, suddenly terrified. He focused, listened. If Cat heard him coming or if he miscalculated and she sliced Susan's throat or even cut her just a little bit. Or if Susan heard. And flinched. And Cat knew it. Couldn't risk it.

He ducked back into the trees to think. Lightning flashed and thunder sounded and a sudden downpour drowned out his senses. He peeked out, watched them return from the houses, fixated on Cat's scowl. He saw her stop and flip Susan toward the lighthouse, then fidget with the ties on Susan's legs and push her in front up the stairs and into the shelter. He twisted and looked and noticed that Inspector Johnson and Constable Anderson and Vern were jetting across the harbor and he breathed relief and then sunk to terror as he realized the men were coming to help but they were also placing Susan in more danger. The knife! So he rushed up to the lighthouse. And saw Cat's face peek through the entrance. She saw him and their eyes met and she leered, then disappeared into the building. He almost paused, feared for Susan, but he'd committed himself so he rushed forward and into the lighthouse and Cat was ascending the stairs, forcing Susan forward, almost dragging her as she tripped up and struggled, and he spun to peek back out to make sure the men knew where they'd gone. But their boat was speeding out of the harbor as if they were heading to Marsh Harbour.

Dan shoved his hand into his pocket. He'd not grabbed his phone when he rushed out of the house earlier. So he pulled his body back into the lighthouse and raised his head and yelled, "Cat."

She kept climbing, then stopped and answered, "What!" Not a question, more of a rebuke.

435

He paused. He wanted to remind her that she had nowhere to go, that this was a lost cause for her, that the police were coming (which would apparently be a lie), that he would...but none of this would accomplish anything and might push her to hurt Susan. So instead he bounded up the stairs, ignoring their fragility. Cat shoved Susan forward and they continued. Around and around and at last Dan glanced up toward them and they were gone. He sprinted up the last round of steps and ducked out onto the widow's walk.

Cat had backed toward the far west end of the platform, toward Marsh Harbour, as if she thought that would somehow help her reach freedom. She'd forced Susan in front of her and pressed the knife again against her throat. Her leg was bleeding. Cat's. Cat's leg was bleeding. She'd been the one who'd been shot. And then he realized she'd been limping as he saw her move toward the back of the boat and then as they hiked up toward the buildings and finally the lighthouse. Barely, but she'd been limping. He'd been so focused on Susan.

"So what's your plan now, Dan?" Cat sounded winded.

"I think that's more of a question for you. You're the one who's trapped."

"How am I trapped, silly? I have Susan. And a knife. I just have to..." She pulled the knife gently toward herself. Blood broke onto Susan's neck.

"Cat!"

"Oh calm down. She's fine. Aren't you fine, Susan?"

Susan didn't answer.

"You want another slice? I said, 'aren't you fine, Susan?'"

Susan nodded, barely. "Yes. I'm fine."

"See. All I have to do is pull the knife across her throat." She nodded back. "Or just throw her over the edge."

Cat sneered. "You'd hate that, wouldn't you Dan? You're probably a wreck just being up here."

"I'm fine."

"Yeah, sure you are. Don't you think I noticed how much you hated being up here that first day."

"I said, I'm fine."

"Well, good. Then you won't mind moving a bit closer to the railing."

Dan glanced at the lantern room. He hadn't realized how close he was standing to the enclosure itself and how far he'd positioned himself from the outer railing. Torrents of rain splashed around them.

"I said move."

Dan shifted.

"Now, climb over. Go ahead...over...Just make sure you hold on though, silly. Wouldn't want you to fall. Yet. And this rain? Kind of slick."

Dan lifted his right leg over the railing, straddling the metal, then brought his left foot across and pressed his toes as far to the extreme under the steel fence as he could. He glared at Cat.

"There. I'm on the outside. Happy?"

"Getting there. Now raise your hand."

"What?"

"Dan." She rolled her eyes. "That wasn't a tough instruction. Lift your coward hand off the railing and raise it."

He loosened the fingers of his left hand and pushed his arm to the sky. Lightning flashed and thunder sounded and wind whipped by him.

437

"Higher."

He stretched his hand farther into the air. A gust of wet air rushed into him, and he immediately threw his hand back onto the railing.

"No!" Cat yelled. "Up. Get your hand back up."

"Cat. There are no—"

"Up!"

He thrust his hand toward the sky. The grip of his right hand tightened.

"Happy?"

"Yes. Although, happy isn't really the word now, is it? But, you've kind of forced my hand. I hate that I have to make you feel so uncomfortable…we always had that special something. Have I told you, Susan? How sexy I think Dan is? But…Dan, up… but what choice do I have? I don't get it, Dan. We used to be on the same side. When you needed me I was there to help you. I put up with your constant come-ons. So annoying."

Dan glanced at Susan. More wind blew into him and he started to flip his hand back down.

"Eh eh eh."

"I didn't come on to you, Cat."

"Oh really? You didn't show up to my house one night, drunk, crying about how you and Susan were getting a divorce?"

She nudged Susan. "Did he tell you that? Oh, he was pitiful. How could I say no to him then? Of course, that was after he killed Victor so, naturally, I was afraid of him. He can have quite a temper. But, you know that. Don't you, dear?"

Cat kicked Susan. Dan flinched. Snarled.

"Don't you Susan?"

Susan didn't respond. Cat turned to Dan.

438

"Of course she does.

"You know," she continued. "I don't know how you put up with this woman as long as you did. Talking to her is like talking to a wall. She never answers. So annoying. Maybe I'll just finish her—"

"No!" Dan yelled.

"Oh, that got a response."

She bumped Susan with her shoulder. "I think he likes you."

She glared at Dan. "I wish he liked me."

"Cat, just let her go. Just let her go. You're really just mad at me."

"Really, Dan? Are you seriously going to make this all about you?"

"Fine, Cat. It's not all about me. It's all about you. But, it's not about Susan. So let her go."

"Oh but it is. You just don't see it. You wouldn't stop loving her and just love me. You even pretended to get jealous that my Dad and me had a relationship." She shook her head. "I was so stupid for believing you."

"Cat, if you expect me to believe that all of this is because I didn't love you..."

"Oh, Dan. This is boring. Just jump." She motioned to the ground with the knife. "Just let go with your other hand. There's nothing there to stop you. It'll be quick. I'm tired of this. I'm tired of you."

"I'm not leaving Susan."

Cat glanced up. She shrugged.

"Okay. Then Susan will leave you."

Cat shifted the knife back to Susan's throat. Dan sprung forward, vaulting himself over the railing and shouting, "No!" picturing the blade slide against his wife's neck and ending everything.

439

"Sarah Wilson."

Cat froze. She dropped the hand holding the blade to her side and peered over the edge of the widow's walk. She blinked. And shifted. Rain wetted her hair, but the storm had softened.

Dan twisted and glanced behind him, toward the ground. Inspector Johnson called out again, "Sarah. It's over. Just stop."

Johnson stood to the right of the entrance with Constable Anderson and Vern. After a moment, Daniel came through the opening that led to the lantern room. He stood straight.

"You killed my father."

"Daniel, no," Dan said. "I prom—"

"Not you. Her." He indicated again. Dan saw that he was pointing at Cat.

"Johnson told me everything."

"Sarah," Inspector Johnson said. "We know about yer dad. And yer boyfriend. Yer mom told the authorities everything before she died."

Dan stepped forward. "Cat, what's he talking about?"

Cat lifted the knife again and hovered the blade against Susan's throat. She hesitated, then:

"Mom's dead?"

"Wait, your mom is alive? Was...a-l-i...?"

"Really, Dan?" She sneered. "That's the part you care about?"

"Cancer," Inspector Johnson said. "But you probably knew that already. About the cancer. Isn't that why your brother came to find you?"

Dan stopped and squeezed his eyes closed. He swallowed.

"Ed? Ed was...you killed your own brother?"

"Oh, don't act so high and mighty Mr. *Oh look at me. I'm so great and everybody loves me.* You can't judge me. You're a philanderer. You're nothing. What was I going to do? Let him expose me?"

"So, Sarah," Inspector Johnson said. "We know ye killed yer father. They have evidence about yer boyfriend. They want to prosecute ye for his death too. Add to that the three murders here in the Bahamas.

"There's no place to go. I saw blood dripped on the path. I can see from here yer bleeding. I reckon the choice will be made for ye pretty soon anyway. Just let Mrs. Harris go."

Cat gazed into the distance, toward the clouds surrounding the lighthouse. She peered into Dan's eyes.

"You're right."

Then she leaned back and toppled over the railing of the lighthouse, still clutching Susan. Dan lurched forward and grabbed at the arm that held the knife pressed to his wife's throat. He was too late to stop the fall but the action was enough that the knife bumped out of Cat's hand and flew over the edge of the platform to where Dan had been standing. The blade sliced his shoulder as the weapon whipped by him. As he fell, he stretched out and strained to wrap his arms around Susan's legs but her feet struck him instead and his head knocked back and he watched the two women tumble over the edge and fall from the widow's walk.

Dan leapt to his feet and spun, knocking Daniel into the railing at the side and diving through the small opening into the lantern room and down the stairs. He jumped over the cement stairway and sprinted across the grass surrounding the column. Inspector Johnson and Vern were clutching at Cat, stuck in a clump of sea grape bushes. She

441

was silent. The grass and wet ground were covered with broken branches and leaves and palm fronds. Dan could see a scrap of Cat's shirt caught along the side of the lighthouse structure. Constable Anderson hovered over Susan. Dan knocked him back. He stood and slipped in the soft mud.

"I'm okay. I'm okay," he heard her say. "...ish. I think I broke my leg or my ankle. Something. It really hurts."

She grimaced, then grinned, then let out a too-real sounding whine and squeezed her eyes closed. After a moment she opened them.

"But, I'm okay. I rolled."

Dan let out a quick laugh. "You rolled?"

She nodded.

He pressed his lips against hers and held them there. An overwhelming sob rushed into him and she pressed him away, peering into his eyes.

"Dan, honey. I'm okay. I'll live."

"I just...you're the best thing in my life."

Forty-Three

Dan crossed to the sofa. He smiled at his wife, then leaned over the back cushions and kissed her, long and upside down. They both looked as if they'd just been released from triage. His shoulder was bandaged, as was his hand. His side had finally been officially treated. Susan wore some fetching bruises and a cast that she'd somehow managed to turn into a fashion accessory. She'd used colored markers to draw geometric designs on the oddly colored plaster. In addition to her fight with Cat, she'd bumped against the side of the lighthouse as she'd fallen and bounced through some of the brush and growth at the bottom—all that knocking had certainly slowed her descent enough to save her life. Miraculously, his wife had not broken any bones, but she did have a very serious sprain. She wasn't going anywhere for a while, which was just fine with Dan. She also had a thin scab across her neck. Cat had not been so fortunate. She'd lived, but she'd be recovering for quite a while—in a prison medical facility.

Susan had spent the week since the lighthouse reading through two of the journals of Edward Hawkins (she and Dan had also managed to fit in some personal time). At the moment, she was absorbed in the third. Dan held her hand as he walked around the sofa and plopped down next to her. She bounced.

"Ow. Dan." She whimpered, then smiled. "You gotta be careful. I'm delicate."

443

"Yeah," he said. "Sure you are."

She set the book to the side and pressed her hand into his. She rested her head back and closed her eyes.

"These are great. You were so lucky to find these. I just want to…I just want to be there with Edward Hawkins and hear first hand from him what that time was like and how he endured everything he went through. I mean, really Dan, his story is incredible. Kind of puts these last couple of weeks in perspective."

"Because they were nothing to worry about?"

"No, silly." She looked exasperated. "I mean…oh I don't know what else to say instead of silly."

He'd asked her never to use that term of endearment again. At least not for a while.

"How about My Lord?" he said.

She grinned, and squinted. "I'll keep thinking."

She went on, "But really, this is the story you should write."

"Are you saying my writing doesn't stand on its own?"

"No." She flashed and kissed him on the cheek. "Your writing is brilliant."

"His is just better." She smirked, then planted another peck, this time closer to his mouth. "Kidding."

She kissed him again. They'd re-entered the honeymoon phase. In yet another ironic twist, Cat had brought them back together, circling and tormenting them until they knew that not only did they want to be together, they didn't ever want to be apart again. Dan snuggled up to Susan's side.

Cat, or Sarah, as events had informed them, had led her own rather criminal life before coming to Hope Town and adopting the persona of a woman from Oregon. She was, as was the real Catherine Smith, the daughter of a preacher.

Where their paths diverged, however, was in the fate of their parents. Catherine's mother had died, as Cat had claimed. But Sarah's father had been the one to die. And she'd killed him. Her mother had confessed, had rescued her daughter from facing any consequences, likely thinking her husband's murder was a one-off, retribution for years of abuse (which, apparently, were real). But, certainly unknown to her, that act of self-sacrifice would ultimately result in Sarah's killing her own brother. When the woman had found out about Ed's death, she'd immediately recanted and spilled everything. As Inspector Johnson had shouted at the lighthouse, Cat was also suspected in the disappearance and, the authorities had just discovered, death of her boyfriend, Steve. Not Scott. Whether or not there was ever a Scott was something Dan would likely never know. And he felt no need to.

A knock on the door interrupted Dan and Susan's nuzzling. He pulled back and smiled into her.

"Should I just ignore it?"

"No, get it. It could be that constable finally coming to apologize for falsely arresting you."

The *arrest*. Inspector Johnson had gone along with Dan's incarceration, he claimed, to protect him. He'd been suspecting Cat for a while, but was worried about so many deaths starting to stack up. He figured that if she thought the police had a suspect in custody, she might stop and nobody else would be in danger. He'd turned out to be wrong, but (after he'd some time to process the ordeal) Dan could mostly see the logic behind what the inspector had done.

Inspector Johnson had apologized for the subterfuge and had insisted that he'd planned to inform Dan of the strategy, but needed to tell him one-on-one—the inspector didn't trust that Constable Anderson wouldn't blab the details to Cat/Sarah in a moment of flirting; he wasn't the most dependable policeman. Dan's escape, and then Jamie's murder, had prevented the warning from ever happening. Between cataloguing and detailing the coffee house crime scene and informing Jamie's parents, the inspector had stopped by the police station and decided that it was more important that Dan be home to protect his wife. The inspector's urgency had likely saved Susan's life.

Dan held his lips motionless against his wife's cheek, then got up and jogged to the entrance and pulled open the front door. Jamie stood on the landing, holding some luggage. Dan stared at him for several long moments.

"Jamie!"

He shook away his shock and rushed forward, throwing his arms around the boy.

"Ow, ow, ow," Jamie said and shifted back.

"Oh, sorry."

Jamie leaned forward and wrapped his right arm around Dan's back.

"I can't tell you how happy I am to see you," Dan gushed. "I thought...I didn't know...you really scared me. I thought I'd lost my new best friend."

Jamie beamed. He grew suddenly serious.

"Listen." He started batting his eyes. "I'm really sor—"

Dan shook his head. He whispered, "None of that matters. I..."

Dan motioned for Jamie to step inside and then twisted and called out, "Susan, look who's here."

"Jamie," she said, motioning to the cast on her ankle.

446

"I'm not saying I should be your favorite. Necessarily…" Dan pretended to whisper. "But I *am* the only one who got up to greet you."

Susan smirked. "Oh, don't listen to him. Come here, Jamie. Give me a hug. I think you've made Dan's year."

Jamie flashed at Dan, paused, then dropped his bags and hurried across to Susan. He hugged her, then stepped back.

"What happened to you?"

"Cat," she said. "Well, I guess she's Sarah now."

"What?" Jamie glanced at Dan.

"You haven't talked to Inspector Johnson?"

"Eh, yes," Jamie said. "But…"

Dan sat on the wrap-around end of the sofa and patted the cushions.

"I'll fill you in. A lot has happened. But, first, sit. Tell us everything…I'm so relieved you're okay."

"Well," Jamie said. "I guess it was close. They said I'd lost a lot of blood. They said if it wasn't for you fastening your shirt around me, I probably wouldn't have lived. So…" He stopped, dropped his head.

Dan slid to Jamie's side. He hugged the young man's neck. Then he scooted back to his part of the couch.

"So," he said. "I guess the more important question is, did you read my book?"

"Dan!" Susan said.

"I'm kidding, of course." He nudged Jamie and grinned. "That's second.

"Really, though, Jamie. I can't tell you how glad I am that you're okay. I thought…" His eyes began to water and he jumped off the couch and crossed to the kitchen. "Drinks? Can I get either of you anything?"

"Well, Jamie," Susan said. "I think I'll have a glass of wine. Will you join me?"

"Uh, sure. I guess. Thanks."

Dan filled two goblets and crossed the room. He handed each their drinks, then returned to the kitchen and poured some water from the fridge into a glass and joined them again.

"So, how are things with your parents?"

Susan's phone rang. She glanced at the display, then eyed her husband. "Dan."

She answered. After a moment, she covered the microphone.

"You never called your agent. He says you never called him."

"Oh." Dan pulled his lips back. "I completely forgot."

He pivoted to Jamie. "Do you mind if I see what he wants? It will only take a second. He's probably wondering why I've not made any progress."

"No." Jamie sipped his wine. "Go ahead."

As Dan crossed into the bedroom to take the call, he heard Susan say, "So, did Dan tell you about my dad?"

He closed the door partway and lifted the phone to his ear. "Hello, Mike. Sorry I've not gotten back to you. Things have been a little crazy. You're probably wondering about the book."

"No," Mike said. "Well, yes. But...I just...I wanted to talk to you about Ryan. I know you said not to look into the hit and run, but one of the heads of the agency hired a private investigator. He lost a son once, too. He wanted to help you out."

Dan inhaled. "Okay. Does this call mean you found something?"

"Yes."

448

The phone was silent for a moment.

Mike continued, "Does the name John Stephenson mean anything to you?"

Dan stumbled back against the bed as if he'd just been hit in the chest and had the breath knocked out of him. "Yes."

"Well, we…"

"What are you saying, Mike? Did he have something to do with all this?"

"He…now, listen, Dan. Don't overreact. This is all preliminary. But—"

"Just tell me!"

"How sure are you the car that hit Ryan was blue? Could it have been gray?"

"Um." Suddenly Dan felt as if he'd been tossed back against the pavement again, cradling Ryan and staring into the distance as a gray car spun around a corner and disappeared. He could hear the gasps, the scraping, the devastation circling around him. His breath pushed into rushing. He stood and paced in the space between the bed and the dresser.

"Yes. Why?"

"You're sure?"

He yelled, "Just shut the hell up and tell me why!"

The room around him rocked and any solid ground he had been pressing against now felt more like marshmallow, sucking in his feet and morphing his body into tile. He couldn't move.

"The license plate, at least, the parts you were sure of…they didn't match any blue cars that fit your description. So we had this detective…Jim, his name is Jim…we had him look into other cars. Colors we thought might have been ambiguous or looked different, depending on the light. When I saw that one of the cars, a gray one, was registered to a John Stephenson. I thought this was too big a coincidence. Isn't this the guy that Susan—"

"Yes. It's him. So…" Dan glanced to the side out at the lighthouse across the harbor. The afternoon had ended and the sun was setting into the horizon. The beam from the lantern was…visible? Dan squinted. Maybe not. Maybe it was still too light.

"How—" Mike began.

"Mike, I have to go."

"Dan, what do—"

Dan hung up Susan's phone and sat on the bed, staring at his hands for several minutes and breathing, gasping at times, feeling lost and dizzy. He pushed himself against the mattress and walked into the living area and took in Susan and Jamie, talking, animated and smiling at each other. He sneered. They acted as if nothing had changed. He stared.

"How are you guys on drinks?"

They both turned to face him. Susan smiled. "We're good. Thanks. Or I am. Jamie, are you okay?"

The boy nodded. "I'm good. Thanks, Dan."

Dan crossed to behind the couch and tossed Susan's phone into her lap, "Here. Mike says hi."

"Oh," Susan said. "I almost forgot. I talked to Wally and Bea, let them know everything was all right. And get this. Cat…Sarah…whatever…she'd somehow swiped the book you had me get. I guess she saw the package when I had my bag open at customs. It was at her house. So after they arrested Cat, Bea went back there and took it. You should have heard her tell me all about it." She grinned.

"That woman cracks me up."

Jamie giggled.

"Oh," Dan said, monotone, and spun to the kitchen. He pulled out a goblet and filled the glass to the edge with wine. He sipped, then gulped, pausing to relish the sensation before he topped off his drink and lumbered out of the kitchen, past the sofa and toward the doors leading to the deck. Susan said:

"So, Jamie has agreed to come live with us. How great is that?"

"Good," he said and kept walking.

"Where are you going?"

"Outside."

"Oh, that sounds nice. Jamie, would you mind helping me get up?"

Jamie started to move. Dan spoke over his shoulder. "No. You two stay here. I want to be alone."

He continued to the door. Dan heard Jamie whisper behind him. "Is he mad about me staying with—"

Dan twirled and beamed. "No, Jamie. Really. That's great. I'm really happy about that. We'll celebrate later." Then he pivoted back and stepped through the opening. He pulled the doors closed behind him.

The afternoon shone brighter than it should, given the advanced hour, given the dropping sun. He looked to Hope Town and crossed to the edge of the deck. He lifted his wine to his lips and drank, letting his eyelids flutter and fall closed. Then he dropped his hand and searched for the beam from the lighthouse. He shook his head.

"Too early."

He stared into his glass at the red.

ABOUT THE AUTHOR

David Taylor Black is an aspiring best-selling author who began his career at nine with the script of the as-yet un-finished film, *In the Backyard*. The premise may or may not have been a bit of a rip-off of a James Bond movie—with lots of running. He lives in Phoenix, Arizona with his partner, Dion, and his too-big-to-be-a-lapdog dog, William.

Made in the USA
San Bernardino, CA
10 April 2018